SUMMER SECRETS

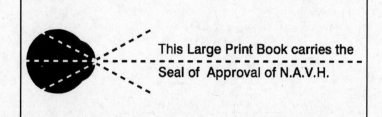

This Large Print Book carries the
Seal of Approval of N.A.V.H.

SUMMER SECRETS

JANE GREEN

THORNDIKE PRESS
A part of Gale, Cengage Learning

GALE
CENGAGE Learning·

Farmington Hills, Mich • San Francisco • New York • Waterville, Maine
Meriden, Conn • Mason, Ohio • Chicago

LIBRARY OF CONGRESS CATALOGING-IN-PUBLICATION DATA

Green, Jane, 1968-
    Summer secrets / Jane Green. — Large print edition.
        pages cm. — (Thorndike Press large print basic)
    ISBN 978-1-4104-7747-7 (hardback) — ISBN 1-4104-7747-9 (hardcover)
    1. Self-actualization (Psychology) in women—Fiction. 2. Self-realization in women—Fiction. 3. Familly secrets—Fiction. 4. Large type books. I. Title.
PR6057.R3443S86 2015b
823'.914—dc23   2015017018

Published in 2015 by arrangement with St. Martin's Press, LLC

Printed in the United States of America
1 2 3 4 5 6 7 19 18 17 16 15

ACKNOWLEDGMENTS

To the many who shared their Nantucket stories with me, in particular Maryellen Scannell, Kari England, Mary Michetti, and Elin Hilderbrand.

The entire team at St. Martin's Press, Pan Macmillan, David Higham & Associates, and Fletcher & Co., including the dream team of Jen Enderlin, Geoff Duffield, Jeremy Trevathan, John Karle, and Katie James, and everyone else who works on my books; Sarah Hall, Meg Walker, Danielle Burch, Lisa Marie Gina, Lisa Senz, and India Cooper; never forgetting my spectacular agents, Christy Fletcher and Anthony Goff.

Karen, Franklin, and Jake Exkorn; Jeff and Wynter Warshaw; Maggie, Deirdre, Kim, Jeff R, Sam, Joe, Mark, Susan, Sunny, and my other family in the "Tower of Power" — you know who you are. And much gratitude and love to Tricia and Maureen, who brought me into the fold all those years ago.

My London media gang from the old days at the *Express:* Sam Taylor, Vicky Harper, Lisa Sewards, Gerard Greaves, and Narelle Muller. My Westport gang — too many to mention but I love you all.

Patrick and Tish Fried at Write Yourself Free; Michael Ross, Mark Llamos, and Annie Keefe at the Westport Country Playhouse.

Dr. Tanya Futoryan, Dr. Charlotte Ariyan, and all at both Westport Dermatology and Memorial Sloan Kettering Cancer Center for their diligence, skill, and kindness — thank you.

If I haven't mentioned you, it is only because memory has failed. So very many people have contributed to this book, to the stories, to the life that had to be lived in order to write it.

I end by thanking my children and my husband. I couldn't have done any of it without you. Actually, maybe I could have, but it wouldn't have been nearly as much fun. I love you the most.

Gratitude unlocks the fullness of life. It turns what we have into enough, and more. It turns denial into acceptance, chaos to order, confusion to clarity. It can turn a meal into a feast, a house into a home, a stranger into a friend.

— MELODY BEATTIE

PROLOGUE

London, 2014

Lord knows, most of the time, when I'm facing an evening on my own, I am absolutely fine. If anything, I relish that alone time, when my daughter is with her father; the luxury of eating whatever I want to eat, the relief at not having to provide a nutritious meal for a thirteen-year-old picky eater.

I can curl up on the sofa and watch things my daughter would groan at — documentaries, news, a great three-parter on the BBC — or putter round the kitchen listening to Radio 4 with no one complaining or demanding I put on a radio station that plays nothing but pop music.

Tonight I seem to have itchy feet. Tonight I am restless, and restlessness is always dangerous for me. Restlessness has a nasty habit of leading me to places I'm apt to regret. I have learned from bitter experience that when I feel like this, I need to keep busy.

I have been told to watch out for H.A.L.T. When I'm hungry, angry, lonely, or tired, it means I have to do a better job of taking care of myself. Tonight I am definitely hungry; tonight, like every other night for the last eighteen months, I am definitely lonely.

I phone the Chinese restaurant at the top of Elgin Avenue and order some noodles and spare ribs, then get up and open the kitchen cabinets. I've been putting this job off for months. My former husband is fanatical about order. He was the one who kept everything neat and tidy, all the pots and pans organized. Since he's been gone, the place is a disaster.

It looks perfect when you walk in, but open any cabinet and you have to immediately catch the bowls and dishes that come tumbling out, freed from the restraint of the solid wooden door.

I start with the cabinet that holds the sieves, amazed at how I have managed to amass seven sieves and colanders of various shapes and sizes, when I am now only cooking for Annie and me. I put five of them on the charity pile and keep going.

Breadboards are added, bowls I have been

given as presents that I've never liked but didn't have the heart to give away. Cracked dishes, chipped glasses, all go on the pile. As the boxes fill up, I start to feel better, busy, useful. It is almost meditative, as if cleaning out the clutter of my cabinets is somehow cleaning out the clutter in my mind.

I reach to the very back, feel something round, pull it out, and freeze.

A bottle of vodka.

Half full.

I have no idea what it's doing there, didn't know, hadn't remembered. It must have been there for months, maybe years. When I was married, my vodka had to be hidden, every nook and cranny in the house turned into a hiding spot for my secret shame.

I haven't held a bottle of vodka in a very long time. I can't tear my eyes away from the glistening glass in my hand. I listen to the sloshing inside the bottle, so comforting, so familiar, and my heart starts to pound.

I can almost taste it, poured over ice cubes and left to sit until it is ice cold, a twist of lemon if possible, no problem if not.

I feel it slipping down my throat, the silky smoothness, the slight burn as it hits my chest, the warmth that instantly rises, removing the loneliness, the hunger, whatever pain is lurking there.

I know what I should do. I know I need to pour this down the sink, but before I do, let me just sit here a while longer, worship at the altar of the god to whom I was once enslaved.

Surely that won't do any harm.

ONE

For as long as I can remember, I have always had the feeling of not quite fitting in, not being the same as everyone else.

I'm certain that is why I became a writer. Even as a toddler, at nursery school, junior school, I was friendly with everyone, without ever being part of the group. Standing on the outside, watching. Always watching. I noticed everything: how a sideways glance with narrowed eyes could say so much more than words ever could; how a whisper behind a delicate hand had the ability to destroy you for the week; how an outstretched hand from the right girl, at the right time, would see your heart soar for hours, sometimes days.

I knew I was different. The older I grew, the more that difference felt like inadequacy; I wasn't pretty enough, or thin enough, or simply *enough*. I couldn't have put words

13

to it, certainly not when I was very young, other than looking at those tiny, perfect, popular girls and wanting, so desperately, to be on the inside, to be the girl that was always picked first for sports teams, rather than the one left until last.

When adolescence hit, I became the friend the boys all wanted to talk to, to confide in, to find out how they could possibly make my best friend, Olivia, interested in them.

I was such a good friend, even though I fell head over heels for every last one of them. Adam Barrett afforded me two months' worth of daydreams about how he would realize, as we were sitting on the floor in my bedroom, the Police playing on my record player in the background, that Olivia was not the answer to his dreams after all; he would suddenly notice the silkiness of my hair (always far silkier in my daydreams), the green of my eyes, the fullness of my mouth, as he woke up to the fact that I was so spectacularly beautiful (which I wasn't), how had he not noticed that before?

After Adam Barrett it was Danny Curran, then Rob Palliser, and of course, Ian Owens. None of my daydreams came true, and at fourteen I finally discovered a great way of easing the pain of all those unfulfilled dreams, those unfulfilled longings, those misplaced hopes.

Gary Scott was having a party at his house. It was a sleepover, the boys sleeping on one side of the giant loft, the girls on the other. Everyone was ridiculously excited, this being the first mixed sleepover. Looking back, I can't quite believe the parents allowed it, given the raging hormones of fourteen- and fifteen-year-old teenagers, but I suppose they thought we were good kids, or that they had it under control.

The parents were there, of course. They were having a small gathering of their own; the laughter of the grown-ups and the clinking of their glasses made its way over to us, at the back of the garden with a record player and a trestle table stocked with popcorn, plastic cups, and lemonade.

Ian Owens was my crush at the time. He had become my very good friend, naturally, in a bid to get close to Olivia, who was, on that night, standing under the tree with Paul Johnson, her head cocked to one side, her sheaf of newly highlighted blond hair hanging like a curtain of gold over her right shoulder, looking up at Paul with those spectacular blue eyes. Everyone in that garden knew it was only a matter of time before he kissed her.

Ian was devastated. I was sitting on the

15

grass talking to him quietly, reassuring him, praying that I might be second choice, praying that he might lean his head toward mine, might brush my lips gently with his, spend the rest of the night holding me tightly in his arms.

"I took this," he said, gesturing to his side, where a bottle of vodka was nestling under his thigh.

"What? What do you mean, you took it? From where?"

"I found it in the garage. Don't worry, there's tons more. No one will notice. Want to?" He nodded his head in the shade of the trees, to a private corner where we wouldn't be seen.

Of course I wanted to. I would have done anything to keep Ian Owens by my side a little longer, to give him more time to change his mind about Olivia and fall in love with me.

I got up, brushing the pine needles from my jeans, aware that there was a damp patch from the grass. I was in my new 501s. Olivia and I bought them together and went back to her house to shrink them in the bath. Hers were tiny, and looked amazing when we were done, drain-piping down her legs. Mine flapped around my ankles like sails in the wind. I had a small waist but great big thighs, so I had to get a big size to fit, which meant they had to be clinched in at the waist with a tight belt and were huge all the way down.

I never looked the way I wanted to look in clothes. I had a new plaid shirt from Camden Market that I really liked, and had smudged black kohl underneath my eyes. Peering from beneath my new fringe — I had cut it two days ago — my eyes looked smoky and sultry, the green sparkling through the kohl. I liked the way I looked, which wasn't something that happened often.

Maybe tonight was going to be a first for me. Maybe Ian would like the way I looked too.

I followed him into the small copse of trees at the end of the garden, as he brought the bottle out and took the first swig, grimacing as he sputtered, then spat it all out.

"Christ, that's disgusting." He passed the bottle to me.

Of course I didn't want to do it. Watching the look on his face, how could I ever have wanted to taste something so vile, but how could I back down? I gingerly took the bottle, swigged it back, felt the burning going down my throat, then swigged it back twice more.

"Wow!" Impressed, he took the bottle back, this time managing to swallow.

Within minutes, I felt like a different person. Gone was the shy, awkward, ungainly adolescent, and in her place a sexy siren. Suddenly the curves I had always hated so much became sexiness personified, my new fringe a sultry curtain from behind which I could peer with bedroom eyes.

The warmth in my body spread out to my fingers and toes, a delicious tingling as I lost my inhibitions and flirted with Ian, stunned that he responded, that we moved from awkwardly standing next to each other to lying on the ground, heads resting on our elbows, my hair dropped over one shoulder in what I hoped was a pretty good imitation of Olivia, both of us giggling as we passed the bottle back and forth.

"You're really pretty," he said suddenly, the smile sliding off his face, the bottle sliding to the ground as he leaned his head forward, his lips inching closer to mine, his eyes starting to close, my own eyes closing in tandem. And there we were, kissing, as my heart threatened to explode.

It was everything I had dreamed of, his hands snaking through my hair, my own wrapped around his back, unable to believe

I had been given license to touch this boy I had loved for so long, license to hold him, to slip my tongue in his mouth, listen to him sigh with pleasure. He pushed me onto my back, lay on top of me, kissing my neck as I looked at the stars, knowing that if I were to die tonight, I would finally die happy. I would have done anything in my power to make that moment last all night.

We heard a noise, someone coming, and he jumped off me as if stung by an electric shock, refusing to even look at me, pretending we had just been out there drinking, nothing more. The disappointment was like a dagger, which twisted and turned as the evening progressed and he didn't come near me again.

What could I do other than pretend I was having a great time, and how could I not have a great time with my new best friend, vodka, when vodka had made me feel so good? Maybe vodka would take away this searing pain, make me feel beautiful again.

For a while, it worked. I danced, and laughed, and attempted to flirt with other boys to try to make Ian jealous. I remember laughing hysterically at something, then all of a sudden the laughter turned into wracking sobs. I don't remember anything after that.

It was my first introduction to booze, blackouts, and the transformative effect alcohol would have on my life.

Alcohol made me beautiful in a way I never felt the rest of the time. It filled me with a confidence that had always been missing. Alcohol made me fit in. And if the night ended with a period of time that I could never remember in the morning, well, so what. I never seemed to make too egregious a mistake, nor do anything so terrible I was ostracized forever. If anything, it cemented my reputation, not as a shy, lonely girl who was always standing on the outside, but as the center of the party. In fact, it wasn't long before everyone knew that a party didn't get started until Cat arrived.

The drinking became a little more of a problem when I went to university. My parents had never been particularly present while I was growing up, so one might presume if I was going to go off the rails, why not do it at home, but I saved it for when I went away.

I was enough of a disappointment to my father. I didn't need to give him yet another excuse to help me understand I was not the daughter he wanted.

My mother had left her native America

when she fell in love with my dad while working for a year as an au pair in Gerrards Cross. She seemed happy when I was very young, then spent most of my teenage years in what I have always thought must have been a deep, albeit undiagnosed, and possibly clinical, depression.

I can understand why.

What I couldn't understand is how she ever ended up with my father in the first place. He was handsome, and I suppose he must have been charming when they were young, but he was so damned difficult, I used to think, even when I was young, that we'd all be much happier if they got a divorce.

I would sit with friends who would be in floods of tears because their mother had just found out their father had been having an affair, or their parents had decided they hated each other, or whatever myriad reasons drive people apart. And these friends would be crying at the terrible fear of their families breaking up, and all I could think was: I *wish* my parents would get divorced.

It seemed to me that if ever there were two people on the planet who should not have been together, it was my parents. My mother is laid-back, funny, kind. She's comfortable in her skin and has the easy laugh you expect from all Americans. She was brought up in New York, but her parents died very young, after which she went to live with her Aunt Judith. I never knew Aunt Judith, but everything about those days sounds idyllic, especially her summers in Nantucket. You look at pictures of my mum from those days and she was in flowing, hippie-ish clothes, always smiling. She had long, silky hair, and looked happy and free.

In sharp contrast to the pictures of her with my dad, even in those early days, when they were newlyweds, supposedly the happiest time of a relationship. He insisted she wear buttoned-up suits, or twinsets and pearls. Her hair was elaborately coiffed. I remember the heated rollers she kept in the bathroom, twisting her hair up every morning, spraying it into tight submission, slicking lipstick on her lips, her feet sliding into Roger Vivier pumps.

If my father was away, she left her hair long and loose, wrapping a scarf around her head. She'd wear long gypsy skirts with espadrilles or sandals. I loved her like that most of all. I used to think it was her clothing that changed her personality, that in the gypsy skirts she'd be young and fun, dancing around the kitchen with me, singing the

Carole King songs she loved at the top of her voice. But of course it wasn't the clothes, it was my father's absence. When he was away, she could be herself, not having to worry about pleasing anyone.

I like to think that my mother had no idea what she was letting herself in for when she married my father. We never talked about it until after he died. My mother prizes loyalty above all else. I didn't know that, of course, during all those childhood years I spent praying for their divorce, but now I realize she would never have left him, however unhappy she might have been, however many days the depression was so dark, so debilitating, she didn't get out of bed.

There was nothing I loved more than going to a friend's house, because their mothers were around. I loved my mother more than anything, but the house would be empty and quiet when I got home. I would help myself to something from the fridge before traipsing up the stairs to my parents' master bedroom, pushing the door open to find my mother lying propped up on pillows. On a really bad day, the curtains would be drawn, the room in darkness. Often she'd be asleep, and I'd pad over to her side of the bed and stroke her arm. She'd rouse, giving me a sleepy smile, pulling me down for a kiss and a hug, wanting to hear all about my day, her only access to the outside world. I couldn't stay long, though. She didn't have the capacity for too much stimulation, and on those days, the bad days, I always saw the relief in her eyes when I said I had to go back downstairs to do homework.

Still, even during the darkest of times, I never doubted her love for me.

On a good day the sunlight would be streaming in through the window and she might be reading magazines, or a book, sipping a glass of iced tea. On those days I could stay for hours, or at least until my father got home. We both always knew, half an hour before he was due to arrive (and thank God he was always punctual), we had to maintain the status quo: The curtains had to be drawn again, the TV turned off. My father would go in to kiss her, and the metaphorical shades over her eyes would be drawn again. I saw it happen over and over, and I knew, even then, that it wasn't glandular fever, or *mono,* as she said, but something else.

And I knew, even then, that my father was, if not the cause, a major contributing factor.

My father could be fun, but it always felt

like an act. However lighthearted he might have seemed, it was entirely eclipsed by his need to control everything around him.

There were times when I felt loved by him, but only when everything in his environment, including me, was absolutely perfect. When my hair had been blown out and rolled into soft curls, held back by a pretty ribbon; when I was in a ruffled, feminine dress, patent Mary Janes, and lace-trimmed ankle socks; when I was quiet, well behaved, respectful.

The other Cat: the wild, tearing-round-the-garden-with-her-friend, disheveled, ample-thighed, growing into surly adolescent Cat? That Cat he hated. Perhaps hated is too strong a word for it, but from the moment I turned thirteen, I don't remember ever feeling loved by him.

He would look me up and down, with little attempt to hide the sneer. "You're going out in *that*?" he'd say, and I, who had looked at my new Doc Martens in the mirror with such pride, such excitement that I could show them off to my friends, would feel instant shame. "You look ri-*di*-culous." He'd shake his head to himself and mutter, as my cheeks would turn scarlet, and I would want a hole in the ground to open up so I could disappear.

"You're never going to get a boyfriend," he'd say, behind his paper. "Wearing those ri-*di*-culous clothes. Can I remind you that you are, in fact, a girl?" And I would want to claw his eyes out in rage.

I hated him for how he treated me, and I hated him for how he treated my mother. He did exactly the same to her, telling her what to wear, berating her for saying or doing the wrong thing, so she made herself disappear in the best way she could, by going to bed. For years.

And me? How did I deal with it? With my friend vodka. And a whole host of other new friends if vodka wasn't available. There was gin, with whom I had a brief but intense relationship while I was at university. Gin and tonics seemed the height of sophistication, but consuming the best part of an entire bottle of gin on its own was not. Even now, at twenty-nine, I can't touch gin. The very smell of it makes me think of the hours and hours of deadly bedspins, the hours and hours of throwing up the next day. If not gin, there were many, many happy times with tequila, including, yes, the infamous worm on a beach in Mykonos one summer.

There was always wine, and beer, although somehow beer didn't seem to count. My tipple of choice was hard: I would always choose a bottle of Jack over a bottle of champagne.

My father couldn't stand my drinking. And I couldn't stand him, so in that sense I suppose we were compatible. Once I finished university and moved up to London to do a journalism internship, which led to this job on the women's desk at the *Daily Gazette*, I barely saw him.

My mother was a cook when I was very tiny, before my father had worn her down. She filled my toddler years with baked treats that reminded her of home: apple pies; muffins, and not the English kind, the American, cakey kind; chocolate chip cookies, which, to my friends who were being raised on chocolate Bourbons, Jammy Dodgers, and Garibaldi biscuits, seemed the height of glamor.

During the dark years, if she cooked, which wasn't often, it was bland and dull, a reflection of her life with my father, a reflection perhaps of how she felt about him.

When my father was diagnosed with cancer, I had an immediate sense of him not lasting long. I have no idea how I knew. In the beginning all the specialists were saying things like prostate is the good one to have, very slow growing, etc., etc., but I knew he wasn't going to be with us for more than a year.

I didn't feel bad about it. Which I still feel bad about. I remember calling my mum one day from work, just a few weeks before he died, and he'd been rushed into hospital because he was spiking a fever. My mum had to go because he was barking at her about what to bring him from home, and I remember hearing his harsh voice in the background, and closing my eyes, just for a few seconds while I said a silent prayer: "Please put him out of his misery," I said. "Please let this be the end."

It wasn't. He clung on for another three months. I went to see him a handful of times. It had been awkward between us for years, and the penultimate time I went to see him I had to fortify myself with booze or I might have ended up saying something I'd regret.

I had a bit more than I intended, and I'll admit, I was extremely . . . happy when I walked in the room.

"You're drunk," he managed to sneer, through the tubes. I just looked at him, the booze having exactly the intended effect. His comment floated over my head, and I kissed him on the cheek, steadying myself on the bed railing because I very nearly fell on top of him, all the while having no reaction at all.

The last time I saw him was awful. In the three weeks since the last visit, he had shrunk to half his size. His hair had gone, leaving a few wisps of white; his face entirely sunken. He was in a drug-induced coma by then, the pain medication knocking him out most of the time, although occasionally he would rouse for one of the nurses to feed him ice chips to assuage his thirst.

I had absolutely no idea what to say to him, this man I had struggled with my entire life. I wanted something seismic to happen at the end. I wanted him to wake up so we could somehow forgive each other, say we loved each other, move on with some sense of closure, for I knew this would be the last time I saw him, but he didn't wake up, and nothing was said. I just sat awkwardly in a chair I pulled up next to the bed and looked at him. After a while I slipped my hand into his and stroked it, remembering how strong I thought he was when I was a little girl, how much I had loved him when I was tiny, when he thought I was perfect, before I grew old enough to fill his life with disappointment. I remembered slipping my tiny hand into his when I was small, how he looked at me, his eyes filled with . . . well. Not love, exactly.

Sometimes love, but it was always mixed with a little confusion.

"Who *are* you?" he'd sometimes say, affectionately. "Where did you *come* from?"

"This is my changeling," he'd introduce me to people, which made me feel special until I grew old enough to read fairy tales myself and realized a changeling is a fairy, elf, or goblin baby who's put in the crib to replace the stolen, perfect baby.

I did cry, though, that day in the hospital, holding his hand. Horrible as this is to admit, I think I cried less because my dad was dying than for the dad I had never had. I cried for the missed opportunities, for not having a dad who loved me unconditionally and unreservedly. I cried for not having a dad who accepted me exactly as I was.

And I think, in amongst the tears, I cried with relief.

My mother grieved appropriately for a woman who had lost her husband of almost thirty years so tragically, and then, after six months, she blossomed.

Looking at her now, you would never imagine she had ever experienced a day's unhappiness in her life.

TWO

The first thing my mother did after my father's death was put our big old house in Gerrards Cross on the market and buy herself a gorgeous, light-filled flat on Marylebone High Street.

My mother has come alive again. She has filled the roof terrace with terra-cotta pots, geraniums and honeysuckle spilling over, clematis climbing up the trellis that hides her from her neighbors and allows her to sunbathe naked, which she does whenever the weather gives her the opportunity.

She has a cat (my father hated cats, which, really, should have been an instant warning sign — never trust a man who doesn't like children or animals, and it seemed to me that my father didn't particularly like either), a wardrobe of beautiful clothes, most of which are picked up downstairs in the Whistles sale, and a busy social life with her new townie friends.

31

We have plans to meet this morning at Sagne, which is something of a tradition on a Saturday, even though I am usually, as I am this morning, suffering the effects of the morning after.

It wasn't quite so bad last night, though. No parties. I had dinner with Jamie, my on-again, off-again person. I can't call him my boyfriend, because he is most definitely not my boyfriend, but he's also most definitely more than a friend. What he is, most of all, is convenient. Jamie's the person I can call, anytime, if I'm feeling horny, or talkative, or simply bored. I still can't quite figure out why we haven't been able to take the next step, because we do have great sex (although, honestly, most of the time I barely remember), and we do have great conversation, and it seems this should be enough, particularly given that neither of us seems to be able to name the one thing that is missing that would seal this deal.

He's already left, for which I am grateful. I know what I look like first thing in the morning after a night of drinking, and it isn't pretty. Although Jamie's seen me like this many times before, I keep thinking I won't do it again, and because he and I both know that's not true, he's taken to leaving while I'm still asleep. It slightly protects our integrity.

Last night we walked down to Regent's Canal and had dinner in that restaurant that's on a barge. It was lovely and romantic, and I wish to God I hadn't polished off the martinis and all the wine, because the streets along the canal are at their most beautiful at this time of year, and I really would love to have strolled through, enjoying them.

If I recall correctly, it was more of a stumble than a stroll. Jamie had to keep catching me and steering me straight. I have no idea whether we had sex or not, but he says he usually stays now just to make sure I'm okay. Of course I'm okay.

Hang on. Something's coming back to me. Last night. We had a fight. On the way home. Oh God. I groan and bury my face in the pillow, as if that will somehow make this memory go away, but it won't; it's still here, and I wish I didn't have to remember.

Jamie is worried about my drinking. He started to tell me I was drinking too much, and I went ballistic on him. I shouted at him all the way along Blomfield Road. I don't remember what I said, only his stricken face.

He didn't stay the night. Now I remember. He said he wasn't going to do this anymore, that he couldn't watch me destroy myself in this way. He said all of my friends were worrying about me, and that at twenty-nine I was still acting like I was ten years younger, and it was time for me to grow up and start becoming responsible.

I remember screaming something about being responsible, I owned a flat, for God's sake, and I had a steady job, and he knew nothing about me.

I open one eye and look over at the right side of the bed, which is, unsurprisingly, empty. Of course he didn't stay the night and creep out early. He made sure I got home, and — I look down at myself, in a T-shirt and pajama pants — yes, undressed me, and then he left.

I am awash with shame. I may be on my own, but my cheeks are burning. He's right. I can't stand this. I can't stand waking up every morning feeling like shit. I can't stand waking up every morning swearing that I will never do this again, that today is the day I stop drinking, and then, at five, or six, or seven o'clock, I tell myself it's only one glass of wine, or one beer, or a quick drink, which surely won't hurt, and then, bam! Cut to the next morning, waking up with spotty memories about what happened the night before, and always, always, feeling like shit.

I pick up the phone and call my mum. "Can we make it eleven?" I croak when she picks up the phone. "I'm not feeling so good."

"Oh God, Cat. Again?" She's used to these Saturday morning phone calls.

"I know. I'm sorry." To my amazement, my eyes then well up with tears as my voice starts to crack.

"Mum? I think I need some help."

An hour later I'm sitting opposite my mum in Sagne, fortified by several strong cappuccinos, four aspirin, and an almond croissant. I know they say the best cure for a hangover is a full English fry-up, but the thought of greasy bacon and fried bread, ever, is enough to make me throw up. A meltingly buttery almond croissant, with just the right amount of marzipan filling, does it every time.

"So," says my mother, gazing at me with concern. "You need help with your drinking?"

Suddenly it doesn't seem quite so urgent. When I spoke to her this morning my head was pounding, my mouth felt like three thousand squirrels had died in it, and I felt entirely desperate. Now, buoyed by painkillers, coffee, and sugar, I'm realizing that I completely overreacted.

"Sorry about that." I am sheepish. "You caught me at a particularly bad moment. I was feeling like complete crap when I called, but I'm fine now." I expect her to smile with relief, but when I look at her, she is frowning.

She is so very elegant, my mother. Her hair, dyed to within an inch of its life when my father was alive, was left to turn its natural salt and pepper once my father died and now, three years on, is a soft shade of whitish grey. She has it cut in an elegant bob, her skin still soft and smooth, her eyes that startling shade of green, which — thank you, God! — I have inherited, the one thing I have inherited from her.

It is no surprise that my father called me the changeling, because in truth I do not look like either of them, with the exception of my mother's eyes. My father had that classically pale, wan British skin, a nose that was slightly beaky, although he always described it as aquiline, and thin lips.

My skin is naturally olive, hiding a multitude of alcoholic sins. Even when I am horrifically hungover, practically comatose with exhaustion, I never look pale or pasty or ill. My lips are full, and my hair is dark with streaks of gold that come out in the sun on summer holidays to hot places. As a child, I detested my looks, longing for mousy brown hair, pale skin, blue eyes, and thin lips. Now, at the ripe old age of twenty-nine, I am becoming more accepting, occasionally, only occasionally, looking at myself in the mirror and feeling both surprised and pleased at the face that stares back.

Still, it is not a face that resembles my mother's. At twenty paces, and despite her having spent the vast majority of her life in this country, you would peg her for an American. Something in the way she holds herself, a confidence, her smile: and yes, she does have great big perfect white teeth (another thing, thank you, God, I have inherited).

She is slim and tall, and even in a pair of jeans and V-necked T-shirt, with an antique gold belcher chain around her neck and ballet flats on her feet, she is almost ridiculously elegant. More so now that she is able to dress as she wants. Her style is simple: she wears shades of greige, never a color, and always looks immaculate, even without makeup, even though she appears to make little effort.

I find it hard to believe she is my mother.

But she is, and I know her, and I know this frown, which is not a good frown.

I take a deep breath. "I really am fine. I just had a bit too much last night, and I always wake up feeling awful, but I don't need help. I mean, clearly I've been drinking too much." She looks up then, surprised I have admitted it. "I know I'm drinking too much, and I'm going to stop. I can't stand waking up feeling the way I've been feeling, so I've decided that last night was the last time. That's it. Today no more alcohol."

I wait for her relieved smile, but it doesn't come. Instead, she is still frowning, and now she is looking down at the table, as if she is figuring out what to say next, and I know it's something bad when she finally gives a big sigh before meeting my eyes.

"Cat," she says slowly. "There's something I've never told you. Something I should have told you years and years ago, but I could never find the right time. I am so sorry. I thought I was doing the right thing for you, but now I think I've done you a great disservice in keeping this from you."

My heart is pounding. What on earth is she talking about?

"What is it?" My voice sounds strange

given the buzzing in my ears, the pounding in my chest. Whatever is about to come next, I have the strangest sense it will be life altering in the most unchangeable of ways.

She sighs again before looking up.

"It's about your father."

THREE

London, 1969

Audrey gazes out the car window at the lines of redbrick semi-detached houses, all identical, all built after doodlebugs dropped on London during the Second World War destroyed lines of houses, as she tries to suppress the tiny jolts of excitement in the pit of her stomach.

She turns to look at her husband, his large hands resting on the steering wheel, his elegant jaw as tense as always. "You must be nervous, darling," he says, not taking his eyes off the road.

"A little," she lies, as he reaches over and pats her leg reassuringly, briefly turning his head to give her an indulgent smile.

"I might try to come out for the third week," he says. "Although with work right now it's terribly difficult. I know you don't want to go, but your aunt needs you. This is absolutely the right thing to do."

"I know," says Audrey, who cannot believe she is being allowed to go back to her country, to America, for almost an entire summer, on her own, with no husband for whom she has to perform.

Five years ago Audrey left New York, as a nineteen-year-old single girl, to come to Buckinghamshire in England, to work as an au pair. Just a few miles away, in London, everything was swinging, life was being lived at a pace never seen before, none of which was apparent to Audrey, out in the suburbs of Gerrards Cross, minding children while their parents drank G&Ts and hosted dinner parties for neighbors and friends.

Audrey had always delighted in everything English, had grown up losing herself in the books of Jane Austen and Charlotte Brontë, had wanted nothing more than to find herself a crumbling stately pile and a dashing lord of the manor to go with it.

It wasn't that she planned to meet the love of her life when she first signed up with the au pair agency, but she couldn't deny that every night leading up to her departure was filled with elaborate fantasies. She stepped onto that Pan Am flight at JFK, her head positively exploding with hopes and dreams.

The Wilkinsons — Pam, Tony, and their

two children, Stephen and Lizzy — were delightful; their large, detached, Edwardian house on Mill Lane equally so, it was all a little quieter than Audrey had expected.

She had a room under the eaves on the top floor, thick white carpet and a record player in the corner of the room, a window that looked out over the trees, a view that made her happy.

The children — Stephen, ten, and Lizzy, eight — were delicious, and her evenings, initially spent curled up in her bedroom reading a book, soon grew busy.

She became friends with another au pair who worked up the road; Anna from Sweden. The two of them would dress up and go into Uxbridge for a night out, or pop into town for a drink at the Packhorse Inn. Which was where, one night, Richard found her.

Despite not being lord of the manor, he was dashing, and charming, and so fantastically handsome in his slim-cut suits and narrow Italian shoes. He swept her off her feet, even without the stately pile.

He treated Audrey like a princess, clearly adoring her, affectionately teasing her about her American accent, which she tried hard to eradicate, managing to soften it to a Mid-Atlantic drawl.

Richard was an estate agent, moving into commercial property as Audrey met him, his charm and good looks bringing him more and more success. He swapped his Triumph TR7 for an E-type Jaguar and swept Audrey up to the West End for glamorous Saturday nights out.

He knew enough people to gain access to all the best places. They rubbed shoulders with everyone from Marianne Faithfull to Prince Philip, from Twiggy to Vidal Sassoon, drinking champagne at Hélène Cordet's Saddle Room or Tramp, playing roulette at Les A.

She met his friends after these dazzling nights out, for eggs and bacon at the Golden Egg in Oxford Street, wondering if they'd spy one of the Kray brothers, feeling impossibly glamorous, eating breakfast in the early hours of the morning, at the center of the entire world.

London came alive in the sixties, and Audrey came alive on those Saturday nights, guided by Richard, stepping carefully down the iron staircase into Annabel's, where Louis greeted Richard with a handshake, Audrey with a kiss.

Of course she fell in love with Richard. She had never met anyone like him in New York, where the men could have done with a little of his debonair grace. She had never felt so fully alive as with Richard. Her au pair job stretched to two years, after which she told Richard she had to go home.

He proposed. She said yes. Because their life was in England, because her parents died long ago, her Aunt Judith flew over for their tiny wedding at the town hall. Audrey wore a floaty Biba dress, hot-ironed curls into her long straight hair, and she was happy.

A few months later, Richard came home one evening, to their small terraced cottage near the railway station, giddy with secrets. He handed her a key, led her to the car, and drove her up the road to a large, beautiful Edwardian house on Mill Lane. It was May and the flowers were blooming, Richard refusing to tell her why they were there, walking her up the garden path, hand in hand, then gesturing for her to use the key to open the door.

"Who lives here?" Audrey had whispered, gazing around in awe.

"We do. Happy anniversary, darling. Welcome to our new home."

Audrey had been breathless as she walked through the house; huge square rooms, flooded with light from the leaded-glass windows, old paneling on the walls. It was a house that begged to be filled with children, with dogs, with memories.

"Do you like it?" Richard asked finally.

"It's the most beautiful house I've ever been in," she said, thinking of the small Upper West Side apartment she had grown up in, with its herringbone parquet floors and layer upon layer of old, yellowing chipped paint.

"We're going to fill it with children." He pulled her close to him. "This is the house our family is going to grow up in. This is the beginning of the rest of our lives."

Audrey allowed herself to be held, and raised her chin up to be kissed as she knew she was supposed to. The truth was, it *was* the most beautiful house she had ever seen, but it didn't feel like a house she was supposed to live in; it didn't feel like home.

She loved the railway cottage, loved how snug and cosy it was. This house felt like a mansion; she had no idea how to decorate it, what she was supposed to do.

"We'll get someone to help you," said Richard, who found a woman who lived in Denham, who swiftly filled the house with furnishings and accessories that Audrey thought were exquisite, even though they still never felt like hers.

"It will be a wonderful house for our family," Richard told everyone and anyone who would listen.

"Are you pregnant?" Someone would invariably turn to Audrey, congratulations on the tip of their tongue, slight embarrassment as she shook her head. "Not to worry," they'd say. "You've got plenty of time."

Three years of marriage, and no sign of a baby. Three years of marriage, and Richard didn't seem quite so glamorous anymore. The nights in the West End had dwindled, at least for the two of them as a couple. Richard still seemed to have meetings that went on for much of the evening, but when the two of them went out it was usually to the picturehouse to see a film, or a weekend picnic at the pond.

Their friends were having babies all around them, and each month, when it was clear no baby was on the way, Audrey told herself that next month would definitely, certainly, be the month it would happen.

God knows she needed something in her life. Now that the glamor of an English husband had worn off, Richard had revealed himself to be somewhat less charming than he first appeared. He was, in fact, controlling and rather bullying, she thought in her darker moments, wondering if it was just the culture clash, that it was because he was English and English women were, perhaps, more passive. She did not like being told what to wear, what to cook, how to act, but she was getting used to it, was trying so hard to be a good wife, to be the wife he wanted.

He did love her, of that she was certain. Or at least, he loved who he thought she was, who she had turned herself into in order to be the wife she thought he wanted. He told her how beautiful she was, how lucky he was to have her. He showed her off like an exotic trophy, knowing he had won the game of attractive wives.

But wasn't every marriage like this? Audrey looked around her, searching for validation, searching for hope that she wasn't alone. And she wasn't alone. Her newfound friends rolled their eyes about their husbands during their coffee mornings, tittered about their idiosyncrasies.

Audrey used to feel like one of them, until the babies started coming, and she lost her new friends to Babyville, leaving her more alone than ever before.

The letter from Aunt Judith could not have come at a more welcome time. Aunt Judith had always been more like a mother to Audrey, particularly after her own parents died, one after the other, when she was in her early teens. Aunt Judith's children were older, had moved, one to California, one to Michigan, had families of their own that kept them busy, too busy to look after their mother, leaving Audrey as the sole responsible child.

I miss you, dear child, Aunt Judith had written. *I'm thinking of selling the house in Nantucket. It has been a long, hard decision, but with all you children now gone, it seems pointless to have this big old house just for me. Abigail said she'd fly in from Michigan to help me, but of course now her children need her, and Michael's much too busy to leave his job in California. I know how busy you are, but if you felt in need of some Massachusetts sunshine, I could use the help! I'm planning on going out right before Memorial Day, and I'll be there, packing up, for the summer. You could come anytime, with Richard or without. Dearest girl, it would be so lovely to see you.*

Audrey had handed the letter to Richard over dinner that night, her heart pounding with anticipation as he read it distractedly, then put the paper down.

"Well?" she said. "Should we go?"

"I can't possibly go," he said. "I've got that huge deal on the car factory, which is likely to keep me tied up all summer." He looked down and took another bite of his steak Diane.

"Well, should *I* go?"

"Do you want to go?"

Audrey thought for a few seconds. She wanted to go more than she had ever wanted anything in her life. While her parents were alive, they always visited Aunt Judith for a couple of weeks in the summer, and after they died, Audrey would go for the entire summer. Nantucket was the place she had always felt most at peace, a place she now found herself thinking about, missing, as she went about her life in the pretty green suburbs of England.

She wanted to smell the ocean air and walk along Main Street, stopping for the papers at the Hub. She wanted to have coffee at Cy's Green Coffee Pot and wander the aisles of the hardware store next door. She wanted to step back to a time in her life when she felt happy, joyous, and free.

"I don't know," she lied, nervous that obvious enthusiasm would make him suspicious, nervous he would say no. "I don't want to leave you, but I feel like I ought to go. It's going to be a lot of work — she's a terrible old hoarder — but she doesn't have anyone else, her kids are disasters, and I owe her so much. I do think it's the right thing to do."

"I suppose you should go," Richard said. "I don't really want you to, but it won't be for long, yes?"

"I would think she'll need me for around a week. Maybe two. The absolute most would be three."

"Try to make it two," he said as Audrey nodded, reaching for a glass of wine to quell the butterflies of excitement that jumped inside her stomach as soon as those words left his mouth.

The excitement never went away. From April 14, when she received her aunt's letter, to May 31, when she flew out to New York, she found herself either itching with excitement or terrified that something would get in the way, that Richard would change his mind.

He didn't. He was as loving and distant and busy as he always was. Their relationship was as pleasant as it always was. What did I expect, she sometimes thought, in the middle of the night when she would wake up unable to sleep, worrying about whether she made the right choice, what her future might hold, whether she should be happier. Her parents, she realized, set an example that few could match. They loved each other with a fierce, all-consuming passion, even after years of marriage, even after Audrey came along, to the exclusion of all others, including Audrey. It was no surprise her father was diagnosed with heart disease shortly after her mother died, no surprise he deteriorated so very quickly once she had passed — neither of them wanted to carry on without the other.

The surprise, perhaps, was that her own marriage wasn't like that of her parents. She knew this, of course, before she got married, that what she and Richard had wasn't the same, but she thought that kind of devotion might grow, becoming stronger as the years went by. She hadn't expected this lack of conversation, the way Richard would sit at the table and read the papers while she sat there quietly chewing, wishing he would talk to her, pay her attention.

He was so animated with his friends, when they went out for dinner with other couples, the life and soul of the party, but on their own, behind closed doors, he barely seemed to notice her.

I am lonely, she would think, those nights when she would tiptoe downstairs at three in the morning and make herself a cup of tea. I never dreamed I could be lonelier in my marriage than I ever was as a single girl.

Children would change that, she knew.

Children would bring them closer together, give her a purpose. Richard wouldn't allow her to work — none of his successful friends had working wives, all of them consumed with hairdresser visits, manicures, shopping, and children — so Audrey floated around the house all day, desperate for something to do.

She got a puppy, a Maltese, that she would take to the common and walk for hours and hours, looking at her watch wondering how it was time passed so slowly.

They needed a child. She had absolutely no idea why it hadn't happened, and no idea what to do about it. She had a suspicion, based on nothing other than instinct, that it was Richard's fault, but she could never say that out loud. He had questioned her fertility, though, countless times, and she was doing all the things she was supposed to be doing. She had even given up smoking, after hearing of one mother who got pregnant as soon as she quit. But it wasn't their time, not yet. At least, that's the line she would always use when people asked.

A child would stop the loneliness, she knew. Imagine her days being filled with waking the baby, warming a bottle, spoon-feeding the baby rice and wiping up around a high chair. Imagine pushing the baby in a pram up the High Street, stopping to peer in the windows of all the shops as she had seen other mothers do, chatting with other mothers as they pass, inviting them over to drink tea as their babies crawl around the living room.

Imagine Daddy coming home from work, his face lighting up as a toddler toddles to the front door to greet him. Imagine her own face, beaming with love as she watches Richard throw his daughter up in the air as she squeals in delight, catching her and swinging her round with joy, holding out an arm to embrace his wife, his eyes filled with love and pride.

Imagine a second child, a third. Imagine this house buzzing with children running up and down the stairs, children's parties with entertainers, paper bowls of Twiglets and Smarties down the center of a trestle table set up in the garden, the grown-ups standing at one end with their gin and tonics and their devils on horseback, smiling indulgently as the magician arrives to delight their children by pulling rabbits out of hats.

The days ticked by to her trip to New York, and again her period came. I need this break, she told herself. Maybe I'll even see a doctor in New York. She trusted them, had heard there were doctors over there who knew the secrets to getting pregnant.

This trip will change my life, she decided, will change my future going forward. The butterflies came back, on the flight, at the airport, in the car Aunt Judith had sent to drive her to Hyannis to catch the ferry, and then finally, as the boat plowed along the water, she glimpsed Nantucket Harbor, whereupon her heart caught in her throat with nostalgia and joy.

FOUR

Nantucket, the little island off the coast of Massachusetts, made famous by whaling in the mid-nineteenth century, had been discovered in the 1950s by developers who encouraged wealthy vacationers to visit the island with its cobbled streets and pretty grey-shingled houses, trellises weighed down with roses and hydrangeas.

People came here to get away from the noise of Boston and New York, to enjoy the beauty of the pretty village, the beaches, the harbor, in a place the locals referred to as Fantasy Island.

Aunt Judith had bought her own house, a Federal off the top of Main Street, in the late 1950s, just as they were starting to build on the island, just as the island was starting to become popular. Her house had been inhabited by an elderly couple and hadn't been touched for years. She was one of the first to see the beauty in the place, a house that shocked her children, who swiftly forgot their reservations over the dark, peeling wallpaper when they were brought in to help, given sledgehammers to knock down walls between the parlor and the kitchen, opening up the house, choosing their own paint colors for their rooms.

Aunt Judith planted hydrangeas along the front of the house, and replaced the rotting shingles on the front with new white cedar ones. She built vegetable beds in the tiny yard and filled them with tomatoes and lettuce.

In Nantucket, Aunt Judith found out how to be happy. Divorce was frowned upon in the New York suburb of Rye, where she had been living with her husband, until she discovered he was having a long-term affair with his secretary. It all ended very quickly after that. She wanted a fresh start, and had spent a handful of happy vacations on Nantucket; it seemed like a place where you could reinvent yourself, cast aside the dull suburban detritus of your housewife life in Rye. Nantucket was a place where Aunt Judith could discover the inner bohemian she hadn't realized was lurking until she shed her staid uniform of neat skirts and pumps, embracing loose-fitting clothes and sandals that made navigating the cobblestones, if

not entirely pleasurable, at least manage-
able.

The house wasn't big — four bedrooms,
two and a half bathrooms, all under the
eaves — but as she always said to Audrey, it
was big enough.

The house looked the same. Of course,
thought Audrey, as the car pulled to a halt
outside. It's only been five years since I was
last here, why would it have changed? The
gravel was thin, a few weeds pushing
through, the paint on the windows peeling
again, but the house was still pretty, with its
classic lines and peaked roof, the window
boxes still filled with geraniums.

The station wagon was gone, which meant
Aunt Judith was out. She had said she was
leaving the key under the pot, which Audrey quickly found, as the driver hauled her
suitcase up the steps and deposited it on
the porch. She thanked him and sent him
away.

The door opened, a wave of déjà vu washing over Audrey as she stood for a minute,
drinking in the smell, the feeling, of being
home. Little had changed. The table in the
hall was new, fresh-cut peonies in the vase
as always. Aunt Judith always had pitchers
and vases filled with flowers all over the

house; it was one of her signature touches.

The suitcase was heavy, but bumping along every step, Audrey managed to get it up the staircase, breathing heavily, dragging it along the narrow corridor until she reached her room and pushed the door open to find the bed made up with crisp white sheets, an antique dusky rose quilt spread across the foot of the bed, an old wooden blanket chest at the bottom. The armchair she had always loved was in the corner, her old blanket from childhood draped over the back, more peonies in a blue-and-white-spattered pitcher on the dresser.

Crossing the room, Audrey opened the windows, the view so familiar, the trees, the sound of the birds, the smell of salt in the air, and found herself smiling as she turned to unpack, pulling out a pair of shorts and a sheer cotton top, dying to get out of what she thought of as her English clothes, dying to feel the sun on her legs, the wind blowing the fine hairs on her arms. She pulled on the shorts and top, scraped her long dark hair into a messy topknot, and started to put the clothes away in drawers, instantly feeling younger, lighter, almost as if her marriage, the last five years of her life in England, had never, ever happened.

Her clothes were almost all put away, the dresses hung, the tops and shorts in drawers, when she heard the door downstairs and rushed to the stairs, a huge smile on her face in anticipation of seeing her beloved aunt.

"Hello!" She clattered down the stairs and burst into the kitchen, all legs, arms akimbo, bare feet, stopping short at the sight of a man standing at the counter, unpacking two paper grocery bags.

"Hi!" He grinned at her. "You must be Audrey. I'm Brooks Mayhew." He put the eggs he was holding down and reached over to shake her hand, apologizing for the paint spatters across his fingers.

"It's fine," said Audrey, wondering who this man was who seemed completely comfortable in her aunt's house. Not a boyfriend, he was far too young, and not an advisor, in his loose, paint-spattered shirt, his baggy seersucker shorts and canvas shoes. His hair was almost shoulder length, his skin tanned, his smile easy and wide. He looked almost as if he could be one of the boating boys, yet the paint didn't make sense.

"I'm working on a new painting. I promised Judith I'd run out and get groceries for her, and time got away from me. She warned me you might be here. She's had to go off island, by the way. Said she would be home for dinner, that there's plenty of food in the fridge and pantry if you want to get something ready."

"I'm sorry," Audrey found herself saying, a habit she had picked up since living in England, apologizing for everything, even when it quite clearly was not her fault, "but who *are* you?"

He started to laugh. "Are you wondering if I'm Judith's secret lover?"

"I'd be terribly impressed if you were."

"I'm the neighbor. I'm renting the house next door, and I've got a studio down on the wharf. I'm an artist, in case that wasn't obvious." He brandished his shirt and hands as evidence. "Judith has become my best friend in a matter of weeks. She feeds my cats when I'm at the studio, and I . . . well . . . I try to help out. I go shopping for her, or fix things around the house." He gestured at the window. "I've replaced the frames in here, slowly working my way around the rest of the house."

"It needs it."

"You haven't been here for a few years?"

"Five. I live in England now."

"I hear. You've got a bit of an English accent."

"Give me a day or two and the English will be wiped out completely."

"When in Rome," they both said at the same time, and started to laugh.

"Can I get you a drink?" he asked.

"I was going to offer you the same thing." She walked to the counter and pulled a six-pack of beer from one paper bag. "Not that I knew if we had anything to offer you, but I'm the one who should be the hostess."

"That sounds very formal. I've forgotten about gracious hosting since living here."

She cracked open a beer and handed it to him, then opened one for herself, leaning against the kitchen counter. "Where are you from?" she asked. "Here?"

"No. New York. Well, Long Island, to be precise. Locust Valley. Lattingtown."

"Fancy!" Audrey said, proferring her can. "I suppose I should say cheers."

"Cheers." He grinned, clinking cans. "It is fancy, and, as you can see, I am not, which is why I am now living in Nantucket, which is about as unfancy as you can get."

Are you married? Audrey found herself thinking, swiftly followed by wondering why it should matter, why she should even want to know.

"I also broke off an engagement," he said, as if reading her mind. "We were going to be living in a big house in Mill Neck, gifted to us by my father, and I knew I would die out there."

"Did you leave her standing at the altar?" Audrey is intrigued.

"Not quite, but almost. A week before. I knew it was wrong from the beginning, but she was the girl I was expected to marry, from the right family, and it became a freight train, gathering steam. There was no way to stop it."

"But you managed."

"I took the coward's way out." He stopped smiling then, a glimmer of shame in his eyes. "I left a note. Horrible. I still can't quite believe that's how I did it, but I knew if I tried to do it in person, Clarissa would convince me to stay, and I knew that if I stayed, I would die."

"Clarissa." Audrey turned the name over in her mind, picturing a slim, elegant blonde, steel blue eyes, hair in a tight chignon, immaculately dressed in Galanos or Balenciaga, purse matching her pumps, the quintessential Waspy American wife.

"She does look exactly as you would expect a girl called Clarissa to look," he said, as if reading her mind again.

"Tall, slim, beautiful? Blond with blue eyes? In Balenciaga?"

"Galanos. But yes. The rest. I don't even want to think about what I did to her."

"Is there any possibility that just as you knew it wasn't the right match, on some level she might have known too?"

"I would like to think that's true. In many ways, I do believe that she may realize that it was never me she was in love with, but what I represented. I could never be the man she needed me to be. Wow." He shook his head with an embarrassed laugh. "I don't usually reveal this much to anyone, let alone someone I just met."

"I'm a good listener."

"So it seems."

They smiled at each other, the mutual gaze lasting a second longer than was altogether comfortable, Audrey looking away, confused. It wasn't done, surely, to reveal so much about oneself to a stranger. Where was the small talk? Where was the polite conversation? How did they get to such big, important stuff so quickly?

And what did it mean?

Don't be silly, she told herself. It certainly doesn't mean what you think it means. This isn't attraction. I am very happily married. Just because a single man who happens to be attractive is standing feet away from me and makes me feel instantly comfortable doesn't mean I have to start acting like a giddy schoolgirl. Grow up, Audrey. Don't be so childish.

"You must be busy. Please don't let me keep you." She snapped into more formal mode to hide her embarrassment at that gaze, that look that held a hint of something more.

"Okay," he said with an easy shrug, draining the rest of the can. "It was good to meet you. I'm next door if you need anything." And with a wave, he was gone.

In the fridge Audrey found a packet of ground beef. She grated an onion, mixed eggs into the beef, added crushed saltines and some dried herbs she pulled from the spice rack. She sang as she used her hands to mix the meatloaf together, as carefree and happy as a young girl.

She found the loaf pan — there was always a loaf pan — and placed the meatloaf on the middle shelf of the oven. She was not an expert cook but had developed a range of recipes to keep Richard happy: meatloaf, creamed chicken, meatballs. She had learned how to make a traditional Sunday roast, complete with Yorkshire pudding, and had delighted him with American-style fried chicken.

Today, for the salad, she arranged large leaves of iceberg lettuce on a plate, carefully peeling a pear and placing the pear halves on top, dousing them with lemon juice to stop them from turning brown. In the cavity she placed a spoonful of mayonnaise, adding grated cheese over the top, before putting it in the fridge.

The sun streamed through the kitchen windows in a way it didn't seem to in England, fresh and clear. She had got used to the endlessly grey drizzly days, had even grown to love them in a strange way, certainly to love how green everything was, how lush, until this moment, being back in Nantucket, back in the place she had always loved.

She took a glass of wine with her to the driveway, where she busied herself pulling weeds, smiling at passersby, most of whom — the islanders at least — stopped to chat and introduce themselves.

At six o'clock, Brooks pulled up next door in an old F-150 truck, cherry red, giving her a cheery wave and smile as he headed into his house. She tried to quell the vague disappointment that he didn't come over, didn't show any signs of wanting to continue their conversation, but as she was mulling it over, Aunt Judith's familiar old station wagon pulled into the driveway, tooting the horn in welcome, as Audrey flung herself down the steps and into her aunt's arms.

Home.

Aunt Judith's solidity had always felt like home to Audrey. Her hair was grey and curly, her eyes a soft blue, her body seeming to be smaller and rounder than it had been before. "I was built for comfort, not for speed," Aunt Judith had a habit of saying, and it was true; when Audrey imagined her, she was always sitting comfortably somewhere, knitting, reading, or doing something equally cozy.

Her roundness and coziness and warmth had always comforted Audrey, who found herself leaning her head on her aunt's shoulder, as, without her knowing why, tears started to leak down her cheeks.

"You look unchanged," Aunt Judith mused over a glass of wine later that evening after they had eaten, cleared up, and were sitting on the porch watching the fireflies buzz around.

"Apart from the English accent?"

"I can't hear it anymore. You look exactly the same, but you seem . . . quieter." She peered closely at Audrey, who said nothing, just looked into her glass and took another sip of wine.

"How is Richard?" Aunt Judith asked next, perceptive as ever.

"He's fine." Audrey looked up at her aunt. "He's charming, handsome, polite, and . . . distant."

"Isn't that how most men are?" her aunt asked, a twinkle in her eye.

"Is it?" Audrey thought about that afternoon in the kitchen, the ease she felt around that man, Brooks, how she felt a connection, a closeness, even though she didn't know him at all. "Perhaps," she said. "Richard is very English, I think. But I presumed things would change once we got married. I thought he would let his reserve down, that we would grow closer, he would be more of a partner, but . . ." Her words trailed off.

Her aunt waited a few seconds. "It sounds lonely, child."

Audrey, surprised, blinked back tears as she forced a smile. "Sometimes it is. But he is a good man. I am a lucky girl."

"Who are you trying to convince? Me? Or yourself?"

Upstairs, in her room, getting ready for bed, Audrey thought about her day. She thought about Aunt Judith, all they talked about, the conversation flowing in and out, back and forth, from laughter to seriousness and everything in between.

She thought about Brooks, the charming man from next door who made her feel a slight jolt, the likes of which she hadn't felt in a very long time, the likes of which she wasn't expecting to feel again, and certainly not from anyone other than her husband.

It's just because he's familiar, she told herself. Of course you felt comfortable with him, you *know* him, if only because you are from the same place, you share the same culture, you understand each other's backgrounds. She hadn't realized just how out of place she was in England until this day, coming back home, meeting someone unexpectedly and feeling an instant connection merely because, surely merely because, they were fellow countrymen: they understood how the other thought.

She pushed thoughts of the handsome artist out of her head, remembering her wedding to Richard, how he looked at her with such love and pride, thinking of the life they had built together and how, in his own way, he treated her like a princess.

Thoughts of Richard led her gently to sleep.

■ ■ ■ ■

Jet lag hit Audrey in the middle of the night. She was wide awake at two in the morning, padding around the house, trying to immerse herself in a book, not worried about the lack of sleep because the next day she had nowhere to be, nothing to do, and if she chose to sleep all day, even though that would be the worst possible thing to do, to give up a moment of her precious time on this island, she knew she could.

She wandered down to the harbor to watch the sun come up, yawning her way back to the cottage as tiredness finally hit, and at 6 a.m. she crawled back into those sweet, white sheets and fell fast asleep.

When she awoke for the second time, it was almost noon. The sun was high and bright in the sky, and Aunt Judith had left a note to say she had a bridge game and would be back this afternoon.

It was a perfect day for a walk, and perhaps the beach. No one had a suntan in England. A few people they knew had ventured to places like Acapulco or Majorca for their honeymoons, but travel was exotic and expensive, and there was little hope of turning golden brown in the weak English sun.

She stretched her legs out, pale in her cutoffs, and grabbed some baby oil from the bathroom cabinet, squeezing it into her straw tote next to a towel and a book. She put on the crocheted bikini she'd bought on Carnaby Street on a trip up to London, unsure when she would ever wear it, but knowing it would be a good investment if she ever went on vacation again.

Twisting her hair into a loose braid, she pulled a T-shirt over the bikini, grabbed her bag, and headed out the door.

FIVE

Main Street looked exactly the same, as picture-book perfect as it had always been. Audrey wandered along, looking into all the store windows, smiling and saying hi to everyone she passed, stopping to chat to the people she knew, all of whom knew she was coming from her aunt's, all of whom were delighted to see her.

She made her way down Straight Wharf, pausing outside one store, its windows filled with canvases, gorgeous seascapes, propped up against one another, a few nudes, reclining women on mussed-up sheets, their faces turned away from the artist. And as she stood, thinking how beautiful they were, she noticed movement behind, and there he was, Brooks, waving at her to come in, a wide grin on his face.

"Hey!" He put down the canvas he was holding and walked over to her. They both paused, Audrey feeling the unexpected urge to hug him, but how could she, she barely knew him. They stood grinning at each other, unable to wipe the smiles off their faces. Brooks eventually extended a hand, which she shook, laughing as she glanced around the room.

"I guess I've stumbled upon your studio! These are so beautiful, Brooks. You're so talented!"

"You're surprised?"

"No. I guess I thought your work would be more abstract, I have no idea why. Look at how you've captured Nantucket! Are they for sale? I'd love to buy one!"

"Which is your favorite?" Delight was in his eyes.

"Let me look through. May I? Is that okay?"

"We'll look together."

They wandered round the studio, Brooks telling Audrey about the paintings, what inspired him, funny stories about how they almost got sabotaged. His sleeves were rolled up, his arms tanned, the hairs a golden brown. Audrey found herself staring at those strong arms, recognizing she was feeling feelings she should not have been feeling; hoping that they would go away, even though they felt so very, very, good.

Her husband might have been very handsome, but Audrey's appreciation of his looks had always been intellectual. She *knew* Richard was good-looking; it just didn't necessarily have much of an effect on her.

It certainly never caused her to catch her breath, a jolt inside her body when his arm brushed hers, as was happening each time Brooks touched her accidentally, or placed a hand in the small of her back to guide her elsewhere in the studio.

When he talked, she turned to him, her eyes running over his thick, dark hair, streaked with gold from the sun, the dimples in his cheeks when he smiled, the way he moved with an extraordinary ease, as if he were a man entirely comfortable in his skin.

He wore paint-streaked jeans, an untucked white shirt. Audrey had a vision, suddenly, of him walking across the bedroom, naked. She inhaled sharply, aware of an unexpected stirring in her loins.

"I love this one," she said quickly, turning away so he didn't see the deep flush rising on her cheeks. She went over to a small, delicate watercolor of the Sankaty lighthouse. "I love the big ones, but this one is so delicate, so pretty, so perfectly captures the essence of this place."

He picked it up, examined it, then handed

it to her. "You have great taste. The watercolors are my favorites, and this one particularly. I always thought I would keep this one, but I couldn't imagine it in better hands."

"Really? Are you sure?"

"Completely."

"How much is it?"

"It's yours. A gift." He bowed.

"A gift? But . . ."

"Yes. I won't hear anything else about it. Say, what are you doing now? Do you want to get an ice cream from the Paradise?"

Audrey broke into a wide grin. "I can't imagine anything I'd like to do more."

"Don't you look happy." Aunt Judith looked up from where she was sitting in the garden, reading the newspaper, a small folding table next to her with a glass of what might have been iced tea, a bowl of nuts beside it.

"I do? I feel pretty happy." Audrey, in fact, felt more than happy — she felt giddy. A perfect day with a man she might not be able to have, but his attention, his flattery, the way he had made her laugh, had her feeling like a teenager, light and free, without a care in the world.

"Where have you been? I was thinking perhaps tomorrow we can start making headway with sorting out the attic. How would that be?" She peered at Audrey. "You've caught the sun, and I noticed the baby oil was missing. The beach?"

"Yes. Actually I ran into Brooks, your neighbor, this morning, and he ended up coming to the beach with me." Audrey looked away as she said this, not wanting her perceptive aunt to see anything in her eyes.

"What a treat!" Aunt Judith spoke without judgment. "He's delicious, isn't he? If I weren't so old I'd fall head over heels for that man."

"He's terribly nice."

Aunt Judith sat back and gazed at her niece. "My sweet girl, I think you deserve to have some fun, and I'm delighted you've found a new friend who makes you smile. You seemed weighted down by the world yesterday, and today it is as if I have got my Audrey back. If being in the company of my neighbor does that for you, then more power to him, I say."

"You don't think it's dangerous?" Audrey asked, after some hesitation.

Aunt Judith smiled her familiar smile, her eyes twinkling as she tilted her head. "I think we are only here for one life," said her aunt. "I think we cannot tell what our future holds, but we should seize happiness where we find it. Do I think you should leap into bed with him? Well, no. Of course not. But nor do I think you should avoid someone with whom you have a connection. Have fun, Audrey. You deserve to have fun, my darling. That's all."

Audrey skipped over to her aunt and leaned down, kissing her on the cheek. "Thank you," she said. "I won't be jumping into bed with him — I am a happily married woman, after all — but thank you for blessing our friendship."

"You're welcome." Her aunt watched thoughtfully as Audrey hopped up the wooden staircase and back into the house.

Audrey felt herself bubble over with excitement. She might not have been thinking about jumping into bed with Brooks, but she couldn't stop replaying their day together. Their walk to the ice cream parlor, then wandering around looking at the boats, and finally the beach, where they sat and talked about everything under the sun.

Everything seemed brighter, the trees greener, the sun stronger, her world in sharp relief as her insides fizzed with possibility. She hadn't thought about her husband all day, her other life, her staid suburban-housewife life back in boring old England.

She looked at herself in the mirror. She had indeed caught the sun. Freckles were emerging on her nose, as they always used to do. She had left the rollers and hair iron behind in England, was leaving her hair loose and long, hanging below her shoulders.

She slipped a tunic over her head and slid her feet into sandals, calling to her aunt that she would be going for a walk, suppressing the knowledge that actually she was going to find Brooks, was hoping against hope she might run into him again, just wanting to see him smile, to continue feeling the high she had felt all day.

She skipped down the front steps, out onto the street, pausing as she heard a murmur from next door. There in the doorway was Brooks, with a young woman. Audrey froze behind the tree, her heart pounding as she watched them, watched Brooks reach out a hand and lay it on her arm, saw the woman throw her head back and laugh.

A wave of misery washed over her as she silently turned left instead of right. She heard her name, heard him call a hello, but she didn't want to see him, felt betrayed, and ridiculous for feeling that way. What did she expect, she asked herself as she rounded the corner, that he had fallen in love with her? That he had no life and was waiting at home for her to appear?

You are being childish, she berated herself, then: *You are a married woman; what on earth are you thinking?* She was stunned at the depths to which she sank, so quickly, merely from seeing a man she didn't really know with another woman. What business is it of mine? she muttered, forcing her thoughts to her loving husband, which didn't make her feel better at all, the entire day clouded in misery.

At the Hub, at the end of the day, she picked up a postcard and sat on a bench, writing to Richard. *Darling Richard,* she wrote. *Aunt Judith is fine, and we're starting to organize tomorrow — have been getting over jet lag! Sun is shining and lovely, but I miss you terribly. Your loving wife, Audrey xx.*

Her spirits were lifted somewhat in writing this, as if writing down she was a loving wife, would make it so: would change the fact that she was sitting on a stoop deep in misery at a perceived rejection by a man who wasn't her husband.

She took the postcard to the post office to stamp and mail, feeling better.

Richard.

She must think about Richard.

How lucky she is, what a good life they have.

Deep in thought, she walked out of the post office, and straight into Brooks.

"Audrey!" He frowned, reaching out his hands to steady her. "I came to find you. Didn't you hear me? I called to you from the porch, but . . . you didn't hear."

"I'm so sorry." Audrey took a step back, glancing at him, then over his shoulder, as if she had places to go, people to see. "I must have been in another world." She didn't want to look at him too closely, didn't want to give him back the power he had over her earlier today, when the rest of the world dropped away, when all she could look at was him.

"She's a client," he said quietly. Urgently. "The wife of a client, actually, buying a painting for her husband's office."

"I don't know what you're talking about."

"It was business," he said simply, as Audrey flushed a deep red. "It wasn't anything else."

"It's none of *my* business," Audrey said eventually, shuffling with discomfort, unable to look him in the eye.

"It is, though," he said. "You and I both know it is."

After that, Audrey had no idea what to say, the glimmer of warmth in her body spreading and growing until she felt bathed in sunlight and happiness, all over again.

"Do you want to go to the Club Car?" he asked. "We could have cocktails."

Audrey, not trusting herself to speak, nodded as they set off down the street, neither of them looking anywhere but straight ahead.

Halfway into her second Gibson, Audrey realized she was drunk. Her third was untouched, sitting off to the side; she knew if she ventured further, she might well fall asleep.

As it was, she was filled with a gorgeous, happy buzz. She went to the bathroom and looked at herself in the mirror above the sink, astonished at how she was glowing.

She walked carefully along the side of the bar, concentrating on walking in a straight line, on placing one foot in front of the other, and sat on her stool, giggling.

"I've had too much to drink," she said, playing with the stem of her glass, not wanting this to be the end of the evening, but knowing she couldn't handle any more.

"Really? You're a lightweight," said Brooks, who didn't seem even tipsy, despite coming to the end of his third. "One more for the road?"

"For you," she said, sliding her third glass over to him. "Not for me."

"What about some food?" He peered at her. "That will help soak it up if you're feeling bad. They have great fish here. Want to eat?"

Audrey realized suddenly that she was starving, but Aunt Judith would be waiting. "I can't," she said. "Aunt Judith. I have to get back."

"I saw her on the way out. I told her if I found you I might whisk you out for cocktails. She knows. She'll be fine."

"In that case, I'd love to." Audrey found that once again, she couldn't wipe the smile off her face.

Dinner out had never been so much fun. They ate shellfish with their fingers, Audrey leaning forward and laughing, giddy with excitement, surrounded in a vague alcoholic haze, which did, she was relieved to discover, get better over dinner. Brooks ordered a bottle of champagne, but Audrey didn't touch her glass, watching him demolish the bottle, not the slightest bit the worse for wear, before moving on to wine.

"Black Irish," he confessed, halfway

through the meal. "It's the blood. Same with my father and grandfather. We don't get drunk. This? Alcohol? Mother's milk to us."

"I'm impressed," said Audrey, thinking fleetingly of her staid husband and his one vodka gimlet before a meal, with perhaps a shared half bottle during dinner. She had never seen Richard drunk, and although Brooks was not drunk, he was looser than he was earlier, funnier, more exuberant, although perhaps, she thought, we are both more relaxed as we are getting to know each other.

"So how is life in England?" Brooks asked.

"Are you asking me how life is in England or how married life is?"

A grin spread on his face as he sat back, his hands in the air. "Okay. You got me. How is married life? We've talked about everything under the sun except that."

"I know." She paused. How would she answer this? "Well. Married life is . . ." Audrey had no idea what to say. "It's fine," she said lamely. "Good."

"Good? That's it? What's your husband like?"

"He's very good-looking," she said, which was about the nicest thing she could think of to say about him. "And he's a good person. I think."

Brooks raised an eyebrow. "You think?"

Audrey visibly deflated. Sick of pretending everything was fine, sick of pretending to be happy, sick of being the downtrodden wife, she looked Brooks in the eye and took a deep breath. "He's pompous. And cold. And distant. And I've never been so lonely in my life."

They looked at each other in shock. And Audrey started to laugh. Peals of laughter, tears streaming down her cheeks. She had no idea why she was laughing, only that she couldn't stop. Until she felt Brooks taking her hand and holding it gently, and when she looked at him he was not laughing with her. In his eyes she saw empathy, and kindness, and a longing that she instantly recognized; she felt the same way.

This excitement cannot turn into anything more, she told herself, excusing herself to go to the bathroom, seeing her bright eyes in the mirror. It is just a lovely new friendship. Whatever is going on here — and it was clear to her by that time that they both had feelings that could be dangerous — it cannot lead to anything.

They were the last to leave. As they walked up the street, Audrey still slightly unsteady on her feet, brushing shoulders with Brooks, bumping into him every few steps, their hands sliding together, as her fingers intertwined with his, neither of them looking at each other, neither of them saying a word.

I shouldn't be doing this, she thought, feeling his thumb rub her hand, her breath almost stopping. But she couldn't remove her hand, couldn't speak, couldn't do anything other than relish the feeling of her hand in his.

And when they reached Aunt Judith's, and he turned and pulled her in, placed his hands on the side of her face and gazed into her eyes, his head moving closer and closer as her heart threatened to leap out of her body, she still couldn't say anything, couldn't think of anything other than his mouth landing on hers.

And when he took her by the hand and led her not up the garden path to Aunt Judith's but next door, through the gate and up the path to his house, when he stood before her in the living room, lifted the tunic over her head, traced his fingers down the side of her neck, over her breasts, hooked them into her panties, leaving her naked and yearning, still she couldn't speak.

"Audrey," he whispered, scooping her up and carrying her to his bedroom, laying her on the bed as every nerve and fiber in her body jumped and tingled, as if electricity were coursing through her.

And still she didn't speak.

However she imagined he would look naked, it could not possibly have been as good as how he felt. His skin was warm, his lips so soft as he kissed, licked, sucked, murmured, nibbled every inch of her body, his tongue reaching into places Richard had never gone, as Audrey quivered and moaned, reaching for him to kiss, over and over.

She had never known what she had been missing.

She had never known how it was supposed to be.

Six

London, 1998

"What *about* my father?"

What? What could she possibly tell me about my dear, departed father that I don't already know? That he was a controlling, narcissistic bastard? That everything was all about him? That she hated him? My mind races. Maybe she's going to tell me he had affairs. Not that it would particularly surprise me, just give me a reason to hate him more. Now it's my time to frown. Oh God. Perhaps he beat her up? Perhaps his bullying crossed the line into physical abuse.

"What is it, Mum?" She still hasn't spoken, and now I'm worrying.

"I'm sorry. I don't know how to tell you this. Your father . . ." she stops. "He wasn't your father."

And everything falls into place.

Of course he wasn't my father. Didn't I

always know I was different? Didn't I always dream that he would turn out not to be my father? Because I never felt close to him, never felt a connection, never understood how I, with my dark skin and wild (at times) personality, could have come from his loins.

Still, I am stunned. I sit and look at my mother as she starts to talk, to tell me about an artist called Brooks Mayhew, about one perfect summer in Nantucket, about how she knew, when I was born a month early, weighing eight pounds three ounces, much to my eternal shame, for what kind of a monster baby is born a month early weighing more than most babies at full term, how she took one look at my olive skin, my screwed-up features, and knew exactly who my father was, and that it wasn't her husband.

"I don't understand," I keep saying, trying to process everything, trying to figure out how on earth you process, after twenty-nine years, that nothing you thought about yourself was true, that in finding out your father is not your father, it makes everything else a lie.

Even when that's not a bad thing, even when you are grateful and relieved that your father wasn't your father, you feel, immediately, that you are standing on shifting

87

sands. That nothing in your life is real, and nothing in your life will ever be the same again.

"Which bit don't you understand?" My mother is flush with reminiscing about a man I can see she loved. Which makes me know, instantly, how little she loved my father.

"Why didn't you stay with him? Why didn't you go back to Nantucket?"

Sadness crosses her face. "Things were different in those days. The shame of having an affair was something I couldn't face, not to mention the shame of divorce. Back then it would have been a tremendous thing, and to walk out of a new marriage was just something I couldn't face. You have to remember, my darling, I didn't have supportive parents. I didn't really have anyone, other than your father."

"You had Aunt Judith."

"True. And I thought so much about what would happen if I left and went back to Nantucket. I dreamed about it, often. I just couldn't muster up the courage to leave. I was also" — she looks down, ashamed — "terrified of your father. Whenever I thought about leaving, about saying the actual words, I would see his face screwed up with rage. I imagined him taking everything, taking you, making sure I was left with noth-ing."

"Which he would have done," I agree. "Although he wouldn't have wanted me if he knew I wasn't his. He didn't really want me anyway."

"I'm sorry." She reaches out a hand, and I see her eyes are filled with tears. "I am so sorry. I thought I was doing the right thing, giving you a stable home, a family, with a father who was able to support us, to give you the life I wanted you to have. Brooks was from a wealthy family, but his trusts were tied up for years. He didn't have anything, not then. And I didn't even know if he wanted me, or the responsibility of a child. I doubt he would have done."

I blink at her in horror. "You never told him?"

"I didn't want to disrupt his life any more."

"So when you left Nantucket you never spoke to him again? That was it?"

"He wrote to me, care of Aunt Judith, so your father never questioned the writing on the envelope. But I didn't write back. I couldn't. I had made my decision and I had to live with it. I thought I was doing the right thing for you." She shakes her head. "God, I wish I'd left him years ago. The only

89

thing that kept me there was fear."

"You were doing the best you could," I reassure her. "It wasn't such a bad life. Who knows how it would have been had you made a different decision. We can't look back." Even as the words leave my mouth I am impressed with how wise they sound, how calm I sound, given the turmoil going on inside me.

I am alternately elated and devastated. It feels surreal to suddenly know that I have a father I have never met — quite possibly a whole other family. I may have brothers, sisters. I may suddenly get to have the life I have always wanted, one filled with siblings and noise and laughter.

But what if they don't want me? What does this mean? What happens next? My mind is filled with thoughts, my body flooded with feelings that bounce back and forth, from excitement to fear, delight to trepidation. I am in another world, forcing myself back to reality only when I hear my mother say something.

"I'm sorry. What did you say?" I look at her.

"The drinking," my mother says again, quietly.

I immediately jump on the defensive. "Really? Are we back to that? You've just given me the most important news of my life and now you're going to start haranguing me about the drinking?"

"No. I meant *his* drinking. Brooks. It was another factor, another reason why I decided to leave, to come back to England. He drank so much. Every day. I worried about him, his future. Even when I fantasized about leaving and taking you to Nantucket, the memory of how much he drank always stopped me. I couldn't rely on him, and it scared me."

"Was he horrible when he drank?"

She smiles. "No. He was much the same. He used to say he had black Irish blood, which meant liquor was like mother's milk to him. It didn't matter how much he drank, he never got drunk."

"Great," I grumble. "I got his black Irish skin but not his ability to drink and stay sober. Thanks." I raised my eyes in a sarcastic thanks to the gods who might be listening.

"Yes," she says quietly. "You did get his liking to drink. I know you don't want to talk about this, but I think there's a genetic component to this. I believe what you said to me this morning on the phone, that you need help. And I believe that you do want to stop drinking, as you told me. I think

91

you believe it too, just as you believe that today is the first day of your sobriety. But I also know you. And I think that at some time today, probably late afternoon, that resolve will be gone and you will tell yourself you will be able to have one small glass of wine, and then . . . then all bets will be off." She leans forward and places a hand on top of mine, again, for I am doing what I always do when anyone points out one of my deficiencies — I have shut down, refusing to look at her, trying to spirit myself away to somewhere else entirely.

"Look at me, Cat," she says. And I do.

"You can't help it. This isn't your fault. That's what I'm trying to say. This is genetic, and it's time for you to get help."

"What about my father?" I change the subject, aware there is a flash of anger in my voice. "What am I supposed to do about him?"

"I don't know," she says. "I think maybe I should write to him and tell him about you. I know you'll want to get in touch with him, but I need to let him know first."

"Really?" I hate myself for the sarcasm dripping from my voice. "You *think*?" I catch myself, take a deep breath, apologize. I can't believe what she has just told me, and yet, of course I can believe.

And for the first time, everything in my life now seems to make sense.

Seven

My mother is entirely wrong. I'm on day four of not drinking, and while I can't say it has been exactly easy, I'm doing it, and without help, at that.

I told all the girls at work, so they don't encourage me, and this week I've opted out of the press launches, because while I'm delighted at this newfound willpower, I know it's only going to work if I stay away from situations where I might be tempted.

More than anything, I can't believe I'm not drinking given what I now know about my life. Drink has always been my first port of call when anything emotional happens in my life, and I'm being forced to feel these feelings, reconcile myself with the fact that I have a different father, without anything to numb me, to help me slip into a state of calm oblivion.

Actually, that's not strictly true. Sam, at work, slipped me some Valium this week, which has helped enormously. I'm only supposed to take one a day, but they wear off so quickly I've found myself taking them every few hours, although yesterday he kept asking if I was okay, terrified, I think, that I had overdosed. Jackie eventually sent me home straight after lunch because apparently I was in a daze. Sam called all evening to make sure I was alive. Just for the record, I have always adored this good-looking, stylish gay man on the fashion desk, but now I think he may have become my official gay best friend.

But I'm doing so well that when all the girls announce they're going to the wine bar across the street after work, I announce I'm going too.

"Are you sure?" says Poppy, who is my closest friend at work, peering out at me from behind her blond fringe. "You did ask us to help you not drink, and the temptation might be too strong."

"I'm fine!" I say. "Bring on the Diet Coke!" I ignore Poppy's worried look as I start to clear my desk.

I have worked here, at the *Daily Gazette,* for eight years. Even *I* am astounded at how I've managed to hold down the same job for eight long years, but perhaps it has something to do with the fact that the women I work with, the other feature writers on the women's desk, have all become my greatest friends.

There are eight women on the desk, including the editor, Jackie. And I consider every one of these women to be my best friend, although Poppy is the best of the lot. I consider myself unbelievably lucky that I get to go to work every single day with my best friends.

When I started, in my early twenties, we were all single. God, the fun we had back then. Every night there was a press launch, or a party, or a premiere, and the whole desk would raid the fashion cupboard across the aisle for fabulous shoes, designer clothes, free samples of makeup, and the whole glittering troop of us would fortify ourselves with a couple of glasses of wine (or four) before piling into a cab, on expenses, and going off to a party.

I was renting a flat in Kensal Rise back then, which in hindsight was a bit of a dump, but it was the very first place of my own, with no flatmates, and I loved it. There was a hideous, garish, swirly carpet of red, orange, and yellow roses with leaves in a particularly hideous slash of green, which everyone thought hilarious. The girls at work ended up giving me a bag full of terrible joke sunglasses to keep on the hall table to help people deal with the pain of that carpet.

I had a sofa donated from an ex-boyfriend (the only good thing to have come out of that particular relationship), and my mum had taken me to Habitat for pretty much everything else. We threw a sisal rug on top of the floral confusion in the living room, added pretty cushions and bookshelves, and it really didn't look too bad.

But the bills were crippling me. I suspected I might have to take in a flatmate, which I really didn't want to do, even though there was a perfectly nice second bedroom, which was completely empty, and I was trying my damnedest to save on the food bills by eating out at the press launches.

There was always so much food! So much drink! I'd make sure I hit the food table, or grabbed enough canapés at the beginning to line my stomach, before hitting the booze.

We were always together, the traveling pack of sparkly hacks, a mixture of blondes, brunettes, redheads (my late twenties saw me going through my red phase), tall, short, large, small, from entirely different backgrounds, with entirely different accents, all of us knowing we would do anything for our group: We were each other's family.

There have been a few changes. A couple defected over to the *Daily Mail,* a couple to the women's glossy magazines, and we have seen the addition of Sam, who may not be a woman, and may not work on the features desk, but is an honorary member of our girl gang if ever there was one. Jackie, Poppy, Gina, and I have been together since the beginning, have watched each other's lives change and grow over the years.

Although my life hasn't actually changed that much. True, I did manage to move out of the terrifyingly carpeted flat a couple of years ago and buy my own garden flat just down the street on Shirland Road. And I have lost my puppy fat, finally, able to easily wear a size 12, and sometimes, depending on the designer, a size 10. And I no longer have red hair but my natural dark locks, with the streaks of gold helped a little by a very nice hairdresser in South Molton Street.

Poppy, my partner in crime in those early single days, both of us drinking and partying, making sure we had each other's backs, then fell in love with Will Simons on the news desk. They got married five years ago in a picture-perfect stone church in the Cotswolds, with roses climbing over every available surface, and all of us her bridesmaids, whooping it up at what we all feared might be the final hurrah.

For a while Poppy dragged Will to all of our bashes, until they got busy having cosy couple dinner parties, Poppy immersing herself in Jamie Oliver recipes as they entertained. They got a cat, then another one, then, finally, a baby. Well, obviously, they didn't "get" the baby, they "had" the baby. George. I am his godmother, and he is the most delicious little boy I have ever known. But even though I adore him, I have to force myself not to dwell on how much he has changed our friendship, on how different our lives are now.

I still consider Poppy my best friend, but we never go out partying anymore. She works from home on Fridays, and her desk sits empty beside me, which always feels unsettling. After work she'll occasionally come for a drink, but it's only one, and she won't really be focused on what's going on. Her body may be in the wine bar but her head is with the baby, and how quickly she can get back to him. Which she does. Usually after a few sips. I don't blame her. I get it. I understand that her life is different now, that she's living an incredibly happy, cozy, domesticated life, and that hanging out with a single girl who likes to drink and party doesn't really fit in with that lifestyle.

She says she loves my stories, that they enable her to live vicariously through me, and I do believe a part of that's true. But if I wished for anything at all, it would be to have what she has.

I am so good at pretending that I have the perfect life. The parties! The launches! The premieres! And for years, throughout my twenties, it was the perfect life.

But, really? At twenty-nine I'm still doing the same old shit? Could I not have found a man like Will? Should I not be living in a two-bedroomed garden flat in Notting Hill instead of my one-bedroomed, very small, and somewhat dark flat on the wrong side of Maida Vale?

Maybe that's why I drink. To dull the pain. I used to think it was to dull the pain of not fitting in, but I fit now! My friends love me! I'm good at work! Maybe the alcohol helps me not to focus on how utterly wrong my life is.

Because everyone is settling down. It was like this huge biological clock struck for everyone on the women's desk of the *Daily Gazette* at exactly the same time. The only one who's still single is Jackie, but she's fifty-four and lives in Sevenoaks. It isn't exactly conducive to hanging out and having a good time.

Gina's married to Alex, Sally's living with Robert, Victoria's married to Mark. The other three girls on the desk are full-time freelancers, and even though they're completely included on our nights out, on the rare occasions we have them these days, we're all a little more reserved with them because we know they probably won't be around for long. And by the way? They all have husbands or boyfriends too.

So I am left the sad single girl, pretending to be happier than any of them, without ties, without commitments. They tease me about how jealous they are that I can come home and eat a bucket of hummus and eighteen Kit Kats for dinner if I want, and I pretend to love the freedom of choice I get, despite not having anyone to cuddle me when I'm feeling down, or help me out when there's a leak in my flat, or just talk to me when I'm almost crying with loneliness.

Tonight, when they have all finished their glasses of wine, they will all be going home to cook dinner for their husbands, or, in some cases, eat delicious food cooked by their husbands, before curling up to watch some BBC drama on the telly.

And I will be going home to eat a bucket

of hummus and two Kit Kats. But I will pretend otherwise, even if tonight I won't be going on to the parties I tell them I'm going on to, if nothing else then to save face.

The wine bar is crowded, everyone from the features desk and showbiz, and a few from news, besides us. Jackie has secured a table in the corner, even though it takes me twenty minutes to get there. Jasper and Olly from the showbiz desk are chatting up the new intern on news, whose name no one seems to know, but whose enviable figure, in sky-high heels and tight short skirts, everyone seems to either envy or ogle.

Roy from the picture desk grabs me on the way in.

"My favorite women's desker!" he says, his face ruddy with alcohol, his eyes gleaming. I've had a long-standing flirtation with him, which ensures I get the files before anyone else, but it would never, ever lead to anything more. Trust me. No matter how much I drink.

"Favorite picture editor!" I lie, planting a kiss on his cheek.

"Let me buy you a drink!" he says, half turning toward the bar.

"No! I'm fine! Off the alcohol!" I attempt, seeing his face crease in confusion.

"Off the alcohol? What for?"

"Just needed a break," I say, for I haven't actually formulated a reason. "Doing a bit of a cleanse."

"You don't need a cleanse," he leers, his eyes flicking up and down my body as I shuffle slightly, wanting to get away, grateful for my high-necked shirt today. "You're perfect. Go on, love! Glass of chardonnay?"

"No, really. I'm fine."

"I know that! I'm getting you one!" And before I know it, a glass of chardonnay is in my hand.

I don't drink it. It takes just about every ounce of willpower that I have, but I take it to the table, and when everyone's face falls, I slide it over to Jackie, and tell them Roy had insisted but I am not touching it.

"Good!" says Jackie. "Because that would have been a wasted Diet Coke." She slides the glass over to me as I thank her and take a gulp, feeling absolutely nothing as it hits my stomach — no familiar buzz, no warmth, no indication that I'm about to start feeling a whole hell of a lot better. Nothing.

"Are those shoes what I think they are?" Sam, absurdly handsome in his skinny blazer, tortoiseshell glasses (which I am sure are fake), and Hermès tie, looks down at my feet, and I grin. We are all completely obsessed with shoes, and up until a couple of weeks ago, I had never even heard of Manolo Blahniks, and now they're all everyone on the fashion desk is talking about, thanks to a big piece on him in one of the women's glossies. Of course Sam, our style guru, knows exactly what they are.

My mum, it turns out, has two pairs she's never worn, and these patent, strappy Mary Janes are about the hottest thing on the planet right now. I extend my legs and show off the shoes as everyone oohs and aahs.

"Darling! I'm impressed! I can't believe your mother has these!" says Sam, practically salivating over the heels. "That tells me your mother is someone I have to meet. Gorge!"

"You would adore her," I say. "And can you believe it? It was like striking gold. Most of her clothes are leftovers from the seventies."

"Really?" Gina sighs, for she is well known for loving vintage. "If she ever wants to get rid of anything, make sure I get first dibs."

"No," I say. "I get first dibs," and I watch as she downs the dregs of wine in her glass and stands up, about to get another round.

All I can taste suddenly is wine. All I can think about is getting hold of a glass of wine. Everything in the room recedes, and all I can see is the dregs of wine in Gina's glass, and it is all I can do not to grab it and drain what little there is left.

Sam goes off to the bar to get another round. I turn to Poppy and say, quietly enough so no one else can hear, "I think I might just get one glass of wine."

"No!" she says, her face immediately stricken. "You said no alcohol. Don't do it, Cat. You'll regret it later."

"I really don't think I will. It's just one glass." I eye up her own glass of red, the temptation to take it almost overwhelming. I have to forcibly bring myself back to the present to hear what Poppy is saying.

". . . come back? Will's cooking, and you know what he's like, he always makes enough for an army. Go on, join us. Please?"

I think about what that would entail. I love being at Will and Poppy's, even though George will be fast asleep. I love being part of their domestic bliss. I love Will's cooking, and their gorgeous flat. I love the laughter involved whenever it is just the three of us. But Poppy won't let me drink, and however much I want to be nurtured by people I love, I want to drink more.

"I have a launch tonight," I say, even though I wasn't going to go. Channel 4 has a new television drama set in France, and they've taken over Chez Gerard in Charlotte Street for their launch party. Joanna Lumley is starring, and who knows, she may grant me an interview. More important, the french fries will be hot, crispy, and copious, as will, and this is really the clincher, the wine.

"Not that Channel 4 thing?"

"Yes. I wasn't going to go, but I realize I really need to try to lock down a chat with Joanna Lumley. I can't *not* go. In fact" — I make a big show of looking at my watch — "I really have to leave now."

"You're going to drink, aren't you?" Poppy's worry is all over her face.

"I don't know, Pops. I might. But you can't worry about me. I'm going to be fine."

"You asked me to stop you," she says, which is true, and I need to say something to appease her.

"Okay. I won't. Really. You're right. I'm going to stay on the wagon." We both know I'm lying, but we also both know there's nothing more she can say.

The cab seems to take forever, and I am fidgeting like crazy in the back, itching to have just one glass of wine, hell, maybe even half a glass, to take the edge off this. I don't have to have more, but that one glass of wine is like scratching an unbearable itch, and I really can't live with this itch, not when a remedy is so close at hand.

And finally we are driving down Charlotte Street, crowds of raucous people gathered on corners outside pubs, pints and glasses and cigarettes in hand, laughter, and merriment, and shouting, and then I am at Chez Gerard, and within one minute of signing in, I have a glass in my hand, and everything, *everything,* starts to immediately feel better.

EIGHT

The first thing that strikes me as unfamiliar is the smell. My laundry detergent smells like white linen. Even after a week there is always the faint smell of cleanliness, and before I even open my eyes, I'm aware that my sheets don't smell the same.

My next thought is: What the hell am I lying on? It feels like I'm sleeping on my back (which, by the way, I never do), on a stick.

The thought after that, once I have opened my eyes, is: Where the hell am I?

I try to sit up, but can't, and I reach behind me to feel a slab of bristles. There is a broom tucked into my T-shirt, and I pull it out, letting it clatter to the floor, clutching my pounding head as I wince, wishing that clattering of the broom didn't make so much noise.

I look around me at this bedroom, which definitely isn't mine, and definitely isn't Jamie's, and I have absolutely no idea whose it is, which would frighten me, if it weren't for the terrible headache that's threatening to blow my head apart.

If I weren't in so much pain, I might possibly appreciate the bedroom. The sheets are blue, the slatted wooden blinds a dark, masculine cherry. There is an antique desk pushed into the corner of the wall opposite, bookshelves next to it. I have no idea whose bedroom I'm in, but I'm pretty sure it's a man's.

An ajar door lends me a glimpse of a bathroom, and I creep in, opening the medicine cabinet to find, thank God, a big bottle of ibuprofen. I tip four into my hand and hold my mouth to the tap to swallow them, looking at myself in the mirror with such shame that I have done it again.

I remember arriving at Chez Gerard. I remember having a long chat with the Channel 4 press officer. And then I don't remember much else.

Thankfully, it could be worse. I am in all my clothes, so presumably I didn't have mad, unconscious sex with a stranger. But it could be much better, and I don't even know who to ask.

There is another door. I push it open and find myself squinting in a large, bright living room. On one side is a sectional sofa and coffee table, on the other a dining table and chairs, with an open-plan kitchen. Huge floor-to-ceiling windows, the light streaming through. My eyes make their way painfully back to the sofa, where there is a man lying wrapped in a bedspread, only the top of his dark hair visible.

Whoever he is, he has to be something of a gentleman, as I am pretty certain we didn't have sex. I'm completely ashamed to say that while it isn't a regular occurrence, there have been occasions where I have woken up, like this, in bed with someone I do not know. Naked. Having had a wild night. I presume, for I rarely actually know for certain.

And it's happened more than once.

Still, whoever this guy is, I don't want to have to talk to him. I have no idea what my behavior was like last night. I have no idea what I said, what I did, how I ended up here, and I really don't want to have to face this guy who may have seen me do anything.

If I knew where my shoes were, I would leave here immediately, but I can't find them, and there's no way I'm leaving those Manolo Blahniks behind.

There they are, a glimpse of a spiked black heel under the coffee table. I pad over, trying to make no noise whatsoever, refusing

110

to look at the sleeping man because if I look at him he will surely, despite being unconscious, feel my eyes on him and open his own, and I reach for the shoes, then practically scream in fear as I hear "Morning."

Damn! I can't believe this. I was so close to getting out of here. I meet his eyes, sheepishly, and say good morning back.

He sits up, the covers falling away, revealing boxer shorts and a T-shirt, and I can't deny the fact that sitting right before me is a fine figure of a man. He yawns and stretches, his T-shirt riding up to reveal a flat, tanned stomach, the traces of hair disappearing into his boxers, and I feel an unexpected jolt of . . . something. Something unexpected. I quickly look away.

I don't even know this man. This is ridiculous.

"Want some breakfast?" he asks, standing up to reveal he is much taller than me, and I'm no shrinking violet at five-eight.

"Um. No, that's okay. I have to go."

"I'm Jason, by the way." He comes over and shakes my hand. "I already know you're Cat. I'm making breakfast anyway, so you might as well stay. I know you won't turn down my offer of coffee." He grins, his hair mussed up, his eyes a warm brown, and I am so disconcerted by his offer, by how nonjudgmental he seems to be, I find myself, against all my better judgment, nodding.

"Sorry about the broom," he says, pulling eggs and bacon out of the fridge, tipping fresh ground coffee into a cafetière. "I was worried you might throw up while you were asleep, and I didn't want you to choke on it. When I was at university we used to stick brooms down people's clothes to stop them lying on their backs."

"Was I horribly drunk?" My mortification is real.

"You were horribly drunk. You wanted to go home, but you couldn't remember where you live. I don't usually bring strange women back to my flat, but it seemed like a safer option than leaving you collapsed in a doorway in Charlotte Street."

"Do you often rescue drunken strangers?" I attempt a smile.

"It does happen from time to time. I'm quite good at helping those in need," he says, cracking the eggs in the pan. "Especially when they're damsels in distress."

"I'm really sorry," I say. "I don't usually drink like that. It's been a rough few days."

"Oh? Anything you feel like talking about?

I know you don't know me, but sometimes it's easier to talk to strangers." He flips the bacon in another pan and slides four slices of whole-grain bread into the toaster.

"I might be able to talk to you if I knew just a little more about you," I say, sipping the coffee and starting to feel vaguely human again. "Just so I know you're not Jason the Ripper or anything."

He lets out a bark of laughter. "I'm definitely not Jason the Ripper. I'm Jason Halliwell, television director extraordinaire. Right now I'm working with Channel 4 on the series we launched last night. Where we met. Chez Gerard. Do you remember that?" He peers at me as I gratefully nod. "Okay. Good. So, I was born in London, brought up in Primrose Hill, before, by the way, it was Primrose Hill."

"You mean before it was overrun by celebrities?" I think of all the pictures of Liam Gallagher and Patsy Kensit, Jude Law and Sadie Frost, Jamie Oliver, all living their lives in the leafy green of Primrose Hill.

"Exactly. The most famous person there when I was growing up was Alan Bennett, and he wasn't even technically Primrose Hill. Gloucester Crescent. Camden." I nod. Even Alan Bennett sounds impossibly glamorous, Primrose Hill being my second choice, after Notting Hill, for where I would live now if money were no object.

"What else?" I push, but what I really want to know is, do you have a girlfriend? Are you available? Might there be any possibility that you could be interested in me, because my God! You are just the sort of man I could see myself with, thank you very much.

"I'm thirty something years old, have two sisters, and parents who have retired to the Cotswolds. This flat used to be the living room and drawing room of the house I grew up in. My parents converted it into flats, and I ended up with this one."

I swivel on the stool and look out the window, noting the pretty pastel-colored terraced houses. Of course it's Primrose Hill. As if it could be anywhere else.

"What are the three most important things to know about you?" I ask, although that isn't what I want to ask. All I want to know right now is whether he has a girlfriend.

"Hmmm. Good question. Okay. I love chocolate. Seriously. It's a huge addiction of mine that means I have to have chocolate every day."

"Milk or dark?"

"Milk?" He grimaces. "I wouldn't touch that crap if you paid me. Dark. The darker, the better. I'm embarrassed to tell you I'm a member of a gourmet chocolate club. Every month they send samples of chocolate."

"Do you have any?"

His face falls. "No. I finished it off last week. But —" His face lights up again as he joins me on the stool next to mine, two plates filled with eggs, bacon, and toast in his hands. "I'm expecting a new delivery later this week, so you can try it then."

I resist the urge to leap up from the stool and do a dance of joy. Surely he would not have said that if he weren't the tiniest bit interested in me? Surely he wouldn't be suggesting we see each other again if that were not the case?

"What else?"

"I love cats. I know, I know, it's a terribly unmasculine thing to admit to, but I'm afraid it's true."

"I don't think it's unmasculine. I think it shows you have a sensitive side."

"That's what I was hoping you'd say." He grins.

"So where's the cat?" I look around the flat, expecting to see one, but nothing.

"Albert is usually outside, hunting. He comes back when he's hungry. Sadly he's turned out not to be a cuddly sort of cat at all, so I'm thinking of getting another one who might turn out to be a better sort of companion."

"How do you know what they're going to turn out to be like?"

"That's the problem, you don't. Not when they're kittens. I thought if I rescued an adult cat that would probably be the best way of knowing."

"So now I have two things that are starting to indicate you may be the perfect man. What's the third?"

"I'm a recovering alcoholic," he says, taking a bite of bacon and reaching for a sip of coffee as if it were the most normal thing in the whole world, having no idea that my ears have started to buzz.

Why did he have to ruin the most perfect morning I have had in years?

"I've been sober three years, eight months, and sixty-eight, no, sixty-nine days," he says, not an ounce of shame about it. "Best thing that ever happened to me."

"Do you think I have a drinking problem?" I say, my voice as cold as steel, because I know exactly why he brought this up. I have no idea how he knows, but seeing me shitfaced last night must be why he brought me home. He's not interested in me, other than because I remind him of how he used to be and presumably he knows the answer to all my problems. I feel a flash of anger and put down the knife and fork, am about to pick up my bag and walk out, because I really don't need this shit. Not from my mother, and certainly not from this guy I don't even know.

No matter how cute he may be.

He looks at me, bemused. "I don't know anything about you. I have no idea whether you have a drinking problem or not. I, on the other hand" — he grins, and the tension disappears — "have a serious drinking problem. Note that I said recovering," he explains. "I'm never actually going to be recovered. The only thing I know for sure is that it never stops at one drink. And I was bad." He shakes his head at the memory. "When I got into recovery I'd been kicked off two television shows, and I was almost entirely yellow, my liver was so fucked. Seriously, they said if I'd have carried on I would have been dead within a year."

I look at him, this picture of health, and I feel slight disbelief, coupled with relief. I've held the same job for eight years, and I'm not the slightest bit yellow. Clearly I'm absolutely fine. Although . . . the bit about not being able to stop at one drink . . . that certainly resonates. But just because I happened not to stop at one drink last night, after I said I would, doesn't mean I can't. It just means I didn't last night. Tonight will be different. Today I'm going to start again, and particularly given I've just met this guy. If he's not drinking, all the better. How much easier will it be for me?

"Did you go to rehab?"

He nods. "And now I go to meetings every day. During the week I go before work, but on Saturdays the meeting's at noon. AA, obviously."

"Obviously. So you knew you had a problem?" I say.

He shakes his head. "I didn't think it was a problem. I was convinced I could stop at one drink, except I never could. I'd wake up in the morning and have no idea where I was or how I got there."

Oh shit.

"Like me," I mutter, eventually, and he just looks at me, with a look of such understanding and compassion I almost burst into tears.

I have never felt more self-conscious in my life than I do right now, in this room full of people, milling round, helping themselves to coffee from the machine on the trestle table in the corner of this room in the basement of a church in Paddington.

I don't want to be here. Except I do. I wouldn't be here had Jason not mentioned that he was coming, and I didn't want to leave him. He has an exuberance and happiness that are infectious, and I figured either I'd have to go home and see my mum at some point later in the day or I could spend the day with Jason.

But I didn't really think about what it meant, coming with him to an AA meeting. We climbed in his old Citroen and drove through the park as he told me his story. The full version. The bit about blackouts, and strange women, and how he had alienated everyone around him. The bit about all his friends trying to talk to him about his drinking and how worried they were, and his absolute refusal to listen. How he jumped on the defensive, cut them off, filled with shame at what he was doing. He talked about the chaos of his life, the self-centeredness, how every time he'd decide to stop drinking, which he decided on practically a daily basis, so fed up with waking up feeling like shit every single morning, his vow would be broken by the evening.

He talked about sitting with friends, in

bars, naturally, nursing a tonic water, and he couldn't hear any conversation, couldn't join in, couldn't do anything other than plan how to get away so he could carry on drinking in the privacy of his own home, so no one else would know.

He talked about all of this cheerfully, with no remorse, no shame, and I had no idea how, because every time he said something, all I could think was, oh my God, this is *me*. This is my story, and how is it he gets to talk about it like this, as if it is the most natural, acceptable thing in the world, when all I want to do is dig a hole in the ground and disappear?

He talked about getting into Alcoholics Anonymous. He talked about letting go of ego, turning things over to a Higher Power. He talked about letting go of control, of learning humility, of learning to accept life on life's terms, and I started to seriously regret getting in the car with him, knowing that it was too damn late to make my excuses and leave.

So here I am. In this hall, where everyone is hugging everyone else, and although I don't know anyone here, and in fact am terrified I might run into someone I know, they do seem like a friendly bunch.

Jason left me on a chair to go and talk to

one of his sponsees, whatever that might mean, and so far three people have come over and introduced themselves to me with big smiles, which is completely weird, but rather nice.

"I'm Jeff," says a big guy, sitting next to me with a cup of coffee in one hand and a paper plate in the other, filled with cinnamon buns from the trestle table. "Want some?" He proffers the plate as I shake my head.

"I'm Cat. Hi."

"First time?"

I nod. "I'm a little nervous. Not sure I belong here."

"None of us are sure we belong here when we first get here. Don't worry, you don't have to say anything. You can just listen. You're not going to relate to all of it, but they say take what you like and leave the rest."

"Okay," I say, as Jason walks over and sits down, and everyone in the room takes their seats.

He said I didn't have to speak. They all chant a preamble, something about the only requirement for membership is a desire to stop drinking, and AA is not allied with any sect or anything, although frankly, there is definitely something eerily cultlike about the smiling people in this room, and how their primary purpose is to stay sober, or something like that.

Then comes announcements, and apparently there's a new speaker meeting, whatever that is, in Queens Park that needs some help, then anniversaries. Two men and one woman stand up and proudly announce, in turn, ninety days sober, two years sober, and then nine years sober. Huge applause, and hugs all round, then a few words from the person leading the meeting.

And then, oh God! *Are there any newcomers?* There is a silence as I look at the floor because I do not want to say anything, I'm only here because Jason said I didn't have to say anything, but I make the fatal mistake of looking up and pretty much every single person in that meeting is looking at me with an encouraging smile, and oh shit, now I have to say something.

"Hi," I say, my voice shaking with nerves. "This is my first meeting."

"What's your name?" a couple of people say.

"Sorry. Cat. I'm Cat." I think about every film I've ever seen that features a 12-step meeting and how they always introduce themselves by saying, "I'm Cat, alcoholic." Or, "I'm Cat, a recovering alcoholic." Or, "I'm Cat, a grateful recovering alcoholic." But I can't. I can't qualify my name with anything else because I'm really not sure I belong. I'm really not sure I have that big a problem with drink. Or at least, not a problem I can't fix by myself.

"Welcome!" the group chimes in. "Keep coming back."

Riiiiight. I give them all the smiles they seem to expect, then shrink back into my seat, grateful for the reassuring rub on my arm from Jason. I turn to look at him, and he smiles and nods, as if he's really proud of me.

God, he's just yummy, I think, and suddenly I'm pleased that I'm here, and I settle back to listen.

It seems this is a "step meeting," and today is step 2: *Came to believe that a Power greater than ourselves could restore us to sanity.*

A thin blue book is passed around, and we move around the circle, reading step 2, and I think, once again, that I am definitely not in the right place, because all this talk about a Higher Power just seems ridiculous.

Perhaps I should not be admitting this, but I have never really understood the whole

God thing. My mother, in her distant past, was apparently Episcopalian. She went to church with her parents, but Aunt Judith was completely antireligion and wiped out whatever my mother had had. And my Dad . . . Well. I can't really call him that anymore, except I don't know what else to call him. Richard. My mother's husband. The man I thought was my father. He was Catholic, which was enough to put me off for life. Because he went to Mass, I refused, and even though he forced my mother and me, once the depression hit she didn't have to go, and although he made me go with him for a while, the older I got the less I went.

I am definitely not a huge fan of organized religion, and as for God? I'm not entirely sure. I do remember feeling terrified on holiday when I was young. In a strange bed, in a strange villa in Portugal, I would lie in bed screwing my eyes shut, desperate not to look at the window, which had no curtains, and all I could see when I pictured that big black window was a face, a rictus of horror pressed against the glass, about to come in and carry me off, the changeling, taken back to where she belongs.

The only thing that helped me deal with that terror, which was so all-consuming I remember actually being paralyzed with fear, unable to even jump out of bed and go and find my mother, the only thing that made me feel a little better was God.

I pictured him then as a big old man with a huge white beard. Presumably Charlton Heston was my inspiration. He had twinkly eyes and a kindly smile, and he loved me. I would lie in bed, my eyes screwed up, reciting made-up prayers that incorporated snatches of proper prayers I had heard over the years.

"Our father, who art in heaven, hollowed be thy name, please protect me and look after me. Please keep me safe and keep the monsters away from me. Deliver me from evil and badness and monsters. Look after me and protect me and keep me safe in this room, for thine is the kingdom, the power, and the glory. Amen. Please. Thank you, God."

And I suppose, during times in my life that have felt particularly hard, or frightening, I have whispered a prayer, or asked whoever might be watching from above for help.

But to ask for help with my drinking? That seems ever so slightly ridiculous.

We finish reading and the leader starts to speak.

"I'm Grant, alcoholic," he says, and I look at him and think, *he doesn't look like an alcoholic.* Neither does Jason, for that matter. And then I wonder what I think an alcoholic looks like. When I was growing up in Gerrards Cross we had a neighbor who was an alcoholic. I only know this because my parents used to talk about it. Everyone used to talk about it. His name was Terence Miller, and he was forever being driven home by the police, having been found asleep in the car park after hours.

I always remember him as being very nice, but he definitely looked like an alcoholic, especially when I'd see him stagger out of the police car, shouting at the very policemen who had been looking after him. Then you'd smell the booze from about a mile away. If you got up close you'd see his face was always red, broken blood vessels all over his nose and cheeks. His eyes would be glazed and watery, and he couldn't focus on anything, would blink at you slowly, slurring his words and hiccupping.

That's what an alcoholic looks like, I thought. Not like Grant, who is the yuppiest of yuppies ever, in his Ralph Lauren polo shirt and cashmere sweater, with a great big Rolex on one wrist. There's no way he's an alcoholic.

"Wow," he continues, shaking his head. "I always get exactly what I need to hear when I come to a meeting, and I really needed to hear about turning things over to a Higher Power. My meetings have been dropping off recently, things just got really hard at work . . ."

Jason leans over to me and whispers, "He's a huge merchant banker. *Huge!*" I look at him, and we both exchange impressed glances, as if, how can a huge merchant banker also be an alcoholic, and I really want to just sneak out of here with Jason and gossip with him about it, but I force my attention back to Grant-the-merchant-banker.

". . . haven't been to as many meetings. And every time I do this, because this is not the first time" — everyone laughs in acknowledgment, as if they too do this all the time — "I start to take back my will, and when I take back my will, that's the beginning of a very slippery slope."

There is a murmur round the room, and I notice a number of people nodding, and I have absolutely no idea what he is talking about.

"I tried for years to stop drinking. My wife threatened to leave me, I almost lost my job, and every time I thought I could do it myself, because *I* was a master of the universe; I could do everything myself. The things I tried!" He laughs a little. "I always decided that the best way for me to stop drinking was to go to a health farm. I figured a week of drinking lemon water and broth, massages every day, and I would miraculously come home and be dried out. The first time I went to Grayshott I left on day two to find the nearest pub and hid bottles of vodka under my bed. And still I thought I could do it. I went to Champneys two months later and it was the same story. I'd stagger into the massages, then pass out in the lounge. And this went on for years, but still I thought that it was just about finding the right amount of willpower. My ego was so huge, I thought I was in control of everything. I had a huge house in Regent's Park, a wife with a wardrobe full of beautiful clothes; my kids went to the best schools, and I couldn't understand how I could have achieved all of this, this beautiful life, but I couldn't stop drinking. My ego ran everything, and I had to get humbled to understand I couldn't do it." He shakes his head at what looks like an uncomfortable memory, and I sit forward slightly in my chair.

I didn't like the Higher Power stuff, didn't

understand it, but I'm always up for a good story, and so far this is turning out to be a good story.

"My wife used to issue ultimatums all the time. Sometimes she'd scream at me, other times she'd cry, and most of the time she'd say she would divorce me if I carried on, and I never believed her. And she didn't know the half of it." He shook his head, as if in disgust at himself. "I was a terrible husband. I was unfaithful, and with the worst kind of women. I thought nothing of paying for sex. I spent fortunes in the kind of clubs I'm now ashamed to admit I went to. My wife didn't know, until I gave her a sexually transmitted infection." He says all this without emotion, while my mouth has practically hit the floor in shock. This handsome, beautifully dressed, rich guy slept with hookers? And admits it? And what's more, not a single person in the room appears to be shocked. Except me. They're all nodding their heads as if they too have all slept with hookers and given their partners STDs. I feel like I'm in a parallel universe in which everything is completely and utterly bonkers. I turn my head and look at Jason, thinking he'll catch my eye and we'll exchange one of those mutual looks, that he will be as stunned as I am, and I see him nodding, just like the others, and now I really do know I'm in Bizarro World.

"It all came out," he says. "The women. The drugs. The booze." Wait. Did he say drugs? What drugs? Did I miss something? I try to picture him shooting up heroin, but no, it doesn't quite compute. Maybe he'll say more. By this time I am not only riveted, I am also curious as hell. If this guy is a huge merchant banker, this would make a fantastic story. Not that I would, obviously, go off and write something about him without his permission, but imagine if I could? I could freelance it out, because frankly it deserves a bigger audience than the *Daily Gazette.* The *Daily Mail* would go into raptures.

Maybe he would *want* to tell his story, I think, picturing myself chatting to him after the meeting, and him agreeing, wanting to help others going through the same thing, which would be, in fact, exactly how I'd pitch it.

"She divorced me and took everything I had."

Oh, this just gets better and better.

"I ended up sleeping on a friend's sofa, until even he had enough of my drinking, and stealing, and lying. I lost my job, my children wouldn't have anything to do with me, and I ended up in a hostel in Waterloo."

Are you kidding me? I need to come to AA meetings more often. This is like *Storytime* on steroids. I want this guy to keep on speaking for hours. I want to hear all their stories. I am completely and utterly rapt.

"That's where I got sober. I hit bottom. I just couldn't carry on anymore. I remember the night I fell to my knees, quite literally fell to my knees, and I was not a religious man, I never gave God a second thought, but I fell to my knees and cried out, 'If there is a God, you need to help me. I need you to change my life.' And I swear to God" — he laughs, and rolls his eyes as the room joins in — "I swear to God I felt, suddenly, an enormous peace come over me, and I knew, beyond any measure of doubt, that I wasn't alone. And I also knew that he would help me, and if I took the right steps, and asked for help, it would always be provided. My first meeting was the next day, and I have been sober since then." There is a round of applause from everyone in the room, with a couple of whoops.

"*I* didn't do it," he says. "I *couldn't* do it. I tried to do it for years, and nothing worked. My sobriety is due to my Higher Power. And more than that, the phrase 'could restore me to sanity.' When I was drinking, I had no idea that my life was insane. I was a mass of neurosis, insecurity, inadequacy, self-righteous indignation, anger. I would fly off the handle at everything, was permanently angry, critical, judgmental. Everything in my life was confusion and chaos, and I thought that was normal." He shrugs. "My dad was an alcoholic. It was all I knew. I spent my childhood vowing that things would be different when I was a grown-up, that I would never do to my children what my father did to me, and here I was, re-creating the hell of my childhood almost down to the letter, the only difference being that I never laid a hand on my kids, and because of that, I congratulated myself on being such a good father. Now . . ." He takes a deep breath. "I have been restored to sanity. I occasionally lose my temper, but it doesn't last long, and I immediately make amends. I have a wonderful relationship with a woman who is in Al-Anon and works her own program, and I am seeing my kids again. Not as much as I would like, because they're still skeptical about my change. But I take it a day at a time. I have a career again, and my life is good." He looks around the room, choosing, embarrassingly, to fix his gaze on me. "My life is good," he says again, nodding to punctuate it. "This program changes lives, and if you're new here" — God! I wish he'd stop looking at me — "if you're new, know that miracles happen in these rooms. Don't leave before the miracle happens."

Finally he looks away, as the room starts to applaud.

"It's your meeting," he says. "For a topic, I'm asking what are the miracles that have happened in your life as a result of getting sober. But feel free to share about anything you'd like. Thank you."

I sit back, exhausted from the concentration, exhilarated by the story, the only fly in the ointment being that although I heard him say he couldn't do it by himself, that only a Higher Power could do it for him, I know that's not the case for me.

I understand this program clearly works for some people, but I also know that I can do this by myself. After all, that's how I have done everything else.

We go for lunch after the meeting, Jason and I, and I think how nice this is, having lunch with someone. I am so used to being single, to phoning up Jamie for sex when I feel like it, to going out with the girls or, of late, given that all the girls are now in cozy relationships, to doing things by myself, I had forgotten what it feels like to be in a relationship.

Not that I'm in a relationship! My God! I can't even believe I just said that. Obviously I'm not in a relationship, but as we sit in Raoul's, our paninis in front of us, with fresh orange juice and salads, I am aware that looking at us from the outside we do indeed look like a couple, and what a delicious, perfect feeling that is.

Because along with that sense of never quite fitting in, I have always felt lonely. Not that this has ever particularly made sense. I have never been short of friends, I lead an active life, but I have always felt this tremendous sense of loneliness, of being alone, of having to be self-sufficient because of that aloneness.

I have had moments of not feeling quite so alone, and those always happen with men. At university I met my first love. Dave Reynolds. We were together most of the freshman year, and I remember sitting with him in pubs and thinking, oh! This is what it feels like! To be normal!

I feel that way now. With Jason. Even though, obviously, I don't actually know him, but there is, I am sure, a connection. There is something about him, and he would never have asked me to have lunch if he wasn't interested. In fact, he didn't actually ask, he just seemed to assume, which is absolutely fine with me.

"So what did you think?"

"I'm fascinated by Grant!" I say. "What a story! I would never have believed it from looking at him!"

"I know! We're not really supposed to talk about what people share in meetings or who we saw. But I won't tell anyone." He grins. "Did you hear anything you related to?"

"Absolutely!" I nod my head vigorously, lying. "So much."

"So, do you think you're interested in getting sober?"

"Absolutely!"

"You need to get a sponsor," he says. "And the best way of doing it, the way I did it after rehab, is to do ninety in ninety. That's ninety meetings in ninety days. It will change your life."

"Okay." I'm not quite sure how that would possibly work in my life, but I don't need to say that out loud. "So, a sponsor. Would you be my sponsor?" I'm slightly embarrassed asking him that, but who else am I supposed to ask, given that I don't know anyone else there.

"I can't." He frowns. "Two reasons. First, they recommend you have a sponsor of the

same sex. Otherwise it can get complicated."
I hope to God he doesn't see my face fall.
What does that mean? That it would be
complicated if we got involved with each
other? That he's not interested in me? I feel
a wave of disappointment, which will
undoubtedly turn into depression, wash
over me, followed by a wave of disgust with
myself: Why did I create this fantasy of a
perfect life with this perfect man? What the
hell was I thinking?

"Secondly," he says, "I want us to be
friends, and I can't be your friend if I sponsor you."

Great. Friends. Fan-fucking-tastic.

"Actually" — he leans forward sheepishly
— "I'd much rather be more than friends.
But if you're going to get sober, they recommend no new relationships for the first
year."

A year? I can wait a year! My heart is soar-
ing so high, I don't even realize I have a
huge, soppy grin on my face.

"Friends?" I say, reaching out my hand,
and he takes it, as I wonder just how long it
will take me to persuade him otherwise.

We leave Raoul's and walk along the canal
and into Regent's Park. Neither of us can
stop talking, and I'm aware both of us have

been smiling all day. Nothing has happened, and clearly, if I'm to get sober, which I now have to do, nothing will happen, but still, it feels like the most perfect romantic day imaginable, like something out of a Richard Curtis film, like the kind of day that only happens on a big screen or to other people.

It is such a perfect day, the earth-shattering news that my father is not my father doesn't even feel quite so important. I tell Jason all about it, because it is one of those days where the laughter and fun devolve into something deeper, more meaningful, and I realize I want him to know everything about me.

"That's pretty big stuff," he says, when I have finished and we are sitting on the grass by the bandstand. "You're going to get in touch with him, presumably?"

"Yes. My mum wanted to write and let him know, and hopefully he'll write back. I suppose I have this fantasy of going over there and finding out I have this amazing family who all welcome me with open arms. It probably wouldn't be like that, but I have to believe I'd have more in common with him than I did with the man I always thought was my father."

"Do you have siblings?"

"I don't know. It's a lot to process." I turn

to him. "My whole entire life I wanted brothers and sisters and I can't quite get my head round the fact that I may have them, that I may finally have everything I've ever wanted."

"It sounds like this could make an amazing book. Depending on what happens, of course, but I could see you writing a memoir."

I sit back, a light going on in my head. I have never thought of writing a book, but isn't that every journalist's dream? Gina ghostwrote a book for a pop star a couple of years back, although I'm not sure that counts, and Jackie has cowritten a couple of self-help books, but I never really thought about it.

I *could* see myself writing a book, though. And I could write a memoir, now that my father is no longer. I drift off into a fantasy of Nantucket, of finding the perfect family who welcome me into their heart, of writing about the hell of my childhood, and the joy of finding this new, improved family.

It's a brilliant idea, and soon Jason and I are planning the logistics of my new, improved life.

I am dropped home just after nine. We spent the afternoon in Regent's Park, before walking down to Baker Street to watch a film. Everything about the day had been perfect, and after the film, Jason phoned a friend "from program" and asked her to sponsor me.

Not that I need it, but I will do it for Jason. He's already said that although he won't sponsor me, he will be my "friend," and that the primary purpose of anyone in AA is to stay sober and help other alcoholics to achieve sobriety.

I'm not an alcoholic, but I do believe that today may mark the beginning of a whole new world.

For starters, not for one second today did I think about alcohol. We went to All Bar One before the film to grab something to eat, and not only did I order a ginger ale, I didn't then spend the rest of the evening looking around me at others drinking and wishing I could do that too.

When I got home I went to the fridge and pulled out the bottles of wine and beer and did the unthinkable. Opened them and poured the contents down the sink.

I may not be an alcoholic, but if I stand any shot at all with Jason, I have to get sober. I'm not doing this for myself, I'm doing this for him, but the end result is the same, and taking a quick bath, still smiling the whole time, I replay every moment of the day, astounded at how life can change so quickly, how I have met someone who feels like he's going to be significant, and how I am absolutely certain that from here on in, things are only going to get better.

I can't sleep. I think it's the excitement of the day, until I realize that I have not climbed into bed without some kind of alcohol for . . . well . . . I don't actually remember the last time I did that.

And I am slightly shocked at the realization. I have no idea how people sleep. I open a book and read, thinking that at some point I'm going to get sleepy, and I watch the clock move through midnight, and then the early hours. If this were a weekday, I would probably be so stressed I would go and get a drink, except I no longer have a drink in the house, and actually, every time I think about that, I then picture Jason, and I know I won't be doing that anymore.

So it's a very long night. But sometime after four, with a smile on my face, I finally fall asleep.

NINE

There was once a freelancer at work who used to sit on the desk and fill all her spare time with personal phone calls. It never particularly bothered me, but Jackie used to go nuts, eventually getting rid of her rather than tell her to stop making the calls. We all learned a valuable lesson, which was, essentially, do not take personal calls unless it is absolutely necessary.

The truth is, outside of family, very few people call me at work. I love the phone, could sit on the phone for hours and hours, and on the weekends usually do. I make myself coffee, sometimes — well, often — with a splash of Baileys to soothe the headache, then sit on the sofa, feet curled under a cushion, talking about everything under the sun. More often than not, it's Poppy on the phone, or Gina, so at work we don't have to worry about taking precious work time to talk on the phone. If anyone needs something we just wander down to the cafeteria for a coffee, or the bar for a drink.

Years ago, when I first started here, I couldn't believe the freedom we had, until I realized that when we work, we work hard. Why shouldn't we be allowed free time too?

Today I'm working on deadline. One of the magazines printed a photo of Kylie Minogue with an ankle bracelet, and now the editor of the paper wants a thousand words on how trendy ankle bracelets are, with Kylie, naturally, as the inspiration. I have to find other celebrities wearing ankle bracelets, and we all put our heads together, Poppy, thankfully, remembering seeing Madonna in one, and Jackie sending me down to Roy at the picture desk, convinced both Cameron Diaz and Julia Roberts have been wearing them of late.

I find enough pictures, then sit, tuning out the buzz all around me, scribbling notes on ankle bracelets. God only knows how I'm supposed to spin a thousand words out of ankle bracelets, but I start by naming the celebrities spotted wearing them, making my descriptions of their outfits as lengthy as possible.

Ankle bracelets, I say, are the hottest thing to have hit town, and all the beautiful people are showing off their delicate ankles with thin strands of gold. The more creative the artist, the more unusual the design, Madonna with her beaded black leather band.

Four hundred words. Bugger. Now what. I take my fingers off the keyboard and sit back, desperately trying to think of what else to write. History! I get on a computer and quickly look up the history, discovering the ancient Sumerians in the Mesopotamian region wore ankle bracelets, possibly to signify the wealth of their husbands. It doesn't really matter whether it's true or not, it's going in, padding out the story and making it seem substantial.

Egyptian royalty wore anklets made of precious stone and metals! I ring down to the picture desk to call up a file on ancient Egyptian royalty. Thank God, the story's now coming together. Only a couple of hundred words left to go.

Everything we write, however flimsy, has to be padded to make the *Daily Gazette* reader feel intelligent. We can spin an article out of an opinion, but we have to get an expert to back it up, to authenticate it, to leave the reader feeling she's learned something new.

My go-to girl for pretty much all my

articles is the psychologist Robyn McBride. She wrote a couple of books on couples and how they communicate, which got her on all the talk shows, with a reputation for being an excellent talking head. Which is what I love about Robyn. Despite her degrees and the letters after her name, she is nothing if not populist. I can ring her up about anything, even something as seemingly prosaic as ankle bracelets, and she'll not only have an expert psychological opionion about them, she'll make it sound brilliant.

"Robyn? It's Cat here. From the *Gazette*."

"How are you, Cat?" We have never met, but from the warmth in her voice, you would think we were old friends. I do, in fact, feel that she is almost a friend, at the very least someone I would absolutely talk to if ever I felt I had a problem and needed some help.

"I'm okay," I say. "Writing about ankle bracelets today! Can you give me a quote, maybe about women using jewelry to attract the opposite sex, and maybe something about the ankles being a long-forgotten erogenous zone?" I am quite impressed with myself, having just come up with the idea about ankles, and Robyn laughs.

"Absolutely," she says. "But let me just check in with you. Usually you say you're great, and today you just said you're okay. Are you okay? Anything you want to talk about?"

And this is why she feels like my friend. Or perhaps my unofficial therapist. Because who else would be able to ascertain, from two words, that I am completely preoccupied with the changes in my life?

Not that they're bad. For the last few weeks my life has, in many ways, been better than it has been in years. I'm seeing Jason pretty much every evening at an AA meeting, and afterward, we'll go out and grab something to eat, or see a movie. Often there will be others with us, and it's the first time in my life I haven't actually felt like I'm standing on the outside; it's the first time in my life I feel like I fully belong.

Although it's not all perfect. Technically I do have a sponsor, but I have no idea what I'm supposed to do with her. She said I had to call her every day, but I don't call *anyone* every day. Not even my mother. What am I supposed to say to her? What if she tells me I have to *do* something?

I'm definitely drinking less. I tell them I'm counting days, but I've had a couple of . . . slips. A few. But I'm not drinking every day, and that's definitely progress.

It's not the drinking stuff that keeps me

coming back, though. It's the camaraderie. And if I'm honest, it's wanting to see Jason, and of course keep him happy. He seems so proud of me not drinking, I'm trying to do it for him, and what he doesn't know won't hurt him.

I had no idea how lonely I was before I met Jason and started coming to these meetings. Not at work, I was never lonely at work, and after work I tried to fill every evening with launches and parties. When we were all single, it was a blast. I wouldn't change a thing about my early twenties, but even I know that to expect to live the same life, do the same thing, as you approach your thirties is just a little bit sad.

The girls are all with their boyfriends or husbands, and I'm still going to the parties, still drinking, only now I think I really do want to stop. These past few weeks I've had a glimpse into a different way of life, and I'm beginning to think it looks better.

Given what I now know about myself, that I am not the woman I always thought I was, that I have this other family, I am even more amazed I'm not getting blasted every night.

Because I'm scared.

I know my mum has written to him, but what if he doesn't write back? What if he wants nothing to do with me? What if I'm left completely fatherless? Even though, clearly, up until a few weeks ago I thought I had already been left fatherless. Could I go through that sort of rejection again? After the way the man I thought was my father rejected me his entire life by withholding affection, support, love?

The very thought of it makes me want to drown my feelings in a very big bottle of vodka. Which I have done, but not every night, not those nights I go to meetings and hang out with Jason afterward, and hope and wish and pray that even though he has been quite clear he will not get involved with me during my first year of sobriety, I can somehow make him change his mind.

Do I want to talk about it? Professionally? I saw a therapist once, years ago, because I felt . . . lost. She was a very old German woman in a big stucco house in Belsize Park. She was very nice, if entirely clichéd. The house was filled with abstract paintings and interesting sculptures. When I say interesting, I don't mean beautiful. She would sit in her big leather chair and just look at me, her face blank, and I had no idea what to say, and would blurt out stuff about my father because I was sure that's what she wanted to hear, and I didn't want her to think I was wasting her time.

Oh, but it was such a waste of time.

I felt a constant vague embarrassment at telling a stranger things I hadn't said to anyone before. I'm sure I made some of it sound a bit better, because I didn't want her to think too badly of him.

I have no idea what she thought of him. She was, I suppose, of the school of thought that a therapist is there as a, what do you call it? Tabula rasa. A blank slate, there to help me understand my life through her silent stares and occasional nods.

It didn't work for me. If I were ever to have therapy, and I'm going to tell you this, I'm frankly extremely uncomfortable with the idea, but if I were to, it would need to be someone with whom I had a dialogue, someone who felt like a friend, someone who would actually give me advice, direct me, shed some light on why I am the way I am.

If I were to see someone, Robyn McBride is exactly the sort of person I would see. I could, in fact, very clearly imagine sitting on a small sofa in a cozy yellow office, chatting away and telling her everything. But I'm not going to. At least not today. I have an article on ankle bracelets that needs to be sent to the subeditors in thirty-five minutes, so I reassure her I'm fine, and she gives me, as she always does, the perfect quote.

I have finished the article, sent it to the subeditor, am just about to tap Gina on the shoulder and ask her if she wants to grab a coffee downstairs, when my phone rings and it's my mum.

"Darling," she says, her voice happier than I have heard in years. "I'm so sorry to trouble you at the office, but I wondered if you and I could meet for a coffee after work?"

"Did you speak to him?"

"I did. Too much to talk about over the phone, so let's try to get together."

My heart stands still. What does that mean, too much to talk about over the phone? Was he happy? Shocked? Angry?

"What does that mean?" I manage to get out.

"It's all good," she says, hearing the anguish in my voice. "Why don't you come over after work today and I'll tell you all about it?"

I think about what I have planned today after work; a meeting with Jason, then up to the Everyman in Hampstead for some Gerard Depardieu film I'm pretending I've been dying to see because he's been talking about it for days, even though I've never heard of it.

"Tell you what." I look at my watch. "Why don't I come over now? We could have lunch."

"Wonderful!" she says, and I put the phone down, scribble a message on a piece of paper to leave for Jackie, and head out the door.

I stop at Waitrose and pick up a sandwich and a salad for Mum. Her American-ness seems to show itself mostly with her food choices. She has never ordered a meal in a restaurant without asking for something to be on the side, or for a substitution — salad instead of mashed potatoes, and she always, *always* eats the salad first.

The only safe thing, in fact, to ever buy my mother for lunch is salad, and sure enough, as soon as she opens the door and takes the Waitrose bag from my hand, her eyes light up at the salad in the way mine would at a huge bag of caramel popcorn. Or vodka. Take your pick.

"Salad!" she exclaims in delight, as if it were a chocolate éclair. "Yum! Come in, sweetie. I've set the table."

I smile at how pretty she has made it; white linen napkins, sparkling crystal glasses, and a vase of creamy pale pink roses in the middle of the table. All this to eat salad out of a plastic container and a sandwich.

"So what did he say?" I can't wait until we sit down, patience never having been a particular virtue of mine. "How did you tell him? Did he remember you?"

Her smile fades slightly, and she nods. "I knew you'd want all the details. Let me try to remember everything. I had written to him, you know that. I told him how terrible I felt and that I was too young and too stupid to realize he deserved to know he had a daughter in this world. I told him about you." She smiles again then. "In the letter I told him you have inherited his dark skin, his dimples, and his creativity, only you express it through words rather than paintings. I told him a little about me. That it hadn't been a particularly good marriage, but that I never felt I had another choice. I told him that I had never realized, until you were born, how unkind he was. And particularly to you." My mother blinks back tears as she says this, and I have to swallow a lump in my own throat. "He was not a good father, and I didn't protect you. I am so sorry."

"It's okay, Mum." I want her to carry on

with the story. I know she's sorry, and I don't bear any grudge against her for not protecting me from my father. She did the best she could, and it has never occurred to me to blame her for any of it.

"I sent him a picture of you. Three, actually. One when you were very tiny, then another from that holiday in Disney World when you were about eleven, and finally one from your birthday last year. I said you knew about him, that I had just told you, and that I had done you both a tremendous disservice in keeping you apart, and if he wanted to change that, as I very much hoped he would, this was the number to call."

"Your number."

"I thought it might be too much to give him your number from the get-go. What if he'd been angry and taken it out on you? I needed to check the lay of the land before anything else."

"When did he call?"

"This morning. At eleven. Which is six a.m. his time. He said he'd been away in New York for a show and had only just got back to Nantucket to find the letter. He'd phoned immediately. I think he's stunned, and happy."

"What did he say? I mean, what *exactly*

did he say?"

"I don't know exactly. He said he had read and reread the letter. That you looked exactly like his two daughters there, who are just slightly younger than you. He said he wanted to talk to you, and wondered if you might consider going over to Nantucket to see them."

"Oh my God!" My heart threatens to flip with joy. "Are you serious? Nantucket? And I have sisters?"

She nods. "Do you feel ready to talk to him?"

"Yes!" I leap up from the table and fling my arms around my mother in an impromptu hug. "I can't believe this!" I say. "I can't believe how easy this is!" My mother disentangles herself and pulls the phone over.

"You're sure you're ready?"

"Ready as I'll ever be." I grin, jiggling my knee in excitement as she pulls out a piece of paper and dials the number written down.

"Brooks? It's Audrey again. . . . Good, thank you. Look, I've got Cat with me. She came over for lunch. . . . Yes. Right here. . . . Sure. Hang on." And she hands the receiver over to me.

"Cat?" His voice is deep, exotically

American. My mother's accent is no longer exotic, as familiar as it is to me, but this is something that sends jolts of longing, a little girl finding her father, something entirely unexpected and discombobulating.

I can't speak.

"Cat? Are you there?"

"I am. Sorry."

"Oh wow. Listen to you!" I can hear the smile in his voice. "With your English accent!"

"I, um, *am* English," I say, somewhat pathetically.

"I know, I just didn't think. Your mom still sounds American, and I just didn't think about it. And you look so like my own daughters, I mean, my daughters here, that I guess I expected you to sound like them. Stupid, I know." He trails off. "Well. This is some big news, isn't it?"

"You think?" I say, and he laughs.

"Big, but *good* news. I'm delighted to have found you. I only wish it had happened a long time ago."

I don't say anything, not wanting to point the finger at my mother, even though I am thinking exactly the same thing.

"I haven't talked to the girls, but they're both here this summer. We convene every year at the house here on Nantucket. Ellie

154

comes with her kids, and Julia is always here, usually with whatever boyfriend she has at the time. I was thinking perhaps you ought to come out here and meet all of us."

I am gobsmacked. So much, so fast. All of it wanted. "I would love to," I say, unable to wipe the smile off my face. "But maybe you should talk to them first. I don't want to cause any trouble."

"You wouldn't be causing any trouble," he says. "But I'll talk to them. Do you have a number where I can reach you? You and I have an awful lot to catch up on."

"Of course." I give him my home phone number, and the office, although I warn I can't often chat when I'm working.

"I want us to get to know each other," he says. "Make up for lost time. Does this sound like something you'd be interested in?"

As if I'm going to say no.

I am so lost in thought, I barely notice that my mum is also smiling, in a way I'm not sure I have ever seen her smile before, and it dawns on me: My God! This is her first love! He mentioned talking to his daughters but not a wife. Maybe he's divorced. Maybe he's single and available. Maybe he never got over my mother, and now they've reconnected, maybe they'll get back together.

Maybe I'll have the family I've always wanted, in this entirely unexpected of ways. I look at my mother's face, and she is positively beaming, and I realize in all of this, I haven't once thought about my mother.

God knows I know how miserable she was with my father. After he died, and especially after she left the suburban boredom of Gerrards Cross, I was convinced she'd find some wonderful man in London, but it hasn't been the case.

She refuses to join a dating agency, and friends have occasionally set her up, but she always ends up becoming great friends with them, and says she's happier that way. They take her to dinner, the opera, the theater, but nothing ever happens beyond, and it's not for want of them trying.

Maybe this really is the man she's been waiting for her entire life. Maybe it's not too late for miracles to happen.

"Mum?" She looks up at me. "Does Brooks have a wife?"

"They're divorced," she says. "He told me earlier."

"So he's single?" My eyes gleam.

She shakes her head, snorting with laughter. "He's single, and it was lovely to connect with him, but I know exactly what you're thinking, and no, I'm not the slightest bit interested."

"He just invited me out to Nantucket. Well, provisionally, after he's talked to the other daughters. But why don't you come with me? Why don't we both go? You can't let an opportunity like this go unexplored."

"It's not unexplored." She smiles. "But what happened between us was years and years ago. We probably wouldn't have anything in common anymore."

"What if you did? What if you had everything in common?"

"It's unlikely. Anyway, I have my life here. I'm not the slightest bit interested in uprooting again."

"Who's talking about uprooting? I'm talking about a summer. Maybe a week. See what happens."

She shakes her head. "This is your time to get to know him. Not mine. I've just joined the board of the museum, and I have much too much to do. But I can't wait to hear how it all goes for you."

TEN

"You're what?" Jason is staring at me, as if he can't believe what I'm telling him.

"I'm going to Nantucket to meet my family."

"Okay. I mean, that sounds amazing. What an insane story."

I laugh in disbelief. We are grabbing a quick coffee on Praed Street before the meeting. "I feel like you don't think this is a good idea."

"Meeting your long-lost family? I think it's probably an excellent idea. I'm just worried about what's going to happen to you, going away now."

"Why?"

"They usually advise you not to make any big changes during your first year of sobriety."

I don't tell him that I'm . . . struggling with my sobriety. I need him to think I can do this; I have done this. The thought of his disappointment, of what he would say if he knew how I was letting him down, not as sober as I appear, fills me with terror. If he knew, then he would leave, and I'm pretty clear Jason is the best thing to have happened to me in a very long time.

"Please tell me you're not going to tell me not to go. This is my father! My sisters!"

"I know, I know." He has the grace to appear embarrassed at the very thought. "You'll need to find meetings."

"Absolutely." I nod vigorously, although frankly that's the last thing I'm thinking about. I need to find my family. Everything else is just gravy.

"You should talk to your sponsor about it. How's that going, by the way?"

"Great," I lie, making for the door. "Come on, we're going to be late."

In today's meeting, someone talks about pulling geographics. Apparently every time life got too painful, or she had alienated too many people, or fallen out with someone, or not wanted to deal with whatever was going on, she moved. She moved from London to Edinburgh, then to Cardiff, Bristol, Glasgow, and finally, when she was ready to reinvent herself entirely, back down to London again.

The group nodded, murmurs of self-knowing laughter, and I turned to find Jason looking at me with a raised eyebrow, as if that's what I'm doing, which is completely ridiculous. I haven't alienated anyone, my job is great, and the only thing that might be difficult to deal with, the meeting of my newly discovered family, I am dealing with head-on.

It is ridiculous that he seems to think I am pulling a geographic. Shaking my head at him with what I hope is a derisive look, I get up to go to the bathroom and take a break.

And once outside, in the hallway, I realize I really don't want to go back in. I don't want to listen to those people anymore. I don't want to hear their stories or stand around the room at the end holding hands and saying the Serenity Prayer.

What I really want, what I really, *really* want, is a drink.

No, Cat, I tell myself. I don't. I don't want to let Jason down. Don't want to let myself down. But nor do I want to listen to any more of this crap, and it is all starting to sound like crap. I whisper to Jason that I'm not feeling well, slip out the door, and make my way home.

ELEVEN

I am beginning to realize, at the ripe old age of twenty-nine, that one of the problems I have in life is a tendency to completely romanticize how things will be in the future, which inevitably leads to disappointment because it's pretty much never, never, what I expect.

Not that I dwell on the bad stuff particularly. If anything, I tend to move on pretty damn quickly, but sitting on the plane as I make my way over to meet my family on the island of Nantucket, I'm alternating between thinking about Jason and how disappointed I am that things haven't worked out the way I was so certain they would, and imagining what it is going to be like having my dad pick me up at the airport, meeting my sisters, being embraced by this new family.

First, Jason. He came to see me before Mum picked me up to take me to the airport. In a very short space of time he has become someone I know I can absolutely rely on. He said he'd drive me last week, although there's no way my mother would allow anyone else to take me when this trip is so momentous, and even though I know we're just friends, I'm also pretty sure I'm not imagining the chemistry between us. And even though I know he will not do anything about it, at least not until I'm sober a year, my God, how am I supposed to wait a year? And more to the point, how is he? I know something's going to happen soon, and something should happen soon, and once it does, there'll be no turning back.

So in my fantasies, I had thought the great send-off might be the time something would happen. I could see him helping me out to my mum's car with my suitcase, putting it down next to me and hugging me — which isn't unusual, because we're big huggers — and as we pull apart he stands, a little closer than usual, just gazing down at me. Then maybe he reaches up and tucks a strand of my hair behind my ear (I told you I had a tendency to romanticize), and there's this jolt in my stomach as the smile leaves his face, and then he'll shake his head with that twisty smile he does, and his face will move closer, and although he knows this is a bad idea he just won't be able to help himself, and then we'll be kissing, and he won't want me to leave.

Of course, I will leave, and then he'll miss me so desperately that by the time I get back from Nantucket he will realize he has fallen madly, but madly, in love with me, cannot live without me, and the rest of my life after that will be one great big fairy tale, lived together, in sobriety and love.

Then there's the second part of my fantasy, which is landing in Nantucket to have my family all come to the airport to meet me, maybe with homemade welcome signs, which I would find completely mortifying but would secretly be thrilled about.

My dad's going to take me in his arms and I'm going to feel safe, and exactly where I belong, and Ellie and Julia are going to be instant best friends, we're going to sit in the car on the way to the house and none of us are going to be able to stop talking, unable to believe how alike we are, and the rest of my life will be . . . well. Yes. You probably already guessed, one great big fairy tale.

I have to say, the farewell with Jason didn't quite go as planned. He'd been haranguing me slightly about making sure I find meetings on Nantucket, but honestly, there'd been so much to do I hadn't actually got round to it. I did find a number for some AA service place in Massachusetts, and I had been meaning to call to find out more info, but life got in the way, and I had looked it up online, but I forgot to go back and revisit the site, and all in all it hadn't been a priority. Even though he apologized this morning and said he wouldn't ask anymore, that it was up to me and he couldn't control what I did or didn't do, I could tell he was pissed off.

All of which didn't feel very good. I hate that feeling of knowing someone is unhappy, particularly the man you are pretending is your new best friend when actually you have a giant crush on him.

We chatted, obviously, as I raced around my flat, making sure I had my passport, my money, but it felt perfunctory, and a little forced. When my mum phoned to say she was on her way, he apologized. He said he was just nervous for me, that going away on a big trip, particularly one with such an emotional component, was a much bigger deal than I seemed to realize, and he was worried I'd fall off the wagon and lose everything I've gained in the weeks we'd spent time together.

I reassured him I was going to be fine,

and things were easier after that, but our hug good-bye did not involve any simmering, longing looks, or tucking hair behind an ear, or anything other than a completely platonic hug and kiss on the cheek.

Yes, I was disappointed.

So now I'm on the plane replaying all of that stuff, and when I'm bored of that, I'm projecting meeting my family, but I'm realizing I really have to stop, because there's absolutely no point, and all that I'm doing is setting myself up for disappointment.

I pull out the book I bought at the airport and, with great effort, manage to stop the squirrels in my head for the next hour.

I love flying. I love airplane food, in compartmentalized trays. I even love puffy synthetic sponge cakes for dessert that taste of little other than chocolate that has been artificially manufactured in a factory somewhere. I love gloppy sauces on chicken breasts, and dull, overcooked green beans.

I love that you have absolutely nowhere else to be other than captive on a great big soothing plane. I love how friendly the stewards and stewardesses are. I love that sometimes they hand out ice cream. I love that you can step onto a plane not knowing anyone and emerge a few hours later with a new best friend.

And I love that they keep pouring wine. At least, I did, before I met Jason. I shake my head when the stewardess offers wine the first time around, as the people on either side of me have a glass of white.

Oh, for God's sake. Why would I not have a glass of white wine on a plane? It's tantamount to orange juice. I'm on holiday. Ridiculous that I wouldn't celebrate a trip with one glass of white wine. It's only one. Maybe two. Three at the most, but hardly three, in those little plastic cups. Three of those might equal one and a half glasses of wine. Hardly excessive.

"Excuse me?" I call down the aisle to the stewardess, who turns, bottle poised in hand.

"Actually, I will have a glass of white wine. Thank you."

The guy sitting next to me smiles his approval and gives me a "cheers" when my glass is in my hand. I'm not becoming best friends with the guy next to me today, that's for sure, but we raise our glasses before I let the cool wine slip down the back of my throat. It is more cloying than I would have chosen, but delicious nonetheless. It is the perfect addition to this flight; I have my book, my magazine, movies, and the task of stilling the fantasies in my head, which, I'm very clear, are to hide the fact that I'm actually nervous as hell. And I will take any distraction over my thoughts.

Because what if they don't like me? What if we have nothing in common? What if they find my Englishness obnoxious? Or superior? Or alien? What if Brooks Mayhew turns out to be difficult? Or arrogant? Or drunk?

He doesn't sound like he's going to be any of those things, from our phone conversations. He doesn't sound like he was ever any of those things, from what my mum has now told me about her summer with him, even though, as she kept pointing out, it was such a very long time ago.

I'm not going to think about it anymore. I'm just going to try to focus on the flight, the movie, the book, the food, the wine. I'm going to focus on getting to JFK and finding my connecting flight to the tiny airport on Nantucket. I'm going to try to focus on staying in the moment and not, absolutely not, allowing a single fear, or fantasy, to creep in.

TWELVE

The flight is long, but feels short. Eventually I abandon all hope of distracting myself and give in to my thoughts. There is so much to think about, so much anticipation, it is all I can do not to get up every few minutes and tear up and down the aisle, just to get rid of some of the nervous energy.

I know a bit more about them all now, my father having written to me and told me about my long-lost family. I have learned that Ellie is twenty-seven, married to Robert, who is a banker. They live in New York, in a brownstone in Chelsea. They have two children, the light of his life — Trudy, a newborn, and Summer, who is four. Ellie is much more like her mother. She is frighteningly organized, heavily involved in the 92nd Street Y, where Summer goes to preschool. From Brooks's description in his letters, she sounds, honestly, a little uptight, but obviously I'm not going to say that. They apparently hold lots of fund-raisers in their very lovely home, and she is an excellent mother. He says the place she really lets her hair down is Nantucket. Although plenty of her friends have summer homes on Nantucket, she chooses not to be part of the scene when there, leaving her New York airs and graces behind and reverting to the island girl she once was.

The younger daughter is Julia. At twenty-six she is, wrote Brooks, a free spirit. She wants to be a writer, but in the meantime is juggling a ton of jobs: a waitress at the Downyflake, cleaning houses, occasional bartending at the Anglers' Club, and scalloping when she has a morning off.

For a few years she went over to Cape Cod for the summers. She grew very close to an English woman, Denise Holyoak, who lived in Boylston for most of the year, and Yarmouth for the summers. Denise loved gardening, the royals, and English chocolate, and apparently passed those loves on to Julia, who would help Denise in the garden, and beg her for stories of growing up in Rushden, England. I think of the Cadbury's Dairy Milk bars in my suitcase — half for Julia and half for her to send to her friend Denise.

Julia struggles to support herself, he said,

so he helps her. I went quiet when I read that. Not that there is anything in life I want that I don't have, except perhaps a nicer car, and only because mine is always breaking down, but because she has someone to turn to. Of course, my mother would help me, financially or otherwise, if ever I asked her, but what would it have been like to have a father who took care of me?

I remember, when I was young, friends' fathers saying they had to save up for their first car, and as soon as they had the money — scrimping it together from Saturday jobs and babysitting — the fathers would tell them that actually the car would be a gift, and they should keep their money for something else. My father never actually got that last bit. He told me I had to save, and I did, confident that once I actually had that fourteen hundred pounds together he would buy me the Triumph Spitfire that I was so desperate for, and let me use that money to help get me through university, just like everyone else's dad did, but he didn't. I called him up to announce that I had finally saved up enough for the car, and he said, good, I should go and buy it then.

I kept thinking he'd surprise me, but he didn't. As if I should have expected anything else.

Julia freelances for whoever will take her work when she has a free moment, which is rare. She also writes his catalogs. I can't be sure, but I think she's his favorite. She's the one who has inherited his creativity, he says. And me, I think. She's also, he says, an incredibly talented artist. One of the things he's encouraging her to do is write and illustrate children's books. She is something of a lost soul, he says, and he wishes she would settle down. She lives on the island, although he worries it's too small for her, that she needs to spread her wings, move farther afield to find where her happiness will lie. She has a knack of picking bad boyfriends, unfortunately.

"She will walk into a room filled with a hundred men, and the one she will end up with will be the addict or the alcoholic," he wrote regretfully. "Not that it's hard on the island. You'll discover we islanders have a unique relationship with alcohol."

She has a new boyfriend, a sous-chef up for the summer, about whom Brooks is cautiously optimistic.

Both girls look like me, especially Julia. He promises to send photographs.

And me? Knowing all this about a family I have never known? If I could have found a way to teleport myself there the minute I found out all of this, I would have done so. As I peer out the window of the plane, high above the clouds, I remember the things Brooks wrote about Nantucket, his description of the cobbled streets, the pretty architecture, the boats bobbing on the water.

I read about driving over to Sconset, for ice cream in the village, to get the papers on Main Street and walk down to the harbor, and everything about my life feels grey and dismal and dull, and the only place I want to be is Nantucket, where everything will be better, I absolutely know it will.

That feeling I have carried my entire life, not fitting in, standing on the outside, never quite belonging, whoever I'm with? Once I'm in Nantucket with my family, I know it will disappear. It already has.

Nantucket airport really is tiny, especially after the noise and bustle of JFK. As soon as we took off from New York, I realized I couldn't quiet the nerves anymore, and even though the wine helped, now that we have landed, now that I am minutes away, I find my hands shaking.

This is it. I'm about to meet my father. As the full impact hits me, I want to throw up with anxiety. I twist in the seat, but there's no aisle service on this tiny puddle jumper, no drinks available. I turn back and try to concentrate on deep breathing in the hope this will calm me down.

My legs are shaking slightly when we disembark. By the baggage claim there are a couple of people with signs, although he wouldn't need a sign, surely, having seen pictures of me, both of us emailing back and forth these past few weeks.

There is no sign of him inside, and my heart sinks. He definitely said he'd come pick me up. I grab the handle of my suitcase and make my way outside, wondering if I should find a taxi. It's a small island, I have his address. Worst-case scenario I'll just show up at his house.

I can't miss him.

Parked outside is a big old blue car, with wooden sides, and getting out of it, looking exactly as he did in the photographs he sent me, is Brooks. My father.

I stand still. He turns and sees me, and his mouth drops open, instantly creasing in a smile that overtakes his entire face. He opens his arms, and seconds later I find myself completely enfolded. It is every bit as wonderful as I had fantasized; I'm held tightly in his arms, am laughing even as the tears stream down my cheeks, and when I pull back for him to hold me at arm's length and look at me properly, I see that he is doing exactly the same.

For once in my life, it all came true. Exactly as I hoped.

"Look at you!" he says, wiping the tears off his face, then my own, before clasping me back in his arms. "Look at you!"

And I say nothing, so happy to be held like this, so grateful to finally have the dad I always wanted.

So grateful this father seems to want me too.

"Ellie is on her way back to the island today," he explains, as I study him in the car. He must have been a handsome man; although his cheeks are ruddy, his age shows. His hair is slightly wild, curling over the collar of his shirt, mostly grey, a sprinkling of dark. He looks like he has lived hard. I don't know if this is a bad thing. He looks utterly familiar, which is unexpectedly poignant, and I find myself blinking back tears every few minutes.

"She had a function in the city last night, so she took the girls, but they should all be back by now. They took the ferry over earlier. And Julia's back at the house with Aidan. It's his night off at the restaurant, so the two of them are cooking for us, lucky us!"

I smile, my body half turned in the seat so I can keep looking at him. Everything I never felt with my father, the man I thought was my father, I feel looking at this man. An absolute recognition of who he is and where I came from. I have his nose, his chin. When he smiles at me, as he does repeatedly, reaching out a hand and squeezing my knee, I see my own smile. His salt-and-pepper hair, sprinklings of gold.

"How do they feel about me coming?"

"I think they're excited."

Think? What does that mean?

He hesitates before speaking. "It has been a lot for them, suddenly discovering they have a new sister. Not that it hasn't been a lot for all of us. Julia's fine with it, she's easygoing, but Ellie's finding it a little . . . harder. You mustn't worry. It's all going to be fine. Ellie's just a harder sell." He turns his head and looks at me. "You look so like them." He shakes his head. "It's extraordinary. Your mother's eyes, though, but the rest of it? Well, there's certainly no doubt."

We ramble along the main road, detouring slightly so he can show me the town, which is exactly, but exactly, like something out of a picture book; the pretty shops, the boats, the tanned, gorgeous people in shorts and flip-flops, the blue hydrangeas spilling out of window boxes and flower beds.

He points out the lay of the land as we head to the house, pulling up in front of a faded grey-shingle building on a narrow street, roses scrambling over the picket fence and up the walls, geraniums spilling out of the window boxes.

Beyond the house is another, smaller house at the back of what must be the garden.

"Welcome home," he says, and I get out of the car and just stand, smelling the salt in the air, unable to believe what a storybook existence this is, unable to believe that this is now my storybook existence too.

"It's so beautiful." I turn to Brooks, my dad. I still have absolutely no idea what to call him. "The flowers!"

"Nothing to do with me, I'm afraid. My former wife was the gardener, and now Kim, who cleans for us a couple of times a week, looks after the plants. I'm afraid I'd turn everything to dust. I never had much of a green thumb. I'm putting you in the guest cottage." He gestures to the smaller house at the back. "Do you want to freshen up first, before coming in to meet Julia?"

I nod meekly, relieved that I can get a few minutes to myself to digest everything. Brooks goes in front of me, carrying my suitcase, which is embarrassingly heavy as I had no idea what to pack, so brought everything, just in case, and leads me to a tiny cottage, more roses, a white wooden chair on the little porch outside, and a bottle of champagne on the table.

"To welcome you!" He smiles. "We definitely have much to celebrate!" He opens the French doors to reveal a surprisingly large room, the ceilings vaulted into the roof, a pretty bed covered in a white quilt and piled with blue and white cushions at one end, a living room arrangement with a small kitchenette at the other.

"It's perfect!" I say, walking over to the walls, to the beautiful seascapes there. "Are they yours?"

He nods. "Whatever I don't sell gets repurposed, either here or given as gifts."

"They're beautiful!"

"Thank you. I'll leave you alone now. When you're ready, come up to the house!" And with a jaunty wave he lets himself out.

When I'm ready? I'm not sure I'll ever be ready. I circle the room, looking at everything, before sinking down on the sofa and hugging myself tightly, a huge smile on my face, not sure whether I'm on the brink of laughter or tears.

Perhaps a bit of both. I feel, suddenly, completely overwhelmed. And scared. All of this is unfamiliar, all of it new, and although Brooks couldn't have been more kind, more welcoming, I am a fish out of water. I have never been anywhere so beautiful, but being here, at his home, makes it real, and suddenly I'm not sure how I fit in, whether I fit in.

I hoist my suitcase onto the bed and start putting things away. Everything I brought seems suddenly far too dressy. My holidays are in the Mediterranean, where we wear strappy colorful sundresses and platform sandals. Don't think I didn't notice how casual everyone here was, the dressiest women I saw in tunics and shorts, still with flip-flops on their feet.

I feel wrong. I want to go shopping, to try to blend in, buy shorts and T-shirts just like everyone else. I have always prided myself on my chameleonlike ability to blend in, but there's nothing I hate more than getting it wrong, and as I pull one dress after another out, it is clear I got it wrong.

I do have one pair of denim capris, so I pull them on with my sneakers and a gauzy purple top. It will have to do. I wash my face, dust on some bronzer and lip gloss, shake out my hair, and it's about the best I can do right now. I grab the bottle of champagne to take it up to the house, and take a deep breath. Time to meet the rest of the family.

Julia wipes her hands on her apron and walks over to me, a curious smile on her face. I don't know whether to hug her; it feels completely different than meeting Brooks, not as natural, more reserved, and definitely more frightening. I want her to like me. I so want her to like me. I try to mirror her smile, aware that my heart is pounding.

"Hi." She stands looking at me curiously as I extend my hand to shake hers. She takes it and grins, her eyes roaming all over my face. "Wow!" She starts to laugh. "This is so weird! You could be my twin!"

It's true, she and I are almost identical. I'm a little taller, heavier, but our faces are so alike, it is disconcerting. Behind her I see a dark-haired man turn from the kitchen sink and walk over.

"Wow!" He lets out a whistle. "God, the two of you could be sisters!" He has an Irish accent, and he grins at me outrageously, breaking the tension, as I start to laugh.

"I'm Aidan." He leans forward and shakes hands, and I am instantly at home with him. "Let me take that." He takes the champagne from my hand. "I like a girl who comes prepared."

"More than prepared," I say, reaching into my pocket and handing Julia a bar of Cadburys as her face lights up. Then a clatter of small feet down stairs, and a small blond girl is standing in front of me.

"Hi!" she says, twirling in her pink tutu. "I'm Summer, and I'm four. Do you like my dress?"

"I do." I crouch down. "I think it might be the most beautiful dress I've ever seen."

"Oh shit!" yells Julia, dashing back to the kitchen. "The onions!"

"Don't curse in front of Summer," says a cool voice, and I look up to see a woman coming down the stairs, the picture of elegance in her hippie-ish but clearly ridiculously expensive white tunic, chunky gold jewelry, and gold-streaked hair swept up in a clip.

Ellie. It has to be. Everything Brooks said about her fits. There is an air of imperiousness about her as she glides over to me, although it may also be that I think that because I am still slumped in a crouch,

180

pretending to be admiring her daughter's tutu, looking up at this vision of ice-princessy loveliness.

She is dark skinned, like both Julia and me, but more refined than either of us. Her nose is tiny, petite, her lips full, prettily parting to reveal large, perfect white teeth. She reminds me of someone, but I can't think who, until it suddenly comes to me. Of course. Audrey Hepburn. The delicateness, the prettiness, as if someone had Photoshopped me down to a daintiness and size that few people in real life ever attain.

But she is real. And coolly appraising me. I stand up, wishing I were not wearing this purple top from Warehouse that looked incredibly good when I bought it three years ago, but many washes in has clearly seen better days. I wish I weren't wearing old sneakers that were once white but are now distinctly grey. I wish I had a smaller nose, thinner thighs, slender wrists.

In short, I wish I were exactly like her, because the very perfection of her instantly makes me feel entirely inadequate.

"I'm Cat." I shake her outstretched hand, hoping for a warm welcome like the one I got from Julia, but I know as soon as I look at her that the chances of that happening are not very likely, and I'm right. She just looks at me.

"I'm Ellie. And this is a surprise," she says. She smiles then, but the warmth definitely doesn't reach her eyes. "You met Summer, obviously, and Trudy is upstairs having a nap. You'll meet her later."

Julia comes whirling back from the kitchen, her energy instantly lifting the room. "Isn't it weird, Ellie? Doesn't she look just like us? Like me?"

"She looks like you," Ellie says, and it is clear she not only does not think I look like her, but that the very prospect of that would fill her with horror.

"Champagne!" says Aidan, appearing behind Julia with a silver tray filled with full champagne flutes. "Time to celebrate!"

I hesitate only slightly before taking the champagne. Everyone takes a glass. How can I possibly be the only one to decline? How rude! Not to mention that any fears I had have been confirmed by Ellie's coolness. This isn't going to be the straightforward perfect family reunion I had hoped for, that much is clear. It's not like it's vodka, anyway. It's champagne, which is completely different. I'm certainly not going to be the one to spoil the fun.

"To family!" says Brooks, raising his glass. "To my newfound daughter, the lovely Cat.

How grateful we are that you have now found us. Cheers!"

"Slainte!" murmurs Aidan, standing behind me. I turn and toast him, and he winks. "Don't worry about Ellie," he says quietly, leaning forward so I'm the only one who can hear him. "She's a bitch on wheels. It's nothing personal."

"Thank you," I say with relief. "She's the one I was terrified of meeting."

"Everyone's terrified of her," he says in his soft Irish brogue. "Drink up. There's nothing like a bit of champagne to chase the terrors away." He's right, I think, so I nod, and I do.

How I love this new family of mine. Instantly and unreservedly. I'm almost sickeningly envious of them growing up here, in this house, although Ellie went to boarding school in Massachusetts. But they got to grow up at the top of a cobbled street that leads to boats bobbing on the water, with a dad who works at home, has a studio next door, was always present, and most of all, loving.

For I can see, even in one night, how loving Brooks is. We were still having cocktails when Summer came in, now out of her tutu and in a proper princess outfit, complete with tiny cowboy boots and cowboy hat, and climbed on his lap with a book. He had been talking to Aidan, and I watched as he immediately focused all his attention on Summer, stroking her hair and talking to her with such sweetness and love, it almost broke my heart.

I watched him read *Goodnight Moon* to her. Every time she stopped him to point out something in the picture, it led to another conversation, and his patience took my breath away.

My father, the man I called my father, only ever read to me if my mother was sick, which was much of the time. I was never allowed to ask questions, or interrupt, or he would start tutting and sighing, putting the book down and saying that as I clearly didn't want him to actually read the story, he might as well stop. And he would indeed stop and leave the room, and not come back. Seriously. That was the kind of father I had. So I learned to lie in bed as quiet as a mouse, biting my tongue while he sped through the story, not pointing out to him that I knew he was skipping whole pages, huge chunks of the book, in order to get out of there as quickly as possible. Oh, I knew.

How different would it have been to have

Brooks as a father. How wonderful it must have been to have someone so patient, so attentive. I look at Julia, through the doorway in the kitchen, as Aidan pulls her to him by the pocket on the front of her apron and kisses her, and I am instantly and horribly envious.

I want to be her. I want to have this father, to have had this upbringing. I want to have a boyfriend who adores me. I want to be a whirlwind of energy. I turn my head and look at Ellie, who has been perfectly polite and pleasant, if not exactly a bundle of warmth and acceptance. I have felt her eyes following me all evening, and I have been on my best behavior.

Even with the champagne. I'm not drunk. Brooks has been drinking all evening, first a glass of champagne, then endless glasses of scotch, but he's not drunk either. I have had three, maybe four glasses of champagne, and I will not have any more. I won't mess this up, don't want to do anything I either won't remember or will need to forget.

Jason and the AA meetings already seem very far away. The prospect of my having a problem with drinking seems very far away. If I had a problem, I wouldn't be able to stop after three or four glasses, and I have absolutely no desire to have any more.

This, right here, right now, feels more real to me than anything in my life these past few months, this family. These girls have each other, have a loving father, and my pain at having been excluded from this is only assuaged by the fact that I have it now.

I have it now.

"Come help me with the washing up," says Julia, and I obediently follow her into the kitchen, grabbing a dish towel as we stand next to each other at the sink.

"I still can't get over it," she says, handing me a sudsy bowl, which I stare at before handing back with a laugh.

"You have to wash the soap all off," I say, laughing only because the reason I dry rather than ever, ever wash is because I have no patience and am always being told off for not washing off the soap.

"I hate washing," she grumbles, taking back the bowl. "I always dry. I just want to get it all done as quickly as possible, so everything's always soapy."

"I'm the same way," I say. "Surprisingly."

"What else?" She is delighted, suddenly holding out her hand. "Look! We have the same hands. Isn't that weird?"

"It is. But I don't know how similar we are. You seem . . . I don't know. Much more together than me. You're, what, three years younger? Four? But already you have a self-possession I never had."

"Are you kidding?" She turns to me, aghast. "You're completely confident! For starters you just flew in, not knowing anyone, and already, in one night, you feel like you totally belong. You don't have any anxiety, or fear —"

I sputter. "I was so terrified when I got to the airport I practically couldn't walk."

"It didn't show."

I pause before deciding to ask about her sister. "I have a question. What's Ellie like? Are the two of you close?"

Julia turns to check we are alone, lowering her voice. "I love her, of course. She's my sister, and if ever she was in trouble I'd be the first one there to help her, but . . . we're very different."

"I can see that."

"You have to understand it's all insecurity on her part. Not that I'm not insecure, but she covers it by being cool and superior, when she isn't actually like that at all. We have different mothers, you know that, right? My mom was with my dad for most of my life, and by the time they split up I was an adult; it didn't have the same impact. Ellie's mom and my dad split up when she was a baby. Her mom had lived here, on

Nantucket, before moving to Boston after the split. Ellie was always here for summers, and I think of her as my sister, not half or anything like that, but I recognize she's very different from me. Her mom's . . ." She lowers her voice still more. "Difficult."

"What kind of difficult?"

Julia checks that no one is coming into the room. "Her mother was a big social climber. Huge. I'm not supposed to know this, but she was totally from the wrong side of the tracks. She thought my dad had fortunes, didn't realize it was all tied up in trusts, and I guess by the time she discovered she wasn't going to be living a life of luxury with homes on Nantucket and in Boston and on St. Barth's, it was time to leave."

"She sounds ruthless. Ellie was a baby, you said?"

"Yes. And the mother, Lily, was on a mission to find another wealthy husband. She found one almost immediately, so Ellie was whisked into this life of luxury, but I know deep down she's terrified people might discover she doesn't actually deserve it."

"It sounds like the dream life."

"Ellie got lavished with everything she wanted, except love and attention. Except when she was here. Lily's now on her fifth husband. Every time she gets married she focuses all her attention on the man, nothing on her child, or the children that came after Ellie. Ellie always used to say when she was with her mom she felt unwanted. Pretty much the only place she felt safe, and loved, was here with my dad."

I think about my own childhood. "I can definitely relate to the feeling unwanted," I say.

"I'm sorry. The awful thing is the older she gets, the more like her mom she is. I mean, not here so much. When she's here she's usually able to let go of the superficial shit. My dad would give her such a hard time if she turned up filled with airs and graces, but she's married to a banker, and they have this huge life with a huge house in New York, and, like Lily, it's all about seeing and being seen at the right functions. She has a closet that, I'm not kidding, is bigger than my bedroom here."

I turn and look at the kitchen, this house that she is staying in for the summer, that she stays in every summer, and I know that even though every fiber in my body is recoiling at what I'm hearing about Ellie, I also know she can't be all bad, not if she stays here.

This house is cozy, and worn, and

comfortable. The kitchen hasn't been redone in at least thirty years. The table is scrubbed with years of use; cookbooks fill the shelves on either side of the range, and not one looks like it was printed after 1984.

This is not a house that a precious princess would stay in unless she has a very different side.

"Yet she loves it here," I say, turning back to Julia and taking a plate.

"She does. Which is bizarre because she's never walked into a hotel room without complaining and asking for an upgrade. Let me tell you, it's Four Seasons all the way for her. But that's also her insecurity. Strip away the armor and she's incredibly loyal. And strong. And a doer. She never talks about doing stuff, she just gets it done."

"That's good to hear. I have to be honest, she's so pretty it completely intimidates me. And she's been kind of . . . cool with me."

"That's Ellie. She always takes time to trust people. But once she's won over, she's yours for life. And it's worth it."

"Good to know." I smile at her, wondering how on earth I am ever going to manage to win Ellie over, because right now it doesn't seem like she trusts me at all.

Aidan walks in, brandishing a bottle of whiskey. "Who'll crack open this bottle with me? Julia? Cat?"

Julia makes a face. "I hate whiskey."

"I'm fine," I say, because the truth is I have never particularly liked whisky either. "Although if you were talking vodka, that would be another story entirely."

His face falls. "Well, that's no fun. The only other person who'll drink it is Brooks, and last time he finished the entire bottle himself." His face lights up. "Tell you what! How about we go to Ropewalk for a drink instead?" He checks his watch. "Come on, Cat! We'll show you a bit of what we call nightlife here on Nantucket!"

I don't want to be the killjoy here, but I realize I am suddenly exhausted. The emotion of the day, the travel, the time difference, all of it has caught up with me, and I am so tired I can hardly speak.

"Ah, but you're suffering from the jet lag." Aidan's voice is all concern. "Here, give me that cloth and I'll finish up the drying. You go and get yourself off to bed. We'll do the nightlife tomorrow. Maybe everyone will come to the restaurant for dinner, then we young'uns will go out after?"

"That sounds great. Thank you." After hugging everyone good night, I walk down the path, stopping only to breathe in the night air, letting myself into the guest cottage and trying not to think of what time it must be in England right now.

THIRTEEN

I sleep the sleep of the dead. A sleep so deep that when I wake up I have absolutely no idea where I am. I lie for a while, blinking, drifting back into consciousness before remembering the events of the day before.

My family. The dinner. The laughter. The feeling of belonging. Champagne. I remember there was champagne. Oh God. It must have led to something bad, but as I lie quietly playing over the events, searching for some embarrassing thing I must have said or done, I realize there was nothing.

Shame is not here to greet me at the start of this beautiful new day.

I didn't draw the blinds, and light is streaming through onto the bed. I sit up slightly and look down to the water, as a feeling of absolute happiness washes over me.

I have found my place in the world.

Bounding out of bed, into the shower, I

brush my teeth, discard all my clothes, and resolve to go shopping today. I pull on yesterday's jeans and a simple white T-shirt, sliding my feet into flat Indian sandals, and pull my hair into a ponytail, literally bouncing out the guest cottage and up the garden path.

"Where is everyone?" I was expecting the house to be filled, as it was last night, with people, with noise, with coffee, but it is spectacularly quiet.

Brooks, sitting at the kitchen table with a coffee, holds a hand to his lips. "All sleeping."

"Sorry," I whisper. "What time is it?"

"Six a.m."

"Six a.m.!" I yelp, then apologize again. "I thought it was practically lunchtime."

"It probably is where you come from." He smiles. "I'm up at this time a lot. One of the problems of old age — you stop sleeping. I figure this is my peaceful time. I make myself coffee, then go for a walk."

"Oh God! I'm so sorry!" I start to back out of the room. "I didn't mean to disturb your peaceful time. I'll go. Sorry."

"Stop! I'm thrilled you're up. I barely spoke to you last night with everyone here. How about you grab yourself a cup of coffee and come on my walk with me?" He gestures to the coffeepot on the counter, and I help myself, pouring into one of the carry cups I find in a cupboard.

"Will I be okay in these shoes?" I point out the flimsy sandals, thinking I really ought to go back and put on sneakers.

"We'll do an amble today. And we'll take it slow. You'll be fine."

I am, as it turns out, fine. It helps that I don't have to do much of the talking. Brooks is a wonderful storyteller. He tells me stories of his childhood, his parents, his life. He fills in all the blanks.

After a while he asks about me, but I'm not used to telling stories about my life, nor downloading my résumé, as it were, so I tell him a little, with an uncomfortable shrug, and turn the subject back to him. It's not that I don't want him to know me, I do, but there's so much I want to know about him.

I feel like my brain is a computer, trying to slot all the pieces together, and it still feels surreal, that I have this father, this family, and if I can get all the pieces straight, figure out how they do in fact all fit together, then I will know how I belong, and I so, so want to belong. I want to be just like them.

Brooks (and a part of me so badly wants

to call him Dad, although even as I think this I picture Ellie's eyes narrowing in disdain, and I know it's too early, realize it might never be comfortable for me to call him Dad) offers to drive me around and show off the island.

We get home, I grab my purse and climb into the big old wagon, and we take off, down to Sconset, then all the way to the other end of the island, to Madaket, where we park the car and walk, marveling at the prettiness of the fishing boats bobbing on the water.

We head back to Main Street, and he drops me off, disappearing round the corner to do some errands while I take pictures of the old wagon selling gorgeous bunches of huge hydrangeas and roses on the corner, the shops that are far more enticing than Oxford Street could ever even hope to be.

I take careful note of what everyone is wearing. I worry my chameleon tendencies display a lack of sense of self, that I am always willing and able to change myself into whoever I need to be. I marvel at people like Poppy, who is always herself, who dresses only ever to please herself, who never feels the need to change her clothes or hair or voice in order to fit in.

Clearly this London girl does not fit in

here, not yet, and I am desperate to do so. Part of my romanticizing my life includes the false assumption that if I look right, then I will *be* right. Despite the twenty-nine years of experience proving otherwise, I still naively believe that this might actually be true.

I find shorts and strappy white tank tops in one of the tourist shops, and colorful tunics a little farther down the road that I know are perfect, pink and green, orange and turquoise, shimmery beads glinting sunlight around the neckline. I find white cutoff cargo pants that are almost exactly like the ones Ellie was wearing yesterday, and exotic leather sandals that have tiny gold and turquoise starfish sprinkled all over them.

In London I wear makeup. A lot. I have always loved makeup, loved the way it can transform a blank canvas into a thing of beauty. I do not think I have ever left my house in my adult life without a full face of makeup. With makeup, I can be very attractive. People have said pretty, although that has always been hard for me to believe. Ellie is pretty. I am not. Without makeup I detest what I look like. I have always been terrified of the morning after the night before, largely because I am convinced that should whoever I am with see me without the benefit of artfully applied eye shadow and contour-creating blusher, he will shrink in horror at my plain face.

But no one here wears makeup, or at least not makeup that is noticeable. They hide their unmade-up eyes behind sunglasses, and I find a cheap pair of excellent Ray-Ban copies in a store next to the bike shop down by the water. I almost laugh as I put them on, already wearing one of the new tanks and the new flip-flops.

If you didn't know better, if you didn't hear me speak, you would look at me and think that I belong here. You would think that I had been here all my life. And indeed, within a few short days, I feel as at home as if I had been born here.

The days pass, sleepy when everyone is out at work or at the beach, doing what they normally do, and riotous when they are all here at the house, crammed in, everyone jumping in to lend a hand with cooking, cleaning up, setting tables.

I fit right in. I fit as if I have always belonged here. The only person who hasn't accepted me is Ellie. I have tried and tried, but at best she is coldly polite. Julia's warmth, Aidan's kindness, and my own father's attention, however, more than make up for it.

Early morning walks with Brooks have become part of the daily routine. We wander to the beach, then finish up at the Hub for coffee and the papers, Brooks stopping every few feet on Main Street to greet people he knows. And to introduce me, his daughter, to everyone's surprise and delight. A third daughter they never knew about, but look at me! So clearly a Mayhew if ever there was one! And with an accent! Welcome to Nantucket, they say. You will never want to leave.

They may be right, all these strangers. The longer I stay here, the more I think I don't want to leave. I know it's a holiday, I know people don't really live like this the entire year, except . . . I think that maybe they do here. They work really hard, but they play hard.

Which is the hardest part for me. How can I possibly stay sober when everyone around me drinks as if it were nothing? And maybe it is nothing. Sobriety suddenly seems like a really bad idea. I'm on holiday, for God's sake. On Nantucket, where I am supposed to be having fun.

"Look at you!" Aidan lets out a long whistle

as I walk into the kitchen in one of my new outfits, bought the other day. White capri pants and a turquoise tunic top, beaded prettily around the neckline. "Is that outfit new? You look like you've done some serious damage in town."

"Does it still count as new if it's five days old?" I grin, hiding my slight worry at the amount I have been spending, although given the exchange rate it really isn't that bad at all. At least that is what I will continue to tell myself. "What do you think?"

"You finally look like an islander!" he says, walking over to the fridge and pulling out two beers, cracking them open and handing me one.

"Isn't it a bit early?" I take the beer, for it would have been rude not to, but I have always tried not to drink before lunchtime.

"It's five o'clock somewhere," he says with a shrug and a grin, clinking his bottle with mine and a hearty "Slainte," so what else am I supposed to do other than drink up?

Everyone is out, Brooks at his studio, Ellie with her children and nanny at the beach, Julia visiting a friend. It is just Aidan and I, and the more beer we both drink, the better time I find myself having.

He, like Brooks, is a storyteller, but this time the drink loosens my tongue, and we try to outdo each other with stories of our outrageous drinking behavior.

"Well, I once woke up on a ferry on the way to Ios in Greece, with absolutely no idea how I got there," Aidan says. "The last I remember I was in a nightclub in London. The next I was in my underwear on the deck of a bloody great boat."

"You win!" I shout, as we both collapse in giggles.

"No more bloody beer." Aidan peers into the fridge. "Shall we make a start on the vodka?"

"Yes!" I stumble ever so slightly on my way to get glasses as Aidan goes to get the vodka, and for a second, just a second, the disappointed, disapproving face of Jason flits into my mind. And for a second, just a second, the church hall flits into my mind, the chairs pulled into a circle, the eager, earnest faces of the people who all talk of the hell of their former lives, and how they have found happiness, and peace, in these rooms.

But I push those thoughts aside with a loud, internal "fuck it." I'm on holiday. If a girl can't drink on holiday, what the hell is the world coming to? I drain that glass of vodka in about two seconds, to loud cheering from Aidan, who follows suit, and we both refill, both equally delighted at having found a partner in crime.

"Jesus!" I open my eyes, taking a while to focus on a stern-looking Ellie, who is shaking me with a look of abject disgust on her face.

"Wha?" I try to sit up, dizzy, drunk, knowing that I cannot let her know how drunk I am. That whatever I do now, my future depends on it. I have to do everything in my power to hide quite how much we have had to drink.

Her face contorts into a sneer. She turns. "Summer?" I see her daughter behind her. Oh God! Her daughter! Of course. "Go upstairs. You can play in Mommy's room. There are toys under Trudy's crib." Cheering, Summer thunders upstairs as Ellie turns back to me with a sneer. "You're drunk," she says, and I find myself squinting, then opening my eyes wide, in a bid to get her face into focus.

"I'm not drunk." I sit up. "I'm just a bit tipsy. I took some headache pills, and I think they reacted with the beer."

She reaches behind her and picks up a vodka bottle that looks like it's just about empty. "That's not beer," she says.

"Oh, leave her alone!" I am relieved that Aidan has now swum into my focus, leaning on the doorjamb of the kitchen. "We had a few drinks, that's all." I register that Aidan does not seem to be as drunk as I am, which is a good thing. Perhaps it means that I did not drink as much as I fear, that I just don't hold it as well. "She's on holiday," he continues.

"And she's a guest in our house," says Ellie, her voice icy. "As in fact are you, even though you're not actually staying here. This is unacceptable, Aidan. Where the hell is Julia? How can you have spent the entire day getting drunk? Both of you. I'm just appalled." She turns back to me, shaking her head in disgust, and I am so filled with shame I want the ground to open and swallow me up.

"I'm sorry," I mutter, trying to stand up, except the floor starts swimming, and even though I am desperate to get away from the grand inquisitioner, it doesn't seem that it's a very likely proposition right now. It's far easier to slump back down on the sofa. As soon as I do, my eyes start to close, which is one way, I suppose, to turn down the noise.

"Wake up!" hisses Ellie, shaking me awake. "You need to get to your bed."

"Right," I agree, although my body doesn't seem able to move.

She hoists me up by my arms, and once I am up, I narrow my eyes to stop the room dancing and walk, very purposefully, and in as straight a line as I can manage, to what I think is the door, which unfortunately, once I get there and search for the handle, turns out to be the fireplace.

"The door's over there," says the wicked witch disguised as Audrey Hepburn.

"I knew that," I say, in as imperious a way as I can manage, stopping as another person walks into the room, this time Julia. I steel myself for more criticism and judgment, but Julia just starts to laugh.

"Oh God!" she says. "Both of you? Hammered? Really?"

"I'm not hammered," disputes Aidan, putting his arm around her and pulling her in for a kiss, and I'm really quite impressed with how non-drunk he seems. "I am quietly merry, as is Cat, who is also on holiday and therefore entitled to have some fun."

"Isn't it a bit early?" asks Julia, who does not push Aidan away in disgust but instead folds into him with an indulgent smile. "Even for you?"

"I don't have to be at work until later," he says. "I'll have a nap and be as right as rain by the time I have to work."

"I'm speechless," Ellie says, her features contorted with rage. "Once again your boyfriend has shown a complete lack of respect. As for . . ." She looks at me, and I know she can't even bring herself to say my name. "Her. What kind of a person shows up to visit her family, who she's never met, and gets so shitfaced she can't even walk properly?"

Aidan lets out a bark of laughter. "At least you know she's related to you!" he says. "No question about that."

"And what the hell is that supposed to mean?"

"Oh come on, Ellie. Get that poker out of your arse. The number of times I've been here and seen your father drunk as a skunk. Not that there's anything wrong with that, I might add. It's a family trait, and one I heartily approve of, by the way, my family being much the same way."

"How dare you tell me to get the poker out of my arse? And how dare you talk about being drunk as if it's something normal, something fun? I grew up with it, with a father who's always drinking, and I know just how damaging it is for everyone around them." She turns to Julia. "I get it, Julia. I get why all of your boyfriends are

205

alcoholics or drug addicts. I get this is all to do with our father, but keep it out of the house, for God's sake. I have young children here. Keep it out of the goddamned house!" Her voice isn't loud, but as cold as ice as Julia disentangles herself from Aidan.

"Don't you dare say a word about my father. I'm lucky to have him. Jesus, *you're* lucky to have him, especially given the mess your mother made of your life. You're always so damned judgmental, Ellie. Everything in your life is always so perfect; you look down your nose at everything and everyone around you. Including your own family. It makes me sick. So what if Aidan's drinking? Or Cat? Or me, for that matter? We're young. We're supposed to. Just because you're on your high horse and living the life of a fifty-year-old Park Avenue matron doesn't mean the rest of us have to. Get over it."

I want to applaud, and then, with slight dismay, I realize that everyone is looking at me in horror. Oh *shit.* That thought somehow moved into my hands and I realize I actually did applaud. I stop. Quickly. And Ellie lets out an anguished groan and runs upstairs.

"Let's get Cat to bed," Julia says, and as I refuse all help, weaving my way out of the room, one sober and sobering thought makes its way into my head: *Nothing is as perfect as it seems.*

FOURTEEN

I wake up with the familiar pounding head and no idea where I am or what time it is. I am completely disoriented, it is dark, and it takes a few seconds for the full mortification of what I have done to set in.

I cannot believe I got drunk today. I cannot believe I showed myself up like that with my family, gave them such a terrible impression of me so soon after arriving here. I can't believe I drank that much, after these past few weeks, after determining never to do that again.

What is the matter with me? Why didn't I stop after two beers? Or even three? What the hell is wrong with me that I am so easily influenced I dived into that bottle of vodka with barely a second thought?

I lie in bed, disgusted, utterly disgusted with myself, awash with shame. How do I ever face Jason again? How am I supposed to tell him what happened? I can't. I couldn't. The look on his face would be unimaginable. After all the effort he's put into me, taking me to meetings, finding me a sponsor, what kind of a terrible person must I be that this is how I repay him?

I should find a meeting. Right now. That's what I should do. I should get myself off to a meeting, confess my sin to a roomful of strangers, and go every day while I'm here so I can get off the plane back in London and feel something other than this horrific mortification.

There is a knock on the door. Julia. With a glass of water and three pills.

"I hoped you were awake. How are you feeling? I brought you some Advil."

"Advil?" My voice is croaky as I try to sit up.

"Painkillers."

I manage to sit up, overcome with a sudden bout of dizziness and a wave of first hot, then cold. I leap out of bed and make it to the bathroom just in time, practically falling on top of the loo as I throw up, my stomach heaving until there's nothing left to come up. I lay my head on the seat, as unsanitary as it is, feeling the coolness, knowing that in a little while I will feel better.

"Are you okay?" she asks, coming into the

209

bathroom and stroking my back, and I think that even though I barely know this girl, I might actually love her.

"I'm so sorry," I croak. "I'm so embarrassed. I can't believe I did that."

"First of all, I'm more than used to it. We all like a drink. Apart from Ellie, obviously. I'm really sorry for everything that she said. I guess we react to the drinking very differently. She has always been disgusted by everything to do with alcohol, and people drinking, and getting drunk. When we were kids and my dad would have too much to drink, she would behave in much the same way as she did with you this afternoon. She'd stand there and scream at him, try to shame him into not drinking. *If you loved us,* she'd shout, *you wouldn't do this.*"

I raise my head and turn to look at her. "You didn't feel the same way?"

"I tried to make everything better. I was never a shouter. I think I thought that if I behaved better, if I was better, maybe that would make him stop. And then when he didn't, I'd be the one that ended up looking after him. No surprise, I guess, that every man I've ever dated has liked the booze, or drugs, a little too much, and I'm always the one that ends up looking after them."

"Aidan's so nice," I say. "He seems to look

210

after you too, although maybe in different ways."

She smiles. "That's why I love him. He does. Very occasionally I think our partying might be a bit much, but what the hell. We're young, we're supposed to be having fun, right? This is the time to party, before settling down, before kids, real responsibilities."

"Exactly," I say, thinking of Aidan and understanding exactly why she forgives his transgressions; thinking of Jason and wondering if he would forgive mine. And then I think that Julia would probably know if there were AA meetings on the island, and if so where I might find them, and I mix the words around in my head hoping to formulate a sentence that would come out without me wanting to die in shame, and I can't figure out a way to do it, so I end up saying nothing at all.

"It's nine o'clock," says Julia. "At night," she adds helpfully, seeing my confusion. "Ellie's so furious she's checked everyone into the Wauwinet, which is what she always does when we have fights, so I thought maybe you and I could go down to Aidan's restaurant and grab some dinner."

"Where's your dad?"

"Tonight's his night at the Chicken Box.

He'll doubtless get a ride home and roll in sometime in the early hours. We tend to stay out of his way on nights like these."

"Will you give me a minute to get ready?" I say, really not wanting to go out, nor have dinner, food being the very last thing on my mind, but experience has told me the best way to go about getting rid of a hangover is painkillers and food in my stomach. And hair of the dog. But I'm definitely going to give that one a miss tonight. This is it. No drinking from now on. It's just not worth the shame.

I don't drink. Well, I don't drink anything hard. Beer doesn't count. It isn't easy, but I sip my beer as everyone around me drinks vodka and tequila, as the night grows more raucous, and I am the one who ends up driving everyone home, which is something of a first.

The next morning, I wake up with no hangover, feeling bright, happy, and excited to see what the day brings. I am thrilled with myself for not drinking the hard stuff last night when everyone around me was; I'm determined to keep this up, to put my best foot forward, not to embarrass myself again with my family.

I can do this. I can absolutely do this. I

can be the sister, the daughter, the friend they need me to be.

The days pass in a haze of sunshine, boats, walks, and great food thanks to Julia and Aidan, who seem to spend most of their time at home in the kitchen.

I manage to stay away from the booze. Mostly. A few drinks here and there but nothing unmanageable. Nothing drunken. No blackouts and no hangovers. Hey! Maybe I can do this after all. Maybe I don't have the problem I thought I had.

Julia is the unexpected delight. I came here to get to know my father, and while Brooks is warm and kind, and exactly the sort of father I always wanted, it is Julia I find myself gravitating toward.

I'm in the kitchen when Julia comes downstairs, two rolled-up towels under her arms and a straw bag over her shoulder.

"I'm taking you to the beach." She opens a drawer and takes out a bottle of Hawaiian Tropic. "It's a beautiful day, and you and I need to get tanned."

"You're already tanned." I point out her dark skin.

"Never tan enough," she says. "And as my sister, you should really be doing the same thing, in solidarity."

"What about Ellie?" I ask dubiously, for Ellie's skin is lighter, Ellie goes nowhere without a hat, and does not, as far as I know, sit on the beach unless covered by an umbrella.

"That's the point. She's freaked out about the sun aging her skin, I need someone like you to live on the wild side with me. You ready? Let's get moving!"

We climb on bikes and cycle down to the beach, a boom box stuffed in Julia's straw basket, Julia chattering away, shouting back over her shoulder as I laugh, unable to hear half of what she says. I love this girl's energy. I love her enthusiasm and warmth, and that it feels as if I have known her forever.

"Tell me more about you." She stretches out her arms and sighs with pleasure at the warmth of the sun hitting her oiled-up skin. "Boyfriend? Dating? What's the story?"

I tell her about my disastrous love life, and then mention Jason, my un-boyfriend, my hopefully future boyfriend, Julia hooting with laughter when I recount the story of how we met.

"You actually don't remember how you got there?" In anyone else I would expect to see shock, because God knows waking up in a stranger's bed is not exactly something I'm proud of, but Julia thinks it's hysterical.

"That's wild!" she says. "Imagine if he's the guy you end up marrying! What a great story to tell your kids!" And she goes off into peals of laughter while I smile.

Imagine.

We talk, and laugh, and giggle, and confide secrets. I don't remember the last time I did this with anyone; I had forgotten just how much fun girlfriends can be. I have had it at work, with Poppy, with Jackie, but they're all so busy now with their boyfriends, husbands, other couples, I had forgotten how great it is to just hang out with someone just like you.

"It's just a weak Bloody Mary, for God's sake," says Aidan, sliding it off the tray and putting it on the table. "I promise you I'm not going to get you drunk again. And I'm really sorry for that, by the way. But I can tell by looking at you that you need a drink. Hell, everyone needs a drink. Isn't life just more fun with a drink under your belt?"

He's right. Life is more fun with a drink under your belt. I've managed not to drink anything for ten days now. Surely I deserve one small drink as a reward?

"I'm just going to have the one," I say, first to him, then to Julia, who is reaching out for a Bloody Mary of her own.

215

"Whatever." She grins. "Cheers!" And we clink glasses and my God, but it feels good. Who would give this up by choice?

One leads to another, to another, and soon whatever mortification I felt the other day is forgotten, and whatever shame I felt has disappeared, and life is not only good again but huge amounts of fun, and Aidan is working, and Julia and I sit together and laugh and share stories, as Aidan brings us drinks, and food, and I love life again, and most of all, I love that I have finally found the one thing I always wanted: a sister.

The restaurant has closed; the staff is sitting around, all of them drinking, smoking, telling funny stories. It is late, and I am drinking, and thinking I should stop, although I'm not sure why, when the peal of the restaurant phone interrupts the raucous telling of stories, and Julia is called to the phone.

"Shit. My dad just passed out at the bar. I have to go and get him." I realize Julia, standing at the table, who I thought had drunk just as much as I have, is actually completely sober, and I have no idea how she did that.

"We'll come," says Aidan, who is definitely not sober.

Julia shakes her head. "It's fine. You guys stay. I'll go and drop him home, then come back and get you."

"Don't be silly," says Aidan. "We'll get a ride home. Are you sure you don't want us to come?"

"Absolutely sure," says Julia, leaning down and giving him a lingering kiss. "I'll see you at home. Bye, Cat!" She blows me a kiss and is gone.

More wine. Vodka. The night has got away from me, and I am back to exactly where I have always been, unable to stop, uncaring that I'm unable to stop, and I don't give a shit. Nothing matters anymore except that I am young, I have no responsibilities, and I am happy to party the night away. Now that Ellie has gone, and Brooks is off doing his own drinking, who is there to judge me? Who is there to point out the error of my ways? Who is there to tell me that this isn't what I wanted for myself, that I am not just letting myself down but all the people in my life: my mother, my friends at work, my friends at the AA meetings, Jason.

Fuck it. I'm young, free, and single, much as I would like it to be otherwise, and I have found my family, and nothing is as perfect as it first appeared, and that's okay because me and my friend vodka have been reunited, and just as it always does, it eases the pain, rubs out the disappointment, makes everything in my life good.

At some point, I am aware that Aidan, who is in similar shape to me, ushers me to a parked car, someone else driving, and we squeeze into the backseat with three other people, staff from the restaurant, and I have to sit on Aidan's lap, which would be massively awkward if I were sober, but as it is, I fold into him and am delighted that he runs lazy circles on my back with his big hands.

I don't say anything the whole way home, just sinking into a warm body feeling the circles, and when we both get out of the car, we both stumble up the path, giggling, and he's holding me up, although I think I'm holding him up, and we get to the door of the cottage, and I turn to say good night, and I have absolutely no idea how this happens, but suddenly we are kissing, and my insides have turned to mush, and I don't remember anything that happens next.

Except when I wake up the next morning to a scream, to Julia standing in the doorway, tears streaming down her face, and to me and Aidan, both naked, both in my bed.

FIFTEEN

London, 2014

My fingers fly across the keyboard as I cradle the phone between my neck and my shoulder, tap-tap-tapping everything the woman on the end of the phone is saying, trying to ignore the creeping pain in my back, which always happens when an interview goes on a bit longer than I expect.

The door slams, and damn, Annie is home, which means I have to get off the phone, have to hang up my journalist coat and go back to being Mum. I can't interrupt her, though, my interviewee, not yet, not until there's a natural break, but I'm willing her to hurry up, so I can go and catch up with Annie on the events of the day.

Since my divorce, and to try to make up for the kind of mother I was for most of my marriage, I have tried to be present for her when she comes home. I'll never be the kind of mother who sets out elaborate teas, an assortment of cakes, biscuits, sandwiches — trust me, there are plenty of mothers around here who do actually do that — but I try to have something nice for her to eat, a hot chocolate in winter or lemon squash in summer. Even if I don't often have something homemade, I will at least get the biscuits that she likes.

"Mum!" she yells through the flat, even though she knows I'm where I always am if not in the kitchen: in the tiny cupboardlike office at the end of the corridor.

"Coming!" I say, finally telling the woman on the phone I have to go, saving my document, tidying the papers on my desk that manage to spread over every available surface, every day, and joining my delicious daughter in the kitchen to finally be the mother I always hoped I would be.

Every day, after school, I sit at the kitchen table and marvel at the child I have created, this person who is, in looks, a combination of both me and my ex-husband, but in personality is all her own.

I would like to tell you I knew what her personality was from the beginning, but the truth is, for a very long time I never bothered to stop and look. For a very long time, the only thing I cared about was numbing everything in my life with alcohol, and as ashamed as I am to admit it, it wasn't until I got divorced that I finally woke up and realized the mess my life had become.

Of course, I recognize the irony of writing feature after feature about divorce, and feature after feature about being a single mother, and even — yes, I will admit this — a first-person piece in the *Daily Mail* about the shame of being a mother who drank, which, by the way, garnered over a thousand comments online, almost all of them filled with a vitriol and hatred that felt like someone was twisting a knife in my stomach. There I was, trying to be honest, to own my part in it, to admit my sins in the hope that I would emerge renewed, and all those people could see was my deficiencies, what a terrible mother I'd been, what a terrible person I was.

Well, duh. Tell me something else I didn't know. My sponsor had warned me about writing the piece, but I went ahead and did it anyway. You are only as sick as your secrets, I had heard, over and over in AA meetings, and I knew I could only be properly cleansed if I told my secrets.

I had this grandiose notion of helping people, that if I was honest there would be tons of women reading my story who would realize the mess they were in too, might be inspired to do something about it.

There were a few. But the notes thanking me, sharing their own stories, washed over my head while the criticisms and insults lodged their way into my heart. At least for a week or so. Since then, I've learned first of all not to reveal quite so much of myself in my articles, and secondly not to read the bloody comments.

"So how was school?" I ask, sliding gingersnaps onto a plate and watching her devour them as soon as the plate hits the table.

"Do you want an apple?" I slide the fruit bowl over, seeing her grimace. "You're having dinner with your dad tonight, so don't fill up now."

"Oh, yeah. He texted me. He's picking me up at four thirty. We're going to Cara's sister's for dinner." She rolls her eyes, and I am secretly glad, although pained as well, at how difficult this new girlfriend of her father's is for her. And for me.

"How was school?" I change the subject, resisting the temptation to quiz her, as I sometimes do, about Cara, and her family, and the general all-round horribleness of her.

Annie shrugs. "Fine. But Lucy's being a bitch again."

"Oh God." I do wonder if I should berate her for her language, but it's not like I'm a paragon of virtue in that arena, so I let it slide. "What's happened now?" Lucy is her best frenemy. They are either as thick as thieves, together all the time, or they hate each other. Lucy is one of the popular girls, so Annie has to vie with others for her attention. I see her open up in the sunshine glow of Lucy's gaze, shrink with despondency when Lucy chooses to shine her glow elsewhere.

Not that my daughter is entirely innocent. I am quite sure Annie is not the easiest person to be friends with — she is demanding and all-consuming — but Lucy, girls like Lucy, have always scared me a little, and I would so love for Annie to find a different set of friends, girls who are a little less glamorous, a little less compelling, a little more ordinary and stable.

"I went to sit with her and Mary at lunch and they started whispering about me and giggling. I hate her."

"I'm sorry, darling. Could you sit with Pippa instead? She's a nice girl."

Annie shrugs. "Pippa's really boring. There's no way I'm sitting with Pippa. She's still obsessed with One Direction, which is just so *yawn.*"

Annie grimaces with disdain, and I think now is not the time to point out her bedroom wall is littered with posters of Harry Styles.

"Do you have homework?" Some days, Annie comes home filled with chatter, and I delight in listening to her, the two of us able to sit at the kitchen table for hours, but other days, like today, it is like squeezing blood from a stone.

"A bit," she says.

"Why don't you get it out? I'm going to start making dinner for tomorrow night."

"What's happening tomorrow night?"

"Sam's coming over. He's turned pescate-rian, so I thought I'd do salmon."

"Can you do risotto?" The only kind of fish my daughter will eat is the kind that is disguised by carbohydrate.

"Maybe," I say. "Although I was thinking of doing something simple, then making ice cream for dessert."

"He'll definitely eat the ice cream," Annie says, knowing full well that Sam is always on some kind of ridiculous diet, all of which goes out the window when it comes to dessert.

Sam has progressed from my gay best

friend to my gay husband. He often commissions me, bless him, and since he and his long-term partner split up a couple of months before Jason and I did, he understands exactly what I have gone through. Although he is the one I invariably turn to for advice, I do believe we have become each other's ports in the storm. The only thing he doesn't quite get is the AA stuff. He drinks. Not excessively, unless it's a celebration, but he doesn't understand why I can't have the occasional glass of champagne.

We have learned to agree to disagree. After I got sober, this time, I let go of a lot of people, the relationships I had that were based on drinking. I didn't want to be around unhealthy people anymore. Sam isn't exactly unhealthy, but if I didn't love him so much, I might have reconsidered his constant urging to "go on, just a glass." Luckily, I have been sober enough for long enough that it doesn't bother me. I am never tempted these days, and quite happy to keep wine at home for when Sam comes over.

It helps that Annie completely adores him. The three of us have formed an unlikely family of choice. Birthdays, Christmas, Easter, Sam is always first on our list.

Annie looks at me. "What kind of ice cream will you make?"

"I thought maybe banana."

Annie makes a face. "Or I could do coffee chocolate chip." She grins — her favorite ice cream, and even though I know I shouldn't, for she will doubtless finish the tub within the next day, even though I know I should be trying to encourage her to stay away from the devil that is sugar, she's my daughter, and this makes her happy, and the guilt I have long carried over the years I was not the kind of mother I should have been, not the kind of mother anyone would have wanted, is enough to make me give her ice cream every day for the rest of her life, if that will make her happy.

Sixteen

I have now spent years trying to make people happy after that disastrous summer when I left Nantucket, left so much unhappiness in my wake.

I have now spent years trying to figure out how to make myself happy, how to come to terms with who I am.

Who am I?

I am an alcoholic.

Today, I am a grateful, recovering alcoholic, but it was not always the case.

My first foray into the world of recovery was in my early thirties, just after I met the man who would become my husband, against his better judgment, against, perhaps, everyone's better judgment.

I slept with my long-lost sister's boyfriend, although I have no recollection of it. My father, who I had only just found after twenty-nine years, kicked me to the curb. He did so kindly, and with tremendous regret. He did so even while admitting that he recognized himself in me, the drinking, the terrible behavior that I refused to see.

He had, he said, done enough damage to his own family with his drinking, and it wasn't fair to continue to bring more destruction by letting me stay. Plus there was the small fact of my sister refusing to ever speak to me again. It was better, he said, if I left. And I did.

I came back to months of heavy drinking. Jason tried to get me sober, but it was much easier to drown my shame and sorrow in alcohol. We lost touch, although he would check in every few months, leave a message, send a text.

I lost my job when a new editor came on board, a new editor who didn't look so kindly on the long, liquid lunches. Nor did he see the point of separate features and women's desks. He consolidated, and two of us were left without a job. Everyone there felt terrible, and as a result loaded me up with freelance work. I made more money freelance than I had ever made on staff.

And then, for a while, I stopped drinking. I went to meetings. I took it seriously, and found Jason again, at a meeting, naturally. This time, because I was sober, had been sober for over a year, we found ourselves continuing what we had so nearly started first time around.

From being worthless and awful and depressing as hell, my life turned around. I woke up in the morning looking forward to the day. I woke up feeling alive, energetic, looking forward to whatever the day might bring instead of wanting to stay in bed with the covers over my head, tired, hungover, and dreading doing it all over again.

I had work, happiness, and a boyfriend! Not a handy shag or a drunken conquest, but an actual boyfriend who loved me and treated me well and understood me, for who better to understand an addict than another addict himself.

I was happy, peaceful, filled with hope. Jason's recovery was so inspiring to me. We, as a couple, were so inspiring. We did, eventually, find our own meetings, separately, but that first meeting, in Paddington, was one we always went to together, and even though we didn't sit together, and if you didn't know we were together you probably wouldn't have been able to tell, everyone knew. We were the couple that all the singles aspired to be.

We were happy. Happy enough that one weekend we drove up to Sissinghurst, to see the famous gardens, and in the white garden

Jason sank to his knees and pulled a ring box out of his pocket, and my heart exploded with excitement and disbelief as he asked me to marry him.

We married at the town hall on Marylebone Road, and the room was packed, with my friends from the media, and old friends of us both, and tons and tons of people we knew from meetings.

For a while, life was better than I could ever have imagined. Settled, calm, peaceful. I worked my program, we both did, and I knew that I would never go back to drinking again. It actually amazed me, that I could go to a party where the first thing someone would do would be to offer me a glass of wine, and not only could I decline, I could continue a conversation with someone without thinking about that glass of wine, without hearing it whispering my name, over and over, until I had no choice but to give in.

It felt like a miracle, that for the first time in my life the drink wasn't calling me. We even kept wine at home, for when friends came over. Not a lot, but a couple of bottles of red and white in the garage, just in case we needed it, which we rarely did.

I didn't miss it. As long as I kept going to meetings, kept doing what I needed to do to keep sober, it seemed that alcohol wasn't a part of my life anymore, and I was certain it wouldn't ever be again. The pink cloud of sobriety.

Oh, how little I knew.

When Annie was born, life changed again. I remember, clearly, the night I thought it would be fine to have just one glass of wine. I could do it again, I thought. All these years of being fine meant that I was cured. Also, I hadn't been going to meetings for a while. Jason still went, but I was so busy with Annie, and she had been such a colicky, difficult baby it was all-consuming.

I think she was four, and it had been a particularly bad day. She had thrown a massive tantrum in Wagamama, where I was meeting friends for lunch. It was the first grown-up lunch in a nice restaurant I had had in ages, and I was really excited, and Annie was going to be a big girl with one of the other girl's daughters, Ruby, and it was all planned.

But Annie didn't like the food. Or the restaurant. Or the people. Even though the last time Jason and I had taken her, on our way to buy her clothes in Selfridges as a treat, she had loved it. This time, she literally threw herself down on the floor and screamed at the top of her lungs. My friends pretended it was fine, that they had all been there, but I knew they hadn't, and from the disapproving looks all around me, the tut-tutting and shaking of heads, I felt awash with the kind of shame I thought I had left behind a long time ago.

Annie didn't calm down, and didn't calm down on the bus home, and when I phoned Jason, in tears, he said I knew he'd be late home because he had some important meeting, and he was really sorry, but that maybe I should just put her to bed.

Well, I tried that, but she pounded on the door, screaming and screaming, and by the time she eventually went to sleep, I was at the end of my tether.

I went into the kitchen — we had a little house in West Hampstead by that time, the most beautiful little carriage house that had a big conservatory on the back which doubled as a sunny kitchen, and I sat in that sunny kitchen sipping my tea, as an image of a glass of wine crept into my head and I could not get it out.

I could taste it. I could feel it slipping down my throat, feel the sweet relief, the tension of the day slipping away. I tried everything to get that thought out of my head, but it was all I could think about.

When I say tried everything, I will confess

I didn't actually do the things you are supposed to do when you are a recovering alcoholic and the alcohol is calling you: I didn't make a program call, or call my sponsor. I didn't pick up the Big Book or a daily reader and let it open naturally, knowing it would inevitably fall open at the one story that would help me not drink. I didn't do any one of the myriad things they tell you to do when you are a recovering alcoholic, and part of the reason why is that sitting at that kitchen table, able to smell and taste and feel the wine, I decided I was not a recovering alcoholic.

I decided that it was so long ago, my out-of-control drinking was entirely due to my unhappiness and my being single. And my God, it wasn't like we weren't all doing much the same thing. Of course I was drinking to excess, and of course I did unimaginably terrible things when drunk. Doesn't everyone?

But look at me now! There I was, in my late thirties, happy, settled, with a wonderful husband and wonderful family. Everyone I knew drank, and no one I knew drank to excess. My friends would laughingly call it the witching hour, that time of day when looking after an unruly child, or unruly children, is all a bit much for us and a glass or two of wine is the perfect antidote to the stress of carrying all of this life, all this responsibility, on our shoulders.

How insane, I remember thinking, at that kitchen table, that I too should not be able to do that. How absurd that I have spent all these years thinking that I am somehow different, that I cannot do what all my friends do and have a glass of wine, or perhaps two, during the witching hour. And God knows, today of all days, I deserve a glass of wine.

I won't have much, I remember thinking. In fact, I won't even have two. I'll just have one, because it's been a hell of a day, and because I can, and because after all these years, I absolutely know that it won't be a problem, that I am exactly the same as everybody else.

SEVENTEEN

Jason came home that night, late, after his very important meeting, to find me passed out on the kitchen floor, empty bottles of wine, and yes, not bottle but bottles, on their sides beside me.

I would like to tell you I was so horrified by my behavior that I climbed straight back on the wagon the very next day, but that phrase I had often heard in meetings — that it is much easier to stay on the wagon than to climb back on — turned out to be a truism that colored my life from that day until the day Jason finally had enough and moved out.

That day was the start of a binge that lasted over a year. Then Jason and my mum staged an embarrassing and awful intervention, which included Poppy and Jackie and other people who had known me for years. I went to rehab, got sober, came home, and started drinking again. I couldn't ever get sober in the way I had been before; it never seemed to want to stick.

I used to think of it like a light switch. The first time I got sober, I knew, I *absolutely* knew, that this was it: My drinking days were over. It was as if a switch had been flicked in my head. I loved how I felt when sober.

When I was drinking I always felt filled with shame, blaming everyone else for my problems, resenting everyone. I was this great ball of anger and resentment and shame, which disappeared when I got sober. I felt like I was, for the first time, filled with peace and acceptance and tremendous clarity. If a friend did something that pissed me off, instead of hating them, and cutting them off, and being consumed with rage whenever their name was mentioned, I found myself able to sit down and calmly say things like "I felt disregarded when you invited Poppy to that and not me." People loved this new me. *I* loved this new me. Jason loved this new me.

After I lost my sobriety, every time I tried to get sober, I knew it was temporary because I could never get that switch to flick on again. I didn't know how to do it. Our life was an emotional roller coaster, in and out of rehab, drinking, not drinking, pretending to not be drinking but actually drinking. It was secrets and lies, and I knew Jason was pulling away.

There was one night, yet another night I had determined not to drink. Jason was coming home at eight, and I'd planned to make dinner, to have a romantic dinner in the kitchen, with candles, after Annie had gone to bed.

I was making chicken stuffed with mushrooms and spinach, and halfway through the recipe I realized it was cooked in white wine.

I didn't have any. I could have cooked it in stock, but the recipe called for white wine, so white wine it would be — if it wasn't cooked in wine, it would be a disaster. And by the way, if you're wondering why two recovering alcoholics would eat anything cooked in wine, the alcohol burns off if you bring it to a high simmer for one minute. At least that's what I told myself that night.

I bundled Annie up in her stroller and walked to the supermarket up the road where I bought the cheapest bottle of white wine they had. I knew, as soon as I picked up the bottle, that I'd be drinking it. I toyed with the idea of not, especially as I'd had three weeks of not drinking under my belt, but I knew.

We got home and I poured a small amount into the chicken dish and the rest into a measuring jug. I told myself I would keep adding to the dish, but I picked up that jug like a large, cumbersome wineglass, and drank. And I kept drinking until it was gone.

When Jason came home, he took one look at me and knew. And by then he had almost had enough. Nothing, nothing terrified me more than Jason leaving me, which you would think would be enough for me to actually get my shit together and finally stop, but I couldn't.

That night set me off. Yet again. The vicious cycle of weeks of not drinking, then falling off the wagon with a terrible bump.

I wanted to get sober more than anything in the world. I knew my marriage depended on it, but the pull was too strong. I just couldn't do it.

And Annie. My poor, darling Annie. When I was drinking, I was raging. There were times when I would scream at her, berate her for doing nothing other than what a young child should do. I would scream at her for not closing the fridge door properly, or her bedroom being a mess, and I would watch her little face fall, see how she tiptoed on eggshells around me, in exactly the way

238

I would tiptoe on eggshells in the house I grew up in, terrified of my raging father, and I would be so disgusted with myself, I would shout more, drink more.

In between, when I was sober, I showered her with love, with gifts, with attention, trying to make up for my bad behavior, my guilt. The poor child never knew which mother she was going to get, never knew where she stood. It was as unsafe a childhood as I had had myself, more so, and there wasn't a minute that went by when I didn't hate myself for it.

The night Jason finally said he couldn't do it anymore, he was leaving, I wasn't yet drunk. I was kidding myself that I was just having a glass of wine at the end of the day, and that I would stop after that glass, and that tomorrow morning would, yet again, be my first day of not drinking, because I knew I had to get serious.

"I love you," he said, and he wasn't angry as he so often was, but weary, and my heart started knocking in my chest. "And I love Annie, but I can't do this anymore. I can't watch you destroy your life, and ours. I'm leaving and I'm taking Annie with me."

And he did.

I didn't actually believe he would. I sat in

the chair in the living room, dizzy with despair and vodka, a terrible combination, and saw him get the big suitcase down from the cupboard in the hall and fill it with his and Annie's clothes.

I lost it then. Burst into tears and staggered down the hallway — how ashamed I am to admit I was too drunk to even walk — and sank to my knees, begging him not to leave, crying that I couldn't live without him, but he wouldn't look at me, said nothing, just quietly moved through the rooms, as if I wasn't there.

He packed their things and left me in a sobbing heap on the hallway floor where even in my drunken stupor, I honestly thought my heart was going to break. I stayed there all night, and in the morning, when my pounding head and dry mouth woke me up, I wished my heart had broken. I wanted to die.

Instead, I stopped drinking. That was my bottom. Abandoned by my husband and daughter. There was no place left to go; the switch was flicked, and while Jason and Annie moved in with his parents, I got sober. And this time it was for real.

I had been a terrible mother; I deserved everything I now had. Something in me woke up, and instead of dwelling on all that had been, all the horror and shame of the past, I knew I had to change, and this time it was serious.

I went to America. To the relapse treatment program at Caron Pennsylvania. I had tried the UK rehabs too many times; it was all a well-worn and familiar road that hadn't worked. Getting serious about getting better meant coming to America, and from the first day I walked into Caron, I knew things had changed.

Jason knew things had changed when I finally got back home. He saw me going to meetings, and working the steps, and more than that, saw how different my behavior was.

I was allowed to pick Annie up from school and take her out for tea, returning her to Jason for the night.

And I was there at the school gates, on time, every single day. That alone was enough to tell him I had changed.

"You look different," he said to me one day, when I was dropping Annie off and he had invited me in. We were in the kitchen of the flat he had rented in Belsize Park, with me thinking how weird it was to see our furniture in new surroundings, for he had moved a number of things in — the sofa, an armchair, paintings — and how awful it was that I no longer had a claim to these things, to Jason's life, to Jason.

"Different bad?" I said, for I was taking great pains in my looks every afternoon before hitting the school gates. Not so much to compete with the other Yummy Mummies, although that was definitely part of it, but to show Jason what he had left, to try to tempt him into coming home.

"Different good," he said with a smile. "Your eyes are clear and your skin. You look . . ."

". . . Sober?" I asked, thinking he'd smile, but he just looked sad.

"Yes. Sober."

"I am," I said. "For today." I didn't give him a day count. There had been far too many times in the past when I had used my fifteen days, or eighteen days, or twenty-four days to throw in his face, right before diving into drink again.

Jason nodded, and in his sadness I saw everything he was thinking: *Why couldn't you have done this years ago? Why did you have to wait until our family had been torn apart? Why did you leave it until it is too late?*

I know what he was thinking because I was thinking the same thing myself. I left then, tears leaking down my cheeks all the way home. I got my daughter back, under court supervision, for half the time. But I didn't get Jason back. I had changed, but he hadn't. The damage I had wrought had altered his feelings. He would always love me, he said, but he just didn't have the wherewithal to do it anymore. He was so scared of it happening again, and he didn't trust me, my new sobriety.

So here I am, eighteen months after our divorce, rebuilding my life, interviewing women like the one I interviewed earlier today, about how she threw her life away for an affair, and I have long known that the greatest affair of my life was with alcohol. I love Jason, but I loved drinking more; in my heart I chose Jason, but everything overruled that, and drinking won, every time.

I did what I had to do, all the work successful recovering alcoholics do to stay successful recovering alcoholics, moving through the steps, speaking to my sponsor every day, filling my free time with meetings.

Finally, I reached the one step I was dreading, the step I had been dreading since the moment I first heard of this program. Step 9: *Make direct amends to such people wherever possible, except when to do so would injure them or others.*

I had a very long list, and the big ones, the ones I left to the end, the ones that had haunted me for years, were my family. The other family. The ones I had let down so badly it is still sometimes unbearable for me to think about.

Three years ago, before I got sober, my father died. Brooks. I wrote to Ellie and Julia then, not to make amends, but to let them know how sorry I was, how sad. I wasn't surprised that I didn't hear from them. Just sad. And sadder still that I will never have a chance to make my amends to him.

I have worked my way through the rest of the list. The easy ones, most of whom had no idea what I was talking about. I phoned Jackie and met her for coffee, and I told her I had to make amends for all the late mornings and lying, and late copy, and she just cracked up laughing and told me I was being ridiculous.

I haven't worked my way through the entire list yet. No one explained quite how long it would take. But I have made amends to Jason, and it did make a difference. Not quite the difference I would have liked — he has made it clear that he has moved on, that he and I as a couple are never going to work, but my acknowledgment of the hell I had put him through seemed to ease things between us, pave the way for, if not a friendship, then at least a convivial coparenting relationship.

Although all that may have changed now that Cara has come on the scene.

EIGHTEEN

I buzz the door open and check my hair in the mirror. I may not stand a chance with Jason, our marriage may be well and truly dead in the water, our divorce a fact of life I have to live with every day, but I still want him to feel some regret, want him to look at me wistfully, see me at my best.

While Annie gathered her things, I surreptitiously ran to the bathroom and tidied myself up. Not too much, not enough for Annie to notice, although she's thirteen: She notices everything. Primer to remove the shine and turn my skin into silk, a touch of bronzing powder that glimmers seductively on my cheekbones, a slick of gloss, my hair quickly brushed, then gathered up in a loose bun, tendrils hanging around my face, in just the way he always used to love. I pick up my reading glasses and put them on. I don't really need them — in fact, they make everything slightly fuzzy — but Sam says I look like the sexiest librarian he's ever seen in the glasses, so what the hell. Jason can see me looking like a sexy librarian, even if to me he's just a blurry fuzz.

"Hey, Jason," I say casually, picking up a stack of books, walking through the hallway and waving, as if he had just caught me unawares, as if I had no idea he was coming, as if I weren't nervous at all, and yes, ashamed as I am to admit it, I am nervous. Always. Still.

He is still exactly, but exactly, my type. And his smile still has the ability to completely undo me. And I look at his hands and remember exactly what his hands used to do, how they used to make me feel, and I could cry with my own remorse and pain.

Jason is such a good guy. He has always been such a good guy. I sit around, frequently, with other forty-something women, and they talk of their husbands, or ex-husbands, with disdain, with derisive laughter; they talk of the excuses they come up with to avoid having sex, the holidays they would much rather take with their girlfriends, and I always find myself looking at them as if they are speaking another language, for it was never like this with Jason.

Even when I was drunk, it was never like this with Jason.

When I was drunk, I loved him more. The fact that his eyes registered his disappointment only made me want to comfort him, reassure him in my slurry way that it wasn't his fault, that I was fine, that I still loved him, no matter what.

"Hi, Cat," he says, awkward. Always awkward. It was fine between us for a while, after I made the amends. We had a few weeks where I actually started to think that maybe we weren't dead in the water, maybe we had a chance. On Annie's birthday the only thing she said she wanted was the two of us to take her to see *Matilda* and then dinner at Wagamama — finally a place she loved unreservedly.

We did, and it felt like a proper family, like we were all supposed to be together, in the way we were together when Annie was very small.

Annie spent the entire evening beaming, and even though she had turned thirteen, she walked along between us, holding our hands, constantly looking from one to the other as if she couldn't believe that not only were we together, we were having fun.

And we were having fun. We loved the play, then slurped noodles and drank green tea and delighted Annie by telling funny stories about when she was a little girl, which she has heard a million times before but never gets tired of hearing, and it was actually a shock, at the end of the night, when Jason said good night and went home.

There was a moment, at the end of the night, when he had gone in to kiss Annie good night, as she had asked him to do, and I had offered Jason a coffee, and he hesitated, and our eyes held for just a few seconds longer than was probably necessary, and my heart jolted, and I thought he was going to kiss me. He didn't. He left, but I was certain that look meant he still loved me, still felt something, and surely it was only going to be a matter of time.

It was only a matter of time before he announced he had met someone. Cara. I didn't hear it from Jason but from Annie, who bounced home after a weekend with her father filled with excitement about this amazing woman who had spent most of the weekend with them.

When I say woman, that isn't quite correct. Girl. Or girl-like. I learned, that Monday afternoon when Annie came home from school, that Cara is, oh lucky Cara, only twenty-nine! Twenty-nine! Practically a child! So much younger than Jason. She is blond! said Annie. And beautiful! Well, of course. And so much fun!

I knew it was serious from the outset because even though I'm quite sure she wasn't the first girl Jason had gone out with, she was the first girl he had ever introduced to Annie, and not just introduced, spent the weekend with. Although she didn't spend the night.

I asked.

But she met them at the Wolseley early Sunday morning for breakfast. And went boating on the Serpentine with them. And made them dinner on Sunday night, lasagna, which I never make because pasta, as far as I'm concerned, is nutritionally empty. Even if it is delicious.

It was clearly serious, and yes, I will admit to being sad. And disappointed. But I was also grateful that if Jason was going to have a girlfriend, at least it's a girlfriend who's nice to my daughter; at least she doesn't have a potential evil stepmother to contend with. It was small consolation, but consolation nevertheless.

How wrong I was. What I didn't see coming was Cara's raging jealousy. It didn't emerge for a while. The first time I met her I was going out and Jason had come to pick Annie up, so we all walked out together, and there she was, this very short blond woman in the front seat of Jason's car.

Sober, I am always gracious, or at least I try to be, so I walked over with a big smile to introduce myself. She could barely look me in the eye. It was quite clear, in fact, that she wanted nothing to do with me, and as the relationship has progressed it is clear to me that she is the one who wears the trousers, and oh what demanding trousers they are.

Before Cara, Jason and I were becoming friends. We had had that lovely night at the theater, and then a few other nights, always with Annie as the excuse, but it was starting to feel hopeful.

Suddenly he stopped wanting to spend time with me, started making excuses. I would suggest something, but he was busy. After a little while I stopped suggesting we do things together, but then, if I asked him to take Annie on a night that wasn't his, or babysit her, or show up to something at school, which had never, ever been a problem for him, suddenly he was unavailable. All the time.

It became clear that this had nothing to do with Jason, for Jason had always put his daughter before everything, but was about Cara wielding her insecurity through power, demanding he put her first, their relationship. It has put a tremendous wedge between us these past few months.

I hesitate in the doorway. If the poison dwarf — as I have secretly started to refer to her, but to Sam only; I would never let Annie hear — if the poison dwarf is waiting in the car, her usual sour expression on her face, Jason will be out of here quicker than you can say Snow White.

"Annie's just getting her stuff," I say. "Would you like a cup of tea?"

"That would be lovely," he says, and I almost drop my books in surprise. Clearly she's not in the car.

I move the glasses up to the top of my head. I know I look good in them, but this is ridiculous, I'll never find the bloody kettle, while Jason makes himself at home at the kitchen table.

This used to be our kitchen table. It is a scrubbed pine table my mum found at Alfie's antique market and Jason and I stripped ourselves. It's a bit eighties country, and not the sort of thing that's very in right now — everyone I know has sleek modern maple-and-steel tables these days — but I love this. It feels like I'm sitting in an old farmhouse in the country, and I will never get rid of it.

I put the kettle on and turn to see Jason, his legs spread because they have never fit properly under the table, his hair messy in the way that I have always loved, and my heart turns over. I quickly walk outside into the corridor saying I'll be back in a sec because I don't want him to see the tears well up in my eyes.

Why did I throw this all away?

For a while, I blamed Jason. Why couldn't he forgive me? Why was it such a big deal? He was the one to blame.

I don't think that now.

Now I just wish things were different.

My friends say I'll meet someone else, but all the dates I've been on were terrible. I show up terrified they're going to think I'm awful, and invariably they're the ones who end up wanting to see me again, with me coming up with every excuse in the book not to have to endure a whole evening listening to arrogance, or entitlement, or just plain dullness.

"Sorry." I come back in the room and make the tea. "So how are you? What's going on?"

"Nothing too exciting," he says. "Busy, as usual. Work is crazy. You?"

"Pretty much the same. The usual interviews with women who are screwing up their lives." I realize what I've said. "Clearly a subject I have much experience with."

He has the grace to laugh, ruefully.

"And you're going to meetings?" he says hopefully.

"Absolutely." I had long ago found meetings he wouldn't be at, women's meetings where I was absolutely safe, didn't run the risk of running into him, or having to endure cheap pickup lines, what we call the thirteenth step, from the less salubrious men in the program. "I finally get what the whole living in recovery thing is about."

He nods, and I note the flash of sadness in his eyes, and I get it. Why couldn't I get this before? Why wasn't I able to do this when we were still married?

Or maybe it's just projection. Maybe he's not thinking that at all.

"How's Cara?" I find myself blurting out to fill the awkward silence, instantly berating myself for being so bloody obvious.

"She's good," he says, and I wonder how on earth things got awkward between us, when they had been so good for so long. How is it that we are sitting here, like strangers, when we slept side by side for so many years, produced a daughter, lived and loved and laughed together?

"Daddy!" Annie bursts into the room, her dark curly hair flying behind her, her green eyes sparkling, all puppyish limbs on the brink of morphing into womanhood. Her entrance saves us both, lifting the energy to enable us both to pretend to be normal, to pretend that things are good.

"Sweet pea! Come on. We're going out for dinner tonight. A new place in Notting Hill."

"Great!" she says, coming over and putting her arms round me. My daughter, at thirteen, is entirely unpredictable. There are mornings when she comes into the kitchen with a black cloud over her face. Those days she barely speaks, uttering monosyllabic grunts, radiating contempt for everything and everyone in her life, and particularly, it seems, me.

Other days she is warm and sunny, her arms reaching around me for hugs, as they are now, and I could melt with love and gratitude at those times, my little girl still my little girl, able to forgive me for all I have done.

"Can I maybe keep her tonight?" Jason asks. "It might be late, and I thought it would be easier."

I hesitate. I don't particularly like last-minute changes, and I am not sure if Annie wants to go, for she isn't always thrilled about sharing her father with Cara, but one look at her face and I see she does.

"Sure," I say, giving her one last squeeze. "I love you. I'll see you tomorrow."

They leave, the flat settling into the silence. In the old days, I would dread the silence, the times Annie would be with her father and I would be alone. After all those years of living by myself you would think I would have gotten used to my own company, but I was never entirely on my own when alcohol was involved.

Sober, without my daughter, without my husband, I had no idea who I was anymore. I had no idea what to do with myself without anyone around, without the ability to drown my fears in drink.

I became, in those early months, a television addict. I had never been a big telly watcher, but suddenly it became my salvation, allowing me the ability to lose myself by binge-watching an entire series, sometimes numerous series, without having to think about my life at all.

Whole weekends would pass with me lying on the sofa, consuming giant bowls of popcorn and endless cups of tea as I glued myself to the small screen. I had no idea how life should be, how to live a life. I just knew I needed to get through the days, one day at a time. I went to a lot of meetings, and met program friends, and tried to keep busy, but in my flat, on my own, it was the television set that saved me.

Today, things are different. I cook. I listen to the radio instead of the TV — plays on Radio 4, the show *Desert Island Discs,* which is the highlight of my week. I garden. I have a small garden but have discovered a love of planting things, the rigorous discipline of learning the Latin names of the plants I buy, learning what they need to survive. My happiest moments in the last eighteen months have largely been spent at Clifton Nurseries, where I can browse for hours, testing myself with my plant knowledge, daydreaming of the day I might have a garden big enough for everything.

I go out to the garden now, with a glass of iced tea. In the old days, it would have been a bottle of wine, but as long as I have something cold, I am fine.

I dug up the old paving stones that made the terrace, and created a Japanese zen garden with gravel, a water feature, and long exotic grasses. A large stone Buddha reminds me to be mindful, and even though I am not a Buddhist, not an anything other than a recovering alcoholic with faith in a

Higher Power, I take enormous comfort in my serene, beautiful Buddha.

There are two wicker chairs out there, where Annie and I often sit with our books, where I try to meditate a few times a week, although I am still a work in progress. More often than not, just as I close my eyes to meditate, I will have spied a few weeds, and how can I possibly relax and meditate until I have pulled those weeds out, and nine times out of ten, before I know it, an hour of weeding later, I no longer have time to meditate because I have someplace to be.

Tonight I have no place to be. Tonight it is just me, with the evening stretching ahead of me. I put my drink down, take a few deep breaths, settle into the chair, and close my eyes, focusing only on the breath coming in through my nostrils, cool and sweet; going out, warm and soft.

And I feel hopeful that life can be good.

NINETEEN

The buzzer rings and I go to the door, expecting Sam, only to hear my mother's voice ringing through the intercom.

"What are you doing here?" I ask when she walks through the door.

"I was just passing on my way home from Hampstead. I saw a scarf there that I thought you'd love." She passes me a bag, and I pull out a beautiful shimmery blue scarf that I do, instantly, love.

"Mum! You didn't have to do that! It's gorgeous!"

"Of course I didn't have to do it. I wanted to do it. Where's that delicious girl of mine?"

She isn't talking about me, she's talking about Annie, and I call for Annie, who whirls down the corridor and into her grandmother's arms.

One of the gifts of my newfound sobriety has been my relationship with my mother. It was always good, but when I was drinking, when I was married, it was marred by the disappointment and judgment I saw in her eyes.

For a very long time I would try to avoid her. No one could have hated me more than I hated myself, and I really didn't need to see that reflected back at me. I knew I was a terrible wife, a terrible mother; the more I felt judged by someone, the less inclined I was to see them.

Now, not only do I delight in my own relationship with my mother, I delight in Annie's relationship with her. I never realized how much my mother loves children, how warm she can be. For most of my childhood she was in a deep depression, but now, as a grandmother, and despite having lived in the UK for years and years, her American warmth comes out.

I know that sounds odd, but I have always felt that the English love children as long as they are polite, quiet, and well behaved. Americans seem to love children however they behave. There have been plenty of times I've been in restaurants and seen American children run screaming around the room, and all the English people are filled with horrified indignation, while the Americans just smile indulgently as if to say, oh, aren't they cute?

However Annie behaves, my mother adores her, and accepts her. If Annie is in a bad mood, my mother still loves her, is still loving and affectionate, waiting for it to pass. I, on the other hand, am a disaster. If Annie is in a bad mood, I struggle not to take it personally, not to strike back, not to berate her for not being happy.

"Something smells good," my mother says, poking her head into the kitchen, where she sees the table set for three. "Oh! You have dinner plans. I didn't want to intrude."

"Don't be silly." I pull her into the kitchen. "Sam's coming for dinner, and there's more than enough for all of us. Why don't you stay?"

"Really? You're sure you have enough?"

"Absolutely. Stay."

Sam adores my mother. Everyone adores my mother. Sure enough, when he walks in, as handsome as ever in his slick shorts and polo shirt, his face lights up as he spies her.

"Audrey!" He envelops her in a hug, pulling back to give her the traditional double kiss. I have become accustomed to hugging, me, who never liked anyone to touch her. It's a program thing, hugs being doled out at the end of meetings like candy. It took me a while to get used to, the all-embracing hugs. I have come to not only accept it, but actually welcome it.

"Sam! So lovely to see you! It has been much too long."

We take the pitcher of iced tea outside to the terrace, as Annie tempts the neighbor's cat to come and roll around on the gravel with us.

"You look gorgeously tan," says my mum to Sam. "Have you been somewhere dreamily exotic?"

"The spray-tanning place off South Molton Street," says Sam with a smile. "Not quite dreamily exotic, but I can't seem to get my act together with a summer holiday this year. I wanted to go to Lamu, but I'm worried it's not very safe anymore. Also, summer's not really the time to go to Africa anyway, even if I decided to risk it."

"There's always the South of France," says my mother.

"There is, always, the South of France." Sam rolls his eyes, which I find hilarious because only Sam could find the South of France boring, which he does; he says everyone he has ever met is always in the South of France and it's the most stressful place he ever visits.

"What about you?" Sam turns to me.

"What are you doing this summer?"

When Jason and I were married, we did great holidays. Winters saw us in the Caribbean, and summers renting lovely old stone houses in Provence or Tuscany. Now my budget is something I'm constantly aware of, and even though we are always fine, we are just on the edge of fine, and I never think I have enough money for extravagant things like holidays.

"I'm hoping to find a travel piece," I say, for I am friendly with the travel editor of the *Daily Gazette,* and every now and then he will send a piece my way, often a fabulous and free hotel, and sometimes even free flights too. Last Christmas, Annie and I left on Boxing Day for Antigua, an all-inclusive, all-paid-for holiday. I had to write a thousand words on how fantastic the place was (which it was), and we had a brilliant time, with yacht trips and spa treatments provided to seduce us into writing a decent piece. As if we needed seducing. "The travel editor often knows of a villa somewhere knocking around."

"What a great idea," Sam says. "I should ask our travel editor if they have anything going. Why don't we go away together?" I nod enthusiastically as he turns to my mother. "Audrey, you should come too!"

263

"I'm already going to Greece," says my mother. "A friend's boat. If there was room I'd invite you."

"We'll miss you," he pouts, "but I love the sound of you, me, and Annie going somewhere together. Let's both speak to the travel people we know and see what we can come up with."

"Deal," I say, and pour them all some more tea.

TWENTY

I try very hard to have something punctuate my day so I have to leave my house. If I don't have something, even a coffee at the dingy little café next to the tube station, it is quite possible that I would never get out of my pajamas, and that isn't healthy or productive for anyone.

Often I go to a noon meeting, and today I am on my way when Maureen's number flashes up on my cell.

Maureen is my sponsor. She's one of the all-time great sponsors, at least that's what I have heard: the kind of sponsor that everyone wants. I knew, as soon as I heard her talk in a meeting, that she'd be perfect for me. I never thought in a million years she would say yes. I was newly sober, struggling, and here was this woman my mother's age, who had years of recovery and, I'd heard, tons of sponsees. Why would she ever say yes to me?

Walking up to her after the meeting, I felt sick at the prospect of having to ask, but I also knew I had to do it. "Look for someone who has what you want," they said. And Maureen seemed to radiate serenity, calm, and wisdom. She was everything I aspired to be.

"I was wondering . . . ," I said, turning beet red, my heart beating faster, "whether you might have any availability to sponsor me."

She smiled and nodded. "I do have some requirements," she said. "Working the steps, going to a minimum of three meetings a week, and talking every day, the same time, no matter what. If you can do that, I would be happy to sponsor you."

I almost cried with relief.

Maureen is a therapist. Talking to her every day is like having my own personal 12-step therapist on call. She has brought such wisdom and support to my life that I wonder how on earth I managed without her. I credit her with the reason why my sobriety has stuck this time. She warned me off the pity pot when I felt sorry for myself, and taught me to live in the moment, to accept my life as it is, not dwell on where I thought it should be.

"I've missed your calls, Cat. I'm wondering what's going on that you've been texting rather than calling. We need to speak on a regular basis, you know that. Texting isn't enough. Is now a good time for you to talk?"

"I'm just on the way to the noon meeting. I'm so sorry, Maureen. I've just been crazy busy." This isn't quite true. There is a reason I've been avoiding calling her, even though I knew it couldn't go on forever. "I have a few minutes."

"Good. We need to talk about your amends list."

"Yes." It's why I haven't called her. Why I have hopefully buried my head in the sand, thinking she might forget; thinking I might forget.

"You know what I'm going to say, Cat. There are two more people left on the list before you can move on to the next step, and we have to talk about how you're going to do this."

Of course I knew what she was going to say. I knew she would eventually call me and force my hand. Ellie and Julia are the last two names on my amends list, the two women who are technically my sisters, who have refused to have anything to do with me since I slept with Julia's boyfriend in a drunken haze.

I did stay in touch with Brooks until he

died. I didn't see him again, but we wrote to each other sporadically. He was a kind man, a good man. And I was able to confide in him in a way I really couldn't with anyone else. It has always been easier for me to write my feelings rather than express them in person, and I wrote to him about my life. Sometimes about my drinking. He got it. As a drunk himself, he knew that I was powerless over alcohol, that I sometimes, often, behaved in ways that were shocking and shameful. He was disappointed in me, I think, in what happened that night all those years ago, but he didn't hold it against me. He understood, I think.

But his daughters cut me off. I wrote to them, in the beginning, letters filled with remorse. I have no recollection of sleeping with Julia's boyfriend. To this day, I have no idea if we had sex. I was on the pill, so pregnancy was not an option, but I honestly don't know what happened, if anything, only that he kissed me and we woke up naked. I have to presume we did, and that has haunted me to this day.

I thought I had apologized in writing, immediately after the trip, but making amends is more than an apology. It is restitution for the wrongs we have done, and I have always known that I would never be able to make up for this transgression by letter. This needed to be done in person. So I have worked my way through my amends list, leaving these two until last, knowing I am not going to like what I have to do, avoiding the topic with Maureen, avoiding calling her, in fact, because I know she will tell me exactly what she is about to tell me.

"You know this is the big one. This is the one you have to do in person, and we have to figure out how to do it."

"How am I supposed to do this in person?" I say, which is what I said last time, although as I say it, I think about Sam asking his travel editor for a holiday destination. What if we asked for Nantucket? What if I wrote a piece about revisiting Nantucket? Maybe we'd get a house, or the flights, for free.

As soon as that thought enters my mind, I realize I always knew this was going to happen. I knew Maureen was going to phone and tell me to do this in person, and I knew, as soon as Sam brought up the idea of a discounted holiday, that this would be where we would end up going.

And suddenly it doesn't seem quite as overwhelming, quite as terrifying, as it once did. It seems exactly right.

"They're on Nantucket," says Maureen.

"It's summer. Surely you could find a way to take Annie to Nantucket this summer. It sounds like the dreamiest place in the world, and you've written travel features before. Why not write a travel piece?"

I start to laugh. "Are you actually a witch, or just psychic?"

"A little bit of both," says Maureen. "And I'm also, as you know, a particularly hard taskmaster when it comes to working the steps. We need to get this done. You need to keep moving. Do you know where they live now? I imagine it won't be hard to find them."

Of course I know how to find them. I used to Google them on a regular basis. There were tons of pictures of Ellie, who was as glamorous as ever, who had barely aged since I was there all those years ago. She was always smiling into the camera at fundraisers on the island, flanked by equally gorgeous women. Her crowd seemed to be city people, out there for the summer, bejeweled, with blown-out blond hair, always at Galley Beach, sunbathing at Cliffside, tea at the Wauwinet.

Julia, on the other hand, is an island girl through and through. There wasn't much about her, although I think she had a small store selling handmade jewelry and clothes on Straight Wharf. I think back to all those years ago, to how everyone on the island seemed to have around ten jobs, and I know she has to do other things. The season is only summer; everything shuts up at the end. I wonder if she goes out scalloping like she used to, shucking her scallops at Charlie Sayle's and selling the meat; I remember her talking about bartending at the Anglers' Club, and wonder if she still does that.

And I wonder if she's married. With children. I wonder if she ever saw Aidan again, if she found happiness with someone more stable, someone perhaps who didn't drink, who didn't fall into bed with her sister.

I have thought, often, about whether or not she would forgive me. It was a very long time ago, and I was a different person, a person so selfish, so wrapped up in herself and her drinking, that I never thought about the impact my behavior made. Maureen describes alcoholics as tornadoes: leaving a path of destruction wherever they land. It even says this in the Big Book of Alcoholics Anonymous: *The alcoholic is like a tornado roaring his way through the lives of others. Hearts are broken. Sweet relationships are dead. Affections have been uprooted. Selfish and inconsiderate habits have kept the home in turmoil.*

My life back then was in turmoil, but I'm not sure Julia would understand that. I'm not sure I would understand it if it had happened to me, if someone, anyone, had slept with Jason.

They say that when you make amends, you have to detach from the result. This isn't about gaining her forgiveness but about owning my behavior and doing my best to make restitution. How she deals with it, with seeing me, with hearing me, has to be put in God's hands.

Even though that's the thing that terrifies me most.

"Start looking into travel," advises Maureen. "And call me tomorrow. The usual time."

I have just filed the piece on women's infidelity when Sam's number flashes up on my screen. I texted him earlier, telling him to think Nantucket, and to see what he could do.

"I spoke to Daniel Emory, our very own travel editor, about Nantucket, and he says yes. He found a house in town ready for us on July sixteenth, for two weeks. Apparently they had a last-minute cancellation, because it is literally impossible to get something decent on the island at this late stage. The magazine will cover the cost of the house, thank God, and it's in dollars so it's cheaper for us. All we have to pay for is the airfare. I have a friend at BA who might be able to swing something."

"Are you serious?" I am unsure whether to be thrilled or terrified.

"Deadly. It's time for a holiday. Get your suitcase ready, my love, because America is calling, and we're on our way!"

TWENTY-ONE

Nantucket, 2014

I remember this. The smell of the ocean, the salty wind whipping through my hair, the hazy island in the distance as the slow ferry chugs along from Hyannis.

We ended up flying to Boston, renting a car, and driving up here. There were no direct flights left, and truth be told, it all felt like more of an adventure this way. Annie, standing beside me, her own hair flying around her face, turns to me with a huge grin, then slips an arm around my waist, hugging me close in a rare and treasured moment of daughterly affection. I tilt my head so it is resting on hers, overcome with gratitude for getting my daughter back, for finally being able to be the kind of mother I would like.

"Excited?" I ask, smiling down at her as she nods.

"I can't believe we're in America!" she

says. "Tell me everything again about Nantucket. Everything!"

"We'll be there soon," I say with a laugh. "You'll see for yourself. Why don't we go and find Sam? We're almost there."

The ferry is busy; the snack bar inside has a long line of people waiting to order fried food to pass the time. We thread through, walking up and down until we see Sam, tucked into a booth with paper trays of fried chicken and french fries in front of him. Sam is just about the most elegant man in the world. Even seeing Sam on a ferry is a little disconcerting, let alone with the kind of food he would never ordinarily touch, for his image is everything.

I had booked a Kia Soul to pick up at the airport in Boston, but Sam refused to be seen in a Kia Soul and talked the woman there into upgrading us into a Mustang for an extra ten dollars a day. And I get it. Sam needs to have a cute little convertible, in the same way he needs to dress the part.

He actually went online and ordered clothes from Vineyard Vines while we were still in London, so he could look like the perfect Nantucket vacationer. He is currently wearing Nantucket red shorts, deck shoes, a Vineyard Vines shirt, and a needlepoint belt. He looks preppier than prep. Even I'm slightly shocked when he opens his mouth and an English accent comes out.

There he is, tapping on his iPhone, his Louis Vuitton travel bag on the seat next to him, reaching out every few seconds for more greasy food as my mouth widens in shock.

We slide onto the benches, Annie reaching automatically for some fries.

"Am I dreaming? Is this my friend Sam McAllister eating unhealthy fried fast food? Did I wake up in an alternate universe?" I actually cannot believe that Sam, who lives on green juices and organic food, the healthiest of healthy, who works out in a gym every single day, who expressed slight panic that he might not be able to find a gym on Nantucket, who was only reassured when I reminded him that he could in fact go for a run instead, is eating this crap.

"I know!" He holds a hand up to silence me. "It's a vacation, and when we're on vacation, nothing counts. Isn't that right, Annie?" Annie, her mouth gleefully full of fries, nods in allegiance. "And when you're on holiday and the snack bar only has, basically, fried food to offer, what's a girl supposed to do?"

"Don't keep them all to yourself," I say, reaching out for the chicken and shrugging. "As you said, it's a holiday. Or vacation, actually. Either way, if you can't beat them . . ." And I put a salty, crispy, deliciously naughty tender into my mouth.

It is painfully familiar. The boats, the huge, expensive yachts, the people milling around on the harbor. Dogs everywhere I look: black Labs, brown Labs, yellow Labs. People with designer luggage, wheeling it awkwardly across the cobblestones, others making their way to Young's Bicycle Shop, where they'll rent scooters to get around the island.

"The Juice Bar!" I shriek excitedly to Annie. "I remember that! They have the best ice cream!"

"Can we stop and get some?" Annie asks, not unreasonably.

"We'll come back. Let's get to the house, then we'll come back into town and wander round."

I had forgotten just how beautiful it is here, the streets charmingly cobbled, the pretty stores lining Main Street, then, as we drive farther up the street, the grand old trees, the beauty of the terraced houses, close together, a mix of grey weathered shingle and white clapboard, window boxes spilling over with geraniums and impatiens, clouds of blue lobelia.

We turn onto Cliff Road, driving slowly so we can fully appreciate the beauty of the homes, these large and impressive, each one seemingly bigger and more beautiful than the next. High privet hedges giving an illusion of privacy, crushed oyster shells or gravel driveways, hedges of huge hydrangeas flanking the houses.

"My God, this really *is* like Fantasy Island," breathes Sam, who insists I stop from time to time so he can photograph some particularly beautiful house.

"I can't believe we're staying here," I murmur, knowing from these houses this must be an expensive part of town. We drive past a patch of green. "Lincoln Circle," says Sam, reading from the map on his phone. "Take the next left. There it is. Oh." His voice is flat as I pull into the driveway, not of one of the large, beautiful homes but of a modest grey shingle house, with a single-car driveway and a few weeds growing through.

It does have the requisite hydrangeas, although they're rather sorry for themselves, struggling to bloom in the shade of a gnarled old tree on the side of the driveway.

"*This* is where we're staying?" Sam says, and I know he's disappointed.

"It's not grand but what did you expect?" I ask. "Do you have any idea how lucky we are to find anything? It will be fine. I know you'd like us to have one of those mansions, but this is perfect."

"I love it!" Annie dances out of the car, and I turn to Sam, speaking quietly.

"We're on vacation, Sam. It doesn't matter what the house is like. We'll probably barely be at home anyway."

He sighs. "You're right, you're right. I'm sorry I'm being princessy. I'll stop. Let's go inside."

The house is perfectly comfortable. It's not the white-slipcovered, French-doored, white-marble-kitchened stately home that clearly Sam had hoped for. It doesn't have a swimming pool, or en suite bathrooms (other than the master, which I give to Sam, if only to shut him up for a bit), or a brand-spanking-new stainless steel fridge.

But it is clean, and bright. And it has a screen porch that has an old but incredibly comfortable-looking wicker sofa on it, and I know we will all be perfectly happy here, if Sam can get over his disappointment.

He walks around the house, not saying

anything. He glances at the greige suedette sofas in the living room, and says nothing. He looks at the slightly orangey pine coffee table upon which sit a remote control and a wire basket of fake lemons, and says nothing. He takes his Louis Vuitton suitcase upstairs, then clatters back downstairs minutes later, his face now lit with excitement.

"I've got it!" he says. "I need to dress the house. I'm sorry, darling, I know it's fine for you, but I can't. I just can't. It offends me sartorially, and I need to be happy where I live. It won't take much, just a few things. I already saw the perfect shop on Main Street. It won't take long. I just need to *zhuzh* it up."

I roll my eyes. "Sam, that's ridiculous. You're going to go out and spend money on a house that isn't yours just so you can be happy for two weeks? It's a complete waste of money, and I won't let you."

"Darling, I can have you write a feature about it, so I can expense everything. How to turn your bland rental into a summer palace. Done! Commissioned! And now we're going shopping. Don't look like such a sourpuss. I promise you'll be happy when it's done. And we can go get ice cream at the juice place too."

"Yes!" shrieks Annie from her tiny bedroom upstairs. "Let's go!"

TWENTY-TWO

We start with the ice cream, joining the end of the ridiculously long line at the Juice Bar, with me, the woman who has the patience of a fruit fly, not minding in the slightest that we have to wait. Being back on this island has transported me into a different state of being, one that is infinitely more relaxed than my London persona.

We go into the Sunken Ship and laugh at the crazy hats, Annie insisting on trying each one on, then we each buy a T-shirt imprinted with the word NANTUCKET.

We mosey up Main Street, with memories flooding back. The pharmacy, the bookstore, the Hub, where I remember getting the papers with Brooks all those years ago.

Everywhere we go, I think I see Julia. It seems that every woman we pass is tanned, pretty, my age. Every woman we pass wears shorts and a T-shirt, has the same body type I remember her having, and each time I see her my heart thumps a little bit harder, the relief sweet at it not being her.

I have prepared what I am going to say, but I am not prepared to bump into her unexpectedly. I can't wander down the wharf, going in and out of the tiny stores, looking at paintings, clothes, jewelry, until this is out of the way, until I have made my amends, and although that's what I'm here for, let me enjoy this day, let me try not to think about it until it is actually upon me.

And please, God, let me not bump into her before I am ready.

Sam finds everything he needs in two of the stores. Shell-shaped pots, oversized white clay starfish, blue and white cushions patterned with coral. Woven trays, glass hurricane lanterns with rope handles. Inexpensive bamboo throws that are as soft as cashmere at a fraction of the price. At least for us, given the exchange rate right now. Were it not for that, I suspect everything on this island is actually three times the price that it would be anywhere else.

We all carry the bags to the car, and Annie and I bring our books to the porch while Sam whirls around the house "decorating," coming back in for the big reveal, whereupon both Annie and I start laughing, clapping our hands in delight.

"You should be a decorator!" Annie says. "Not work in journalism!"

"I know." Sam grins. "It's my hidden talent."

"Not very hidden," I say, looking around with pleasure because a few bagfuls of accessories have in fact transformed our rather bland house into a dream beach house.

The orange pine coffee table is hidden by a large woven tray; silver candles and starfish are dotted around on various surfaces. The suedette sofas are unnoticeable underneath the glorious bamboo throws, and the cushions are perfect.

"It's gorgeous!" Annie sinks onto the throw, gathering it around herself.

"No!" snaps Sam in a panic. "It's just for show."

"Tell me you're joking." I turn to him in alarm. "Tell me you didn't actually just say that."

"You're right, you're right. Old habits die hard. Wrap yourself as much as you want. I'm sorry," he sighs. "What are we going to do for dinner? I have to tell you, I'm completely jet-lagged and exhausted. Can we make it quiet?"

"I tell you what," I say, realizing suddenly that I too am exhausted. "How about I run up to the grocery store and cook tonight?"

"Would you mind? That would be fantastic!"

"Of course," I say, grabbing the keys to the car and kissing Annie, who is happy to bury herself back in her book, good-bye.

Stop and Shop for vegetables, Nantucket Seafoods for the scallops I remember so well from all those years ago.

Fresh corn from a farmstand, and on the way back, I check the map, driving along Vesper Lane to scout out where I'm going to be tomorrow morning, at the Drop In Center, at 7 a.m. sharp.

Because I never fit in as a child, I always felt as if I were standing slightly on the outside, looking in, but at this relatively late stage in life, I have been astonished to find that the one place I always fit in, the one place I always feel at home, is in an AA meeting.

It doesn't matter whether it's my regular meeting in London or one in an unfamiliar place. It doesn't matter whether I recognize a soul in there, for wherever I am, as soon as I walk in, I know I'm home.

I remember clearly, when I was here to meet my father, knowing there were meetings on the island but not going to them.

Perhaps if I had found my way to them, what happened with Aidan wouldn't have happened. I can't dwell on the what-ifs, though; I can only make sure I don't fuck up again, and the best way I know to stop that happening is to get to a meeting, as soon as I possibly can.

I get the shopping done, and we make it through dinner, but only just. We are all so tired we can barely keep our heads from falling into our pan-roasted scallops with brown butter and herbs. We don't even bother washing up, just pile the plates into the sink, hug one another good night, and go upstairs to our respective rooms.

Tomorrow is, after all, another day.

TWENTY-THREE

I drifted to sleep last night thinking I would creep out of the house in the morning, not waking anyone up, but of course we are all on British time, and I'm the last one down. Sam is trying to figure out how to use the coffeemaker; Annie gets up from the sofa on the sun porch to come in and give me a hug. She is bikini ready, and I watch her go back to the porch, a little stunned at how womanly she is. I still think of her as such a little girl, yet look at her in this bikini, curvy as anything, her waist a tiny hourglass. She is not my little baby anymore, much as I want to pretend she is

"I've got it!" Sam announces, sliding the filter holder out of the machine and pouring the ground coffee in. "Thank Christ! Finally figured out how this bloody thing works. Annie? Do you still want coffee?"

"What?" I say. "Since when does Annie drink coffee?"

"She said she'd have some when I figured it out. Is that okay?" He looks at me doubtfully.

"I suppose so." I shake my head. "I just . . . I'm realizing she's much more grown up than I think."

"With a figure like that?" says Sam. "You *think*? Where are you off to, anyway?"

"A meeting."

"Here? On vacation?" He grimaces. "Isn't this the time you should just be relaxing?"

"No. This is exactly the time when I need a meeting most! When I'm off my guard. I told you the story of what happened last time. I definitely need a meeting."

"Don't you think what happened last time was because you were young and foolish rather than because you hadn't been to a meeting?" He is as skeptical as he always is when the conversation veers toward alcohol, and I wonder, not for the first time, why he is so resistant to the subject.

"If you stay away from meetings," I say, "you forget what happens to people who don't go to meetings."

He opens his eyes wide. "Ominous! What happens? They get to spend the day on the beach sunbathing?"

"Ha ha. I'm not cutting into sunbathing time. It's six thirty in the morning, for

288

God's sake."

"I know. I don't think I've seen six thirty in the morning in twenty years." He peers out the window. "It's rather lovely. I might go for a run."

"I'll see you later." I blow him a kiss before climbing into the car.

I have never been to this center before, never been to this building, yet I know every person in here. I know the faded Oriental rugs on the tiled floor, the old dark brown kitchen cabinets in the corner, know I can step into the little kitchen and find a pot of fresh coffee and something sugary and sweet.

I know the big poster hanging on the wall, the 12 steps, by heart. I know the needle-points of the Serenity Prayer, and the faded old prints on the wall, all with an AA theme.

And I know the people. I recognize the look we have, all of us who have lived a little too hard, partied a little too long, done everything a little harder, faster, longer. Addicts and alcoholics. People of extremes.

We are, as a group, often too fat, or too thin. We are too tanned. Our fashion sense is out there. But our hearts? Our hearts are as big as the ocean.

Everyone smiles a hello, reaching out a

hand to introduce themselves. I grab coffee, then sink down onto a suedette sofa to one side — what is it with suedette sofas in this country? — as people start to fill up the rows of chairs facing two chairs in front of the sliding French doors.

We start with the Serenity Prayer, then go around the room introducing ourselves. There are a couple of other visitors, but most are islanders, and as I sit, listening to the readings, to people starting to share, I know this is exactly where I am supposed to be, and I know, with a sense of peace, that however Julia reacts when I find her, when I say what I need to say, it will all be fine.

I raise my hand, needing to speak, to claim my place in this room.

"Hi, I'm Cat. I'm an alcoholic."

"Hi, Cat," murmurs the room.

"I just wanted to claim my seat. I'm so unbelievably happy to be here. We flew in yesterday, from England, so I'm completely jet-lagged, and actually I've got no idea what day it is, but the last time I was here was about fifteen years ago. I was newly in program, and I never went to a meeting, and I lost my sobriety right here on the island. It took me over thirteen years to properly get it back. I loved so much of what I heard today; that when you're drinking nothing moves, nothing changes, nothing gets better. Wow. That hit me." I am aware that people around the room are nodding their heads.

"I was drinking for the best part of my marriage, and I screwed that up, blaming him, blaming everyone else, for nothing ever changing, nothing ever getting better, with no idea it all started with me. Anyway, I'm here, on this island, to make amends. When I was here, I was drinking, and I did something awful. I was here to meet family I'd never met before, and I ended up betraying my . . . urgh. I probably shouldn't . . . Well. My half sister. I have no idea how she'll even react when she sees me again, although my sponsor says that's irrelevant. The only way through this discomfort is through it, I suppose. I've been putting it off, but I'm making a commitment here today to try to find her. Today. I need to make this amends so at least I have maybe a shot of enjoying this vacation. *God.* Procrastination is something I've always been very good at, especially when I was drinking. I couldn't stand to be in any kind of discomfort, which of course was one of the excuses I used to justify the drinking. And now I'm learning to live with it, to focus on the present, to trust in my Higher

Power that everything is exactly where it needs to be. I'm just . . . hugely grateful to be here. Thank you."

I sit back, happy to have spoken. When I first came back in, this time, I spent the first two or three months just listening. I wanted to be invisible. I wanted to soak up what everyone else was saying without being seen. Maureen got me to speak. She told me I couldn't be part of the group unless I was part of the group, that I had to claim my seat, that my recovery would grow exponentially when I reached out to others, and allowed myself to be both seen and heard.

She was right. The woman next to me, older, with white hair and a deeply tanned, creased, kind face, reaches over and gives me a reassuring squeeze and a smile, and once again, I am glad I came.

I only ever feel awkward after a meeting. That moment when you're not sure whether to stay or go, who you should talk to, what you should talk about. Occasionally there is someone who has shared something that has resonated with you so strongly, it is easy to walk up and talk to them, tell them how you felt about their share, what you're going through. But often it is, at least for me, weird, and clumsy, and I walk out with my head down, careful not to make eye contact so I won't have to talk to anyone.

I am planning on doing this here, delighted I have heard so much good stuff, determined to come back tomorrow, but not particularly wanting to talk to anyone, but the older woman sitting next to me catches up to me and stops me.

"I'm Abigail," she says. "I really liked what you had to say."

"Thank you. This whole amends thing is a bit overwhelming."

"You know, you've probably heard this a million times before, but the ones you're worried about are usually the people who have completely forgotten whatever it is you're making amends for."

"Oh, I don't think she'll have forgotten," I say. "I slept with her boyfriend. At least, I think I did. Long story."

"Do you want to have coffee?" she asks, and I have no idea why I say yes, other than that she looks like someone I might want to know, but I say yes, and we arrange to meet at Black-Eyed Susan's, in fifteen minutes.

I don't think Black-Eyed Susan's has changed an inch since the last time I was here. In fact, the whole island seems not to have changed an inch, which is both disconcerting and something of a huge relief. Where in the world hasn't changed? I think of London, how different it is today to when I was a child. I remember London when everything stopped on a Sunday, how sleepy it was, compared to today, when nothing is ever closed, when you cannot move down Oxford Street for the hordes of people, a million different languages reverberating in your ears.

The stores here are still, mostly, independent stores, run by islanders. There is the odd chain — I saw Jack Wills and — oh, how happy Sam will be — Vineyard Vines, but on the whole, the stores look and feel much the same as the last time I was here, all those years ago.

I know, of course, Nantucket has changed. I have read about the vast influx of wealth that is now here, and driving along Cliff Road, it is easy to see where that wealth is. The cars in the driveways are Jaguars and Bentleys, but you don't see them in town; you're barely aware of the millionaires who descend on the island every summer.

I read recently that Nantucket is described now as being the island of the Haves and Have Mores. And while I know that it's here, most of the people I have seen are regular holidaymakers, families in shorts and T-shirts, little jewelry, no designer bags in their hands. Other than Sam, of course, who might possibly die without a little bit of luxury in his life.

Nantucket always had the mix. All the great old families had estates here and mixed with the islanders. I remember hearing Julia talk about Ellie hanging out with her prep school friends, who would show up during the summer on their luxury yachts. They were perfectly happy tucking into waffles at Morning Glory, or singing with Scotty round the piano at the Club Car late at night. Everyone mixed with everyone else.

Perhaps they still do, but the truly wealthy, the insanely, new-monied wealthy, the ones with the Bentleys and Jaguars in the driveways, I'm not so sure they're mixing with everyone else, drinking at the Club Car, grabbing a burger at Brotherhood of Thieves. But this is Nantucket, where everything is possible.

Abigail walks in and joins me at our small table in the window, and I realize I am suddenly starving and order huevos rancheros, even though I'm not entirely sure what it is, other than Spanish sounding and involving eggs, but it seems exotic and filling, and both of those things sound good to me now.

Abigail has just coffee, and it turns out she is, as I thought, an islander, and a part-time Realtor, occasional cook, house manager, and sober coach.

"I'm astonished you have any time to breathe," I say, when she has finished describing all that she does.

"Me too." she says, laughing. "Although, you know, we all do that here. We all have a dozen jobs because the season's so short, there's never enough work to keep you going all year."

"What's your favorite out of all the jobs?"

"Hard to say. I used to love scalloping, being out on the open seas early in the morning. At the start of the season three hours will get you five bushels a person. You can really make a lot of money, although you can't go out if the temperature dips below twenty-eight degrees, so this past winter was a hard one and I'm looking for something else. I like the house-managing stuff. That keeps me busy year 'round."

"What does that mean, house managing? Do you look after staff for millionaires?"

I'm joking, but Abigail barely cracks a smile; in fact, she nods. "That's part of it. I do whatever needs to be done. Organize gardening, yard work, repairs. If they're here I'll sometimes plan parties for them, cook dinner, whatever they need. I like doing things for other people."

"I keep reading that Nantucket has been overrun by the super rich. What are they like to work for?"

I steel myself for great stories about entitled millionaires, realizing suddenly that there very well may be a great feature in this for me, but Abigail surprises me.

"I love everyone I work for. If I didn't, I wouldn't do it. That's one of the things I learned in program: Life is where you look. Of course, entitled, snobbish people are here on the island, but if I'm not focusing on them, not only am I not attracting them into my life, I'm not even seeing them. I work for some really important, wealthy people, and my experience of them has been great. Obviously a couple of unfortunate things, but you move on. I raised my son here, and there is nowhere else in the world I'd like to live."

"Is your son still here?"

"He is now. He left for a few years, went down to Boston, but luckily for me, he decided to come home. All my friends' kids seem to be divided into two camps, those that can't wait to get off the island and never come home again, and those that can't stay away. Thank goodness he's one who loves his home. Lucky me."

"Lucky you, indeed. What does he do?"

"A little bit of everything, like the rest of us. Although now he's really doing construction pretty much all the time. He's always done carpentry, but he's building houses now, a couple of beautiful ones down in Sconset. At forty years old he finally seemed to have found his path!"

"You don't look old enough to have a forty-year-old son!" I lie, knowing it's what's expected of me.

"He's forty-two now," she says proudly. "And thank you. I'm seventy-five years young. It's the summers that keep me young," she says. "I love the influx of people we get. Every May I start to get excited that the island's going to wake up again. Granted, I get tired by the end of the summer, but I wouldn't change it. Things used to stop dead after Labor Day, but not so much now. It's a funny thing about island life," she muses. "We can't wait for everyone to leave, then we can't wait for them to come back. We need money, for starters," she says, and I think of my father, painting, selling paintings on the wharf all summer.

"My father's family was here," I say. "You probably know them."

"What was their name?"

"Mayhew."

She nods, entirely unsurprised. "I figured as much. Even before you spoke, I took one look at you and knew you had to be a Mayhew. You and Julia look like twins."

It is like someone has twisted a knife in my heart, and for a second I almost can't breathe.

"You know Julia?"

"Of course! Everyone knows Julia. She worked for me for years, helping out with the houses. She still does sometimes, off-season, when her store is closed. She's the one, then? The one you talked about? Or is it Ellie?"

"Oh God. I'm sorry. I just . . . I just didn't realize you would know my family so well."

"I knew Brooks very well. He was a kind man. Big drinker. Really should have been in program. And Julia I watched grow up, of course. Ellie I only know a little. She always felt like a summer person." She laughs briefly. "Of course, Ellie really was a summer person; she never felt like an islander. You, on the other hand" — she peers at me as the waitress brings over an enormous plate of huevos rancheros — "apart from the accent, you could definitely be an islander."

"What does that mean?"

"It's a compliment. We're a certain type, we New Englanders, and in particular we islanders. The Vineyard or Nantucket, it's much the same. We live hard. There's a lot of depression here, a lot of drinking, family secrets everywhere, and tremendous loyalty. In program we say there are two types of people on the island: those that are in AA, and those that should be." She barks with laughter.

"I guess, if drinking or being in AA is a qualifier, then that qualifies me." I take a bite, and it is delicious, the creamy egg yolks bursting over tomatoes and spicy black beans.

"It's more than that. You're tough. A survivor. Don't ask me how I know, but I felt I recognized you as soon as you walked in, and not just because you look like a Mayhew. Julia's on island, you know. I saw her in the store a couple of days ago. She's usually at Cru for drinks after work, if you want to know where to find her."

"Is there anything you don't know?" I ask.

"No." She shakes her head with a large smile. "Listen, I'd love you to come for dinner. In fact, I'd love you to meet my son."

I sit back with a large smile. "You invited me for coffee because you're matchmaking?"

"Absolutely. I know every single woman on the island, and none of them are remotely right for him."

"But you don't know me."

"I know your family."

There is a huge smile on my face at the way this conversation is going. "You don't know if I'm available."

"Are you?"

"Yes."

"Well, then."

I shake my head, impressed as hell. "I'll make a deal. I would love to come for dinner, but only if I can bring my friend Sam and my daughter, Annie."

"Of course," she says. "The more the merrier."

"So am I allowed to ask about your son? What should I know?"

"He's smart, fun, sober, single, and tall. What else is there?"

"I'm so glad you mentioned tall. That would have been a deal-breaker."

"Also, he loves animals. Especially dogs. He's probably up at Tupancy Links now, walking Brad Pitt."

I stare at her. "He has a dog called Brad Pitt?"

"It is a particularly handsome yellow Lab."

"Well, of course it is. Wow. I got up this

morning thinking I was just going to a quiet meeting, and I'm practically married."

Abigail smiles. "Will you come Tuesday? Seven? I'll write down my address for you."

"I've just realized his fatal flaw," I say, watching Abigail scribble down the details. "He lives with his mother."

"Only while he's doing up his house." She smiles, and I cannot help but burst into laughter at the events of the day, and it isn't even nine o'clock in the morning.

"Are you sure you're not an ax murderer?" I ask her, as we get the check and I fumble in my purse, relieved I thought to take out cash before we left.

"I'm quite sure. Ask anyone on the island about me. They all know me. Now, I'm off to the Take It or Leave It Pile. Do you want to join me?"

"I'm going to go back home," I say, knowing that if I even ask what on earth the Take It or Leave It Pile is, I may never make it out of this restaurant. "We'll see you tomorrow," I say. "Is there anything we can bring?"

"Bottle of wine!" she says, before cracking up laughing. "Of course, that was a joke. Bring yourselves and good humor. See you Tuesday night, if not before, and good luck with Julia!"

Damn. I was having such a good time I

had entirely forgotten to worry about seeing
Julia again.

TWENTY-FOUR

I follow the instructions on the note I find on the kitchen table. They have taken off to the beach, with arrows pointing the way.

I change into a bathing suit, grab a towel, sunblock, and my book, and hesitate over the front door. In London, I wouldn't even walk to the end of the hallway without locking my door. I wouldn't go anywhere without locking the car. There have been plenty of times when I've let a prime parking space go because there's a group of dodgy-looking youths walking toward me and there's absolutely no way in hell I'm going to get out of my car anywhere near them.

But this is Nantucket. I remember Brooks never leaving anything locked. I remember the freedom and safety that came with that. I even remember Julia telling me that everyone left the keys in their scooters and cars. How she and her girlfriends would regularly jump into a Wagoneer parked down by the wharf, feeling above the visors for the keys, then take off to a beach party down toward Cisco, private and secluded enough that they wouldn't get busted for drugs.

They would steal scooters all the time, to go to the Madaket Sham Jam, or the Chicken Box, before heading off to Galley Beach to go skinny-dipping, out of their minds, high, drunk, stoned, buzzing.

I had forgotten all of that. The sharing of stories. The envy I had of the freedom, the way Julia got to grow up. I had forgotten her delight in sharing her stories with me, how much I had liked her, how much I felt we had in common.

I had forgotten how much, for a very brief period of time, I had loved having a sister.

And although I know it was the booze, although I know I was in a horrible place, hesitating by the front door as I debate whether or not to lock it, I cannot actually believe I screwed my life up in the way that I did.

Sam is stretched out, with tiny gogglelike things on his eyes, already beautifully bronzed.

Next to him lies Annie, who has never

been the slightest bit interested in suntanning, who never considered it a proper holiday unless there was a swimming pool for her to jump around in for hours and hours every day, yet is now appearing to take her tanning very seriously.

"You're blocking the sun, Mum!" she says, irritated, as I attempt to lean over her and kiss her hello.

"How did you get so brown already, Sam?" I put my towel next to his and spray myself liberally with SPF 30, passing it to Annie and insisting she do the same when I realize she has covered herself with Sam's SPF nothing coconut oil and will be a rasher of bacon by the end of the day.

"It's all fake, darling," he says. "But good, no? I wouldn't subject the poor people of Nantucket to my pasty white English skin if my life depended on it. They'd be blinded by the light. It wouldn't be fair. I'd have to hand out sunglasses before disrobing. Unlike you." He turns to me and his goggles fall off. I hand them back to him as he continues. "I do not have the skin of a Brazilian, much as I would like."

"What are those goggles?" They are white plastic with tiny black holes to see out of.

"I stole them from the spray-tan place. Aren't they fab? I couldn't bear to have panda eyes again after the whole Ray-Ban Aviator fiasco last summer. So? How was the meeting?"

"Well, oddly enough, it was all rather exciting. Actually, that's not true, the meeting itself wasn't that exciting, although it was really good. In fact, it may have been one of the best meetings I've ever been to."

"Really? What makes a good meeting?"

I always wonder whether Sam is being facetious or whether he is genuine when he asks about AA, but he takes his goggles off and makes eye contact, without a smirk, so I know it's genuine.

"Strong recovery makes a good meeting. Old-timers. People who have been sober for years and years, who are really living in recovery. They work the steps, over and over, for years. They're never not working them. They speak to a sponsor every day, and they have sponsees. They show people like me how to do it a day at a time. Plus I hear amazing slogans, things that just make sense to me, or help me."

I look at Annie, who doesn't move a muscle and has her earplugs in. This may mean she has Bruno Mars at full volume, or may mean that she is pretending to listen while eavesdropping. Hard to tell which. At this moment, even if she's listening, it is fine. I used to have such shame in admitting I am an alcoholic, at anyone knowing I was an alcoholic, at my child, of all people, knowing that not only was I not perfect, but I was as flawed as this.

As if she didn't already know.

I tried to hide it from her, begged Jason not to tell her, but then realized I had to come clean, that it was better for everyone. Now I talk about it openly, and Annie has come to accept it as a way of life. I have no idea whether she will turn to alcohol, whether it is in her blood as it is in mine, but I do know that if she is an addict, whatever her addiction happens to be — drink, sugar, shopping, sex — she will know that there is another path, and for that I am now grateful.

"So what did you hear today?"

I'm not supposed to talk about what happens in meetings. It is a spoken rule, so clear that we end every meeting by saying, "Who you see here, what you hear here, when you leave here, let it stay here."

But for God's sake, I'm human. As long as I'm not saying who said what, surely it's okay to pass on a little?

"Someone used the phrase 'itty bitty shitty committee,' which I thought was sheer bloody genius."

"Definitely genius," agrees Sam. "What does it mean?"

"They were talking about stinking thinking, which is another one that I've always loved. How they thought they always knew best, they were in control of everything. Their itty bitty shitty committee."

He gasps with pleasure. "Can I steal it?"

"Absolutely. It's yours."

"Any other gems?"

"I remember in my home meeting in London, a girl once said she had been dating the same guy for ten years. Only his name kept changing."

"Ooh, that's good. But that didn't resonate, surely? You haven't dated anyone."

"Thanks for that. But no, it didn't resonate, I just thought it was a great concept. Maybe I'll use it in the novel I'll probably never get round to writing. Someone else said who else but them gets to have a meeting with God every day. God being a group of drunks. I quite liked that one. But then afterward I ended up going for coffee with this fantastic woman from the meeting, and . . . ," This time I glance at Annie and do lower my voice. "She's invited us all for dinner tomorrow night and she has a hunky son she wants to introduce me to."

Sam slowly sits up. "Great. You've met a complete stranger who may well turn out to be an ax murderer, and we're going into the lion's den tomorrow night."

"She's not an ax murderer. I asked. She's a Realtor. And house manager. And a few other things, but she's really nice, and anyway, she knows my family."

"But you can't check her out because you're not in touch with your family."

"Trust me. She's fine."

He raises an eyebrow. "She's an alcoholic."

"Oh, ha ha. We're going."

"You're sure you're comfortable flirting with Mr. Handsome with young you-know-who around?" He gestures to Annie, who still hasn't moved a muscle, and so presumably is still not eavesdropping.

It is true there has been nothing physical since Jason. I have never had to think about how Annie would react if I suddenly announced I was going out with someone, or brought someone home she had never met before. I presume she would be fine. I like to think of my daughter as well rounded, secure, polite, but God knows I have heard horror stories from other people about children of divorce who make the second marriages hell.

I wrote a story on it last year. The reason

310

most second marriages break up, I had read, was because of the children. I found three case studies, and each one was heartbreaking. The children hated their new stepparent, resented them, causing more friction than any reasonable person could endure, trying to force their parent into making a choice, so much so that it ended up breaking the marriages apart.

I remember being horrified at some of the things these children, and their stepparents, had done, before realizing that I was in that same boat, or at least hoped one day to be. I hoped to meet someone, to settle down, even to marry again, and naïvely presumed that Annie would be thrilled to have a family again, a man in the house, never thinking that she might do everything in her power to get rid of him.

Sadly, I have never discovered how she would react because there hasn't been the slightest sniff of anything since I broke up with Jason. The one time I actually found someone sexy, a minor actor in a major TV series who flirted with me outrageously at the press launch and demanded my phone number, sending me home in a cab almost delirious with excitement, he turned out to be married.

Thank you for that, Google.

Not that he ever phoned.

I look at Sam. "I wouldn't be flirting. Not tomorrow night, anyway. And even if he is gorgeous, he probably wouldn't be interested in me."

"Now why would you think that? You're one hell of a sexy woman, plus you have the English accent, which over here seems to go down a storm. If I could find out where the gay men congregate, I could have myself a seriously good time."

"What if there aren't any gay men on Nantucket?"

"Don't be ridiculous, darling. There are gay men everywhere. It's just a question of weeding them out. Although it would have been so much easier in P-town. Next time, Cat, we're going to Provincetown. Next time it's all about me."

"I love you." I blow him a kiss as he lies down and places the goggles over his eyes again. "And I thought it was always about you."

"Good girl," he murmurs. "I have trained you well."

We swim in a surprisingly still ocean, although Annie suddenly freaks out about sharks and runs out of the water, refusing to get back in.

"Are there sharks here?" asks Sam quietly, so Annie doesn't hear. "Because if there are, I'm getting out of the fucking water too."

"*Jaws* was filmed in Menemsha," I say. "Which is not very far." Sam looks terrified and starts to move toward shore. "*Jaws* also featured a mechanical shark. We are fine. Anyway, the sharks don't come here. They're all over in Sconset."

"How on earth would you know that?"

"Because Julia told me never to go skinny-dipping there. It's where they fish, so there are always sharks. Julia's friends all used to come over to Galley Beach to swim at night. Much safer."

"What about Steps Beach?" Sam looks around, worried.

"Safe. No fishing."

"I think I'll get out now anyway," he says. "Isn't it nearly time for lunch?"

TWENTY-FIVE

I take them both to Something Natural for lunch. The line is short, miracle of miracles, and we each order sandwiches, bags of chips, and Diet Coke — my one indulgence since getting sober — then go outside to sit at a picnic table, waiting for our name to be called. We watch families with kids play in the boat on the grass, feeling as if we are in the middle of the countryside, this field overlooking a wildflower meadow just beyond an old wooden split-rail fence.

I warn Sam and Annie about staying out of the sun, feeling suddenly like the mother of both. "Just because you spray-painted your skin dark bronze doesn't mean you built up any protection," I say to Sam. "You have to be careful. I think your shoulders are a fierce angry red underneath all the fake tan."

"They are a bit sore," he says, wincing as I press his skin to see the white mark left by my thumb. When I say white, I mean dark bronze, but a definite big change of color.

"You're burnt to a crisp," I say. "Why don't we stay out of the sun for the rest of the afternoon? Maybe we should walk around town. You can buy a baseball hat to protect your face, because your cheeks are lobster red too."

We leave Something Natural, stuffed from enormous sandwiches crammed with turkey, Swiss cheese, avocado, and fresh, juicy tomatoes, and go to town, weaving our way in and out of the stores, and I know where we are heading, I know we will eventually make our way down to the water, to the pretty little stores, in one of which sits, possibly, Julia. But the meeting this morning was the very best thing I could have done, and all of a sudden I am ready, ready to see her again, ready to say what I have to say and get on with the business of vacation.

Deep down I hope that Abigail is right. I hope this is an amends that Julia will have practically forgotten about. "Oh, we were so young!" she might say. "Aidan was a waster!" She will laugh. "You did me a favor!"

Or, "Who?"

We step onto the dock, and a wave of

anxiety washes over me.

"Why don't you take Annie for an ice cream?" I say, trying to communicate with my eyes that I need to do something important.

"Oh! Okay!" Sam says, steering Annie across the street as I walk down the dock, suddenly wishing I didn't have to do this, knowing I have no choice.

There is her name above the shop. Julia Mayhew. It doesn't surprise me that she has her own business, that she is probably successful. Julia struck me not only as creative but as scrappy. She was someone who could always manage to get herself out of trouble. Outside there are mannequins, pretty knitted shawls draped around their shoulders, in fine cashmere, lacy knits. I pick up one and marvel at the tiny stitches, at how beautiful and fine they are. Exquisite beaded necklaces, doubtless beaded by Julia herself, semiprecious gemstones studded with pearls, hang around the mannequins' necks. I pick up a price tag from behind a neck, thinking I might buy one for myself, thinking how lovely it is, but it is thirteen hundred dollars, so clearly it is not destined for *my* neck.

The Haves and the Have Mores, I think. Good for Julia, recognizing she can charge this much, recognizing there will always be people who will pay. I look at the cashmere scarf. Nine hundred dollars. Good Lord.

The Haves and the Have Mores.

I hesitate outside, take a deep breath, and walk into the tiny shop, making eye contact with the girl behind the counter. She is not Julia. It may have been years, but this is not Julia, although in looks they are similar. This is a young girl, too young, it seems, to be working in a shop, although granted, I remember having a Saturday job in a shop when I was fourteen. She has a sweet smile, a familiar smile, as she says hello and asks if she can help.

"I was wondering if Julia Mayhew was around?" My voice catches in my throat, signaling my nerves, if only to myself.

"She's just in the back. Let me get her for you," she says, going to a curtain and poking her head around. I watch her move, almost unable to breathe, there is something so achingly familiar about her. "Jules? There's someone here to see you!"

Jules. I didn't expect that. I realize I was expecting her to say "Mom." Of course she is familiar; she has the same hair as Annie, the same dark skin as me. But it is just co-incidence. Jules. Not *Mom.* She is not my niece.

Julia steps out from behind the curtain, with me unable to take my eyes off her. Age has been kind to her. She is stockier than when I last saw her, and it suits her. She looks more solid, grounded. Her skin is tanned and clear, barely a line on her face. She looks fantastic, far better than I would have expected, although God knows what I expected. That she would have led a hard life, I think. A life filled with drink, maybe drugs, probably countless affairs. I expected her to have had it rough, and I expected it to show on her face.

She was with Aidan when I was here all those years ago, but she was a partier. I realize I presumed her life had followed a trajectory similar to mine, living life hard, squeezing out every last drop.

"I'm Julia," she says, extending a hand with a warm smile, an expectant look on her face as she takes my hand, and I have no idea what to say. And as we stand there, clasping hands, forgetting to let go as we look into each other's eyes, recognition starts to dawn, and I swear to God I watch the smile literally slide off her face as she gasps.

"Oh my God," she says finally. "It's *you.*"

TWENTY-SIX

We walk to the end of the wharf, to Cru, where we grab a sofa in the lounge area, next to the beautiful people who have left their yachts for cocktails under the canopy.

She orders a glass of prosecco. I stick with a seltzer and lime.

"I remember this when it was Morning Glory." She looks around. "When George and Bruce tempted you with these incredible waffles that had cream cheese frosting. I worked here a couple of summers. We had the most decadent staff parties you can imagine."

Is this how it is going to be, I wonder? Small talk? Avoiding talking about the real stuff, keeping it light. Although she is surprisingly warm, which is not what I expected. I thought she would be cold, unforgiving, but she is smiling and sweet.

She looks around the restaurant, cranes her head to see who's sitting in one of the great big wooden wing chairs outdoors, waves at various people across the way, gestures for the waiter, who of course knows her — everyone knows her — to refill her glass.

"You look wonderful," I say, not because I want to flatter her into liking me, but because it's true.

"I feel good. I've taken up running." She looks me up and down, appraisingly. "You look good too."

I take a deep breath. "Thank you." I can't pretend anymore, can't sit here making small talk, can't hold a normal conversation until I say what I came here to say. "Julia, there's a lot I need to say, starting with I'm sorry."

"It's fine." She interrupts me, shaking her head and waving her hand as if it's all irrelevant, as if I don't need to carry on speaking. "It all happened a very long time ago. I can barely remember anything about those days. You don't have to say anything."

She must be uncomfortable. I would be uncomfortable if I were in her shoes, although not as uncomfortable as I am being in my own shoes right now. I remember what Maureen said, that I am not doing this for her, or to get her forgiveness, but so I can wipe my slate clean and move on with a clear conscience. "But I do, Julia. I'm an alcoholic, thankfully now sober. When I was here, all those years ago, I was drinking."

"We were all drinking," says Julia, looking ruefully down at her prosecco. "Some of us still are."

"There's a difference between drinking socially and not being able to stop. I never seemed able to stop at two or three glasses of wine. There were times when I didn't drink at all, which was how I was able to convince myself I didn't have a problem, but when I drank, I had no off switch. I drank until I passed out. But all of this is kind of irrelevant. What's relevant is that I came here to find my family, and I committed the worst kind of betrayal with your boyfriend. I am so, so sorry, Julia. I never ever intended that to happen. I don't know how it happened, and I have to make my amends to you."

I am watching her, and she is looking into her drink, not meeting my eyes.

"I was a horrible person," I say. "Selfish, self-pitying, everything was all about me. I have changed, which probably doesn't matter in the slightest to you, and nor should it, but I have wanted to apologize to you for years. My behavior here has been with me for years. I know you probably want nothing to do with me, but I needed to see you, to do this in person."

I am astonished to see Julia blinking back tears. Instinctively I reach for her, wanting to comfort her, but she shrinks back and my arms return to my sides.

"I'm sorry," I say again, knowing how lame it sounds.

"I don't really know what to say," she says, after a silence. "I suppose this is the last thing I ever expected to happen. It was such a long time ago, Cat. I mean, I appreciate the apology, I do. I think it must have taken an awful lot to come back here and say the things you've said, but there really isn't anything to apologize for. We were young, and God knows I did enough stupid things of my own. I knew you were drunk. I knew you didn't remember, and honestly, you did me something of a favor. I might have ended up married to Aidan, and Lord only knows how that might have turned out. Clearly fidelity wasn't his strong point, so as far as I'm concerned, you saved me. Truly, you did."

I sit back, stunned. "Do you really think that?"

"Oh, Cat," she says through laughter. "Those were crazy times. We all did some crazy shit, me included. Too much coke. Too many drugs. Prescription ones too." She shakes her head with another laugh. "Dr. Feelgood was pretty much my longest relationship."

"Dr. Feelgood?"

"That's what we called him because he doled out so much great prescription medication. I had too much sex with inappropriate men, and probably not enough sex with the appropriate ones. I never got married. The only one who did really talk about getting married and having babies was Aidan, but . . ." She shrugs. "Perhaps that was all part of his Irish charm. That was probably what he did with everyone." She reaches over and puts a hand on my arm. "I am really touched with your apology, but you mustn't feel bad, Cat. We have all moved on."

I pause. "Ellie too?"

"Ah." She raises an eyebrow. "Ellie's still somewhat binary. Once you betray Ellie, or someone she loves . . . Betray!" She laughs again. "I'm sorry, I didn't mean to use such a strong word. But Ellie has never been very good with forgiveness, and she wasn't exactly excited at the prospect of another sister to begin with."

"Is she here, on island?"

Julia peers at me. "She is, but if you're

planning on saying the same thing to her, on apologizing, my best advice to you would be, don't. She won't be interested. I've never been able to bring your name up again."

Why would she bring my name up? I think.

"I've thought about you over the years," she admits. "You blew in like this incredible whirlwind, this sister who seemed so much more like a sister to me than the one I was raised with, and then, poof, it all blew up and that was that."

"I've thought about you too," I say, blinking back the tears that have unexpectedly pooled in my eyes.

"Jules?" We both turn to see the girl from the store. "Mom's on the phone. She wants to know if I'm staying with you tonight. Can I?"

"You want to?"

"You know I want to. I want to live with you!"

"You know your mom would never let that happen. But of course you can stay tonight. You can have some friends over if you want, but don't let me catch any of them with water bottles filled with vodka."

Her face breaks into a delighted grin. "I love you." She skips off with a wave as Julia turns to me. "They think they're being so clever, coming in all polite, holding plastic water bottles, thinking I don't know they're filled with vodka. My God, whatever they do, I did it first, and I was probably better at it."

My mind is whirling as I connect the dots and the dates and why I thought this young girl was familiar, as I realize suddenly who she is.

"She's Ellie's daughter, isn't she. I don't remember her name. The baby."

"That's right. Trudy. She's almost sixteen now. Summer, the oldest, is away at camp."

"Trudy's a little older than my daughter, Annie. They look alike." Like us, I think, but don't say. Like Annie, I think, but don't say; Annie who would give anything to have a cousin; a *"big sister."* Julia dips her head, then looks up at me with a faint smile, saying the same thing without words.

"And Ellie? Is she happy?"

Julia shakes her head. "She's had a pretty rough ride. Actually, it probably wouldn't be that rough for you or me." I note how she links us together, how it establishes an intimacy, a familiarity, and I remember her doing this before, all those years ago, and how good it felt, how it instantly made me feel as if I belonged.

It still makes me feel as if I belong.

"Her husband was convicted of insider trading. I don't even honestly know if he was one of the guilty ones, but he took the hit. The guy who ran the hedge fund encouraged it, it was part of the culture, but there were a handful of guys that had to take the hit for the boss. He was one of them, and they lost . . . well . . . not everything, because some was in Ellie's name, but they lost a lot, not to mention that for Ellie the humiliation was huge."

"Everyone knew?"

"Everyone who happened to pick up the *New York Post*. Her husband went to prison for two years and was fined five million dollars."

I almost choke. "Five million dollars? Who has that kind of money?"

"Insider traders?" says Julia, after a pregnant pause, and the pair of us burst out into guilty laughter.

I remember this. I remember how much I liked her all those years ago, how I felt, instantly, like this was my long-lost sister. And here we are again, all those years later, and I still feel it, I still feel our shared blood linking us, the sister I never had, the sister I always wanted.

"So her life must have changed dramatically."

"It's still not exactly a hardship. The Nantucket house is in her name, so they have that, but, shocker, they were forced to give up their city house and move to a fairly modest house in the suburbs. She tells everyone it's Rye, but it's actually Rye Brook, which isn't quite the same thing. But the move was a good thing for her. It was easier for Ellie to start again without having to face all those hugely competitive women in New York. Everyone knew. I don't blame her in the slightest for running away. I would have done the same thing."

"How are her kids?"

"Summer's at college now. Thankfully there was a trust fund set up for that, so she was fine, and Trudy is, as you can see, amazing. That's the thing with that girl, however much privilege she had, and God knows they had a lot, it never seemed to mean much to Trudy. Summer's different, more like Ellie, she cares more, but Trudy doesn't give a damn. I love that kid. If I had a daughter, that's exactly how I'd like her to be."

"So you're close?"

"We couldn't be closer. I'm the fun aunt who lets her do what she wants."

"That's why she wants to sleep over!"

"Wouldn't you?"

I think back to my childhood, how I would have given anything to have had a fun aunt, an aunt who let me, not particularly do what I want, but perhaps would have let me be me. How I would have wanted it, to have an aunt just like Julia. Lucky Trudy. Particularly with a mother like Ellie.

Julia leans forward. "Listen, it really is good to see you, Cat. But I mean it, you might not want to think about doing this whole amends thing with Ellie. My sister is an expert at holding grudges, I'm afraid. She was kind of suspicious of you from the outset, and after what happened, well, she wouldn't be exactly pleased to see you."

"I did write to her."

"I know."

"Did she rip it up?"

Julia grins.

"So how about you, Julia? Are *you* happy?" I have no idea why I ask this. I hadn't anticipated asking this, and she certainly doesn't owe me any information about herself whatsoever. But I hope she is happy. I hope life is treating her well.

"It's good. It's . . . my life. Not what I expected, but I work hard, I play hard."

"Do you live in the same house? Your

dad's old house?"

"No. I did for a while, but we sold it a couple of years ago to some bajillionaire from New York who paid us a fortune and promptly tore the whole thing down to put up a McMansion. Ellie can't even drive by without crying. I don't mind, though. It gave me the money for the store."

"So where do you live?"

"Right now I'm renting a small house in town. Where are you staying?"

"A house off Cliff Road."

She lets out a long whistle, orders another prosecco. "Fancy."

"It's not. It's the least fancy house in the whole area. Maybe you could come over one night? For drinks? Or maybe we could meet with the girls. I think Annie would love to meet Trudy."

Julia frowns. "I don't know what Ellie would say. I mean, of course it would be great, they're cousins, or half cousins, or something, but Ellie might go nuts."

"I guess it's not something we could keep a secret." I can't keep the disappointment out of my voice, knowing that secrets are no way to live a sober life.

Julia looks pensive. "It would be good if they met. Maybe I can talk to Ellie, make her see sense. Let me see if I can figure it

329

out. God knows I've kept enough secrets for Trudy. Ellie would have a shit fit if she knew even half of what Trudy gets up to. They should meet, you're right. I'll see if I can persuade Ellie."

Cousins. Half cousins. I remember how I loved it that when we met, all those years ago, Julia never referred to me as her half sister, always as her sister, and again I am struck with the loss of something I only had for such a brief period of time.

I think of Annie, how thrilled she would be to meet someone her own age, never mind someone related, how much better this holiday would be if she had someone to pal around with, and I nod, excited. "If there's any chance it could be sooner rather than later, that would be spectacular," I say, as the waitress comes over and we order another drink.

I am on a high for the rest of the day. I am on a high at having found my sister again, at having our "confrontation" be anything but. At having been forgiven. I am on a high because the amends to my family, last on my list, have been hanging over my head like a black cloud of doom ever since I got sober.

I have been carrying this fear, this dread,

for the longest time, terrified of what she would say. It turns out that it is true when people say you have nothing to fear but the fear itself. I cannot believe how much I have dreaded meeting Julia again, expecting her to rage at me, or dismiss me, to be furious, but she wasn't.

I would never have expected her to be warm, welcoming, as comfortable to be with as she was all those years ago.

I could almost weep with joy.

I tell Annie about Trudy later that evening, when I go in to kiss her good night, and she perks up, thrilled at the sudden possibility of meeting a cousin she didn't know about. I explain about Ellie, about how she and I didn't get on, without going into too many details, and explain that Julia is hopefully going to smooth the waters. I tell her not to get her hopes up, but as I say the words I realize how much *I* want this, to give Annie what I never had: a cousin; bloodlines; *family.*

I still don't know what to do about Ellie. Perhaps her agreeing to a friendship between the girls will pave the way for our own reconciliation. I know I have to find a way to make an amends to her, however uncomfortable that might be, however disinterested she is, however much she doesn't want to see me. I put a call in to Maureen, but it goes straight to her machine, unsurprisingly, because I forget it is the middle of the night in England, and I don't leave a message. I've never been much good at asking for help.

If I can figure it out by myself, that's what I'll do. The girls becoming friends has to be a way in. Maybe if Ellie meets Annie and likes her, that will make everything easier.

TWENTY-SEVEN

Julia phones the next day, and the excitement is evident in her voice. Ellie didn't say no. Ellie didn't seem all that interested, which, given how well Julia knows Ellie, means it's okay for the girls to meet. Trudy, naturally, had no idea she had a half aunt who lives in England, nor a cousin a couple of years younger. Trudy, naturally, has always wanted a big family, brothers, sisters, cousins, and is now itching with excitement at the possibility of meeting Annie.

What a gift we will be giving these girls, I think; the gift of sisterhood. Remembering how much I longed for it at Annie's age makes me want to weep.

Trudy wants to know when we can all meet, how soon, and might there be any chance that we could all meet up today?

She is working at Julia's store. Could I bring Annie? Could Trudy meet us properly? And maybe Julia could get someone else in to help for the afternoon so the two girls could go off and get to know each other.

Annie, when I tell her, is just as excited. She's going to have a cousin! Who knew?! What should she wear? How should she act? Should her hair be up or down? She looks like me? How do you know, Mum? You *met* her! This is so weird! Tell me *everything*!

"Oh my God!" yells Trudy, standing up and running over as soon as we walk in, wrapping Annie in a giant bear hug. "We look like sisters!" She turns to me. "I thought it was strange when you walked in yesterday, that you looked so much like Aunt Julia, but I never would have believed you were my aunt! I never would have believed I have this whole other family I never knew anything about!" She flings her arms around me as I laugh — her joy is infectious. "This is, like, the most exciting thing that's ever happened to me! Can I take Annie to the Juice Bar and get ice cream? They all know me in there, so we don't have to wait in line."

I look at Annie, check her expression to make sure she is willing. Boy, is she willing. I can see she has an instant girl crush on Trudy. Frankly, who can blame her? Trudy is so warm, so open, not to mention gorgeous. Piles of dark curls falling well past her shoulder, highlights of gold. Annie's hair is curly, but she hates it, spends hours trying to blow-dry it straight, or scrapes it back in a clip, as she has done today. But where Annie still has puppy fat, rounded thighs, a peachlike bottom, Trudy has legs that are long and coltish in her denim cutoffs. Both of them have the same olive skin, and as they walk off together, their heads close, Trudy chatting away, I have a pang of regret that this didn't happen years ago, that I have somehow robbed Annie of something incredibly special by not getting in touch earlier. Not for me, but for her.

"Well," says Julia, turning to me after the girls disappear into the crowds of people who have recently got off the Hy-Line. "That went well."

"It couldn't have gone better."

"It's weird, you can tell they're family," Julia says. "You can see they feel it."

I nod, because I know what she's talking about. It's exactly how I felt when I met Julia all those years ago. "I'm going to meet my friend Sam and take him on a tour of the island," I say. "Would you be interested in joining us?"

Julia's face falls. "I would have loved that. I couldn't find anyone to help today, so I'm stuck in the store all afternoon. But I'd love to get together properly. Can we maybe do dinner?"

"I would love that," I say, and we spontaneously move toward each other and hug, and I am so enormously grateful for this newfound relationship that when we pull away, my eyes are filled with tears.

"So," says Sam, waiting at the end of the wharf, examining me carefully as I walk up to him. "Who would have thunk it? She didn't spit in your eye and cast a spell on you."

"Quite the opposite. The one thing I never expected was the warmth, Sam. She's as warm and lovely as she used to be."

"Even though you shagged her boyfriend?"

I groan and cover my eyes in shame. "Can you not? I'd really much rather forget about that. Anyway, there's still the sister to contend with. Apparently she has allowed the girls to meet, although no mention of wanting to see me."

"You never liked the sister though, right?"

"She never gave me a chance. But no, she's not the kind of woman I generally warm to. At least she wasn't, all those years ago. She's cold, and imperious. She always made me feel less than."

We cross the cobbled street behind two women in very high wedge sandals. "God!" I whisper to Sam, grateful for my flip-flops. "What are they thinking, wearing heels in Nantucket, for God's sake?"

"They're thinking a twisted ankle would be an excellent souvenir from their trip." He rolls his eyes, and I laugh. "I'm starving, Cat. Can we go somewhere and grab lunch?"

I whisk him off to Sconset, which he completely falls in love with — the gorgeous little village with its pretty store and restaurant, the tiny cottages covered in climbing roses.

We go to the Summer House, which he instantly pronounces his favorite place on the island thus far, partly, I am sure, because everyone here seems to be clad in designer labels equal to his own.

"Now it feels like a holiday," he says, as we find a table next to the pool and watch all the glamorous people having lunch around us. "This is definitely my kind of place. Isn't that John Kerry over there?"

I turn to look, just as my phone buzzes with a text from Annie.

Mum, can I go to Brant Point with Trudy?
She's meeting a crowd of friends. Please!

I pass the phone over to Sam, let him read the text. "What do you think? Okay?"

He frowns at me. "Why would you say no?"

"Trudy's sixteen. She's quite a bit older than Annie. I suppose I'm just worried about Annie getting up to . . . stuff."

"Like you used to do?" He laughs.

"I suppose so. Even though Annie doesn't seem nearly old enough. I just worry that she might be led astray."

"Stop worrying so much. Let her go. This is what you wanted, that she would bond with her cousin and have an amazing vacation with kids her own age. This is going to be much more fun for her than hanging out with us, however much she loves us."

I sigh. "You're right. Of course you're right." I reach out for the phone, tap away on the screen.

Are you having a good time?

OMG! The BEST! She's AMAZING!

Do you have enough money?

Yes. Love you xxxx

Love you more. XX

"And there she goes, out into the big wide world," says Sam when I show him the text. "Boys, booze, drugs. It's all out there waiting for her."

"Oh, fuck off," I say. "Thanks for playing into all of my fears." I take a deep breath. "This is Annie we're talking about. She's not about to launch herself into a life of debauchery. Anyway, Trudy seems lovely. I'm glad she's having a nice time. Why don't you finish the burger and we'll go to the beach?"

I pick Annie up from the beach at Brant Point at six. She has already texted, over and over, begging to stay later, but I tell her we have two weeks for her to see her new friends, and she can always go back later. I have made a reservation at the Galley tonight, and it's special, and expensive, and a treat for all of us. I want Annie with us.

"So?" Sam asks when Annie climbs into the car. "I see there were quite a crowd of kids with you. Nice kids?"

Annie is beaming, in a way I'm not quite sure I've ever seen her beam before. This is

339

my quiet, unassuming, bookworm of a child. She's never been interested in socializing, or partying, or hanging out with groups of kids.

"They were amazing! They were all so friendly, and cool. I had an awesome afternoon."

Sam grins. "Awesome! You sound like an American!"

"Well, duh! I've been hanging out with them all day."

"So how is Trudy?"

Annie is so excited, she sits forward in the car, her arms resting on our seats. "Mom, she is just the *best*. And we have so much in common. Oh my God, it's like, I don't know, it's like suddenly finding a sister."

And I know — I remember — exactly what she means.

I dress up for tonight. Most of my suitcase was stuffed with casual clothes, shorts and T-shirts, but I packed a couple of silk beaded tunics, gauzy trousers, and large gold hoops, just in case.

I don't bother blowing my hair straight — in this humidity it is likely to stay straight for about twenty minutes, if I'm lucky. I gather it back in a loose ponytail at the nape of my neck, letting a few tendrils fall on either side of my face. Already my skin is bronze — thank you, Brooks, for the olive skin — and I glide a large brush with luminescent bronzer over my cheeks.

Beaded flat sandals on my feet, I look at myself appraisingly. I look good. I look like I belong.

Sam gives me a wolf whistle when he sees me. "Extremely gorgeous," he says admiringly. Even Annie comes out to give me her approval. She is in a long skirt but tucks shorts into my bag. "I might see Trudy later, and I don't want to be in a skirt," she explains.

We walk through the restaurant and onto the beach. Our table is on the sand, lanterns casting an apricot glow on crisp white tablecloths as the horizon starts to turn pink, ready for a spectacular sunset, I think.

All around us are the beautiful people. The kinds of beautiful people that intimidate the hell out of me at home. But not here. I'm a stranger here, and I have no desire to fit in. In fact, these last few months I can honestly say for the first time in my life I am learning to be comfortable in my own skin.

"It's like the Chiltern Firehouse, on sand," whispers Sam approvingly. I turn to look at him and actually start to laugh at the dreamy look on his face, for pretend as he might that he is happy in a T-shirt and shorts, happy to grab half a sandwich at Something Natural and eat it on an old picnic table, bleached white from the sun, this is his natural habitat. This is where he belongs.

Two women are at the table next to us, with their daughters, all five of them almost ridiculously beautiful, in that way only very wealthy Americans can be, the daughters long haired and long limbed. I look at one of the mothers. She is probably my age, her skin dark, her hair long and tousled, beachy. She wears a gauzy white top, grey flowing pants, a large gold cuff around her wrist, no other jewelry. A part of me thinks how much I would love to look like her, to wear exactly what she's wearing, to have her style. A part of me remembers all the years I would go shopping, trying to turn myself into someone else, convinced that if I had those pants, that top, that cuff, I would be that person, have that life.

I pick up my glass of seltzer and look at Sam and Annie. "Cheers," I say. "Here's to being comfortable in your own skin."

"Cheers," sighs Sam. "God, I love it here. Look at that table of perfect boho-chic women. Can we please eat here every night?"

"Only if you're willing to expense it." I laugh, and he grimaces, as the waiter shows up and hands us menus.

We have finished our meal, Annie spending the last ten minutes texting furiously, arranging to meet Trudy and her friends. I try to reprimand her, no texting at the table being our rule, but Sam stops me. "We're on holiday," he says. "Besides, she's making plans."

I turn to watch a crowd of people weave their way through the tables to their own, a little way off from ours. They seem to know everyone there, a halo of energy surrounding them.

Tall, handsome men. They look like bankers. They all have that golden glow of success, of wealth. The women may be carrying small clutches made out of bamboo and straw, but you know that confidence only comes from having the sort of money that means you never have to worry about anything in your life.

I look more closely at the woman with hair in a sleek chignon. The sort of chignon I dream of having, except my own personal frizz factor would never allow it. She looks like Audrey Hepburn, and my heart skips a beat. She looks like Ellie. I can't tear my eyes away.

They keep moving, out of sight, and it takes me a while to center myself, to bring myself back to the present, to the people I love, the here and now. It probably wasn't her, I tell myself; I was probably mistaken. It has, after all, been years.

As we leave, I stop in the bathroom, and as I am washing my hands, admiring my suntan in the mirror, the bathroom door opens and in walks the woman with the chignon.

She smiles at me, vaguely, then stops in her tracks, a look of growing horror in her eyes.

I was right.

It is Ellie.

And I freeze.

I have no idea what to say.

TWENTY-EIGHT

The color drains from her face, and she falters, before turning and leaving the bathroom, and I find myself going after her, walking quickly, catching up with her, placing a hand on her arm, which she shakes off, turning to glare at me.

"Ellie. Please. Can we talk?"

"What the hell are you doing here?" she hisses, keeping her voice low, as I wonder what she means: it's not like Julia hadn't told her, it's not like she didn't know about Annie. I am aware people have already started turning to see what is going on.

"Can we go somewhere quiet and talk?"

"I have nothing to say to you," she says, disdain dripping from every word, unable to look at me.

I don't want to be here. I don't want to do this, not here, not in public, and not really at all, but I have heard enough times that you don't get to move on, to fully recover, until you do the steps, and I know making the amends is the most important one. This isn't about getting Ellie's forgiveness; it's about doing everything I can to keep myself on the wagon, to keep myself sane.

"Ellie, I owe you an apology."

She puts a hand up. "Don't. Just don't. I have nothing to say to you, and there's nothing you could say that I would want to listen to."

"Ellie, please. I need to make amends —"

"I don't care," she almost spits. "How dare you! How dare you come back to Nantucket as if you didn't commit the most egregious of crimes." Her voice is rising in anger, and the conversation in the room falls away, everyone straining and craning to hear. "How dare you even talk about . . . what did you call it? *Amends?*" She snorts in derision. "Who do you think you are? You were the cause of my sister's broken heart, you ruined her whole life, and you think you can come and make some sort of an apology, make amends, for that? I don't think so. You have some nerve, coming back here. I don't know what the hell you think you're playing at, but you are not welcome here, do you understand? You are not welcome on this island and you are not welcome in my family. Never again. I don't ever want to lay eyes on you ever again." She is now shouting, and the restaurant is so quiet you could hear a pin drop, and this is it. The worst kind of shame and mortification imaginable. It is everything I had ever feared, and so very much worse.

And it is everything I deserve. As I stand here, my cheeks burning, grateful only that my daughter is not witness to this, that she and Sam are no longer in the restaurant, but standing in the car park, waiting for me to emerge from the bathroom, doubtless wondering where I am, I know that this is it. The penance I have waited all these years to pay.

TWENTY-NINE

I don't know how I manage to get out of there, but I do, aware that everyone is staring at me. I keep my head held high and look straight ahead, eyes focused on the car park I can see beyond the open door, refusing to look to the left or right, refusing to acknowledge the pitying glances.

"What happened?" whispers Sam, who can see I am upset, almost on the verge of tears, but I shake my head, knowing that if I try to speak, I will probably burst into tears.

"Migraine," I say, which saves me from having to speak all the way home. I go straight upstairs and get into bed, playing the conversation over and over, shuddering in humiliation and horror each time I hit the replay button.

Annie texts me that she's going out with Trudy. I should say no, particularly after tonight, but I can't stop this relationship, not now that these two girls have found each other. I need to talk to Julia, need to download this horror onto someone who will understand, someone who may know what I could do to smooth the waters, if not for me, at least for Annie and Trudy, because they have to continue seeing each other and we can't keep it a secret. Ellie is bound to find out.

Secrets have a habit of rising to the surface, like milk gone sour.

I wake up with an emotional hangover so heavy and disturbing that for a few seconds I feel like I must have been drinking the night before. I replay it again, and am grateful that in the bright morning light it doesn't feel so bad.

Yes, it was humiliating, but it's not like this happened in front of anyone I knew. This was clearly the most dramatic and possibly entertaining thing the people in the restaurant last night had seen in years, but I don't know them; they don't know me. It really doesn't matter.

I think of something I heard someone say in a meeting once: Other people's behavior is none of my business. Whatever they must have thought of me has nothing to do with me. It doesn't matter. What Ellie thinks of me is another thing, but really, what did I expect? That she, like Julia, would fling her arms around me and proclaim her forgiveness?

Well, yes. Sheepishly I realize I was holding out for some kind of dramatic transformation. I need to let go, I think, taking a deep breath and picking up my phone to look at the time. I can squeeze in a meeting, I realize, and nothing straightens me out, reminds me of what's important, better than a meeting.

Throwing back the sheets, I climb out of bed and go to get dressed.

The Tuesday meeting is exactly what I needed, and even though I don't share today, by the time I leave, I am centered and calm.

Sam texts me that he's taking Annie to the Downyflake for blueberry pancakes, and a man from the meeting, Stew, gives me a ride there. I walk in and see the two of them there, how grown-up Annie suddenly looks, her skin golden and glowing, her eyes lit up with excitement, and I am filled with love and gratitude.

To hell with Ellie. Look at what I have! Look at my wonderful daughter, my best friend, the life I have managed to build for myself in spite of everything. I walk to the table and give Annie a squeeze, sliding into the empty seat next to her, and I listen to her bubble with joy as she tells Sam about the beach party last night, a bunch of them over at some water tower off Cliff Road.

At least they weren't far.

Most of the kids are at least sixteen, although she assures me there are a couple of younger ones like her. But they are all so lovely, she says. So curious about this new English girl Trudy introduced as her cousin.

"So what do you do at a beach party?" asks Sam as he pours maple syrup over his pancakes. "Are you all snogging?"

"Ew! No! Sam, that's gross!" she says, although she turns red, and Sam meets my eye with a knowing smile. "We just talk," she says quickly. "And, I don't know. Hang out."

I think of the giggling kids I have seen all over town. "Were there any drugs?"

"Mom!" she says. "Don't be daft. Of course not!"

"Sorry." I shrug, masking my skepticism. "I had to ask."

After breakfast Annie comes with us to the bicycle store. We rent three bikes and take off round the island, stopping from time to time to consult the maps. I marvel again, as I did all those years ago, at how such a tiny island can have so many things. The charm and beauty of Sconset, the quaintness of Main Street, the rugged beauty of the working boats bobbing in Madaket Harbor.

We pick up sandwiches at Something Natural and take them to Steps Beach for lunch. At two o'clock, Annie gets a text, and I watch her read it, her face falling.

"What's the matter?" I lean over, concerned. "Is everything okay?"

She looks up at me, her face stricken. "It's Trudy. She says she's not allowed to see me anymore."

And she bursts into tears.

I call Julia, wanting to know why Ellie is behaving like this, if Julia can talk to her but she doesn't pick up.

How do I explain?

How do I tell my child that the reason she is being ostracized is because of me, because I did something so unforgivable, that all these years later I am still paying the price?

But more than that, she is paying the price.

Any way you slice it, that just doesn't seem fair.

I do what I had been planning to do last night, when I got home, when I suspected that the confrontation with Ellie would have ramifications. I go back home, get changed, and go and see Julia.

"I heard," she says as soon as I walk in the store, happy that Julia is there and that she is on her own. "*Everyone* heard," she says ruefully. "I think the whole island is talking about Ellie's outburst last night. It definitely provided a drama that will doubtless keep them all going for days. Possibly weeks." She peers at me. "You're not okay. I'm sorry. I really am. I was hoping you and Ellie would be able to avoid each other."

"But I don't understand. She knew I was here. You told her." Julia looks away and for a second I wonder if she was telling me the truth, but why would she lie? "She has changed her mind about the girls being friends and is refusing to let them see each other."

"What?" To my relief, Julia is as horrified as I was. "But that's insane. And wrong. She may not want to see you, but to get in the way of their relationship is just *wrong.*"

"I know. And Annie's heart is breaking. I left her at home in floods of tears. Julia, I don't know what to do. I understand that Ellie will never forgive me, but I can't bear for the girls to be split apart. Can you do anything? Say anything to make her change her mind?"

"Absolutely. You just need to allow her to let off steam. She'll be fine after a few hours. I'll drop in later and talk to her. She didn't mean it. Whatever she feels about you I know she wouldn't punish Trudy like that."

In the old days, I might have considered lying, but deception hasn't felt very good to me since I got sober. When I was drinking, my life was filled with white lies and half truths and stories I told to save myself. I learned to be honest, open, and willing through my sobriety, learned that rigorous honesty was one of the keys to my life being as good as it is today.

Lying, withholding the truth, feels wrong. I need Julia to get Ellie's permission for this friendship to continue, and I have to trust she will be able to do so.

Do any of us, Ellie included, have the right to ban this friendship? Isn't it better for everyone, and certainly for the girls, that they are allowed to continue discovering each other?

My mind is whirling; I offer a quick prayer that Ellie will come round.

"You think you can change her mind?"

"I've always managed it in the past. We'll figure it out. In the meantime I'd like to get to know Annie too. I know she was supposed to see Trudy tonight. Do you think maybe I could take her out?"

"That would be amazing! She would love it!" I give Julia a huge hug, thinking how lucky I am that Julia is still as wonderful as she always was.

I leave and walk up to the flower stand on Main Street to pick up flowers for Abigail, then to the supermarket for a couple of bottles of sparkling apple cider in place of wine, then come back and crawl into bed for an afternoon nap, which feels like the most delicious luxury of all.

I wake up and plot Annie's evening with her. We will drop her at Julia's on the way to Abigail's house, where she will spend the evening getting to know her aunt. Annie isn't quite as excited as she was about Trudy, but it's a close second.

After a shower, I stand in my room having a full-on clothes crisis: jeans, a linen shirt? Too hot. A floaty skirt? Better. Not with the linen shirt, though. A silky tank? Yes. Necklace? Too much. Smaller necklace? Still wrong. Gold hoops. Perfect. He's tall, Abigail's son, or so she said, so I could wear wedges. But I hate wedges. I only bought them because there was a fantastic sale in Russell & Bromley and I fell in love with them, even though I couldn't walk in them.

No.

Flip-flops.

Yes. That's it.

I am excited. I shouldn't be, I know that being excited is only a recipe for disappointment, that having expectations of any kind is pointless. But it's not really about meeting this man and truly thinking we both might be struck by a bolt of lightning; more about dressing up, about the *possibility,* the realization that after all this time, all these months and months of hoping that Jason and I might find a way back together, I might actually be ready to meet someone new.

Those moments when I think Jason might still have feelings for me are just that, I realize: moments. He probably still does have feelings for me — you don't spend years with someone, have a beautiful baby together, know almost everything about the other without having some feelings for her, surely.

At least, in our case. It wasn't like I had an affair, or he did something awful, so one of us decided to hate the other forever and ever. My alcoholism was awful, but the one thing I absolutely believe to be true is that Jason never saw it as my fault. It's the first thing you learn when you get sober. Alcoholism is a disease, a sickness. You can love the person without loving the disease, and this is how it was for me and Jason. More so, I think, because he's a recovering alcoholic himself.

(A more successful one than I, clearly.)

Those moments when our eyes lock, or when I feel my heart flutter, I know he has separated the woman I am from my behavior, my drinking. I just don't know that he'll ever be able to forgive me. And I don't blame him. I have made my amends, but with Jason it is a living amends. I have to show him I've changed by how I raise my daughter, how I interact with him, the choices I make every second of every day.

But until this relationship with Cara, I thought, *hoped,* if I behaved well enough, if I proved to him just how much I had changed, we would get back together. It seemed so simple.

I didn't want to meet anyone else. I didn't want to be with anyone else. But suddenly the possibilities have opened up. For the first time since my marriage ended, I could imagine myself with someone else.

We're not talking marriage here. Not even dating. Well, maybe dating. But sex! My God! Suddenly, in the sunshine, it is as if my libido has been switched back on. Who knows what the son is like, but really, does it much matter? If he's cute and sexy and fun, maybe I'll have a summer fling! Maybe he'll remind me what it feels like to be young, single, and free.

I call Sam and Annie, and we three troop out to the car.

Abigail greets me at the door of her quaint shingled house and gives me a proper, tight hug before turning to Sam and doing the same thing.

She takes the sparkling cider and the flowers, and ushers us into the kitchen, as we admire the coziness of her cottage.

"I've been here forever," she says. "Almost everything you see is from the Take It or Leave It Pile."

I fling my hands up in the air. "Okay. You got me. What on earth *is* the Take It or Leave It Pile?"

"It's at the dump. Everyone on the island leaves anything they want to get rid of there. It used to be a tiny little thing, but now it's a barnful. Sofas, tables, beds. There's not a day I've been when I haven't found something useful."

"What did you find yesterday?"

"This stool." She points to a small wooden

stool with flowers painted on it. "Can you imagine someone getting rid of that? Isn't it lovely? Ah well. Their loss is my gain."

I peer hopefully around the small cottage, wondering where the son is. Then the back door opens and in walks a tall man, and I find myself smiling and taking a step backward, because although I had thought how lovely it would be if he turned out to be utterly gorgeous, I didn't actually think he would be.

Those fantasies never come true. Except for today.

I turn to look at Sam, who is also gazing at this very masculine, handsome man who is walking toward us with a smile and an outstretched hand.

He is wearing shorts and a polo shirt, and he smells of soap, and clean, and he has perfect white teeth and dimples in his cheeks and short, tousled mousy hair that makes you want to reach up and ruffle it.

His shoulders are broad, his forearms strong. My hand in his makes me feel completely safe and looked after, and looking into those soft brown eyes I almost forget to speak.

"Cat," I manage to get out, just as the back door opens again and a second man walks in, with an equally big smile, and I falter, because I must have got this wrong. It's the other guy that's the son, surely. This handsome one is some kind of ringer, it's the friend, or the plumber. He looks like a plumber.

"Hi!" says the other guy with a wave. He looks nice, but nothing like the Greek god in front of me. "I'm Billy."

"I'm Eddie," says mine, and yes, I'm sorry, but I've already decided he's mine.

"I'm Sam," says Sam, shaking hands with both of them.

"So which one of you is Abigail's son?"

Both burst out laughing. "I'm just here to help fix the grill," says Billy. "Eddie's a genius with wood but doesn't know the first thing about gas."

"Thanks, buddy." Eddie lets out an easy laugh. "Can I get you a drink?"

"Only if you have a beer, which I know you don't." Billy grins. "Nice to meet you all." He looks at us before heading for the door, as I close my eyes and offer a silent thank-you to the gods.

"Come outside," he says. "We're all set up out there, and you can meet Brad Pitt."

I used to hate small talk. I would crease up with anxiety when I found myself standing with someone new at a cocktail party, ease the fears with a few glasses of something.

I don't seem to do small talk anymore. I'm having a very hard time even remembering what it is. Something in me has shifted to the point where I know, very quickly, what the heart of the matter is, and it has brought extraordinary connections into my life.

I think it is because I am now so used to sharing in meetings, and being brutally honest, out of habit I find myself doing the same thing in, well, *civilian* life. I'm seeing a difference in how people are around me. It's as if me revealing my true self, flaws and all, allows people to drop their guard, to feel safe enough to reveal their true selves to me in turn.

It's not unusual anymore for me that when I go to a party — not that I go to a tremendous amount of parties, but when I do go — I walk into a room full of strangers and walk out with a room full of friends, and not just superficial ones, but people who have bared their souls in a very short space of time. I don't necessarily ever even see them again, but we have bonded, have connected in a very real way by letting down our guards.

So it is tonight. We all instantly connect, have real conversations, and all of us are high on the excitement of finding each other. Sam is completely enthralled by Eddie. Who wouldn't be enthralled by Eddie? How is it possible, in fact, that Eddie hasn't been snapped up by some great woman?

Forty-two and still single. Forty-two and never been married. There must be something wrong with him, I think. Who gets to be forty-two and unmarried unless there's a serious problem?

I think of Alex, a television producer I met years ago when I was at the *Daily Gazette.* I did a piece on one of his shows, and we became friends, and he's still, often, my un-official "walker" when I need a date.

We both must have been around thirty when we first met. He was incredibly hand-some, and funny. Oh my God, Alex used to make me laugh more than anyone else I'd ever met. I have absolutely no idea why I never fancied him, because he should have been my type completely, but from the get-go he always felt more like a brother to me.

Plus, Alex dated the most beautiful women in the world; there was no way I could ever compete. I didn't bother trying. He had the most terrible reputation as a heartbreaker, and it was true, he moved through women in the way I move through a box of chocolates — with tremendous speed and purpose, barely stopping to appreciate what I've got.

Until he met Sara. Sara was not his type. She was kind of ordinary. Quiet, even. A bit mousy, as tiny as a doll, with a slightly odd, asymmetrical face, and crazy smart. She is a lecturer in political science, and had she been in a roomful of women that I had to pick out for Alex, she might possibly have been the absolute last person I would have chosen. Too short, too ordinary, too . . . pedestrian. Alex had always been with women who stopped traffic. This woman was almost invisible.

None of it made sense, and I waited for the text to say it was all over and did I know any women to set him up with. It didn't come.

Alex dropped off the face of the planet with Sara. He wasn't at parties, or ringing to ask me to TV awards. There was radio silence for a few months, and the next thing I knew, I had received an invitation to his engagement party. His engagement to Sara. The librarian (which is how I have always thought of her in my mind).

Alex the commitment phobe was making a commitment. All those women, those dozens and dozens of women who had sat on my sofa crying, were wrong about him. It wasn't that he didn't want to make a commitment; it was that he didn't want to make a commitment to *them.*

There was nothing wrong with Alex other than that he picked badly, and as soon as he met the right woman, he settled down. Six months ago they had a baby. In his late forties, Alex is happier than he ever thought possible, and no one, none of us, ever thought this would happen to Alex.

It taught me not to make assumptions about people. It taught me not to look at this perfect specimen of manhood sitting in front of me and assume there must be something wrong with him.

I suppress a yawn — oh God! Please stop me yawning! — and look over at Eddie, wondering if it is the same story. Wondering if he has just been waiting for the right woman to settle down. Knowing that it's highly unlikely that I'm the right woman, but perhaps I could be the woman for right now.

Or perhaps the stirring in my loins, a stirring I haven't felt for a very long time, can be satisfied by Eddie. Not forever. Just for a holiday fling. I blink and swim back into the conversation, realizing I have no idea what he's been talking about for the last ten minutes, my mind far away, on Alex, and commitment, and finally, naughtily, deliciously, on sex.

". . . so my dad died a few months ago, and it kind of feels like I've been set free," Eddie is saying. "My grief felt much more like relief. It's why I stayed away from the island for so long. I came back a free man."

"I felt exactly the same way when my dad died," I say. "Relief. He wasn't actually my biological dad, although I didn't know that until after he died. But that sense of relief, and guilt. I was never what he wanted, he clearly didn't like or approve of me, yet I'm the one who felt guilty!" I let out a wry smile.

"How could he not approve of *you*?" Eddie says.

"I was very different from him, not unsurprisingly."

"But look at you! You're gorgeous, and successful, and sweet. He must have had a big problem."

"He did," I say, but my ears are buzzing. All I can hear is what he just said. I'm gorgeous! Sweet! He, this man to whom I am growing more and more attracted as the minutes tick by, thinks I'm gorgeous! And sweet!

I realize I am high. High on the excitement, the possibility, the flirtation, for that is surely what this is. High on the fact that after all this time, someone as great as this is actually interested in me. Finally!

Abigail comes to the back door and calls me inside.

"Would you mind helping me with this salad?" she asks, sliding a wooden chopping board and a bunch of tomatoes over to me. "Just slice the tomatoes and the basil, would you, Cat?" She peers out the window to where Sam is chuckling over something Eddie has said. "Are you having fun outside?"

"Huge fun," I say. "Your son is lovely."

"He is," she says, a look of sadness crossing her face. "I just wish he would settle down with the right woman."

"I'm pretty sure a divorced mother who lives in London isn't the right woman."

"You are a Mayhew, my dear. You may live in London now, but who knows what the future holds?" She winks at me.

I go to the window, realizing I can hear everything Sam and Eddie are saying.

"She's pretty great," I hear Eddie say.

"She is."

"How do you guys know each other?"

And Sam starts to tell Eddie about how we met.

■ ■ ■ ■

By 8:45 I am more than clear that I fancy Eddie. Fancy him in the way I haven't fancied anyone in a very long time. I love the way he moves, the strength in his arms, his politeness and attentiveness.

When I talk, Eddie looks deep into my eyes. He asks lots of questions, seems genuinely interested in what I have to say, but I have absolutely no idea whether he might be attracted to me. I do know he thinks I'm gorgeous. And sweet. And pretty great.

Is that enough? Does that mean he's interested? Suddenly I feel like a lovesick sixteen-year-old, analyzing every word he's said, trying to figure out if that look means something more.

I'm starting to get tired. I know I'm not supposed to think in English time, but I realize it's after two o'clock in the morning where I'm from, and this makes me yawn even more, which I try very hard not to do, because as we all know, yawning begets yawning.

But I can't stop.

"You're tired! Nearly done. Will you stay for dessert?" Abigail shoots me a concerned glance. I am desperate to go to bed, but desperate for more time with Eddie. Sam, on the other hand, seems to be absolutely fine, and I have no idea how that is possible.

There is now a chill in the air. Eddie stands up and grabs the wrap from the back of my chair and wraps it around me, as a warm glow starts to spread in my heart.

Abigail takes dessert from the fridge, a blueberry pie she made this morning. We decide it's too cold to stay outside, so we'll all go in to the kitchen for dessert. Sam goes to the bathroom, leaving Eddie and me to clear the table. We don't talk, but we smile at each other as we move around the table gathering things up, our hands brushing each other's as we both reach for the salt at the same time, and I laugh, awkwardly.

God. I have forgotten how to do this. I have absolutely no idea how I'm supposed to act, other than like a lovestruck teenager.

"Do you guys want to come to the Club Car?" Eddie says suddenly. "There's a great pianist this evening. It's a fun night, should be filled with islanders. It will give you a taste of what Nantucket's really like."

I want to go. There's nothing I want to do more. I have visions of Eddie and me squeezed together in a bar, sexual tension wrapping itself around us. I look at Sam, wondering if he might possibly bow out, might realize his presence would not be a good thing, but he is clearly considering the possibility.

And I yawn again, and shake my head. There is nothing I want to do more than continue this evening with Eddie, but I can't. I just haven't got it in me.

"I've got to get back to bed," I say. "I'm so sorry. I'm on English time, and the jet lag is killing me. Another time?" I add hopefully.

"Absolutely," he says, turning to Sam. "How about you?"

"You know, I really don't feel jet-lagged at all," says Sam. "I'd love to."

I grab Sam in the hallway.

"How are you not tired? I'm almost dizzy. This is completely unfair."

"I bought something called a five-hour energy drink," he confesses. "I took it at seven. It's great! I really do feel filled with energy."

"Thanks!" I mutter. "You could have got one for me."

"I will next time. Promise to tell you all about it."

"I hate you," I say.

"I know." He puts his arms around me and gives me a hug. "I'll be sure to get home safe."

THIRTY

I wake up briefly when Annie comes in to give me a kiss after Julia dropped her home, then sleep the sleep of the dead, until I open my eyes and look at the alarm clock, and it's 7:43 a.m. After the past two days of waking up at 3 and 4 a.m., this feels like the lie-in of the century. I have missed the morning meeting, but clearly I needed to sleep more.

I open my eyes again and it's 10:24 a.m. Oh my God! I went back to sleep. Annie! Sam! Where is everyone? I jump out of bed, completely bleary-eyed, and go to the stairs.

"Annie? Sam? Hello?"

No answer.

I go to Annie's room and quietly push the door open, and there she is, fast asleep on her bed, her face as relaxed as a baby's. I smile, then pad down the hallway to Sam's room, gently push his door as well, and he

371

too is fast asleep.

It seems the jet lag caught up with all of us.

I slip on yesterday's shorts and T-shirt, slide my feet into the flip-flops by the back door, and jump in the car to go grab croissants and coffee, to bring back to the house.

"Morning!" Sam is almost ridiculously clichéd in the mornings, stretching his arms up like a great sleepy bear, yawning in the doorway as he stumbles into the kitchen.

I have been dying for him to wake up. The croissants are still warm, on a plate on the kitchen table, and I have made a bowl of berries to have with them. I have been waiting and waiting and waiting for Sam to get up, desperate to do the postmortem on last night, to find out what Sam thought of Eddie, whether he thought there was chemistry, and most important, to find out if Eddie said anything when they went out.

I'm sure he did. He must have done. I am desperate to know but have to pretend to make small talk before I go in for the kill.

"Late night?" I say, passing the plate of croissants over to him and pouring him some coffee.

"So late!" he groans. "God, it was completely wild in there. It's good you

372

didn't come, actually. Big, big drinking. Everyone in there, I think. Do we have any painkillers?"

"I think there are some in the kitchen drawer." I go to the kitchen drawer to find a bottle of Advil. "How many? Three? Four?"

"What? Are you crazy?" Sam looks at me in horror. "Who takes three or four painkillers, for God's sake? Two!"

I feel a faint flush on my cheeks. I sometimes forget that I am a person of extremes, that other people, *normal* people, don't overdo everything in their life. I have to do everything in my life to excess or I can't feel it: coffee as strong and thick as mud, everything a little harder, faster, *more.* And then at times like these, I am embarrassed when I realize I have no idea what normal is.

I shake two out into my hand and give them to Sam with a glass of water, watching as he gratefully gulps them down.

"So, was it fun?"

"Oh God. Huge fun. I just wish I hadn't had so much to drink. Lots of singing."

"You? Singing? You must have been drunk."

"It was all Billy Joel and Carole King. Fantastic stuff."

Enough Billy Joel and Carole King. I have

to cut to the chase. "I thought Eddie was gorgeous. Like, really, properly gorgeous. Like, loin-stirringly gorgeous. I think maybe he might have been interested in me. I can't stand it anymore — please tell me he said something about me."

Sam stares at me. "What?"

"I know! I'm behaving like a lovestruck teenager. I know it's ridiculous, but I have this huge crush, and if he liked me he would have said something to you. Come on, Sam, put me out of my misery, did he?"

And Sam stares.

"Sweetie," he says, slowly, cautiously, and after a sigh, "how do you not realize that he's gay?"

I shake my head and start to laugh. "Not this time, Sam. You think everyone's gay, particularly if they're handsome and in good shape. There's no way his mother would have set us up if he was gay. And he's not gay."

"Cat, he's gay. His mother doesn't know."

"Bullshit. He's not gay."

"If I tell you he kissed me last night would you believe me?"

"That's not funny, Sam."

"I know. I'm not smiling."

And he's not. His face is deadly serious, and worse than that, there's a look on it that if I didn't know better I would say was pity.

"Shit!" I jump up from the table, completely and utterly mortified. I know Sam is my best friend, and I know I can tell him anything, and he is probably not looking at me right now thinking I am the biggest idiot in the whole world, but that's how I'm feeling.

I am the biggest idiot in the whole world.

"Cat?" Sam jumps up after me. "I'm so sorry. I had no idea you didn't know. You have great gaydar. How could you not tell? I'm so sorry. I can't believe you didn't . . . Oh God. I'm sorry."

I turn from the stairs, which I am climbing in a bid to crawl back into bed and hide under the covers, never wanting to look Sam in the eye again.

"I cannot believe what a fool I seem."

"Sweetie," he says gently, taking my hand and pulling me back toward the kitchen, "if you knew the number of times I've hit on straight men convinced they were interested in me, you would not be feeling a fool. And he's not swishy. And he's American, and frankly, even I wasn't sure. I mean, I kind of thought he was at a certain point in the evening, but I don't always get it right."

"But how can his mother not know?"

"Apparently his dad was a huge homophobe, and he just decided it was easier to not tell anyone. It's why he moved away for so long. He's planning on telling his mother, just hasn't found the right time, although she's constantly trying to fix him up with women, so he's realizing he's just going to have to bite the bullet and get it over with soon."

"How do you live with that kind of secret from your parents?" I say, realizing, as the words come out of my mouth, that my mother lived with a far bigger secret, one that would have blown her life apart.

"His mother would be fine," I say, knowing that her years in program will have prepared her for this. "Shocked, probably, given that she thinks her son is the most eligible straight single man on the island, but she'll accept it. She has years of recovery. I can't believe he wouldn't tell her."

"He said on some levels his mother is extraordinary, and accepting, and loving, but she's also a devout Christian, and has particularly strong views on homosexuals, as she calls them."

"So he actually kissed you?"

"Are you sure you want to hear about this?" He peers at me dubiously.

"Yes. Now that I am over my utter mortification at fantasizing a future with a gay man, yes, I want to hear all about it."

"Oh my God, Cat," Sam burbles, suddenly as giddy as a teenager. "He is gorgeous! We talked about everything, the whole him being gay thing, but I wasn't sure he was interested in me, and then, when we left the Club Car and were walking down a side street, he just grabbed me, pushed me back against a wall, and started kissing me. It was the craziest, sexiest thing that's happened to me in years."

I pull the front of my shirt away from my chest, fanning myself. "Okay, so I'm not supremely jealous. Given that the last person I kissed was Jason, and that was probably a year and a half ago, I could throw up, I'm so jealous. So it was amazing, yes?"

"Out of this world amazing."

I look closely at Sam. "Did you have sex?"

His hand flies to his chest, a horrified expression on his face. "Cat! What kind of boy do you think I am?"

"A horny one?"

"Well, yes. I certainly was last night, but no, we didn't have sex. Not on the first date."

"Are you seeing him again?"

"I bloody well hope so. He apparently has some kind of social tonight and invited us."

"Both of us?"

"Yes."

"So I can be the big fat gooseberry?"

"Well, it was nice of him to invite you."

"There's no way I'm going to come and be the third wheel in your budding romance. I'll feel like an idiot."

"Apparently there'll be a few single men there. Straight ones. I think we should go."

"I don't know whether I'm interested in meeting anyone. Right now I need to stay focused on raising Annie and being a good mum."

Sam raises an eyebrow. "And that's why you were all aquiver last night at the possibility of Eddie being straight?"

"Can you please not remind me? Let's just move on."

And we do.

Annie emerges, finally, close to noon, black eyeliner smudged under her eyes, her usual sunny demeanor replaced by one that is surly and distracted, and horrifyingly familiar to me.

My God, I think. It happened, finally. My little girl just became a teenager.

I think back to a comedy sketch I once

saw, a sweet little boy sitting with his parents waiting for the clock to strike midnight so he can turn thirteen. On the stroke of midnight he transforms, in a seemingly painful way, into a teenager. His short back and sides grow, werewolf-like, to a long, greasy mess. His smile is replaced with a growl, and his response to his parents is a loud bark: I hate you! Oh, Harry Enfield, I think, how right you were. I just didn't expect it to ever happen to my sweet little girl, and how is it possible that it seems to have happened, literally, in twenty-four hours?

"How was last night?" I say brightly, hoping to pull her out of her funk. "There are chocolate croissants there if you want breakfast, although" — I look at my watch — "it's almost time for lunch."

"It was fine," she says, shrugging, taking a croissant and spraying crumbs everywhere. I resist the urge to reprimand her, instead quietly getting a plate and putting it in front of her.

"What did you do?"

"Went for dinner. Hung out."

"So what does that mean?" I attempt, with a laugh. "Hang out? What do you actually do?"

"Nothing," she barks. "That's the point."

"Okay. Sorry I asked. How was Julia? Is she fun?"

"Totally!" Annie says, in an almost perfect American accent. "She's amazing! Oh, and Trudy called. She wants to see me tonight. Can I go?"

I start in surprise. "Ellie said it was okay?"

Annie shrugs. "I guess."

Wow, I think. Julia really is that good.

Annie sidles over to me, sliding an arm around me and resting her head on my shoulder in a semblance of old Annie, sweet Annie. "Mummy?" she says, and I know this means she is about to ask for something. "Can I sleep over at Trudy's tonight? Her mum is off island tonight and said she can have four girlfriends sleep over, and they really, really want me to go."

"Her mom's not going to be there and she's allowing friends to spend the night? Are you sure?"

"Of course I'm sure. Trudy's completely trustworthy, and they are sixteen."

"I know. That's what worries me."

"Mum! There won't be any boys, it's just girls, and she *is* my cousin. We're going to hang out at the beach today, then go back to Trudy's house. Her mum leaves at lunchtime, and I promise we won't go to bed late."

"There won't be any drugs or alcohol?"

Annie looks horrified. "Who do you think I am? Of course not!"

"Okay, I was just checking. I'm just a little nervous about letting you go somewhere with no adult supervision."

"You let me stay at Emily's house all the time when her parents are in the country."

That's true, but it feels different. I have known Emily since junior school, know her parents, know how she lives. Also, Emily, as lovely as she is, is something of a nerd, a fact I am extremely grateful for. I would far prefer Annie to be hanging out with Emily, trust Emily far more than I trust Trudy. Not that I have any evidence to base it on, but Sam described Trudy as "fast," and even though she is sweet, and has a lovely smile, and is polite, I have an instinct that all is not as it seems, she is not all she seems.

Years ago, I would override my instincts at every turn. I would meet some woman, and have an intuition that she was a little bit crazy, but she would go out of her way to befriend me, phoning me, inviting me places, so that I would soon decide I was the one with the problem and clearly my instincts were entirely wrong.

Except they never were. We would become instant best friends, until something would inevitably happen to prove me right. I would always look back in regret, wishing I had listened to that inner voice telling me something was wrong.

It isn't that the voice is telling me there's something wrong with Trudy, just that perhaps the sweetness isn't all there is. She's *too* sweet. It feels disingenuous.

"Let me think about it," I say, watching Annie's smile disappear, the sullen expression take over her face again.

"You can't say no," she snaps. "You just can't. If you say no this will end up being the worst holiday of my life. I finally have the chance to be part of a group of girls, to actually belong somewhere, and you saying no will ruin that for me. If I don't go tonight, then I will never be part of that group, and everything will be ruined."

I resist the urge to roll my eyes. The drama! Instead I nod, as if I am carefully considering everything she is saying, and pull Sam out to the screen porch to see what he thinks.

"I think she should go," he says, before I have a chance to say anything.

"There's something I don't feel right about," I admit reluctantly. "I know Trudy is family, kind of, but you saying you thought she was fast has really made me uncomfortable. I think you're right. And I worry about what they'll get up to."

"Fast doesn't mean bad, it just means she's a little more worldly. Frankly I think you're incredibly lucky that Annie's had such an innocent ride up until now. What were you doing at that age? I was smoking pot like it was going out of fashion, and I'm pretty damn sure you were drinking your way into oblivion."

"Maybe. But this is Annie! Sweet, innocent Annie. I don't want her corrupted."

"Sweetie, it's going to happen, whether you like it or not. If she's going to experiment with something, surely it's better it happens here rather than London? It's not only safer, it's contained. We're leaving in less than two weeks and then it's over. Plus, this is part of growing up. You can't protect her forever."

I sigh. "I really don't want to say yes, but I know she will never get over it. Also, I do see your point. If she's going to get stoned, let it happen on a beach on Nantucket."

"I'm sure their shit is better anyway," says Sam. "I spent my teenage years rolling joints out of hash. Horrible stuff. Half the time it just made me throw up. At least here you've got to presume they're getting good grass."

"You do realize you're talking to a recovering alcoholic?" I say. "And you're not exactly alcohol-free. Maybe we're the ones who are fucked up? Maybe what you and I think is normal isn't normal at all and we should be saying no?"

And I realize it's true. For a very long time I presumed that all teenagers did what I did, got drunk, were wild, had nights they couldn't remember. I thought it was absolutely normal to drink, to get stoned, it was part of being a teenager, and I fully expected that when I grew up and had children of my own, they would do exactly the same thing.

Then I got sober. And I started to hear other people talk about their childhoods, and they didn't have the kind of teenage years I had. Of course there were fights with their parents, and discord, and hard times, but most people didn't lose their teenage years to a sea of drugs and alcohol. Most people didn't accept that as normal behavior.

It wasn't what everyone did.

"We're not fucked up," says Sam. "Maybe just a bit, but in the best possible way. And despite all of it, neither you or I is doing so badly. Let's not turn this into something bigger. Just let her have fun. It's a holiday, and it's her cousin. Who knows when they'll see each other again, and she'll love you much more for saying yes."

"You're right, you're right." I sigh, and go back into the kitchen to tell Annie she can go.

"I love you!" She jumps up from the table, literally shrieking with joy, flinging her arms around me and covering my face with kisses, the surly teenager just sitting at the kitchen table now replaced by my sweet little girl. "You're the best mum in the whole world!" And even though I know this isn't real, even though I know this is temporary and will only last about two more minutes, I put my arms around her and sink into this moment of joy.

Sam and I walk up and down the docks in Nantucket Harbor, trying to peer into all the boats, amazed at the luxury and beauty of some of them, the size. Every now and then he pauses, whipping out his phone and furiously texting, and I glance over to see Eddie's name. Each time a text arrives, Sam starts smiling like a lovestruck teenager.

"Apparently it's a fund-raiser for the firemen," he says at one point, his eyes lighting up. "Now you have to come."

"Since when has firefighting been a cause close to your heart?"

He stops in his tracks. "Have you ever seen an American firefighter? I have no idea how they do it, but they make them differently over here. They are quite the most gorgeous things you've ever seen. Turns out" — he grins smugly — "Eddie's a volunteer."

"Well, of *course* he is. Is there anything Eddie can't do?" I say grumpily.

"I'm not sure he can knit," Sam says eventually, after appearing to think about it very hard.

I have often thought that you know instantly when something very bad happens.

I have heard stories of people waking up in the middle of the night at the precise time that, on the other side of the world, their mother died. Or the phone will ring, and as you pick it up, you get a wave of premonition, a sense of dread about what it is that you are about to hear.

I am sitting at a trestle table, at the firemen's fund-raiser, moving pasta salad around my paper plate with a plastic fork, when a couple of policemen walk into the room.

I notice them because they're in uniform, and they seem to know everyone here, which is unsurprising, and I wonder if this is a fundraiser for the police too, and if not, why they might be here.

They seem to be looking for someone, but everyone they ask seems to shrug and shake their heads, until a guy we were talking to earlier looks over in our direction and points, at least I think he points, to me.

And my blood runs cold.

"Are you the mother of Annie Halliwell?" I realize my mouth is filled with pasta salad that will not go down my throat, and I pick up my napkin and expel the salad into it as I start to shake. Whatever they are about to say, this cannot be real. This isn't for me. This has to be a mistake.

"There's been an accident," they say. "You need to come with us."

"Where is she?" My voice comes out as a shriek as Sam and Eddie jump to their feet, although I don't see them, don't see anything, the room closing in to a pinprick of black. "Is she okay?"

"She's in the hospital," one of them says gently, taking my arm. "We're going to take you to see her now."

I don't want to ask. I sit in the back of the police car, Sam at my side, holding my hand, stroking my arm, and I can't ask the question that's whirring round and round in my head, waves of nausea each time I think of it.

They would have told me, I think. If she was dead they would have told me. They would have said something like *I'm so sorry but she didn't make it.* They didn't say that. She must be alive. And if she's alive, there must be hope.

Nothing makes sense. A scooter accident? She doesn't have a scooter. She knows she's not allowed to go on a scooter. We're here on holiday, for God's sake, and she is thirteen years old. Where is she going to get a scooter from?

And why? Didn't she text just an hour ago to say they were renting a movie and making popcorn? How did a movie and popcorn turn into a scooter? How did a movie and popcorn turn into police turning up at a firemen's fund-raiser? How did a movie and popcorn turn into me sitting in a police car, about to throw up, more terrified than I have ever been in my life?

I am not, *was* not, a woman of faith. Religion was never part of my life when I was a child, although I always had a belief in God, in someone looking out for me. When I first went to AA, all those years ago, I thought everyone was crazy, talking about a Higher Power. I had no idea of the power of prayer, or of trusting that there is someone, something bigger, who is looking out for us. It seemed like a load of nonsense.

For a while, I talked about the group being my Higher Power. I had heard other people say this, and I felt less ridiculous, less "woo-woo," having something substantive rather than a great bearded man in the sky.

But something shifted this last time I got sober, the last time, I hope, I get sober. I was at rock bottom, had lost my marriage, my child. When I started to pray, I really did feel that I wasn't alone, that I would be okay, and even though I never thought of myself as religious, I have come to find enormous solace in prayer.

So I pray now. The prayers I know. The Serenity Prayer: *God, grant me the serenity to accept the things I cannot change, the courage to change the things I can, and the wisdom to know the difference.*

The Third Step Prayer: *God, I offer myself to thee, to build with me and to do with me as thou wilt. Relieve me of the bondage of self that I may better do thy will. Take away my difficulties that victory over them may bear witness to those I would help of thy power, thy love, and thy way of life. May I do thy will always.*

And then simply *God, help her. Help her,*

God. Help her be okay.

I say them over and over, my eyes squeezed shut, my lips moving, my hand clutching Sam's. Over and over.

We pull up, and I jump out of the car, edgy, jittery, desperate to see my daughter, terrified of what I will find. I am forced to slow down, to not burst in through the doors of the emergency room of this tiny cottage hospital, flanked as I am by the two police officers.

We are led to a room, a curtain is pulled aside, and there is Annie, alive, and I burst into tears.

"Ow!" she cries when I gather her in my arms, shocked at how scratched she is, her arms and legs covered in blood, her face, thankfully, unscathed.

"A broken arm," says a doctor who suddenly appears in the room. "And a nasty gash on her head. We think she may have a concussion, so we'd like to keep her in for observation overnight. She's remarkably lucky. Other than that, scratches and bruises. Her friend just got out of the operating room. We think we've saved the eye. We won't know for sure for a few days. They're both lucky girls. We can't get hold of the other girl's mom."

"Friend?" I look at Annie, who starts to

cry, the hiccupping, sobbing, hysterical crying of a child.

"Trudy," she says. "She was driving the scooter."

The story doesn't come out until later. Their neighbor, who was away, has a scooter, and the movie was boring, and someone came up with the brilliant idea of "borrowing" the scooter and going for a ride around the island. Of course there was alcohol involved. I didn't know that then, that both girls had blood drawn when they got to the hospital, that the police had the results, that there might be further action.

The keys were right there. Of course they were. This is Nantucket, not London. Trudy said she knew how to drive, and Annie climbed on behind her.

The car came out of nowhere. Sailed out of India Street and knocked the bike flying, Trudy diving face-first into a car, Annie on the cobblestones.

My little girl. My little girl buried in books, quiet, nerdy, painfully shy, now stealing scooters and getting into car accidents.

I think about my instincts that morning, how I knew it wasn't a good idea, and I wonder, at what point will I start to listen? At what point will I trust my own voice?

Trudy has a bandage over half her face, is fast asleep. Oddly, she isn't nearly as bloody as Annie, but her wound is more serious. *We think we've saved the eye.* Please God, let them have saved the eye, let this night, tonight, be nothing more than a bump in the road, something from which they will learn, something that will change them, but only for the better.

I pull a chair up to the side of her bed, astonished at how young she is when asleep. This little girl, who could have been Annie. I take her hand in mine and lean over to kiss her cheek, the one that is bandage-free. I stroke her hand and I stay there a while, knowing that if this were Annie, I would want someone, a mother, to sit with her, to stroke her hand, to kiss her cheek and whisper that she is going to be okay. I have no idea if she will ever know, but it is what I would want for my own child.

I go out to the waiting room and call Julia. Where is Julia? Did the hospital just not know to call Julia? There is no response; her phone rings and rings before going to voicemail. I leave a message. "Julia, this is Cat. It's very important that you call me.

Please. As soon as you get this. It's about the girls."

I try texting.

No response.

I have to try to reach Ellie. However furious she may be at having to speak to me, she has to know. I call Abigail, who says she will get hold of Ellie's cell for me, and rings me back two minutes later with her number.

I phone, my blood running cold as the phone switches to the machine and I listen to Ellie's voice. I don't leave a message, knowing she will never call back, knowing she probably wouldn't even listen if she knew it was me.

I try again ten minutes later, and again ten minutes after that. And on my fourth time, Ellie picks up, and I know, before she even says hello, that she is out somewhere drinking, and I suddenly realize that however perfect her image, however much she relays a cool, imperious, impervious persona, there are cracks, and weaknesses, and vulnerabilities, and maybe going to a bar and having a few drinks is her way to ease her pain.

God knows if that is the case, I understand it.

I am not judging. I feel compassion. As terrifying as I have found her, this is a woman who has discovered her husband is not who she thought, who has lost the life that was so important to her, who was humiliated in public. Drinking isn't going to solve anything, but I understand why she might think it will.

But of all the nights to choose to leave the island, to be in the bar, to possibly be drinking, could it not have been any night other than this?

"Ellie, it's Cat. I'm really sorry to be phoning you, but Trudy has been in an accident. I'm with her at the hospital. She's going to be okay, but you need to get back as soon as you can."

"What? I can't hear you. Who is this?" I can hear the slurring in her voice. Perfect Ellie, not so perfect after all, and instead of feeling smug, I just feel sad.

"Ellie!" Now I am shouting. "Take the phone outside."

"Okay, okay. Hang on." I hear her shout to people, then the quiet as she walks out the door. "Who's this?"

"This is Cat."

"What the fuck do *you* want?" The hostility in her voice, in her real feelings coming out when drunk, is almost enough to send me reeling, but I keep going, willing myself to ignore it.

"The girls were in an accident. They bor-
rowed a scooter and got hit by a car. They're
going to be okay, but you need to get back
on the island as soon as possible. I'm at the
hospital with them."

There is a silence, and I know she is trying to digest it, know what a shock this is.

"What girls?" she says eventually, slurring.

"Our daughters. They were together. At
Julia's house. Trudy. Trudy has had an
operation on her eye."

And now she starts to shriek. "What?
What? Oh my fucking God! My baby!" She
starts to wail, and there is absolutely no
point in continuing talking to her because I
can hear the alcohol in her voice. Her wail-
ing is getting louder, so I click off the
phone, praying not only that she gets here,
but that she is sober by the time that she
does.

I go back in to see Trudy, and as I stroke
her good cheek, she opens her eyes and
stares at me, not quite registering who I am.

"It's Annie's mother," I say. "You're okay.
You're in the hospital. They did some
surgery on your eye, but you're going to be
fine."

"Where's my mom?" she croaks, her one
unbandaged eye darting round the room.

"She's making her way back," I say.

"Remember she was off island tonight? I just spoke to her, and she's coming back. Don't worry about anything. I'll look after you until she gets here." Trudy nods and closes her eyes, and I stay until she falls asleep again, when I go back to see Annie.

Sam goes home to get me a toothbrush. The hospital sets up a cot in the room for me, and I go out to the corridor, still feeling dazed, grateful the girls are basically okay when it could have been so much worse, but furious with myself for letting Annie go.

Jason.

I have to tell Jason. It is now almost 4 a.m. in England. The last thing I want to do is disturb him in the middle of the night. Surely it can wait a few more hours, until morning.

And yet, if Annie was with Jason and something happened to her, even if she was going to be fine, as she is going to be fine, I would want to know. I would be furious if Jason didn't tell me until the next day. I might never forgive him.

I go out to the car park and dial Jason's home, praying the poison dwarf won't pick up, taking a deep breath when I hear Jason's familiar, sleepy voice.

"Jason? I'm so sorry I'm calling in the middle of the night. Annie was in a scooter accident today. She's okay," I say quickly, knowing adrenaline will be flooding through his body at the mention of the word "accident." "I'm in the hospital with her now. She has a broken arm and possible concussion, but she's going to be fine."

"Oh my God. Scooter accident? What the hell was she doing on a scooter? She's thirteen."

"I know. I didn't know." Now is not the time to tell him she was also drinking, and the scooter was stolen. Keep It Simple. That's what I learned in the rooms.

"Where are you exactly?"

"Nantucket Cottage Hospital."

"I'm coming. I'll start looking into flights now."

"Jason, that's silly. It's really not serious enough to warrant you coming over here. She'll be fine."

"This is my daughter," he says. "There's absolutely no way I'm not going to be there."

After I finish telling him the different methods of getting here, after I put the phone down knowing he is fully awake and will spend the next few hours organizing flights, organizing his life so he can leave it behind and come out to join us, I have to admit, I am glad he is coming.

Sam is an amazing friend, but no one loves Annie like I do other than Jason. No one understands how awful it is to see your child in pain, in a hospital bed, other than Jason. And even though she'll probably be out of hospital by the time he gets here, even though she will be absolutely fine, there's a part of me that simply wants him here by my side.

Thirty-One

Annie is discharged the next morning, with a list of all the concussion symptoms to look out for, things that would mean an immediate trip back to the hospital. I know we need to have a talk, but not yet; my daughter needs to heal before she deals with my upset.

I see Ellie just as we are leaving, her hair and clothes disheveled, looking more like Julia than Ellie. It is the first time I actually see a family resemblance. I think of walking over to her to say something, but there is nothing to say. I can't make it better, and seeing me here will doubtless make it worse.

I am walking through the car park when I hear my name and I stop in my tracks, unwilling to be shouted at yet again, unwilling to turn and listen to whatever it is she has to say.

But I do turn. I walk slowly over to where she is standing.

"Cat, thank you." Her voice is rasping and rough, but authentic. "Thank you for being here."

"You're welcome," I say, and then she just looks at me, as if she is going to say something else, but she doesn't, and I give her a rueful smile and leave.

I don't know what Ellie's story is. I don't know if she drinks in the way we tend to drink in our family. I don't know if she was drunk last night, or if she just needed to let off steam. I do know it is not my place to judge her. I do know that as I walk into the streams of sunlight hitting the car park, I am filled with gratitude that I am no longer the kind of mother that can't be there for her child; I am no longer the kind of mother who goes AWOL, who finds herself in bars with strangers, is more interested in being in bars with strangers than raising her daughter. I thank God that I am not showing up in the morning drunk, smelling of booze and cigarettes, because my family was never my priority.

How easily this could have been me. This *was* me. For years. Jason protected me from the full horror of how bad a parent I was. But what if I hadn't had him? I doubt I would have been able to be present last night in the way that I was. My daughter would have been "fast," "advanced," because how else do you survive when you do not have a mother? How else do you survive when your mother is too busy planning her next drink, or binge, to know or care what you are doing, until of course the terrible thing happens, when you wail down the phone and fortify yourself with booze on the ferry over, to get you through whatever pain awaits you when you arrive?

Annie is home, being looked after by Sam the nurse. Eddie dropped in with an "Eddie" bear that I thought Annie would discard, announcing she is much too old for stuffed toys, but the Eddie bear is squeezed next to her in bed as Sam runs up and down the stairs tending to her every need.

Here I am, at the ferry, to collect Jason. I have parked a little ways up the street and walk down to watch the boat come in, the hordes of people that swarm off. I never understand where all these people disappear to. It is such a small island, but never feels crowded, although every day I see more people arrive. I'm never here to see the same crowds leave.

I'm in a reverie about where people disappear to when I see Jason, and my heart starts to smile, for he looks so very English in his slim-cut jeans and trendy sneakers, his V-neck T-shirt and cool metal aviators. He looks English, and handsome, and I wish to God, oh how I wish to God, my heart didn't do an involuntary flip. But it does, and I take a deep breath, compose my features into something that does not give away the fact that I still think this man is the most perfect man I have ever seen, and I wave.

"Hey, you," he says, and he puts his bag down and gives me a hug.

I could stay here forever. I give myself the luxury of closing my eyes so I can fully appreciate the loveliness of being in his arms again, if only because he is trying to comfort me, comfort himself perhaps, and when we pull away I try to be very matter-of-fact to hide the fact that even though we are divorced, even though he is now very much with the poison dwarf, he still has the ability to make me come completely undone.

"How is she?"

"Happy to be out of the hospital. Worried about Trudy, her cousin, actually, who is still in the hospital, and very much enjoying having Sam and Eddie run up and down stairs and bring her treats."

"Eddie?"

"Sam's new friend. I know, we've only been here five minutes, but he seems to have lucked out. He brought Annie a huge teddy bear this morning that she engulfed."

He runs his fingers through his hair as he shakes his head. "I can't actually believe our daughter was in an accident. You always think these things happen to other people, never to you. Jesus." He pauses. "How grateful am I that she's okay."

"Speaking of grateful, there are incredible meetings here."

"You're going?"

"Almost every day."

"Cat, I'm so happy that you're really doing it this time," he says, as we reach the car. "You really are so different."

"Thanks," I say lightly, swallowing the lump in my throat, because if I'm so different, if I'm really doing it, how come you still don't want me?

"Daddy!" If Annie hadn't been covered in bandages and stitched up everywhere, if she could have leaped out of bed to jump into her father's arms, she would have done.

"Bobannie!" It has always been his nickname for her after a childhood song: *Annie Bannie Bo Bannie, Banana Fana Fo Fannie, Me My Mo Mannie, Annie!* She would make him sing it over and over, giggling hilariously each time, and Bo Bannie, over time, became Bobannie, which became Bob-any, emphasis on the Bob.

"Daddy!" She nestles into his arms, joy exploding out of every pore. I didn't tell her he was coming, wanted this to be a surprise, and I step back to wipe the tears from my eyes, then go downstairs to make some lemonade.

"Where's Eddie?"

"Gone to fight fires."

"Actually?" I turn to Sam, impressed.

"No. He's gone to get some fish."

"Does that mean to the fish market or out on a boat with a rod?"

Sam raises a withering eyebrow. "You look at him and tell me what you think. Is he mincing round the aisles with a red plastic basket hanging prettily from his very strong, sexy forearm, or is he ruggedly on a large boat, gritting his teeth, his muscles bulging as he hauls in a giant swordfish?"

"Fishing, then?"

Sam nods, then puts down the magazine he was reading, a freebie we picked up on Water Street with a list of houses for sale on Nantucket.

"I was thinking I might buy somewhere here," says Sam, examining the cover, "until

I saw what the prices are. It's insane, Cat. I don't think I could even afford a shed here, let alone a sweet little two-bedroomed cottage."

"Are things already that serious between you and Eddie?" I'm impressed. "You're actually thinking about buying a house here?"

"No, sweetie." He sighs. "It's just what I do. Thank God the only porn I indulge in on a regular basis is real estate porn. You have to look, indulge in the fantasy of what if. What if Eddie and I fell madly in love and decided to live out the rest of our days on Fantasy Island?"

"You do realize he might have to tell his mother he's gay if that were to happen."

"Oh, we've already had that discussion. Many times. I keep telling him life's too damn short."

"Anyway, he's a builder. You don't have to buy a house. If we're going to indulge in fantasy, you could probably buy an adorable piece of land somewhere for next to nothing and have Eddie build you a palace."

"There *are* no pieces of land on Nantucket for next to nothing. There's nothing under a million. Not even land. Also, I don't want a palace. I want a greyshingled house with window boxes filled with geraniums and lobelia, and banks of blue hydrangeas, and a white crushed-oyster driveway, and French doors from the bedroom that open onto a gorgeous little balcony with tons of old terra-cotta pots and a couple of chairs for Eddie and me to sit in when we have our morning coffee or our evening glass of wine."

"Will the balcony overlook the sunset?"

"Well, of course it will!" says Sam. "And the sunrise."

"Oooh. Same balcony? Tricky!"

"Maybe the balcony will be on the roof. What do they call that thing? A widow's walk! So we can just turn the chairs around."

"Or have a backless bench so you can sort of face each other and simply turn your heads one way to watch the sunset, and another way to watch the sunrise."

"I like it!" He gives a slow grin. "I hadn't thought of that. You're good."

"I'm available for decorating services anytime you need."

"Sweetie, the one thing I don't need is decorating services." He gestures around at the new-look house, for even though he swore he would stop at the living room that first day when we went shopping, every time he goes out he comes back with a little

406

something to make the house even better. The kitchen table now has a burlap runner going down the middle of it, and assorted sizes of glass lanterns, and I'm pretty sure those white ceramic bowls on the sideboard weren't here yesterday.

"So." He peers at me. "How is having hunky ex-husband over here?"

"Nice," I say, getting up and making myself busy at the kitchen sink because Sam has a horrible habit of getting the truth out of me, and I'm not sure I'm ready for him to see how much I still care.

"Nice in a you still want to sleep with him way, or nice because you feel supported and it makes Annie happy?"

"Those days of wanting to sleep with Jason again are long gone," I lie, as someone clears his throat in the doorway, and I turn, horrified that Jason is standing there, mortified that he heard, my cheeks turning a swift, startling red.

"Well, that told him," says Sam happily, who loves nothing more than being witness to a horrifyingly embarrassing situation.

"I'm just going to use the bathroom." I dash past Jason, my head down, and up stairs, where I throw myself onto the bed with a huge groan. I can't face him again. I just can't. I grab a hat, tiptoe down the stairs and out the front door, managing to avoid everyone. When I'm safely out of sight of the house I text Sam that I'm going for a walk along the beach and I'll see them later.

I go to the end of the road, climbing the long wooden steps to the beach, taking deep breaths and trying not to think about the fact that Jason just heard me say I wasn't interested in sleeping with him.

I suppose it's marginally better than hearing me say I *was* interested in sleeping with him.

Sleeping with him.

Oh, how I loved sleeping with Jason.

Jason has always made me feel safe. I had never been able to sleep comfortably in a bed with anyone before Jason. Granted, I don't remember most of my one-night stands and brief relationships in my youth, only remember waking up the next morning with a sinking feeling in my stomach, but the few I do remember, I remember not wanting to be touched.

I never understood spooning, for example. How could anyone sleep pressed into someone's hot body? How could anyone sleep even touching someone else? No thank you. I wanted to be all by myself, on my pretend island on my side of the bed.

Until Jason. The first night we spent

together was in my apartment, not his. It wasn't a drunken falling into bed but a sober experience, in more ways than one. I still remember everything about it. How we had spent the evening kissing, and kissing, and kissing on the sofa. How I knew then that this was it, that he was the one for me.

I remember that I got up and went to the bathroom and started getting ready for bed. I brushed my teeth, took my hair down, and got undressed. I pulled on my pajamas and padded back into the living room, where I think Jason was shell-shocked, wondering where on earth I'd gone, what I was doing. He never expected me to come back into the room in my pink and white flowery pajamas.

I walked over to him, sitting on the sofa, took his hand, and saying nothing at all I led him into my bedroom, sat him on my bed, then straddled him, taking his face in my hands and kissing his face everywhere but his mouth. I wanted to remember this. I wanted to remember everything.

And finally, gently, I kissed his lips, back to his neck, and back to his lips, and it was the sweetest, slowest, most loving kiss I could ever remember.

He buried his face in my hair, in my neck, murmuring my name. It had been such a long time coming, Jason and I, friends for so long, this unspoken attraction unspoken for so very long, that allowing it to emerge was an almost spiritual experience.

He unbuttoned the buttons of my pajamas very slowly, kissing all the way down, as I moved my hands under his T-shirt, unable to believe I was able to do this, feel his skin, feel his tongue in his mouth, when it was all I had thought about for so very long.

It was soft, and sweet, and slow. Loving. It was the first time I had ever known the difference between sex and fucking and making love. This was making love, and when he was above me, moving inside me, leaning down to kiss me all over my face, in just the way I had kissed him all over his when I first sat him on the bed, I was astonished to feel tears leaking their way out of my eyes.

He stopped moving. "You're crying. Why are you crying? Am I hurting you?"

I shook my head. I had no words. I had no idea how to explain that these were tears of joy, because I had never cried tears of joy before.

Afterward, he pulled me in tight, spooning into him, and I sank back into his body, wanting to drink in his taste, his smell, his strong arms wrapped around me.

I woke up to daylight streaming in through

the cracks at the sides of the curtains, Jason's arms still around me, still holding me tight, and I had had the best night's sleep I had ever had.

It was how we always slept. No matter how bad things were between us, we slept together, in the middle of the bed, Jason's arms wrapped tightly around me, and however bad things had been, however much we had fought, as soon as I felt his arms, I knew everything would be all right.

I stay on the beach for a long time. I wish Jason hadn't heard me say it. Even though I said I didn't want to sleep with him, what the hell am I even doing putting the words "Jason" and "sleep with" in the same sentence? Surely he'll think I am thinking about sleeping with him. Maybe he'll even laugh about it when he's home, lying in bed with the poison dwarf, both of them feeling sorry for me, the single mother who threw her life away and won't find anyone to love her ever again.

People start gathering up their things, and I realize it's time to go. Much as I would love to stay away forever, we've got days and days more, and Jason's going to stay in the house, and I can't avoid him forever.

The house is quiet, until I hear a burst of laughter coming from the screen porch. Female laughter, and it's not Annie's.

I walk through the kitchen, wondering who in the hell is in my house, and push open the door to find Jason sitting on the sofa, a pitcher of iced tea on the table, with Julia.

They both clearly found something incredibly amusing before I walked in, and I bite my tongue so as not to say something sarcastic, because I am completely discombobulated by seeing the two of them together, the two of them laughing, and oh how I am hoping I am imagining the threads of chemistry I feel weaving around the room.

Instead I look warily from one to the other, disturbed that they were having fun, that I was excluded from the aforementioned fun, and bewildered as to what she is doing here.

"Julia. What a surprise. How's Trudy?" I hover in the doorway, wanting very much to disturb them, to disturb their laughter, whatever fun they seem to be having, but not, obviously, wanting to disturb them.

"Come and join us," says Jason. "I made iced tea."

"No you didn't." Julia shoots him a look as he shrugs apologetically. "*I* made iced tea. You had no idea how to do it." She's smiling, and I'm quite sure she's flirting, and I look from one to the other, stunned, not knowing quite what to do, only knowing that I wish she would leave.

"I have absolutely no idea what's going on here. How do you know each other, and what are you doing here, Julia?" I try to keep my voice light, keep the accusation out of it, but I'm not sure how successful I am.

Julia has the grace to look embarrassed. "I'm so sorry, Cat. I came over to apologize for last night, and to thank you for looking after Trudy. I was organizing a big event over at Quidnet last night, and I didn't even think to check my cell. I thought the girls were staying in watching a movie. I'm completely mortified at what happened, and so upset. And, obviously, so worried about them. I can't believe they stole a scooter and then crashed. Thank God no one was seriously hurt. And there's something else I have to tell you. . . ." She looks away, uncomfortable. "I am so sorry, Cat, but I lied about Ellie saying it was fine for the girls to be together."

My mouth drops open as I look at her in disbelief, even though a part of me thought this might have been the case. I had a feeling, but I didn't want to believe it so I didn't pursue it.

How stupid I have been.

"I just felt so awful that the girls couldn't be friends, so Trudy and I decided not to say anything. I thought I was doing the right thing, but I realize how wrong it was. I'm so sorry."

"Oh my God, Julia," I gasp. "I don't even know what to say. That's such a huge lie." I am gratified that even Jason looks shocked.

"I know, but it truly came from the best intentions. I screwed up."

"Ellie knows you were lying too."

"Yes. Now she does. I've apologized to her."

"Did she go off the rails?"

"No. She's too guilty at not being here, and too relieved that Trudy is okay. I think she's even relieved that you were there. This time she will actually let the girls see each other. She feels horrible, and she knows she was wrong."

Julia looks remorseful, which isn't really the point. I still can't believe she would lie, not just to Ellie, but to me; to all of us. And even though this may have resulted in what we all wanted, the dishonesty behind it makes me wonder how well I know Julia, why she would go to the trouble of lying for my daughter.

"Why did you do it?" I ask. "Why risk it?"

"I did it for Trudy. I know how much she has always wanted a big family, and I didn't think it was right to keep them apart, so I took matters into my own hands. I know I was wrong. I feel horrible about it now."

To give her credit, she does look mortified, but I feel extremely unsettled. Honesty has become such a huge part of my life; if I had known she had lied, I would never have encouraged the girls to get together.

And yet, I stop myself, I did know. On some level, I knew.

But if Julia could lie so easily about that, what else might she lie about? Would she lie that she has forgiven me? Would she be that callous? Does she, in fact, feel the same as Ellie?

"I know what you're thinking," Julia says, standing in front of me now, grabbing my arms. "I hated lying. I'm not a liar, I did this for the girls. For you. I know I made a terrible mistake but this isn't who I am, and I am going to make it up to you. If nothing else, Ellie is pretty disgusted with me right now, but much more inclined to have a relationship with you. She has forgiven you. This isn't all bad, Cat."

I look in her eyes, and I realize she is right. People make mistakes. We fuck up, and what kind of person would I be if I was unable to forgive her?

I close my eyes for a few seconds and nod my head. "Okay," I say. "Okay, I understand. We need to move on from this."

Julia envelops me in a hug. "Thank you. You will never know how relieved I am. And Ellie too, so relieved and appreciative. She said she had no idea what would have happened if you hadn't been there."

How could she not believe it? I think, staring at her. Isn't Julia filled with stories of doing exactly the same thing when she was a teenager? Didn't she regularly steal Jeeps parked by the harbor and drive them to parties all over the island? Didn't she sneak into all the bars underage, chatting up the doormen and sticking her boobs out to get in? How on earth could she possibly think Trudy isn't going to do, if not the same exact thing, then something similar?

How did I not realize? I think. Because I still think of Annie as a little girl. I hadn't realized, until last night, just how much she has grown up.

"I am so sorry, Cat." Julia is standing in

front of me now, and she grabs my arms. "I don't know how I'm going to make it up to you. Ellie is furious with me. She may never talk to me again. But she's feeling a bit warmer toward you, although disgusted with me that I went out to an event and wasn't contactable, and you were the one who showed up."

"I imagine it's the last thing she would have wanted."

"I imagine that's true, although she is relieved and appreciative you were there. Really appreciative. She said she had no idea what would have happened if you hadn't been there."

A glow of warmth spreads inside me, and I realize how much it has bothered me, all these years, being hated by someone for no reason at all. I am a people-pleaser; I need to be liked, and I can't help but feel gratified that Ellie may be changing her mind, even though it took a web of lies to get her there.

"The nurses at the hospital told me you were back and forth between the two rooms all night. I feel awful I wasn't there when it happened. I'm so sorry, Cat. I really don't know how to thank you."

"You don't have to thank me. It's the least I could do, the least anyone would have done. I just wish I had known you weren't going to be around last night. The girls could have come here."

"Ellie would never have allowed it. I was just trying to do the right thing without having the girls feel like they had to lie. I'm sorry."

"Okay. It's . . . fine. I'm just relieved I was able to be there. How is Trudy doing?"

"She's okay. They took off the bandages to examine the eye, and they think it's going to be fine. Ellie's with her. I just left to get her some things from home, and I wanted to drop by and say thank you in person."

"Oh. So . . . have you been here long?" I look at the iced tea, remember the discomfort of walking in to her and Jason laughing.

She flushes slightly again and grabs her straw purse from the floor. "Longer than I should have been. I've got to get back to the hospital. Cat, thank you. From the bottom of my heart, thank you, and again, I am so sorry." And with that my half sister puts her arms around me and gives me a genuine hug. "It was good to meet you, Jason," she says, as he stands up and shakes her hand across the coffee table. I watch his face very carefully as he looks at her, and I forget everything that just happened.

I know my husband.

Ex-husband.

He fancies her.

Fuck.

I know that look in his eye. For once, Cara the poison dwarf doesn't seem like a bad alternative. I walk Julia to the car and come straight back in, standing in the doorway with my arms crossed accusingly.

"You fancy her."

"Oh my God." He starts to laugh. "Are you out of your mind?" And I start to feel a tiny bit better.

"You were totally flirting with her," I say, but even I'm aware there is less conviction in my voice.

"I was not flirting with her, totally or otherwise. Actually I was curious about the sister I'd never met."

"Half sister. You do realize it would practically be incest. And more to the point, what would Cara say if she knew you were entertaining attractive single women in your screen porch?"

Jason makes a face, looks away, then looks back at me, and I know what's coming next, a shiver of happiness running through me in anticipation of the words I know I'm about to hear.

"We broke up."

"What?" I sit down in the chair opposite, shocked in spite of myself, trying to hide the smile that so desperately wants to break out, having completely forgotten the unsettling conversation with Julia, having completely forgotten, in fact, that Julia was just here.

"What do you mean you broke up? When? Why? I thought this was the big one. I thought you were going to end up together." It's too late: The smile has made its way onto my face, and I know how massively inappropriate that is, but I can't help it. I can't stop smiling.

"We broke up about a month ago."

"You didn't say anything?"

He shakes his head.

"So. What happened?"

"It just wasn't right."

"Oh come on, Jason. It's me. I know I'm not your wife anymore, but you have to tell me. Let me guess. You had enough of her telling you what to do."

"It wasn't just that."

"So that was part of it?"

He groans and sinks his head into his hands. "Okay. It was all too much for me. Everything revolved around her, everything had to be done her way. I tried, I really tried to make her happy, but nothing was ever going to make her happy. I'm not sure anything ever will."

"But you didn't end it, surely?" I know Jason. He's a good guy, a people-pleaser. That's why I thought he was so stuck. Even if he was miserable, he'd have to stay to try to make it better, try to make her happy.

"She kind of ended it." He starts to shift awkwardly in his seat. He's not making eye contact, and I realize he must have done something, behaved in a way that made her give him an ultimatum.

"What did you do?"

"Nothing. I didn't do anything!"

I peer at him. "Did you have an affair?"

"*Can* you have an affair when it's just a girlfriend? Don't you have to be married?"

"You're totally evading the question, which means you *did*! You started seeing someone else!" I'm shocked, but convinced this is what he did. It's so typically male. They'll never directly end it, unless of course you're a raging alcoholic and make your marriage a living hell; instead they'll behave so badly that the woman is forced to end it, to say shape up or ship out, offer an ultimatum that enables them to make an easy exit.

"I didn't actually *do* anything," Jason

admits reluctantly. "It was a flirtation, and not even one I started. Someone was flirting with me."

"Who?"

"An actress I was working with. She was sending me some pretty outrageous texts, and Cara found them."

My mouth has dropped open. "You really didn't respond?"

"Barely. I was extremely polite, but" — he looks embarrassed — "I didn't want to be rude and not say anything."

"What did Cara do?"

"It was extremely high drama for twenty-four hours. Lots of screaming and crying. I kept telling her nothing had happened and it wasn't my fault this woman had a crush on me, but she didn't believe me. In the end she said she couldn't trust me anymore and she was leaving, and I had screwed up the best thing that ever happened to me."

"So you got dumped."

"I can't quite think of it that way because I'd been desperate for it to be over for weeks. I just didn't know how to extricate myself. This was like a lucky gift from God."

"Has she been back in touch saying she made a terrible mistake yet?"

He gives me a sheepish smile. "Yes. She said she realized I would never do anything to hurt her and she wanted to give me a second chance."

"And you said?"

"That over the past few days I had had a lot of time to really think about what she had said, and I think she was right, we aren't right for each other."

"You know I never liked her," I say, knowing that I probably shouldn't be saying this.

"She didn't like you either." He grins.

"Well, clearly. She obviously hated my guts. She didn't seem like a very nice person, and honestly, I couldn't ever figure out what you saw in her. She treated Annie horribly. Not in the beginning when she was trying to win her over, but as soon as she felt secure with you, Annie just seemed to become this enormous source of resentment and irritation."

"I'm so sorry," says Jason. "I kept thinking they would figure it out."

"I don't think Cara has it in her to figure things out. Some people battle with jealousy. I think she couldn't ever deal with you having other women in your life. Me, your daughter. It would have been hell for the rest of your life."

He nods, pensive. "Yes. I think that's probably true, and I think I had realized that. I'm sorry I didn't see it earlier."

"Me too."

And then we hear Annie from upstairs. "Mum? Dad? Hello?"

"I'll go." I turn to go upstairs, knowing that the time has come for Annie and me to talk, that she is healed enough. "Won't be long."

I push open the door, heart melting at how vulnerable my daughter looks, in bed, bandaged, like a wounded duckling.

"Hi, darling, how are you feeling?"

"Good. Okay. Better. You know what I really want?" She sits up, pushing the covers back. "I've got a huge craving for ice cream."

I lean over and kiss her on the top of her head, then sit down on her bed. "We can get you ice cream. But first I think we do need to have a talk."

Her face falls.

"Annie, now that you're better, I need you to know that I love you, and I am so relieved that you are fine, but I am also so angry and disappointed that you got into this mess." I am careful to keep my voice flat. In the old days, the drinking days, I would have shouted, screamed, ranted and raved. I wouldn't have waited until Annie got better, would have been a reactive mess.

"You are thirteen. I don't know what to say about you even being on a scooter, let alone stealing one. The lying, Annie. The dishonesty. How am I supposed to trust you?"

"It wasn't my idea," she grumbles, picking at the bedspread, refusing to meet my eyes.

"It was Trudy's idea?"

"No!" She is quick to defend her cousin. "It just . . . I don't even remember how it happened. It was the other girls, not Trudy. They dared us to do it. I knew it was stupid and I didn't want to, but I didn't want to be the annoying bratty little cousin. Mum, I really didn't want to." Now she looks at me, eyes swimming with tears. "Neither of us did, but we didn't know how to say no."

"Okay." I nod. I understand this, understand what this feels like, when you are thirteen, and desperate to fit in, and terrified it might be discovered that you aren't as cool or as fun as everyone else. I don't know that Trudy felt the same way, am quite certain, in fact, that she was an instigator, but I know my daughter. "Okay."

She looks up at me. "What about Trudy?"

"What about her?"

"Can I still see her?" Her voice is tentative, nervous.

I look at my daughter's face. I know Trudy

425

was an influence on her. Not necessarily a bad one, but one who is older, more experienced, who I'm quite certain has seen far more of life than my sweet young daughter.

I want to say no. I want to tell her that there is a consequence imposed for stealing scooters and lying about what you are doing and where you are. I want to be absolutely sure this doesn't happen again.

But this is her cousin, and Ellie has now said it is okay. How can I separate them? How can I get in the way of a family, when I know just how much my daughter craves a connection with this girl, her own age, and her blood relative?

How can I say no?

"Supervised." I give her a stern look, although of course it will be supervised. Poor Trudy is still bandaged up. It is doubtful Ellie will let her go anywhere for a while.

"I love you, Mum!" My daughter flings her arms around me before pulling back. "Now. About that ice cream . . ."

Jason and I take Annie to town. She swears she is up to it, but her arm is in a sling, and we are careful to move slowly, not to tire her out. She wants to look in the stores, sees a pair of sandals she wants, which Jason buys for her.

In the window of another store, I pause, seeing a beautiful silvery grey scarf.

"That would look great on you, Mum," says Annie, seeing what I'm looking at.

"It would," Jason agrees. "Shall we go in?"

We do, and the sales assistant brings me the scarf, and it is quite the most beautiful thing I have ever seen in my life.

"It's pure cashmere," she says as I wind it around my neck, "but so fine it's almost like silk."

In the mirror, I see Jason standing behind me, looking at me. I meet his eyes, and he grins. "It does look beautiful on you," he says. "You should buy it."

I search for the price tag, and see it is $395, and there is no way in hell I have $395 to spend on a scarf, cashmere or otherwise, and I do not let my face register my shock at the price, slowly unwinding the scarf, telling the sales assistant I will think about it.

"Sure!" she says. "We have a few of them. How long are you here for?"

"Another week," I say.

"You're an adorable family," she says, looking from me to Annie to Jason, and I just smile and thank her, not wanting to catch Jason's eye, not wanting him to see the need in my face, the longing, the wishing that we were still an intact family.

"Why didn't you buy it?" he asks as we leave the store. "It really did look wonderful."

"Because it was a fortune," I say, not adding that I'm a single mother who has to watch pretty much every penny, who can't afford to waste hundreds of dollars on frivolities, no matter how beautiful.

We walk down to get ice cream, both of us flanking our daughter, who chatters away, looking from one to the other, and I see how happy she is to have her family complete, to have her mother and father together.

I remember how good we always were when things were good. How good we always were when I wasn't drinking. I remember how good we were on holiday, how well we got on, how much fun we had.

Jason always liked doing the same things I was doing. I had friends who were married to men who hated lying around on a beach doing nothing. When they go on holiday my girlfriends spend all day by themselves while their husbands furiously run from tennis lessons to fishing or sailing, or hike around deserted parts of a Greek island for hours on end.

I have other friends who love walking around cities, spontaneously going into wherever takes their fancy, be it a museum, a gallery, a café, or a shoe shop. Obviously the shoe shop is the most important, but they're married to husbands who refuse to stop, who march from A to B, sullenly waiting outside should their wives give in to the urge to browse, which makes those wives feel guilty, even as they slip their feet into exquisite heels that they would never find at home, and the whole holiday turns into one big stress fest.

Jason and I always seemed to be on the same wavelength on holiday. We would fly over to Paris for long weekends with nothing booked, nothing planned, staying in a tiny little boutique hotel in Le Marais, le Bourg Tibourg, spending all day every day just walking. We would go to the Rodin Museum if we felt like it, or the Musée d'Orsay, and we would walk. We would wander up and down the banks of the Seine, stopping for café au lait and chocolat chaud, entering the tiny boutiques, where Jason practiced his school French on the chic sales assistants.

We would go to the Greek islands, staying in stark white beautiful villas on Mykonos, spend all day lying on the beach, plunging into the Mediterranean, happy to read a book, play backgammon, be with each other. We'd wander back to the villa after lunch, make love, fall asleep with a fan whirring above our heads, wake up in time for showers and dinner.

Then Annie came along, and our holidays changed, but we were still good together.

We were *so* good together.

Walking along these cobbled streets, Annie chattering away, from time to time both of us smiling at each other across the top of Annie's head, it is absolutely clear to me that we are still good together. That our divorce was a terrible mistake.

I don't get an ice cream. Annie does, and Jason does. I abstain, deciding that my jeans may be skinny, but my thighs definitely aren't, and if I want to continue being able to get into them, I have to stop with the ice cream.

Jason holds his ice cream out to me, and I lick it, making the mistake of looking up just as my tongue touches the swirl. I meet his eyes, and the intimacy in this look, in my tongue being out, in a flood of desire washing over me, turns my cheeks bright red, and we both look away.

Why is this happening to me now? How has all this time gone by, during which I have been able to accept that my old life is over, that Jason no longer wants me, that I screwed things up and we have now both moved on, only for me to feel like this here?

Where the hell has this desire come from, and what am I supposed to do with it now?

THIRTY-TWO

It has been a perfect few days. We have managed to spend time together and time doing our own thing. Even though three adults and a teenager should be overcrowded in a house as small as this, somehow it works.

Yesterday, a letter was pushed through the door. I took it into the kitchen and leaned against the counter to read it. It brought me to tears.

Cat, writes Ellie, *I wanted you to know that I am sorry. For how unfriendly and unwelcoming I have always been toward you; for how I never gave you a chance.*

I had no idea the girls were seeing each other before I ran into you at the Galley, and then I wanted to keep the girls apart to punish you. But seeing Annie and Trudy together, the instinctive connection they have, it's quite clear to me that they are family; that you and I are family, however much I didn't want to accept it. And despite my trying to keep them apart, there is an extraordinary bond between them. A bond I never allowed us to have. It isn't easy to admit this, but I was wrong. And I am sorry. It took a lot of changes in my life, a lot of humbling experiences, for me to realize that.

I have learned many things recently, not least that nothing is as important as kindness. I have lost everything I thought was important in my life, only to realize that none of it was important; that the kindness of people is the only thing that has allowed me to get through. I know you're going home, but I would like us to try to have a relationship. I would like us to try to get past this, maybe even find a sisterly friendship in there. God knows at this time in my life I need family more than I ever have before.

I am sending you my gratitude, and thanks, Cat. I would like to see you before you leave. Perhaps we can go for a walk? Ellie.

I exhaled as I put the letter down, overwhelmed by these words of warmth, of something even possibly akin to love; words I would never have expected to hear from Ellie.

This morning, I called her. We went for that walk. We met at the Hub and walked around the harbor, coffees in hand. It was easier to walk side by side, to talk about things, without having to look each other in the eye. She wasn't warm, particularly, but nor was she cold. I think she was mostly embarrassed. She was honest enough to admit her bitterness toward me, that she had always felt she never got enough of her father, had to fight for any attention, and my appearance was one more thing to take her father further away from her.

I understood, and told her a little bit about my own father. She had never been interested in hearing my story all those years ago, had never been interested in me. Today she listened, not saying much, but nodding in the right places.

I made my amends. We didn't fall into each other's arms as long-lost sisters, but we agreed to see how it goes. More important, Ellie agreed to foster this precious relationship between our daughters, this bond that is already so clear to both of us.

"I'm sorry for how I treated you," says Ellie when we are about to leave, and even though I'm still not experiencing waves of warmth, I go to put my arms around her, and she hugs me back.

"I'm sorry for how I treated all of you," I say. And I know that even if we will never be friends, we can now be friendly. And the girls can be the cousins they are so desperate to be.

These past afternoons Jason has been taking Annie to see Trudy at Ellie's house. The girls spend several hours together every day, and when Trudy starts to get tired, Jason picks Annie up and brings her to wherever we are, usually at the beach.

Eddie joins us from time to time, while Brad Pitt frolics in the water, and yes, I will admit it, I still salivate over Eddie's extraordinary body. Of course he's gay, I think to myself drolly. What straight men do I know with bodies like that? I know I'm never going to have him, but what a delightful sight to brighten up a girl's day, particularly when her loins have been reawakened after the desert of the last few years.

I go to my meetings every morning, and Jason goes to his own, later in the day at the First Congregational Church. Abigail and I meet for tea, and I tell her that her son is adorable but there's no chemistry between us, so although I am thankful for her introduction, a romance between us is not on the cards.

"Pffft," she says. "Who needs chemistry? Well, it's nice to see he's made a new friend in your friend Sam."

Indeed.

Suddenly, unbearably, we are two days from the end, and I realize I don't have nearly enough information about Nantucket for my piece. I leave Annie in the care of Jason and Sam and whirl around the island going to the lighthouse at Sankaty, the whaling museum, the Nantucket Lightship Basket Museum, in order to fill my article with things to do on this island.

Although frankly, I'm sure the *Daily Gazette* readers would be just as happy doing what we have done, exploring the restaurants and spending all day on the beach.

Tomorrow is our last night, and I have booked Corazon del Mar, thinking that tonight I will cook a family dinner here at home. I have lobsters in the fridge, their claws surrounded by rubber bands. Although I love lobster, I've never cooked them before. I didn't know, London girl that I have become, I didn't know until I went to buy lobsters, that you have to plunge them into boiling water while they're still alive. It is too late to change my mind, even though I'm not at all sure I'm going to be able to go through with it.

I have made potato salad, and coleslaw,

and shrimp cakes to start, with a cilantro lime mayonnaise. I made a simple peach tarte tatin and have a tub of homemade (not by me) vanilla ice cream in the freezer, and a vase stuffed with blue hydrangeas, clipped from our own garden, in the middle of the table.

The table has been set for four, with Sam's hurricanes lit in the center. It looks beautiful. I'm excited we're going to be home, not least because this, more than anything, is what it used to be like. At least when things were good. Me cooking, setting the table, Jason, Annie, and me sitting down to something homemade. Jason loved my cooking, even though he was no slouch when it came to the kitchen, but he said being cooked for, by me, always made him feel taken care of, made him feel safe. He always said he could taste the love in my food.

Obviously there's no love in the lobsters, but I poured my heart and soul into the shrimp cakes, into the cilantro and garlic, lovingly minced by hand and a very sharp knife before being stirred into the mayonnaise. There was love in the tarte tatin, which has always been Jason's most favorite dessert, served, as it will be tonight, with ice cream fragrant with dozens of tiny black vanilla pods.

I am in the shower when I hear Jason come home, and surprised when, a few moments later, there is a knock on the bathroom door.

"Hang on," I yell, grabbing a towel and opening the door to find Jason there, embarrassed to be exposing quite so much skin, for the towel really doesn't meet properly and I'm clutching it closed, even though it's not like he hasn't seen it all before.

"I'm so sorry," he says. "I just see that you'll be cooking dinner, and I'm about to go and pick up Annie from Trudy's. I thought it might be nice to invite Trudy tonight. She and Annie are so close, I don't know what they're going to do without each other."

"Of course. That's a great idea. If Trudy is up to going out. Absolutely. Why not invite Ellie as well?" I am about to say Julia, but the memory of Jason and Julia laughing over their iced tea still feels uncomfortable to me, even though we are leaving, even though I am probably being ridiculous.

"Sure. What about Julia?"

I look at him sharply, but there is nothing in his voice, nothing in his face, that would indicate that he particularly wants Julia there.

438

How do I say no? How could I be childish enough to not invite my own half sibling because I think my ex-husband may find her attractive? How sixteen-year-old. How puerile. I am better than this. "Of course invite Julia. Great idea," I say, turning so he doesn't see the lie in my eyes. "Pick up another three lobsters, though, okay?"

He leans forward and kisses me on the cheek, and I stand there long after he's gone back down the stairs, wondering why he suggested we have her here, and whether, despite his protestations the other day, despite denying he finds her attractive, how could he not? She looks exactly like me.

And what the hell could all this possibly mean?

THIRTY-THREE

Ellie can't come. She has a long-standing charity commitment that she cannot get out of, but Julia comes. She brings me flowers and a bottle of sparkling cider.

"I didn't know what to get," she says, walking through the door and giving me a stiff hug. "I was going to bring a bottle of wine but then I remembered, obviously, so I stood in the store for ages before deciding on this. I hope you like the flowers, I got some in town but cut a few from my neighbor's garden to add to the bunch, and thank you so much for inviting us, Cat, this is incredibly kind." She is chattering nineteen to the dozen, which makes me realize how nervous she must be, and that, in turn, seems to help me relax. I am the one in control.

I watch Jason carefully to see how he greets her, whether he hugs her, whether she hugs him, but they just say hello with polite smiles. I can't detect anything at all between them. Perhaps I was imagining it after all.

Trudy gives me a hug, poor thing, still bandaged on one side of her face, and thanks me profusely for being at the hospital.

"Don't be silly," I say. "Any mother would have done the same thing." And then I realize, of course, any mother apart from hers, and I wish I had just kept my mouth shut. "I didn't mean your mo—"

"Don't worry," she interrupts me, laughing. "I know you and my mom have made up. It's okay."

"Come in, come in." I usher the two of them inside. "Come sit down. What can I get you to drink. Iced tea?" I look at Julia. "Wine?"

"You have wine?" I hear the surprise in Julia's voice as Sam walks in, going straight to the fridge.

"Of course we have wine," says Sam. "You think I'd last two weeks on holiday staying in a house with no wine? Sweetie, are you completely mad? Red or white?"

"Actually, I'm fine without," she says, and I am glad that she is making the effort, although she does look longingly at the bottle of chardonnay that Sam immediately opens.

"It smells great," she says, walking over to the stove, "and the house is adorable! I had no idea it was so cute inside."

"It's not," says Sam. "It was completely ghastly. I had to redecorate the entire thing."

"It's true," I say. "He has single-handedly revived the economy of the island by purchasing every accessory that's for sale within a five-mile radius. Come through to the sun porch. Let's take our drinks out there."

I had imagined chemistry. I had clearly imagined chemistry. Julia is lovely, as warm and personable as she always was, and I relax and remember how much I always liked her, how good it feels to have a family, to have a sister who is so very like me. I feel a wave of gratitude that Jason suggested this, that even if we don't stay in touch in any meaningful way, the bad blood that I was so certain must have existed has definitely gone.

I would never have imagined Ellie and me hugging, but it happened. I could never have predicted the outcome of this trip, how wonderful it feels to have been forgiven, to have the weight of guilt and shame that has sat on my shoulders all these years now removed.

This is what they mean by making amends, I think. I apologized, and now I am letting go. And it seems, without any guidance at all, Julia had long ago reached a place where she was willing to do the same. She is a wonderful girl, I think to myself. And I am lucky to have her in my life.

". . . which was just like our dad," I tune in to hear her say. "He wasn't exactly known for his sense of responsibility."

Our dad. She didn't say "*my* dad." She acknowledged that we are related, and it is this seemingly tiny thing that warms my heart more than anything else this evening.

"I barely knew him," I say. "Although we stayed in touch. He always struck me as a very loving father."

"When he wasn't drunk, he was the best. Actually, even when he was, he was always fun."

"I was so jealous of everything you had here," I say. "I shouldn't tell you that, but it's true."

"Are you kidding?" Her mouth falls open. "I was so jealous of you! This incredibly sophisticated woman shows up who has this crazy exciting life in London, of all places! You were a journalist! You interviewed celebrities and went to parties and had such a huge life! You were going on vacations all over Europe. The only place I had ever been was Cape Cod, and Boston. And I only went to Boston to get my boobs reduced. Sorry." She shoots Jason and Sam an apologetic look. "We all had giant boobs back in the day. I have no idea why, but that was how we used to get in everywhere when we were underage."

"Did the boob reduction stop you getting in?" Sam is loving the direction of this conversation.

"I didn't have them done until I was twenty-one, so it didn't matter. But I had basically never been out of Massachusetts. You were the most exciting and glamorous person I had ever seen, and you were my sister! I was so jealous, I could hardly stand it."

"Wow." I am speechless.

"Wow," echoes Sam. "Put like that, it does seem Cat's life is rather exciting."

"I was this island girl. I still am. I hadn't been anywhere, done anything. The most exciting thing I'd probably ever done was steal mopeds on Easy Street and take them to Thirty Acres, where we'd get wasted and go skinny-dipping. Excitement was baking up a batch of pot brownies, and stealing clothes from the store my friends' parents

444

owned, and waiting until the guy on the door at the bar was drinking so we could sneak in, one at a time. That was my life, and I never knew that there was anything different until I met you, and I wanted everything that you had. I took off because I met you. Not because of what happened, but because it opened my eyes to the fact that there could be a bigger life."

"That's quite an impact. Did you get to Europe?"

"No! I did go to St. Maarten for a few years. I worked on the boats, but after a while it felt exactly the same as here, just with better weather, and a bit more French." She laughs, then shrugs. "So I came home. But I was the one who was jealous."

"But you had all those years with . . . our father."

"Yes. And when he was great, he was great. But nothing is ever how you think it is looking at it from the outside."

"She's right," says Jason. "Life is where you look, right?"

Julia frowns. "What do you mean?"

"I mean look for the bad, you'll find more of the bad, look for the good, you'll find more of the good."

A smile spreads on her face. "I like it. Life is where you look."

"On that upbeat note" — I stand up — "let's call the girls and go in for dinner."

Dinner is wonderful, in every way. The food is delicious, everyone is relaxed, the girls don't just sit at the end, having their own private conversation, but join in ours, as equals, and I think how perfect this evening is, how happy I am right now, how much I wish this could continue.

It feels like a perfect little slice of life, one that won't last, that can't last. We'll go back to London in two days, back to our flat, and Jason will go back to his, and there will be no more family dinners, no more hanging out on sun porches talking about nothing in particular, and I will go back to being as desperately lonely as I have been since the moment we split up.

Jason being here has been the best and the worst thing imaginable. Every time I look at him I feel a mixture of love and pain. He's here, but he's not mine. He's here, but he doesn't want me.

Or does he? Because there have been moments these last few days when I've really wondered, moments when I am convinced there is chemistry between us, that all is not lost, that we may be able to find our way back to each other after all.

The more time we spend together, the easier it is, the more fun we seem to be having. I can't believe it's all about to be over, and I wonder if there's any chance, if something may happen before we leave.

Oh God! Listen to me! I sound like a teenager. I feel like a teenager. Giddy with happiness at my crush finally paying attention to me. The fact that my crush happens to be my ex-husband feels irrelevant, other than that he belongs with me, we belong with each other, with Annie.

At 9:30 Julia says she has to go. She thanks me for a wonderful evening, hugs us all, and leaves. Trudy decides to stay for a final sleepover with Annie, and I pull out a box of DVDs I found in a cabinet in the living room, so they can curl up on the sofa and watch movies. What a terrible thing, I think, to be grateful for the accident, grateful that it has forced the two of them to be home, quiet, to do something safe where I can keep an eye on them.

I tuck a blanket around them and go into the kitchen to make popcorn. Sam leaves to go meet Eddie somewhere for a late-night drink, and Jason comes in, walks up behind me as I'm shaking the pan, waiting to hear the kernels start to explode, and I am completely still, remembering how he used to do this, used to come up behind me while I was cooking and slip his arms around my waist, rest his head on my shoulder to see what I was doing, nuzzle into my neck to make me laugh.

I am holding my breath, frozen with anticipation, waiting for those arms to slip around my waist as I am so sure they will. I can feel him, right behind me, feel his body heat, as he leans his head forward, until it is almost on my shoulder, but not touching, and I know he feels it too, and I don't know whether to turn, whether this is the moment he might kiss me. I am completely frozen, I am sure he is too, and then, suddenly, he backs off.

"It smells delicious," he says, and the only thing I can think is *fuck.* How did that moment just disappear? How could we have got so close, and yet nothing happened? I know it wasn't just in my imagination; I *know* he was feeling it too.

How do I get it back?

"I think I'm going to go for a walk. I might go to town," he says, stepping out of the kitchen. I wait for him to ask me to come too, but he doesn't, and I realize this moment was probably overwhelming for him. It was overwhelming for me. When Jason is overwhelmed, he needs space, needs time on his own, and the absolute worst thing I could do right now is invite myself along.

Which I wouldn't do anyway.

Not unless I was completely desperate.

Which I'm not.

"Have fun," I say, pretending I am not standing here with my entire body on fire, pretending that lust and anticipation and disappointment aren't fighting a huge battle inside my body, that the disappointment is winning, is so great that I feel a lump in my throat and I am worried I may burst into tears.

Don't be silly, I tell myself, after I give the girls the popcorn and finish the cleaning up in the kitchen. That moment was real. Jason needs to figure it out. You didn't imagine it. It's all good.

And then: If it's supposed to be, it will be. I have to let go. I can't force anything to happen, nor can I be upset that it didn't. If we are supposed to be together, we will be, and if I have learned anything from my time in program, it is that I have to let go and let God; that if it is God's will, it will happen.

I say a prayer, fold the dish towel and hang it on the hook, then kiss Annie good night and go upstairs to bed.

I don't sleep.

I can't sleep.

An hour goes by, then two. Where is Jason? A walk isn't two hours. I go downstairs, pretending I need water, then that I am checking on the girls, and still there is no sign of Jason. I open his bedroom door and leave it ajar so I can walk past and check.

No Jason.

Where is he?

I start to worry.

I never used to be a worrier, until I had Annie. That first year I spent all my time terrified something terrible would happen to her. If I left her with a babysitter and the babysitter didn't pick up her phone, I would have to go back home, to reassure myself that the babysitter wasn't lying unconscious on the floor of the nursery with no one to look after Annie.

If Jason was later than expected, if a meeting ran on, or he told me he'd be home by seven and it was 8:30, I would phone his cell over and over; each time it went to the machine I would literally be picturing his car smashed up on Baker Street, police and ambulance racing to the scene, where they would find my poor, mangled husband.

It was very bad for a while, my catastrophizing, constantly waiting for the worst thing to happen, and then it seemed to go away.

What is the worst thing I can imagine happening now? My daughter being involved in
a scooter accident is right up there, yet it
happened, I didn't go to pieces, and we all
coped.

Which should give me a measure of relief,
but I feel the familiar panic rise up as time
ticks slowly on and there is no sign of Jason. Where is he and what has happened?

Eventually, close to midnight, I text him. I
keep it light. I don't want him to know I am
panicking about him, reverting to old
behavior that used to drive him nuts.

u ok? I type.

There is no response.

Jason? Just wanted to check you're ok.

No response.

JASON? PLEASE RESPOND

Nothing.

Fuck.

Sam is out. The girls are asleep on the
sofa, piled together like puppies. My
adrenaline is pumping and my heart is beating fast. There is absolutely no way I'm going to sleep. Even though I haven't heard
sirens, that's all I can think about.

I have to go and look for Jason.

I know it's crazy, but, as he always used to
point out, rational thought tended to go out

the window once I had got myself into a state of full catastrophizing.

I pull on jeans and a T-shirt, go outside, and stop, cursing. He took the car. Shit. I'll have to cycle, which I don't particularly want to do at night, but I have no choice.

I wheel the bike out, strap on the helmet, and start to pedal along Cliff Road, wishing I could appreciate the beauty of the velvet night sky, and the smells of salt and ocean, but my heart is pounding, and images of flashing lights and broken bodies are all I can think about.

Town is busy. Busier than I would have expected, the odd groups of people, all of them looking like they've been drinking, occasionally careening out of doorways with laughter and noise.

Where would he be? In a bar? Jason doesn't go to bars, not for years, not since before I knew him. He *can* go to bars, he's well beyond the point of being tempted, but he wouldn't go there by himself out of choice.

Would he be by the water? Sitting on a bench, thinking? I hesitate, not knowing which way to go, happy only that there is no sign of any major accident, no sense of something terrible having happened here this evening.

A crowd of people come out of the Club Car, noise and music drifting out with them, and I step aside, letting them pass, before opening the door, something unconscious pulling me inside.

The noise, the heat, the laughter, the piano, the singing. Everything hits me at once in this packed former train carriage, the bar running along one side, packed with people, a huge party, alcohol fueled. Wherever Jason is, he would not be here.

As I turn to leave, something familiar catches my eye. Julia. Seated at the bar, her back to me, leaning in to someone. I can't move. I freeze, knowing it is Jason, and when she tilts her head I see that I was right.

She snakes a hand around his neck, and pulls him down. As if in slow motion, I watch as Jason's head moves closer to hers, and they are kissing.

A wave of nausea washes over me. I have to leave. But I can't move. I see Jason's eyes closed, remember how it felt to be kissed by him, and I don't know whether to tear them apart, slip away, or throw up.

They break apart. I don't see Jason's face because at that moment Julia turns her head, and as if she knows I'm there, as if she is expecting to see me, she looks straight into my eyes.

And she smiles.

I tear out of there, wanting to disappear, wanting to get as far away as possible. I feel as if I am in physical pain, my heart threatening to rip open and tear, and I gulp out a sob, unable to believe what I just saw, unable to believe the pain I am in.

A bar. More people. Light, and noise, and alcohol. I hesitate by the window and look in, at the polished mahogany bar, the stools, the bottles and bottles of vodka, gin, tequila, everything that is warm and familiar and comforting, and it is like a force field pulling me in.

That will make it all better.

That will make the pain go away.

THIRTY-FOUR

London, 2014

This is not my usual meeting. I have taken the tube into town, because I am desperate for a meeting, and not my usual cozy one, where I know all the people almost as well as I know myself, where I will hear them say some variation of what they always say, and it will be as comfortable and familiar as a night out with my oldest friends.

No. That's not what I need today.

I need to be in a room filled with people I don't know. A big meeting. One in which I can be completely anonymous. One in which, hopefully, I will be surrounded by people who have far better recovery than I, who know what to say to ease my pain.

They often say that in meetings you will hear exactly what you need to hear at any given time. I need that to happen today. I need someone or some reading, something that will show me how to get through this day without wanting to drown everything out in a sea of vodka.

I came so close, that night in Nantucket. I didn't go into the bar, but I wanted to. I didn't drown my pain in alcohol, but I came the closest I have come since I got sober, and it was terrifying.

It has set off a craving, one that I thought I had let go of long ago. Pain has always been a trigger. I don't want to feel, which is why I drink: to numb, to make it all go away.

The pain of seeing Jason and Julia together has continued, as has the wanting to drink. I haven't, but I think about it all the time, and I am filling my time with calls to my sponsor, meetings, reading literature, writing the steps; anything to stop the white-knuckling.

I need a meeting that isn't filled with strange strangers, as has sometimes happened when I've tried a new meeting. I don't want one filled with homeless people — forgive me — and nor do I want one with creepy guys that come up afterward and ask for my number.

I know there is a good meeting here, in Soho, and I walk in, a few minutes late, glad the room is packed, every seat taken, both around the table and the second circle pushed back against the wall.

Someone grabs a folding chair for me, and there is a shuffle as they make room. I glance around, see that it's mostly men, a few women, one I have seen before in a couple of meetings. She raises her hand and gives me a smile. I'm not sure of her name. Andrea? Amelia? Something like that.

I close my eyes during the reading from the daily reader, Thought for the Day. Martin, a middle-aged cheerful-looking alcoholic, reads:

"Roselle says: I used to try to deny or excuse the things he did that hurt, but that didn't do anything to heal my hurt. When I came out with my true feelings and honestly 'told' him I was hurt and angry, he came back with his true feelings. The wrongs are never made right, but the love and forgiveness puts them in the past and out of today's 'processing memory.' "

My true feelings. I'm still trying to process what my true feelings are, although I'm pretty sure I know.

I know because I haven't been able to talk to Jason since the night I saw him kiss Julia. I took Annie to Sconset the next day, just us girls, and when we got home I went straight up to bed with a pretend migraine so I wouldn't have to go out for dinner with them. Anything to avoid spending time with Jason.

I couldn't stand it. That moment, him kissing Julia, keeps spinning round and round my head, on a reel, and each time it does I have to fight the tears. And the anger. And the knowledge that Jason was just a pawn, that Julia's smile told me everything. Had I not happened to walk into the bar and see them, she would have found a way to let me know. She would have found a way to rub my nose in it, for she could see, *anyone* could see, how I still feel about Jason, and she had waited years for revenge.

I had always thought that Ellie was the bitch, that Julia was the one I had so much in common with, but Ellie, despite everything, was at least honest. Julia had been holding her secret poisonous grudge all this time, and I never saw it. I didn't know.

Did she even care about Jason? I doubt it. I doubt this had anything to do with Jason other than being the perfect way to get back at me. And Jason was stupid enough to be carried away, to be flattered into seduction, to lose himself in the moment thinking I would never find out.

At least I presume that's what he thought. I haven't seen him since. We had different flights home, and in the three weeks since we've been back I have managed to avoid him completely, out of the house when he comes to pick Annie up, clicking his phone calls over to the answering machine, texting him the briefest, curtest texts when I have no other choice.

Love and forgiveness. How I wish I were in a place of love and forgiveness. But I'm not. I'm in a place of hatred and murderous thoughts.

Martin closes the book and starts to speak, as I wait with bated breath.

"I'm Martin, alcoholic."

"Hi, Martin," from the rest of the group.

"Great reading." He shakes his head slowly, as if unable to believe the magnificence of what he just read. "So much food for thought. So, here's what's going on for me today."

My heart sometimes sinks slightly when someone starts with apologizing for going off topic, or announcing what's going on with them today. It can mean fifteen minutes of something that's totally ir-relevant, at least to whatever the topic is supposed to be.

It can mean, often, venting about the problems in their life, and so it is with Mar-tin, who spends about fifteen minutes talking about some problem at work with his bastard of a boss, and it has nothing to do with the reading, and nothing to do with AA, or recovery, in fact, until he talks about forgiveness. And then I listen.

And when he is done, I realize my hand is up in the air.

Wouldn't you know it, the first person he looks at is me.

Shit. I hate it when this happens. Putting my hand up is like an involuntary reaction when something is bursting out of me, and I sigh and roll my eyes.

"Shit," I say out loud. "I was hoping you wouldn't pick me." And everyone in the room laughs. "I'm Cat, alcoholic."

"Hi, Cat."

I take a deep breath. "Thank you for your lead, Martin. I'm completely unprepared, but I think in today's reading I may have heard what I needed to hear. I definitely needed to hear about love and forgiveness because right now I'm about as far away from loving and forgiving as I have ever been, and that, as we all know, is a recipe for disaster." I grimace and continue. "I just got back from a holiday in which I flew to America, essentially to make amends to my half sisters. It's a very long story, but the last time I saw them I was in my twenties, wreaking havoc wherever I went, blackouts being the norm, and one night, back then, I went out with my sister's boyfriend, we both got completely shitfaced, and the next morning we were found in bed together. By her, obviously. As if it could have been worse."

There is a murmur of pain around this room. However different their stories may be, most have drinking stories of equal horror.

"Clearly, doing my ninth step, this was the big one, so I decided to do it in person. The amends seemed to go okay. One sister, Ellie, wasn't exactly warm and fuzzy, but honestly, who can blame her. She didn't want anything to do with me, but the other one, the one whose boyfriend I slept with, said it all happened long ago and she had forgiven and forgotten years ago. I believed her. Why wouldn't I?" I snort. "She was as warm and lovely as she had been years ago. I remember when I first met her I instantly felt that I'd come home. I knew her. This was my family. And I felt the same when I saw her again. So we forged a friendship, and her niece and my daughter, who are very close in age, became instant best friends, and everything seemed to be great.

"While I was there, my daughter got into

an accident, and my ex-husband ended up flying out too. If it all sounds terribly complicated, it's because it is. Sorry. My daughter was fine, a broken wrist, scratches and stitches, but fine. So my ex-husband . . ." I take another breath, a deep one. "We split up a year and a half ago. Like so many of us, I was the one who fucked up my marriage. The first time I got sober, I got sober for my husband. Every time I got sober after that, I got sober for my husband, because I loved him, and I wanted him to be happy, and proud of me. And because I was never getting sober for me, it never lasted. A few weeks, a few months, I could never get it to stick. So my marriage was a roller coaster. Fantastic when I was sober, and then I'd start drinking, and raging, and we'd start fighting, and I never ever thought he'd leave. I thought we would just carry on like that forever. And one day, he had enough, and he left. And took our daughter with him.

"I got sober, properly. It felt different. I was finally doing it for myself. I have stayed sober for eighteen months." There is a round of applause, which I pause to acknowledge before continuing. "And I have tried to move on with my life. We now split custody with my daughter, and things were pretty great between us, in that we got on, we were co-parenting. I think he knew how different it was this time. And then he got this horrific girlfriend. The poison dwarf." Another ripple of laughter around the room. "And he pulled back. She was jealous of the good relationship we had. And maybe she realized something that I hadn't even realized, not on a conscious level anyway, about how I still felt about him. She hated me, and things were difficult for a while, and I didn't see him much, and then he flew out to Nantucket, just now, after our daughter had the accident.

"And having him there was amazing. It felt like we were a proper family again, only without it feeling precarious. Every time I was sober before, I always knew, in the back of my head, it wasn't going to last. I would white-knuckle through it until I couldn't do it anymore. I had no idea what it meant to live in recovery, to live a peaceful and serene life, until this time. And being with my hus . . . ex-husband, in the place I am today, was amazing. And after a few days, it hit me that I still love him. I'm still in love with him." I pause, my eyes welling up, as someone slides a box of tissues over.

"So there I was, thinking things were great, thinking that it was only a matter of time before something happened between us, because there was chemistry. I know there was chemistry there. Toward the end there was a night where I felt something was going to happen, and it was confusing, I could see it was confusing for him too, so he went out. He didn't come back for hours, and because I'm a woman and a little bit crazy, I started panicking, so I went looking for him. And I found him in a bar, not drinking, he's a recovering alcoholic too, but kissing someone." I pause and take a deep breath. "My half sister."

There is an audible gasp around the room, and it actually makes me laugh. "I know! Right? And not the one who was a bitch, who wanted nothing to do with me, but the one I thought had forgiven me. The one who was pretending to have forgiven me. He didn't see me. But she did. And she looked into my eyes, at my shocked expression, and smiled. I knew instantly that this had nothing to do with him, that her accepting my amends was crap; this was all about revenge. She could see how much he meant to me; she knew that the best way to hurt me was through my daughter, or him. And she did. I have no idea if they slept together. I imagine they did. I imagine she would have had to do the same thing to me as I did to her all those years ago. And had I not showed up at the bar, had I not happened to see them, I know she would have found another way to let me know she had seduced the man I love."

I pause to wipe the tears from my eyes. "I haven't spoken to him since then. I avoided him the next day, and I've managed to avoid him since. I have no idea if he knows anything. Probably not. And I have been sick with grief, and anger, and hatred. Fury with both of them, with her, and so much fury and pain with him. It's my half sister. He knew it was out of bounds. I still can't believe he did it. But I also know that avoiding the pain, avoiding my feelings, avoiding him, is old behavior. If anything was painful, I would just run away, cut people off, pretend it had never happened, and I can't do that now. I can't do that because avoiding all the painful stuff is going to ultimately lead me to picking up a drink, and I won't do it; I have to do things differently. But my God, I have wanted to drink. I get to the end of every day thanking God that I managed not to, because it's all I want to do, to drown the pain. But I haven't, because I know it's a few moments of reprieve, and then the spiral down to hell, and I can't go back there, no matter what's going on in my life.

"The reading today tells me not to hide. It tells me to tell my ex-husband what I know, and how hurt and betrayed I feel. I don't know that I necessarily have to tell him I'm still in love with him, but I have to tell him how upset I am. The only person I'm hurting by keeping this all in is me, and if I want to stay sober, I have to do this. What was it the reading said? That the wrongs are never made right? I can't go back and unsleep with my half sister's boyfriend. And I can't change that she then slept with my ex-husband for revenge. But I can express my feelings honestly, and move on. I can love and forgive, and move on in a place of peace." And as I say these words out loud, it is as if a cloud is lifted, and I know, suddenly, that this is absolutely true, and that by saying it out loud, I *am* able to let it go.

I still have to talk to Jason, though. Not Julia. I'm letting go of her. I wish her well, I know the girls will stay in touch, but there's nothing there for me. She may be related to me by blood, but she's not my family. Maybe at some point in the future we'll be able to work things out, but I can't see it today. Today, we're equal. Two wrongs have not made a right, but they have canceled each other out. It is time for me to move on. I will keep in touch with Ellie. Her honesty has made room for us to have a relationship, and we need a relationship for our daughters.

The meeting continues. More people share. We pass the basket for the seventh tradition, where we make a voluntary donation. I put a couple of pounds in, and I think, once again, how this is my therapy, how extraordinary it is that a group of strangers can make me feel not only so happy, but so completely at home.

At the end, a couple of people stop me as I'm walking out, tell me how my story really resonated with them, or that they hope I'll come back. I thank them and keep walking, and just as I'm at the door I turn my head and find myself looking straight at the last person I want to see right now. The last person I expected to see right now, and the blood drains from my face.

Jason.

Fuuuuuuucccccckkkk.

He was in the meeting. I am rooted to the spot in horror, unable to believe what I talked about, unable to believe how honest I was, unable to believe that he was in here, listening to every word.

How did I not see him? Why did I not check the room more carefully? How did I not realize there was a corner, and more chairs squeezed into the space round the corner?

Oh shit. Oh shit. Oh shit. Oh shit. What am I supposed to do now? I open and close my mouth, like a fish, and then I do what every recovering, serene, self-possessed forty-something woman does when faced with an uncomfortable situation: I turn on my heel and run.

"Cat!" He's behind me.

Go away, go away, go away.

"Cat! Wait!"

I'm sobbing now, the pain and humiliation too much. I just want to get in my car and drive off a cliff somewhere, except I don't even have my car here, I took the bloody tube, and I turn the wrong way and it's away from the tube station and I frantically scour the streets for a taxi but there's nothing, and then a hand on my arm, and Jason has caught me.

"Cat. Stop. Please. You can't just run off. I am so sorry you saw me. And I'm sorry that anything happened with Julia. I didn't sleep with her. I didn't mean to do anything."

I went for a walk and she saw me out the window of the bar and grabbed me. She was drunk, Cat, and I kept trying to leave, and she wouldn't let me."

I can't look him in the eye. "You don't have to explain anything to me," I say. "It has nothing to do with me."

"Bullshit. It has everything to do with you." The urgency leaves his face as it softens. "Cat, I didn't know."

"Didn't know what?" I am so uncomfortable, I'm actually fidgeting, moving from foot to foot, desperate to stop this conversation and get out of here.

"I didn't know how you felt about me."

"I can't." It comes out in a howl, as the tears start to fall. "I just . . . can't. I'm sorry, Jason. I'm sorry you were there. I'm sorry I opened my big mouth. But I can't talk about this. I just can't do it." And this time, when I turn and run away, my whole body wracked with sobs, he doesn't come after me.

THIRTY-FIVE

The only place I can ever kick my shoes off and feel completely at home is at my mum's. It may not be the place I grew up in, almost all of the furniture may be completely new, but when I need to feel comforted by something other than a couple of tubs of Ben & Jerry's ice cream and binge-watching *Celebrity Big Brother* for hours on end, it is to my mother's flat I go.

I tell her everything.

It is not like me to tell my mother everything, and it is not like me to burst into tears on her sofa as she tucks me up under a fluffy throw and brings me cups of hot, sweet tea, and listens. Really listens, murmuring in all the right places.

Her own depression and my father's controlling nature pulled her away from me as a child. When I was in pain, or upset, or hurt, I learned to figure it out for myself. I never doubted she loved me, I just knew I couldn't turn to her for help.

Now, I can turn to her for help.

Where else would I go?

The story comes out in between sobbing like a child, tears spouting from my eyes and my nose running as I pluck tissue after tissue from the box she conveniently keeps on the coffee table.

"How am I ever going to face him again?" I cry, when I have finished the story. "He knows I still love him. It's the most horrific, humiliating thing that's ever happened to me. Mum, I want to die. I swear to God, I actually want to die."

She doesn't say anything for a while, just smiles gently and rubs my back, waiting for my hiccups to go, passing me more tissues.

I think about when Annie is upset, lying on her bed, crying, and how I sit on the bed, just as my mother is sitting on the sofa, and rub her back, and pass her tissue after tissue.

I have a story about my mother, that she was always in bed, that she was depressed, unhappy, wasn't able to love me. I have a story that I was raised by wolves, by a father who didn't want me and a mother who couldn't stand up to him, who in having to retreat from him, retreated from me too.

I have a story that that is why I turned to

471

alcohol. Because I had no one; because alcohol was my only friend. As I lie here, sodden with grief, I remember. I remember my mother doing this when I was a child. I remember her loving me, and looking after me.

I was jealous of Julia and Ellie, jealous that they had a father, but I had a mother. She might not have been there all the time, but it doesn't matter.

I was loved.

I know, suddenly and without any shadow of a doubt, I was always loved.

Which only serves to bring on a fresh set of tears.

"You still love Jason?" my mother asks, when everything seems to have dried up and I am finally able to breathe.

"Yes. Of course. I never stopped loving him."

"So why be humiliated? Lucky him, having someone as wonderful as you love him. You wouldn't have told him under different circumstances. Maybe what happened today is a good thing. You couldn't have gone on avoiding him forever, and isn't it better for everything to be out in the open?"

"But he doesn't love me. He doesn't want me," I moan, suddenly hit by the full fact of my divorce in a way I wasn't in the beginning, too busy getting sober, getting my daughter back, assuming that Jason would come back, assuming he would forgive me because we had been through this so many times, and he always had.

This grief I am feeling is completely disproportionate with what was a pretty bad exercise in humiliation, but was just that: an exercise in humiliation. I, however, feel like my world is ending, and I realize, as I lie here, that I am finally accepting this is over.

Jason is never coming back. I may meet someone else, and he may be wonderful, but he won't be the father of my child; I will never have a whole, intact family again.

I break into a fresh set of tears.

"Do you know he doesn't love you?" asks my mother, when I have calmed down again.

"Yes. Of course. He doesn't. It was clear on Nantucket that he wasn't interested."

"I thought you said there was a moment when you thought he might have been. In the kitchen. Making popcorn."

"I thought that at the time, but two hours later he had his tongue down Julia's throat, so, no. I don't think it was a moment. I think it was my overactive imagination working overtime."

"What if you're wrong?" my mum says

simply. "What if he still loves you? Then how would you feel?"

"But he doesn't," I groan. "If he did, he would have said something. Oh God. It's just so awful. I can't believe he knows."

"It might not be so awful," she says. "It might all turn out to be for the best."

THIRTY-SIX

Jason is now avoiding me. Which is a huge relief. I don't need to skulk around the flat or suddenly find a reason to go out if he's dropping Annie at home, because he's clearly feeling as humiliated as I am, not to mention quite possibly appalled, and is staying as far away as possible.

While I try to get on with my life.

Like an awful flashback, the scene from the meeting, the things I said, the knowledge that Jason heard them, come back to haunt me on a regular basis. Usually when I'm lying in bed at night, and I often throw the pillow on top of my head and groan in horror.

But as the weeks have gone by, it has got a little easier. Not seeing him has helped.

I speak to Maureen, my sponsor, every day, go to my meetings, write my articles, look after Annie, and as the pieces of the puzzle of my regular old boring life have fallen into the same place they were before we left for Nantucket, so the pain has eased.

It is beginning to feel like a bad, but distant, dream.

I even bit the bullet and signed up for Match.com. I didn't want to do it, but Sam threatened to divorce me if I didn't, so even though I haven't met anyone yet, I have spent quite a few evenings winking away and having some . . . interesting chats.

I don't know that I feel quite ready to actually go out on a date yet.

Until I meet Matthew, who has blue eyes, and likes windsurfing, and go-karting, and good wine, and basically we have absolutely nothing in common, except his messages are very quick, and clever, and when he asks if he can call me, I say yes, and his voice is warm and lovely, and when he asks if I'd like to meet for a drink, I say no.

Two or three weeks go by, during which we talk every night. This isn't real, though, I tell myself. Anyone can be anyone they choose during a phone conversation. This means nothing. Who can predict chemistry?

Sam phoned yesterday to see if I would be interested in writing a piece on middle-aged online dating. Great. Everything I write these days has to be prefaced with the word "middle-aged," which doesn't exactly make this middle-aged single woman feel particularly good about herself.

"Get over it," said Sam. "It happens to the best of us."

Tonight, I have finally agreed to meet Matthew for a drink. We're going to the Queens in Primrose Hill, and because this is my first date in years, and even though I'm almost certain he's going to be awful in real life — did I mention we have nothing in common? — I have still put an inordinate amount of time into getting ready today.

I went to the hairdresser this morning and had a few highlights put in. A few more highlights, to be correct. And I got a spray tan, because even though technically it's autumn, it's entirely possible that I just went to somewhere like Marbella for the weekend, and I do look so much better with a tan.

Doesn't *everyone* look so much better with a tan?

I have lost some weight, which isn't a bad thing. Not that I was unhappy, particularly, but I am always convinced that if I were ten pounds lighter then everything in my life would be perfect, and lo and behold, when I went to try on the skirt I was thinking of wearing for the date tonight, it was swimming on me.

Instead I go for the really-much-too-small-for-me skinny stretch jeans that are very dark, and very tight, and possibly, at this point, at least two rather than three sizes too small for me. It takes me about ten minutes to inch them up my legs. They're so tight I have to wear a very loose sweater with them to hide the muffin top, and I already know that within about an hour and a half I will have such bad gas I may have to cut the evening short, but for that hour and a half, I will look absolutely fantastic.

As long as I don't sit down.

Much.

I am nervous. I have just finished putting some makeup on, not too much, it is only the Queens pub, after all, when my phone rings, and it is Sam.

"Change of plan," he says.

"What plan?"

"The plan where you're writing about middle-aged online dating. It's been done to death anyway. I want you to write another piece for us."

"Fine. I hadn't written much anyway. What's the piece?"

"I want you to write about people who get divorced, who still love each other, then get back together."

478

I say nothing.

"Hello?" says Sam. "Are you there?"

"O-kay," I say, because we had a night out a couple of weeks ago, and I told him about what happened, and it does seem a little . . . insensitive, to ask me of all people to write this particular piece given what is going on in my life right now.

"In fact, I'd like to get a bit more specific, if that's okay. I want you to write a piece about a woman who only gets sober once her marriage is over, and then realizes how much she threw away when she was drinking, and once her husband realizes she actually is a different person, she has changed for the better, he realizes that she's always been the only person he has ever wanted to be with, and they go out for dinner, to Odette's, at eight o'clock tonight, and then they live happily ever after. Do you think you could do that for me? By the end of the week?"

There is a very long silence. "What?" I say eventually, because I really don't know what else to say. "What the fuck?" I follow up with, which wouldn't be very professional with any other editor, but it is only Sam, after all. "What the fuck are you talking about?" I am deeply confused.

I can hear the smile in his voice. "Jason

479

called me. He is desperate. He has no idea how to talk to you, and he still loves you, so this is what you're doing. You're going to put on your nicest clothes and get your arse to Odette's at eight o'clock this evening, where your former and hopefully soon-to-be-again husband will meet you, and the two of you can finally figure this thing out. Okay?"

"No!" I say. "I have a date tonight."

"A date?" He is both aghast and intrigued. "Who with?"

"With bloody Matthew who I met on Match.com thanks to the original article I was writing for you."

"So cancel it."

"I can't! I feel really bad."

"Please tell me you're joking. The love of your life and I have conspired to bring you back together tonight, and you would rather meet a lanky, balding, boring guy called Matthew who you don't know?"

"How do you know he's lanky, balding, and boring?"

"I don't. It's a guess. But whatever he is, he's not Jason. You love Jason. And Jason loves you. That's about as happy an ending as anyone could wish for. Go, and enjoy. And write the piece."

"I don't know what to say." I don't. I am

in shock.

"Nothing needed to say. That's what friends are for. And by the way, this is exactly what should happen. It's clear to everyone who knows you that the two of you are supposed to be together. I'm just relieved that Jason finally decided to do something about it."

"Wait! Do you really want me to write this as a piece?"

"No. It's not very us. But it's very *Daily Mail*. Why don't you offer it to them?"

My mind is still racing. "Sam, one more question. When you say he still loves me, are you sure you don't mean as a friend? Because I'm the mother of his child, so he'll always love me, or do you mean —"

He interrupts me. "I wouldn't have gone to all this trouble if it was anything other than the real deal. Go. And phone me tomorrow morning. I expect every single detail."

I put down the phone and squeal as I dance my way up the corridor, my heart threatening to burst out of my body with joy. I pause by the full-length mirror outside Annie's room, and I look at my reflection. I look into my eyes and see how full my life is, how happy, and calm, and present I am. How I am a good mother, a good friend. A good person. And I have never felt that about myself before. I look into my eyes and I see how far I've come.

And smile as I think of how far I have to go.

ABOUT THE AUTHOR

A former feature writer for the *Daily Express* in the UK, **Jane Green** took a leap of faith when she left, in 1996, to freelance and work on a novel. Seven months later, there was a bidding war for her first book, *Straight Talking*, the saga of a single career girl looking for the right man. The novel was a hit in England, and Green was an overnight success. Most weekends see her cooking for a minimum of twenty people in her home in Westport, Connecticut, where she lives with her husband and their blended family. When she is not writing, cooking, filling her house with friends and looking after their animals, she is usually thanking the Lord for caffeine-filled energy drinks.